THE NEXUS

Mike McQuay

BANTAM BOOKS

NEW YORK • TORONTO • LONDON • SYDNEY • AUCKLAND

I'd like to gratefully acknowledge the assistance of Dr. Steve Weiss, Ph.D., in the preparation of this manuscript. Without his insight into the autistic child, this project wouldn't have been possible.

———————

This book is lovingly dedicated to the memory of my grandmother, Blanch Martin, who early in my life recognized and helped subsidize my love of the arts.

THE NEXUS
A Bantam Spectra Book / May 1989

ISBN 0-553-28178-X

Published simultaneously in the United States and Canada

Bantam books are published by Bantam Books, a division of Bantam Doubleday Dell Publishing Group, Inc. Its trademark, consisting of the words "Bantam Books" and the portrayal of a rooster, is Registered in U.S. Patent and Trademark Office and in other countries. Marca Registrada. Bantam Books, 666 Fifth Avenue, New York, New York 10103.

PRINTED IN THE UNITED STATES OF AMERICA

O   0 9 8 7 6 5 4 3 2 1

ACT ONE

Scene 1

EXT—NITE—FORT WORTH, TEXAS. A late-model FORD
VAN is picking its way carefully through the heavy downtown
traffic around the area of the old stockyards and the new
country bars that have taken over that end of town. RAIN is
sheeting down heavily, early summer heat turning Texas into
a giant steam bath.

The van turns a corner into the huge parking lot of BILLY
BOB'S CLUB, a crowd of men and women dressed uniformly
in jeans and Stetsons and checkered shirts with fake mother-
of-pearl buttons is crossing in front of the van, their hats the
only protection against the weather.

The van passes close to our line of vision, the words
WORLD CABLE NEWS stenciled across a representation of
a globe on the side of the thing. The van HONKS at the
slow-moving crowd.

ANGLE—COWBOY IN THE RAIN. He shouts an obscenity,
then turns his back to the van, pulling down his pants to
MOON the passengers.

ANGLE—INT—VAN. Two men sit within the driver's compartment, the rain loud against the hollow interior, the wipers'
shadows passing back and forth across their faces. They are
DENNIS STILLER, the passenger, and FRANK HAR-
GRAVE, the driver, both employees of WCN.

FRANK
(wearily)
A low-yield nuclear weapon dropped around here
would raise the average IQ of the world by fifty
points.

DENNIS
I don't know, Frank. That bastard's butt may be the
biggest story we've covered in a month. Look at that
marbling.

FRANK
Buddy, boy, you're lucky to have stories to cover at
all. What I can't figure out is how come I'm stuck
doin' mea culpas with you.

DENNIS
(turning to stare)
You're just lucky, I guess.

Denny Stiller knew exactly why Hargrave was stuck on the
shit detail with him, but it was the kind of thing you couldn't
talk with the man about. The bottom line was, Frank Hargrave
was crazy. He was a walking exposed nerve with a camera in
tow. When sent out to do interviews, he focused on people's
hands. When sent to cover press conferences he'd invariably
come back with pictures of empty chairs. It made little
difference the night Hargrave walked into a 7–11 hostage
situation armed only with his camera and talked a madman into
giving himself up if all he came out of the experience with was
close-ups of the victims' eyes.

Hargrave was a tornado chaser with an entirely different
idea from management of what constituted "usable footage."
Unfortunately, Stiller's own methodical erosion of esteem in
the eyes of the powers that be was more deeply rooted and far
more demeaning.

"There's a spot," Denny said. "Right near the door."
"It's got a reserved sign on it," Hargrave replied.
"That's how come it's open," Denny said. "Pull in."
"You're the boss."

Hargrave wheeled the machine into the empty space, the
rest of the lot jammed tight with cars and people. Denny

climbed out into the rain, the sound of sharp-edged country music oozing through the walls of the cowboy hippodrome so physically that he could almost smell the sweat. A strange place to be looking for psychic phenomena. But, then, maybe anyplace was a strange place.

He moved to the back of the van, the rain making him angry because it underscored the uselessness of the whole endeavor. He looked down at the arm of his tan sport jacket. It was spotted dark with water. He'd have to do any on-camera work without it.

Hargrave moved around to the back of the van, his limp more pronounced in the wet weather. He put a hand to the rear door, then looked up into the sky.

"Got some damned fine clouds buildin' up there," he said. "See them high ones . . . the ones rushing up on us? That's good twister weather."

"Forget it, Frank," Denny said. "We've got business here."

"Right," Hargrave said, pulling open the back of the van. "We got to chase down faith healers in bars. Uh-oh. Looks like trouble."

Denny turned in time to see a man in his early twenties, dressed like a Texas Ranger, come striding purposefully toward them— one of the parking valets.

"I'm sorry, sir," the man said in a monotone. "You're going to have to move your vehicle." He was real big up close.

"You sound like a cop, son," Denny said.

"That parking space is reserved for the owner," the valet said. "You're going to have to move."

Denny smiled at him, then nodded for Hargrave to begin unloading the equipment out of the van. "We're members of the working press," he said, "Mr. . . . ah. . . ."

"Call me Robert," the man said. "And I'm telling you to move along."

Denny smiled even wider. "We're here to do a story about your establishment, Robert," he said, watching the man for any sudden movements. "Now I'll move along if you want, but how would you like me to do a story about all the drunks and all the fights and lewdness just out here in your parking lot, Robert? And how would you like me to feature you, Robert, prominently in that story? I wonder how your boss would like that, now, Robert? What do you think?"

The man stared at him, a note of uncertainty in his eyes. Denny moved in for the kill.

"Look, you seem like a nice kid," he lied. "Leave us here for just a bit. I promise we'll be in and out in thirty minutes tops, and tomorrow I'll personally call your boss and tell him how nice and cooperative you were."

The valet scratched his head. "Well . . ."

"Good," Denny said, patting him on the arm and motioning to Hargrave to get moving while he had the chance. "You've done the right thing."

Hargrave was already limping through the big awninged doors of Billy Bob's, the tarp-covered camera case stuffed up under his arm. Denny grabbed the covered light stand and hurried after him.

"My last name's Jenkins," the boy called after him. "Robert Jenkins."

Denny waved obliquely. "Sure, kid. Sure." And he had already put the young man totally out of his mind.

He walked under the awning then through the doors, the stale smell of beer the first thing that hit him, followed by the smoke and the gaudy light and the boozy laughter, the kind that comes without humor.

He moved up the steps and into another world—cowboy heaven. Billy Bob's was *the* experience in the Dallas–Fort Worth metroplex, the legitimization of an artificial dream. The place was monstrous, containing ten bars under one roof, plus a large stage with seating for five thousand, a shooting gallery, a video arcade, and a miniature rodeo arena for *real* bull riding.

Tonight, though, no one was going to be riding the bull—they'd be shooting it.

He spotted Hargrave at one of the bars, a large oval freestanding in the center of excess space, with a bottle of beer already in his hand.

He joined Frank at the bar, noticing the stares of recognition all around him. Sometimes Denny loved being recognized. Sometimes, like tonight, it was simply an albatross necktie. He could always tell when he was feeling sorry for himself.

He eased himself up on a high stool, leaning his equipment up against the wooden bar. On stage, a hundred yards distant, a band he didn't recognize cranked loudly into a progressive country version of "Your Cheatin' Heart."

"Why don't you put down a couple of these long necks," Hargrave said above the racket, looking at Denny out of the corner of his eye, "and then forgit this shit and chase some storms with me."

"You've got a one-track mind," Denny said. "And you know as well as I do that if we went out and chased storms, we'd end up chasing new jobs."

Hargrave turned to him. "Hell, Denny," he said, taking a long drink from the bottle. "They've done everything but strip you naked and make you run the gauntlet anyhow. What the hell difference—"

"I'm going to make it work," Denny said. "Things change."

"Right," Hargrave said, turning back to stare at nothing. "Horton was practically laughin' when he gave you this one. The Washington beat to faith healers . . ." he shook his head. "It ain't manly, Denny."

"If I shove it back down their throat, it is," Denny answered, and he forced himself to diffuse the anger that was building up and would affect his performance.

A bartender in western shirt and vest strode up to them. "Get you something?" he asked.

Denny looked at the man. "You got that faith healer here tonight?" he asked.

The man looked at his watch. "Yeah. She's back in the bullring." He narrowed his gaze. "Hey . . . ain't you somebody?"

"Nobody special," Denny replied, Frank snorting around his beer. "Is it some kind of show or what?"

The bartender's young face darkened somewhat. "It gives me the creeps," he said. "There's somethin' . . . I don't know . . . wrong about it."

"What do you mean?"

"Somethin' wrong, that's all," the man said, then turned abruptly and walked away.

"Interesting," Denny said.

"Regional interest," Hargrave said. "Regional fuckin' interest." He swept a lanky arm around the interior of the place. "Maybe this will mean somethin' to history. Hey, barkeep! Another long-neck Bud!"

"No," Denny said, putting a hand on Hargrave's arm. "If you're working with me tonight, you're staying sharp. Just because it's a poop story doesn't mean we don't give it the good treatment."

"You're a fool, you know that?" Hargrave said, his long face deeply lined.

"What does that make you?" Denny replied.

"A camera . . . that's all," the man said, finishing his beer and sliding his lean frame off the stool. "Just a camera. Come on, let's roll some tape."

Denny picked up his gear and watched Hargrave limp off. The man had been a topflight cameraman for CBS during the Vietnam War, his reconstructed leg a shrapnel love tap from a bouncing-betty mine near Khe Sanh. The war had changed him somehow, altered his personality just enough that his view came from just slightly off center. It was enough to keep him off the nets, and probably enough to keep him off the air entirely were it not for people like Denny who were willing to work with him as he was and live for those two or three truly great pieces a year that the man's warped brain was capable of producing.

He followed Hargrave through the smoke haze toward the hallway leading to the small arena, passing the carnivallike shooting gallery where a bunch of truckers in teamster ball caps were war whooping as they made the fake squirrels and mannequin piano player jump under the withering fire from their light-beam rifles.

Both he and Frank had been here before, five months previously. It was right after Ted Gayler, WCN's owner, had busted him down to regional-reporting fillers to be used whenever there was space on the all-news format. Billy Bob's had been his first assignment, his first humiliation as he lined up at the shooting gallery for his turn at the squirrels just as the truckers had. Two weeks before that he'd had a personal interview with the president.

They moved into the dark hallway, a line of strangely quiet people queued up all the way to the arena door. There was something desperate about them, an atmosphere that created a static tension that hung physically in the air. It was so strong, so overpowering, that Hargrave turned to stare back at Denny, brows knit in concern.

He responded by shrugging.

WCN had picked up the story of the Billy Bob's faith healer and finder of lost things, a woman named Tawny Kyle, from a local Fort Worth newscast, Gayler himself calling down to Horton and telling him to put Denny on the story. It wasn't much of an item, just something else to blindside Denny Stiller with and force him to walk out on his contract.

A cheer careened out of the arena and down the hallway,

the atmosphere momentarily lifting, then sinking like a stone again almost immediately. Inexplicably, Denny remembered his childhood and a story his father had told him about a woman he'd seen in Poland during World War II. She'd been afflicted with stigmata and bled from the palms. To his father, it had been proof positive of the existence of God. To Denny, even at age six, it had seemed only a sign of his father's gullibility. Oddly, it had been the last conversation he and his father would ever have.

Hargrave waited for him at the arena doorway, his hands absently uncrating the video camera as he slipped on the battery pack, his eyes searching the confined space for the best place to set up.

Denny moved through the doorway, staring into the crowded arena. It jarred him, just like it had the last time he'd been here. The place reminded him of a Hollywood set. It was an arena, but far too small, its dust-fogged dirt floor no longer and wider than thirty yards. The perimeter was fenced, with bleacher seating for two hundred rising all around, the enclosing ceiling and harsh lighting giving the scene the air and unreality of a sound stage.

Most of the seats were filled. The audience was about half drunken patrons and half poor people in K-Mart clothes, the kind Denny called the "mobile home generation." The drunks hooted and laughed, while the others stared in rapt fascination at the people on the arena floor. There was plenty to stare at.

Two folding metal chairs were set out at the far end of the arena, a spotlight focusing on their occupants. One was a washed-out, middle-age blond with sagging eyes and a sagging face that was too heavily rouged and topped by a beehive hairdo, the kind that Denny hadn't seen for twenty years. She wore tight jeans and four-inch spike heels. She wore an overlarge T-shirt with the name Tawny amateurishly scrawled on it in sequins. She would have looked comical had it not been for the scrawny young girl sitting beside her. The girl sat, rocking sideways on her chair, dirty black hair stringing across her face. Her eyes were large. Even from across the arena floor they were the largest eyes Denny had ever seen. Her eyes stared vacantly, eyes that seemed removed from her body. Both her hands were up in front of her face, her fingers flailing wildly as she looked at nothing. She wore a dirty T-shirt with a ripped sleeve and dirty jeans. She was not in the arena, at least not mentally. It gave Denny a chill to wonder where in the world she might be.

"How do we want to handle this?" Hargrave whispered, the strange couple shaking even him.

"Move around," Denny replied. "Find a good spot. I want the camera tight on them, especially the girl. We'll play it by ear."

"That girl . . ." Hargrave said, his voice hoarse.

"What?" Denny asked, unable to take his eyes from her.

"There's somethin' . . ." the man said, a slightly trembling hand coming up to rub his face around the camera he'd hoisted onto his shoulder. "I had a niece once that was just like her. She was autistic."

An overweight black woman in a gaudy flower-printed cotton dress was being led by a child in a new suit across the dusty floor toward Tawny and the girl.

"You say you *had* a niece," Denny asked, still mesmerized by the girl. "What happened to her?"

Hargrave turned to look at him, his runny blue eyes frail as crystal. "She died in an institution at age twenty-three. God, Denny. She was the most beautiful girl I ever saw. Ever. But she was just . . ."

"Why have you come?" Tawny Kyle asked, taking an envelope from the little boy and dropping it into a plastic trash bag laying beside her on the floor. Denny nearly laughed, and several members of the audience did. The woman had a high nasal twang that was at once comical and grating. This was going to sound awful coming over the air.

"My gramma cain't talk," the boy said, the audience chuckling again.

"You rolling?" Denny whispered.

"Yeah."

"Move around. Find a decent position. I want tight on that little girl's eyes. Do we need the lights?"

"Not in here."

"Can you hear me?" Kyle asked the black woman.

The woman nodded, the flesh on her arms jiggling.

"Then git down heah on yo knees, honey."

The woman knelt, the blond reaching out to clasp a hand around her throat.

"Choke her!" somebody yelled from the bleachers, a small chorus of laughs drowned out by shushes.

Denny took it all in, not sure of the angle here. Was he

there to make fun of it all, to expose yet another fraud, or to play it straight? He couldn't get a feel for it yet. The girl had unsettled him too much.

The Kyle woman reached her other hand toward the girl, pulling the dancing fingers of one hand away from her face, the girl continuing her personal performance oblivious to what was happening around her.

"You are a sinner," Kyle said in a monotone. "But through the power of the Lord, Jesus Christ, Ah will heal you."

The spiel was contrived, the delivery obvious and unconvincing. If the woman was a preacher, she was the worst Denny had ever seen.

The woman shivered violently in her seat for several seconds, both she and the black woman grabbing their throats, gagging, in pain. Then it abruptly stopped. "Rise up," she said. "By the power of God you are healed. Rise up and speak."

The woman got up slowly, staring around for the little boy who lingered nearby.

"Go ahead, honey," the blond said. "Talk fer us."

The woman just stared at her.

"Go ahead now."

The arena quieted to a whisper, everyone staring. The woman put a hand to her throat, croaking as if she were clearing it. Her eyes widened as she stared around the arena, her mouth hanging open.

And a sound came out of her throat, very small and far away at first, then louder, bolder.

"Jaaasssonnn!"

The boy ran to her squealing, throwing his arms around her. She did it again, louder, slurred.

"JAASSON! JASON!"

The crowd cheered, even the cowboys.

"Ahhh cannnn takkk!" the woman said, her tongue thick, as if she'd never used it. "Praissse th Looord!"

The black woman began laughing and making sounds, as if discovering her voice for the first time, her joy unmistakable as she and the little boy danced around, laughing and clapping their hands.

The blond smiled slightly, then leaned over nonchalantly to look inside her trash bag.

Denny's insides were shaking. He'd underestimated the woman terribly. He'd been watching faith healers for years, and most of them were content to overstate their own performance while leaving those they "healed" to perform without sincerity or professionalism. This woman was different. Playing down her own role, she featured the victims. The black woman's performance was flawless. She almost had him fooled.

The woman left, singing loudly off-key, a young, pregnant girl taking her place, she also handing the Kyle woman an envelope, which went into the trash bag.

"What have you come fer?" Tawny Kyle asked.

The woman looked shyly at the ground, then gazed from side to side. "I-I want to know the . . . sex of my baby," she said in a near whisper.

"Come close," Kyle said, and placed one hand on the girl's stomach, the other once again taking hold of her assistant's flapping hand. Then she stared for a moment, her eyes narrowing. She suddenly released the pregnant girl, abruptly reaching into the trash bag and withdrawing the envelope, handing it back.

"You jes go on home now," she said.

"But they said you could tell about the baby. They said—"

"You jest go on," the woman said, turning away from her.

"But I paid you fifteen dollars!"

"You got yo money, child," Kyle replied angrily. "Now go on."

She then raised her hand in the air, one of the parking valets hurrying onto the floor to lead the girl away.

This made no sense. It wasn't set up right. Following the mute woman with a dud like this wasn't good show business *or* good religion. Denny was beginning to get impatient for usable footage. Hargrave, meanwhile, had managed to angle up the side of the arena to within ten feet of the autistic girl, his camera zeroing relentlessly on her face, her hands now flapping wildly beside her ears.

The next man in line was looking for a lost wallet. The healer put her hand on his back pocket and told him it was under the circular saw table in his garage.

"Of course!" the man yelled happily and charged out of the arena full speed, to the amusement of the spectators.

Denny tightened his lips. This wasn't going to do. He and Hargrave could stand there all night and never find an angle or get any footage. If he was going to make it work, he'd have to shake up things himself. If it wrecked her act, that was what she deserved for taking money from poor people.

The next man in line began to walk across the floor, Denny moving quickly into the arena and hurrying to intercept him.

"Sir," he said, taking the man's arm.

The man was big, a farmer in overalls. He looked darkly over at Denny. "What?"

"Do you know me, Dennis Stiller?" Denny asked.

The man's eyes widened in recognition. "You're on the TV," he said, voice awed.

Denny nodded. "I want to get some quick pictures with Tawny Kyle," he said. "If you wait a few minutes, I'll put you on the TV, too."

"Sure," the man said. "Can I say 'Hi' to my grandkids?"

"You bet."

"I'm obliged."

"Thanks." Denny turned and moved toward Tawny Kyle, an idea beginning to take shape in his head. If Gayler was going to send him to a sideshow, he'd have to expect the Stiller approach—direct and uncompromising—the style that had made him famous to begin with.

As he approached the woman, he could hear the murmurs in the audience as recognition spread. For her part, Tawny Kyle merely looked quizzical and, perhaps, a trifle afraid.

He got within two feet of her and stood, looking down. "You're Tawny Kyle?" he asked.

"We ain't doin' nothin' illegal," she said low, her twang strong even in whisper. "Mr. Harrow, he allows us to come in heah and—"

"I'm not the police," Denny interrupted.

"Then what are you?"

"I'm a TV newsman with World Cable News and we want to do a story on you."

The woman puckered her lips, wrinkles etching deeply around her entire mouth. "Ah'm gonna tell you like Ah told them other fellers last time," she said, narrowing her gaze. "You kin do a story about me, but it's gonna cost you, jes like it costs ever'body else."

Denny smiled, thinking of all the times people had offered *him* money if he'd do a story on them. "How much?" he asked.

"Same as ever'body," she said. "Fifteen dollars."

He turned and looked at the girl, her hands still flapping at the sides of her head. Her face was flawless, unlined by any emotion, her eyes deep reflecting pools that were either highly intelligent or simply bottomless. "If I give you fifteen dollars," he said, listening to the crowd get restless all around them, "you'll be able to perform some . . . healing for me?"

"Ah figger to," the woman said, looking around. "But you better crap or get off the pot, honey. Ah'm losin' the audience."

Denny fished a twenty out of his pocket and handed it to her.

She smiled at the bill. "I'll git yo change," she said.

"Keep it," Denny said, then turned to Hargrave at the arena's edge. "Frank! Put that damned thing on a tripod and come over here."

"What for?" the man called back.

"Come on!" Denny said. "The natives are restless."

Frank went into the camera case, Denny returning his gaze to Tawny Kyle. "My friend's got a crippled leg," he said. "I wondered if you—"

"It'll cost him fifteen dollars, too," Kyle replied. "In advance." She held out her hand.

Denny reached into his pockets again and found another twenty, wondering how this was going to look on the expense report. "That girl before," he said, handing her the money. "Why wouldn't you tell her about the sex of her baby?"

The woman put the twenty in the trash bag, this time not bothering to offer change. "Because it don't matter," she said. "That baby's gonna be borned dead, is why."

"How do you know that?" he asked.

"Ah see'd it, that's all," Tawny Kyle said, and tightened her lips again.

Denny nodded. "What I want to do," he said, "is bring Frank over to you, then I'll go and saw a few words for the camera before you do your thing with him, okay?"

"Do what?" she asked.

Denny took a breath. "I'll point to you when I want you to do . . . whatever it is you do."

"Ain't me, it's the Lord," Tawny Kyle said.

"Right," Denny said, Frank walking up to join them.

"What do you need?" the man asked.

"Tawny here is going to heal your leg, Frank," Denny said. "Right on camera she's going to heal you."

Hargrave's face darkened. "This ain't funny, pard," he said low. "I don't want to be no laughin'stock."

"Business, Frank," he said, walking away. "Don't worry about it. We're going to give the folks some hard news to mix with their fantasies."

He turned his back to them and moved to the camera, removing his still-wet sport jacket and hanging it over the perimeter fence.

"I don't like this, Denny," Hargrave called to him.

"Pretend you're Bob Woodward and this is Watergate," Denny said, rolling up his sleeves.

"Who?"

Denny fished the small lapel mike out of the case. "Never mind," he called absently, hooking the mike to his tie. "It'll only take a minute." *Or less*, he thought.

The audience was talking loudly, many of them getting up and leaving.

"Let's git t'movin'," the Kyle woman said loudly.

"Just about ready," Denny said, walking around to peer through the viewfinder of the still running camera. The scene set out nicely, the girl, the strange girl, the focus of attention. Denny stared at her for a moment, wondering if she should be off getting help somewhere. Why was she being used this way?

He gauged a distance through the viewfinder, then walked around in front of the camera to speak. At this point he was going to simply run as much tape as he could. Later, he could edit it to any form he wanted.

"This is Dennis Stiller reporting to you from Fort Worth, Texas's own Billy Bob's," Denny said, falling into his television voice and simply taking it on the fly. "We're here tonight to witness a phenomenon that has been a great success here at Fort Worth's hottest night spot. For those of you out there who think that water and oil don't mix, I give you Tawny Kyle, faith healer extraordinaire, who plies her trade here in Billy Bob's bullring every Thursday."

He made a flourish with his arm and stepped away from the camera so it would show nothing but Tawny, Frank, and the strange girl. He continued talking.

"For fifteen dollars on Thursday nights, bar patrons and local zealots can hoist a few cold ones at one of the establishment's many bars, then come on in here for a dose of healing and salvation as only Texas can dish it up. Tonight, especially for our cameras, Ms. Tawny Kyle has agreed to try and heal the leg of my cameraman, Frank Hargrave, who was wounded in Vietnam."

"Enough already," Frank called. "Git on with it."

The crowd laughed, responding to the camera and the artificial reality it created for all of them.

"Okay, okay," Denny said.

"Now?" the woman asked, looking at her watch.

"Just a minute," Denny said, going back to look through the viewfinder again. Something wasn't right here. He needed more. The leg, that was it. The leg was covered.

"Frank!" he called. "Why don't you pull off your pants for us, so we can get a look at the leg?"

"You can go to hell, too," Hargrave replied angrily. "What are you tryin' to do to me?"

"She's going to heal you, for Chrisake," Denny said. "Let's drag out the offending organ and see what's what!"

Hargrave frowned deeply, the crowd applauding, then clapping in unison, yelling, "Pants off. Pants off."

Hargrave's face settled into a posture of disgust, his hands going to his belt. "You want it asshole," he said. "You got it. But don't be surprised if I take it outta you sometime."

"Lighten up," Denny said, unsure as to why he had carried things to such extremes. He had wanted to put the woman on the hot seat, but he didn't have to do it with Frank.

The man dropped his jeans to the floor; the crowd hushed at the sight. His leg was a tribute to modern medical science, a human jigsaw puzzle with monstrous livid inch-wide purple scars running around his thigh and calf, nothing quite fitting together the way it was supposed to. As he hopped around, trying to pull the pants legs over his cowboy boots, his leg moved strangely, the five pins that held it together at the joints giving it an inhuman-looking agility to bend at odd angles.

The room had become totally quiet.

"Satisfied?" Hargrave asked Denny.

Denny still hunched over the camera, zoomed in on the leg, then pulled back for more detached observation. Without a word, he lifted his hand and pointed to the woman.

She nodded and looked up at Hargrave. "Why have you come here?" she asked.

"Just git on with it," Hargrave said. "I feel like enough of a fool already."

"Come closer," she said, the man complying.

She reached out, running her fingers gently over the scars of his legs. "Lot'sa pain," she said. "Still have it?"

"Some," Hargrave replied, and Denny knew a lot more about his friend than the man would have ever told him.

Tawny took the girl's hand, then ran her free hand over

Hargrave's battered leg, the man staring down in great sadness.

"You are a sinner," she said. "But by the power of Jesus Christ Ah will heal you."

She closed her eyes, rocking with the same motions the girl was using. Suddenly she quaked violently, a loud groan slowly escaping her lips, and it seemed to Denny that the lights had dimmed somewhat.

Frank screamed, loudly and without control, triggering other screams in the audience with its frightening timbre. He jerked away from the woman, his hands going to his leg, terrified cries still spewing from his lips.

"Medic!" he screamed. "Medic! God, help me!"

Then Denny saw it, and heard himself screaming. The leg, the shattered leg was slowly realigning itself, pulling itself together as the scars faded. He could see bones moving around under the skin, pushing themselves back together properly. Hargrave yelled loudly as something fell from his leg and hit the dirt floor. It was one of the pins in his knee!

One by one, the pins pushed themselves from his leg and fell to the ground, Frank's screams turning to whimpers, then moans. And within twenty seconds, it was over.

The man stood, staring down in disbelief at himself. The leg that had a moment before caused anguished cries because of its ugliness was perfectly formed, perfectly normal. Hargrave turned to stare at the camera, an image Denny would never forget as the man's face lit up with a mixture of fright and overwhelming joy in the presence of something beyond belief or understanding.

Not a sound could be heard in the arena as people stared in shocked disbelief, faith rewarded beyond reason, beyond even their dreams or desires. Denny looked at Hargrave, then looked at him again through the viewfinder. He was totally numb.

Someone in the stands began crying, softly, like a baby in the middle of the night.

"You ain't no statue," Tawny said in her offhand way. "Go ahead and git to walkin' on it."

Hargrave turned slowly away from the camera and looked at the woman. She laughed.

"Go ahead," she said.

The man gingerly reached out a foot and took a tentative

step, then another. He turned to Denny. "Shit, man. Oh shit. It's workin', Denny. It's workin'!"

He began walking slowly, then faster, moving around the arena like a prancer in a horse show. Then he ran, yelling in delight, whooping like the teamsters at the shooting gallery as he charged full speed around the edge of the arena in boots and no pants.

He jumped and fell down and jumped again. He did a flurry of Rockette kicks, then danced the twist to the uproarious applause of the audience, singing the tune at the top of his voice, delirious with the moment.

Denny, still in shock, turned and stared at the camera. What in the name of God had he captured on tape?

What?

In the name of God.

He ZOOMED IN on the little girl. She was rocking back and forth, totally oblivious of the excitement around her.

Scene 2

(three hours later)

DALLAS, TEXAS—INT—NITE. We are looking down a long, dimly lit hallway within the studios of World Cable News. At the end of the hallway is a door with a glass cutout set at head level. Light spills through the small window, and we see just the head of a woman talking animatedly, her words muffled by the closed door. Several beats later, the door BANGS OPEN, the woman striding purposefully toward us. Through the open door we see a security guard sitting at a desk for just a second before the door closes again. The woman is MOLLY HARTWELL, WCN producer. As she closes in on us we see that she is smallish, with a lush figure self-consciously hidden beneath a loose fitting dress and lace-up boots. Curly brown hair bounces on her shoulders as she walks.
ANGLE—MOLLY'S FACE. She appears angry, her jaw set hard.

ANGLE—MOLLY'S POV. She moves down the hall, stopping to push open a doorway with a drawing of a large, smiling sun tacked to it. The door opens into the WEATHER CENTER, consisting of a series of monitors set on desktops showing changing weather patterns. Two men sit at the consoles, overlaying computer-generated maps of the United States on the satellite pictures of changing weather patterns.
ANGLE—MOLLY.

MOLLY
You ooon Stillor?

ANGLE—WEATHER CENTER. A short, bald man smiles up at Molly. He is RED BOLTON, meteorologist.

RED
He said to tell you he's in Studio C.

ANGLE—MOLLY. She nods and moves out of the room. We follow her down the hall. It turns, and she passes Studio A and Studio B. Studio B has a flashing red light just above its door, the words ON THE AIR blazing in and out of existence. She stops just outside the doorway of Studio C, listening to the sounds of muffled singing within. She hesitates a beat, tightens her jaw, and enters.
ANGLE—STUDIO INT. The set is dark, an informal talk show with chairs and a coffee table, connected to a kitchen set. Three cameras sit dead and unmanned on their moorings. Frank Hargrave, obviously sloppy drunk, a beer bottle in his hand, is dancing around the set, moving in and out of the furniture, singing loudly.

FRANK
(off-key)
He's got the whole world, in His hands. He's got the whole world, in His hands. He's got the whole world, in His hands (etc.) . . .

ANGLE—MOLLY. She narrows her eyes and sighs deeply. She looks to the right and sees . . .
THE CONTROL BOOTH. Through the wide front window of the booth, she can see Denny moving around within. The

booth is nearly dark, lit only by TV monitors and instrument panels.

ANGLE—MOLLY. She moves up the five steps to the booth and enters.

Denny watched her move into the booth, her rigid posture the usual giveaway that he was in trouble. "Howdy, darlin'," he said in a put-on west-Texas accent.

"Where've you been?" she asked.

"Business," he replied. "As soon as you see—"

"Remember our little hot tub happy hour?" she said sadly. "And our candlelit dinner for two?"

"Molly—"

"Don't Molly me," she said, throwing herself down on a chair in front of a bank of monitors juicing test patterns. "It's always the same, isn't it? Good old Molly sets it up and good old Denny tests the limits of human endurance and understanding by screwing it around. I perfumed my body for you, Stiller. I sat in the goddamn hot tub so long I came out looking like an albino prune. Why do I put up with you?"

He moved to a tape machine and began rewinding the tape of Billy Bob's. "Because you love me?" he offered.

"I love my dog, too," she said in exasperation. "But I beat it when it craps on the carpet. And what the hell is that crazy man doing running around drunk in the middle of the studio?"

He jerked around to face her, pointing out the front of the booth. "That's just the point, Molly," he said. "He's *running* around the studio. Frank is *running*."

He watched her sitting there in the half-darkness of the cramped booth. She began to speak, then thought, her face softening from anger to reflection. She turned her head and watched Frank cavorting around the set, then turned slowly back to stare at Denny. "What the hell is going on here?" she asked quietly.

"I've got something to show you," he said, grinning. "And you're not going to believe it."

He turned on the half-inch tape machine, the picture immediately jumping to the ten monitors on the control panel and the bullring of Billy Bob's took its reality there in the booth.

"It's rough," he said, as they listened to the voice of the previously mute woman. "I haven't edited it yet. I'm trying to decide if I should or not."

"Not edit?" she said, professional interest kicking in.

"Just watch. You're going to be seeing the resurrection of Denny Stiller." He pointed to the screen and sat down beside her, eagerly watching her eyes narrow as Tawny gave a voice to the woman who couldn't speak. "I thought she was faking at first, but look at that exuberance. This is great stuff. I can feel the energy right through the screen."

They continued watching, the light from the screens reflecting off Molly's face as she concentrated on the action with a professional eye. "What's the deal with the little girl?" she asked.

"Frank thinks she's autistic," he replied.

"Why is she out there?"

"Tawny Kyle denied it," he said, picking up a pencil to take down some ideas, "but I think the girl, her name's Amy, is the key to the whole thing here. Do you notice that Tawny takes her hand before she does anything?"

"It could just be part of the act," Molly said, leaning back in the chair.

"*If* it's an act," Denny returned. "Look, here comes the part with Frank."

He found himself drawn into the screen, Molly laughing when Frank had to take off his pants, then gasping at the fleshy jigsaw of his leg. This was the third time for Denny, having seen it once live and once more when he got the tape into the studio, and even after repeating viewings, it was hard for him to believe what he was looking at. He felt it in his head, and he felt it in his stomach. And when he felt the familiar tingle in his nose, he turned away from the screen to keep from sharing Frank's emotions and crying. This was business, and he wasn't about to screw it up by involvement. He had recorded something talked about in history, but never saved for posterity. He had the first, genuine recording of a psychic phenomenon in action. Small sounds escaped from Molly's throat every time one of the pins removed itself from Frank's leg.

When the tape had run its course, she turned to him, breathing heavily, her own eyes moist, mascara smeared. "H-how did you do that?" she asked in a small voice.

He leaned over and took her hands, surprised to find her trembling. "I didn't do anything," he said, and put up a hand. "Scout's honor. This is unedited life."

"I can't believe it."

He stood and moved to the director's chair. "You want me to call in Frank and have him take off his pants again?"

She looked at him quizzically. "You're going to have to," she said. "I don't think I can believe it otherwise."

Denny picked up the headset and juiced the studio speakers. "Frank," he said, the voice loud, godlike, all around them. "Come on in here for a minute."

He took off the headset and swiveled around to face her. "What do you think?" he asked. "Will it help?"

"Help what?" she replied.

He slapped the chair arms. "Help me get back in . . . you know, good graces."

She shook her head, eyes wide and confused. "Denny . . . I don't think I even know my own name right now. My insides are shaking. Don't you know what you've got there? It's an act of God, Denny, a . . . a . . ."

"Miracle's the word you're lookin' for," Frank said from the doorway. He staggered in, knocking over a folding chair and falling onto the instrument panel, a whole bank of lights coming on over the kitchen set. It reminded Denny that he hadn't eaten since lunch.

Hargrave slid into a chair and began idly playing with the control board, the studio coming to life then dying again in small sections. "It's a first-class hand-of-God miracle. There ain't been nothin' like this since Moses."

"Molly wants to get a look at your gams," Denny said, stifling a smile.

Frank wiggled his eyebrows. "Always happy to oblige a lady," he said. His hands left the control board and went to his pants, Molly tactfully looking away as he shinnied them down. "Near as I can figure she restructured the whole shebang: muscles, tissue, blood vessels . . . everythin'. What Charlie and modern medicine did to me, she undid in a few seconds. Take a feel of that leg."

Molly reached out a tentative hand and touched his leg. "Do you swear to me that it looked like it did on the tape and that it was held together with pins?"

The man nodded. "You got it. Most of the doctors wanted to take the son of a bitch off," he said, "and the others told me it'd be a miracle if I ever walked again . . . but they was wrong." He pointed to the leg. "This here's the miracle." He pulled his pants up.

"Miracle is a pretty strong word," Denny said. "It suggests more."

"A purposeful act of God," Molly said.

Denny just stared at her.

"What are you going to do with this?" she asked.

"You tell me," Denny returned. "I'm a newsman and this is news. I thought I'd try and work it up, then see if I could get the exclusive to do follow-ups, maybe several, with management permission."

She frowned, thinking.

"What's wrong?" Denny asked.

"I don't know," she said. "It seems so . . . crass to talk about packaging God in between the sports and the entertainment."

"Stop with the God talk," Denny said. "It just confuses things. Look, Tawny Kyle is no more religious than I am, I'm sure of it. It's all just her package, her way of selling what she does to the rubes."

"If it wasn't God that did this to me," Frank said, "what did?"

"It doesn't matter," Denny said. "Who cares where the power came from, as long as—"

"You really don't get it," Molly said too loudly. "It may not matter to you, but to the couple of billion people who could ultimately see this thing, it's going to make a great deal of difference."

"Fantastic!" Denny said. "So we'll turn big numbers, and if Denny Stiller plays his cards right, he'll have a hand-stamped ticket to network heaven."

"I've been wonderin'," Frank said, draining the last of his Budweiser. "If that little girl can do this for me . . . what else can she do?"

Denny thought about that. If Amy Kyle did, indeed, exercise control over physical laws of Nature, her potential was limitless. He needed to get Tawny and Amy signed to some sort of contract before someone else beat him to it. He looked to Molly again and couldn't understand her lack of enthusiasm.

"What the hell's wrong with you?" he asked finally.

She shook her head, reaching out a hand to touch his, then letting it fall to her lap. "Something just isn't right here," she said, "and I'm not sure what it is. I'm happy and excited about your story, but there's warning sirens blasting away in the back of my mind. It's like, all religious faith and beliefs are built around the idea of the potential existence of this kind of power . . . but the reality of it is something else again."

"You're worrying about nothing," he said. "We live in a

world of wonders—telephones, airplanes"—he gestured around the booth—"television for God's sake. This will be just another source of input among an infinite number of inputs."

"Then let's forget about it," she said, a smile turning the corners of her mouth.

"You know what I mean," he said, getting angry at her deliberate obtuseness. "We just run this thing straight, no religious connotations . . . you know, little girl with the big power. People will get all excited, then forget about it the next time some public figure gets caught with his pants down. Meantime, we milk it."

"Learn your audience, Denny," she said, staring hard at him. "Don't be surprised if people see this and start erecting altars to that girl."

"Then we *are* going to run it?" he asked, finally hearing what he wanted.

Molly swiveled around to face Frank. "Could you take a walk for a while?" she asked. "I need to talk to Denny alone."

"Take a walk," Frank said, slowly uncoiling from his chair. "Can't tell you how happy I am to be able to accommodate you." He tossed his bottle across the room to crash in a trash can. "I need another beer anyhow."

"Don't run off," Denny called to the man as he reached the door. "I need you around in a bit for a testimonial. And for right now, don't tell anybody about your leg."

Frank waved, moving out of the booth, whistling "Amazing Grace."

"Tell me you don't see the possibilities in this thing?" Denny asked her when the door shut.

Molly gazed at the floor for a moment, then suddenly looked up at him. "What would you do if I said I wouldn't run it?" she asked.

"I'd go over your head," he replied. "You're just the producer. I'd take it to Gayler if I had to. Hell, he's the one who put me on to this to begin with."

"He did?" she asked. "I wonder why?"

"Maybe he likes faith healers," Denny said. "What difference does it make? Once we show this, his news division will be talked about all over the world. I've looked at a lot of footage in my time, and I've never seen anything like this."

She got out of her chair and walked over to him. "This isn't just a story, Denny," she said. "Sure, I understand the possibilities. This could be the biggest story in the history of stories." She leaned down and kissed him deeply, Denny pulling her onto his lap, his hands casually stroking her. She sighed, relaxing in his arms.

"Sorry I missed tonight," he said.

She locked her arms around his neck. "It's okay, you brought a note from home. For once, I almost wish you didn't have a good excuse."

"What's your problem with this?" he asked, a hand to her face, touching the softness. "This is the biggest thing to happen to me in years."

"I don't know," she said. "Your demotion . . . this story . . . its implications. None of it makes any sense. It scares me somehow."

"Scares you?"

"What good can this story do?" she asked. "It will just get a lot of the wrong people stirred up."

He straightened, turning her face to his. "It's news," he said. "You remember our jobs? You know, we report, the folks watch, then judge. It's a time-honored tradition."

"It's not real news and you know it," she said. "It's an overblown feature that's just going to upset people for no reason. You can destroy that tape and walk away from this thing clean right now, and the Earth continues spinning in blissful indifference, billions of people living out their nonproductive little lives, happy as pigs in slop."

"What are you saying?" he asked.

"I'm saying that this whole deal is nothing but problems," she answered, her voice tightened up like a mainspring. "I'm saying this is too hot for you to handle. Take it out of the machine, burn it. That tape has trouble written all over it."

He sat up straight, practically dumping her off his lap. "And throw my career right out the window?" he said.

"Don't be childish," she said. "You're overdramatizing and you know it."

"No, Molly. You listen to me for once. I've waited my whole life for this story and none of your 'fears' are going to stop me. I'm beginning to wonder if you're afraid for me to make a comeback." He thought for a moment, then pointed a finger at her, an artificial smile plastered on his face. "Maybe right now you've got me weak and vulnerable, right where you want me."

She climbed off his lap, fighting to maintain her dignity. "That's it, you bastard," she said coldly, straightening her skirt.

"The blood bank is closed for the night. You want your story . . . you got it. We'll run it at eight A.M. as a news feature, then again every half hour until midnight. We'll give you five full minutes. You work it up however you like . . . those visuals will sell no matter what the hell you do. Just don't say I didn't warn you."

"Now, Molly—"

"Look around you, Denny," she said, the electronic mazes flashing everywhere. "This is your reality. You forget that there's a whole world out there that doesn't think the way you do. You can hurt yourself with this thing. And this time I think I'm going to let you." She turned and strode out of the booth, slamming the door behind her.

Denny turned back to the tape machine, forgetting about Molly's tirade the minute she was gone. She'd come around; she always did.

He rewound the tape, playing it through one more time, deciding that it would run better raw and unedited, with extra footage added to the front and back that emphasized the truth of the encounter. That part would have to be strong because all reality tended to blend together on the TV screen.

As he watched the tape the fourth time, his eyes were drawn to the crowd, to the faces set in awe and confusion as they watched the tableau of Frank's leg unfold before them. There was one face in the crowd, an older man dressed in a long raincoat and wearing a hat. He bore a striking resemblance to Ted Gayler, a very striking resemblance.

Scene 3

(the next day)

MONTAGE. We see a swirl of scenes in the early morning, all showing people to whom television is an intergral part of day-to-day existence. Everyone's TV is turned on, all tuned to WCN as Denny's feature progresses and we watch people getting ready for work, mothers making breakfast for their families, a tollbooth attendant with a five-inch screen in his cubicle, a secretarial pool in a large office, an elderly retired couple with coffee, a sweating man in tank top and shorts doing push-ups in front of the TV, and people still in bed turning on the set with a remote control. The only sound we hear is Denny Stiller's voice introducing his taped experience. The sights we see are pulled from the deepest roots of human belief and emotion, as we watch a torrent of faces become transfixed with wonder and confusion at the truth their eyes and ears witness. As the scene progresses we watch, fascinated, as eggs burn in a frying pan and phones go unanswered, human beings caught up in the same mind-numbing paralysis that grips us when we watch newsreel footage of people leaping to their deaths from the top floors of burning skyscrapers. And above it all, Denny's voice drones on in practiced, professional monotone . . .

<u>DENNY</u> (vo)

Since the beginning of recorded history, the civilization called Man has been tied indelibly to notions
beyond its experience, be they religious miracles,
tales of sea serpents and dragons, or the worldwide
phenomenon called UFOs. Though thousands of volumes have been written about preternatural experience and many eyewitnesses have come forward to
testify, the truth of the matter is that no hard evidence of the existence of phenomenon beyond the

natural order has come to light. Religions depend upon faith, many thousands of UFO sightings are not backed up by empirical data or convincing photos, and old sailors' legends make up the bulk of monster stories.

That all changed for me—and for the world—last night. The tape you are watching was recorded just as it happened. My cameraman and myself have sworn affidavits testifying to the fact that our tape was not altered or doctored in any way whatsoever. In fact, I am running the tape unedited so that you will see it just exactly as it happened, and it is available to experts to test for edits or camera tricks. What I believe you are watching is the first true recording of paranormal phenomenon, and in it, a woman, Tawny Kyle, and her daughter, Amy, are performing actions in defiance of the physical sciences.

What this means, I don't know. What I do know is that the story doesn't end here. I will continue to study Tawny Kyle, continue to probe her power and its roots and bring you the story just as it happens. How much can she do? What are her limitations, if any? And what could such power mean to the world at large? The answers to our questions await further study. We are truly staring into the face of something beyond our understanding. It's heady . . . and a little frightening. This is Denny Stiller, WCN News, Fort Worth, Texas.

CUT TO:
CLOSE UP—FRANK'S FACE on tape, twisted in agony as the pins drop from his legs. We PULL BACK to reveal an elegantly furnished office. A man in a silk, pin-striped black suit is sitting behind a large desk, watching the tape. A Bible sits on the desktop, priestly vestments on a hanger dangle from a nearby coatrack.
CLOSE UP—THE MAN'S FACE. The face is smooth and unlined; an impressive shock of silver gray hair is combed straight back from his rugged, handsome face. The man watches impassively, no emotion bleeding through, but we sense something behind those intense quiet eyes—something unsettling. He is DR. JAMES CONNOVER, televangelical

superstar. In the background, the PHONE RINGS. We PULL
BACK as the doctor reaches for the receiver.

<u>CONNOVER</u>
(picking up the phone)
This is Dr. Connover speaking. . . . Oh, it's
you. . . . Yes, I'm watching it now. . . . What do
you think I think? I'll handle it any way you tell me
to. . . . With pleasure. You, too. (he cuts off the call
with his finger, then punches up an extension number) Helen, This is Dr. Connover. Would you get
hold of Larry and get him in here first shot. . . .
Sure. And I want everything you can dig up on that
Tawny Kyle character *and* on Denny Stiller. . . .
Yesterday, Helen. I want it yesterday.

He hangs up the phone and stands, with great dignity and
purpose, moving to a large bookshelf that takes up an entire
wall. He removes a videotape from the shelf and walks to the
television, putting the tape into the machine. Then he returns
to his desk and sits, turning on the tape with a hand control.
ANGLE—THE TELEVISION. Denny Stiller is standing
before a huge amorphous church, a microphone in his hand.

<u>DENNY</u>
. . . called the great white mound by its detractors,
Dr. Connover's home base Church of the Savior itself
cost nearly a hundred million dollars to build . . .

ANGLE—CLOSE-UP—CONNOVER. His face remains impassive as Stiller continues to talk.

<u>DENNY</u> (cont, os)
But it is only one of many strange financial dealings
connected with the operation. Our sources show that
Connover's expenses ran nearly two hundred million
dollars a year for the past three years, including his
satellite systems and overseas brances, while only
generating a little more than half that amount in contributions. An IRS investigation into the matter
seems to have stalled out, but the questions remain—
where does Dr. Connover and his ministry get the
money?

While he listens, Connover's face slowly, imperceptibly breaks into a tiny, satisfied smile.

Denny had to pull off the road two blocks from the entrance to the trailer park where Tawny Kyle lived in the bedroom community of Irving, Texas. The road was jammed with cars, none of them moving, and he decided that an accident must be blocking things up ahead, though he hadn't picked up anything about it on the police band on the dash.

The rain had quit during the night, but had started up again at first light in the form of a fine mist, invisible to the eye, but evident in its results.

He climbed out of the tan Ford with the WCN emblem on the side, sinking into the spongy earth just off the gravel shoulder. Irving was a town of truck drivers and commuters, pickups the main form of conveyance and mobile homes the preferred mode of lifestyle. The road leading to the Happy Times Mobile Home Park was two lane and wooded, all of it vibrant green from the last two weeks of early summer rains. The road was full of cars, all honking, many pulled off to the side just like Denny's.

As he walked, he fought against the lack of sleep and the coffee-generated tension that made him want to scream every time the spongy ground sucked up a foot and wet his sock. The night had been a long one, spent first in preparing the tape for morning playback and then in waking up his lawyer and taking steps to insure that he wouldn't be cut out of the gravy train.

He knew a hot story when he saw it, and considering the way his career had gone with the news division the last six months, he felt justified in trying to protect himself. If he'd understood the reasons for the demotion, things wouldn't have been quite so bad; at least he'd have been able to correct the mistakes. But it hadn't been like that. He'd been pulled from the Washington beat by telegram, the word coming directly from Ted Gayler's office without explanation, and he'd been left hanging just like that, leaving him with feelings of disassociation that he couldn't quite shake. Tawny Kyle and her daughter were going to be his whether Ted Gayler liked it or not. He needed them, for job insurance and for his own self-respect.

He walked the long line of cars, people getting out and wandering into the street to peer down its length. The jam-up was getting seriously out of hand and Denny wondered where all the cops were hiding. A shame the wreck didn't happen near a doughnut shop.

When he reached the heart of the confusion at the entrance to the park, he'd figured to see the wreck, but there wasn't one. Instead there were simply hundreds of cars jammed at the entrance, all trying to drive in. They couldn't because the park itself was jammed with cars and people like some out-of-control street carnival.

He shoved his way into the crowd that filled the place, the trailer homes stuck like small oases in the desert of faces.

"What the hell's going on?" he asked a large, weathered man in faded, torn jeans and a red T-shirt, his large stomach overhanging the waistline.

"That miracle woman lives here," the man said, wiping misty rain form his face and bushy red beard. "I got kin who know people who live here and they said—"

"Miracle woman?"

"Hey . . . wait a minute," the man said, pointing. "Ain't you that newsman who put her on the TV? Hey! Here's that guy that put her on TV!"

The crowd suddenly turned on Denny, pressing in around him, the man in the torn jeans pushing up and getting in his face, breath heavy with chewing tobacco. "My car threw a rod," he said loudly as voices broke upon Denny like surf on rock. "An I sure ain't got no money to get it fixed. Can you get that woman to help me out? I'd sure be obliging—"

"I don't—" Denny began, but a sudden eddy in the flow of the mob carried him away from the man and he was struck by a frightening helplessness in the hands of the longing, demanding faces that threatened to envelop and suffocate him.

Everyone was talking at once, their eyes hollow with need.

"Please!" he yelled. "Please get back!"

But nobody listened. He was borne along, his feet barely touching the ground and he knew if he lost his footing he would by trampled by desperation.

Something hard slammed him on the back, and he found himself shoved up against the side of a '57 Chevy. He reached frantically behind him, his hand finding the door handle, survival to Denny Stiller at that moment reducing itself down to whether or not that door was locked.

He pushed the button, the door catch springing. He pulled out hard against the crowd, using the opening door to force them back, then falling into the front seat when he could squeeze in. He pulled his legs in then, the natural push of the crowd slamming the door after.

He sprang up, pushing the door locks. He sat for a moment, his whole body shaking, his breath coming in rapid gulps. What in God's name was wrong with these people? Tawny Kyle was a woman . . . just a woman.

When he'd regained his composure he looked at the ignition. The key was sitting there. As he slid under the steering wheel and turned on the engine, a million thoughts raced through his mind—the effect of his broadcast, the fears for Tawny and Amy, the animal nature of the crowd. He knew a hot story all right, but this defied belief. His first impulse was to turn the car around and try and drive it out of the madhouse, but his next thought quelled the fear: Tawny and Amy were partially his responsibility after last night and he owed them some help if he could muster it. Besides, he needed to get in there and sign them up before someone else did, mob or no mob.

He dropped the three speed into first gear and clutched his way into the crowd, moving them aside, an inch at a time, with his bumper. The mailboxes had all been knocked down, making it impossible to locate an address, but all he had to do was find the place where everyone was congregating.

The going was rough, people unwilling or unable to get out of his way. But he pushed on, literally carving a path for himself with the car's superior weight, making a sweep of the curving street that defined the park.

Then he saw it, a small, old trailer covered with people like ants on sugar. They climbed on the sides of the thing, several even on the roof as they pushed against it or climbed upon one another's shoulders to try and see in the windows.

Cars were jammed up in front of the trailer, making it impossible to get any closer than thirty feet distant without playing trash masher with the people packed in tight all around the area. He sat there, still breathing heavily, and tried to figure out what to do.

These people were all here to see the woman, all wanting the world for their fifteen dollar investment. The amazing thing was that he hadn't given her address out to anyone; they must have picked it out of the phone book or through word of mouth. He should have thought about that, but it simply hadn't occurred to him that this kind of reaction would be generated from that one piece—and it was still early. This was far better, and far worse, than he'd ever expected.

People surrounded the white, beat-up trailer, all of them

calling out Tawny's name. It was almost ritualistic. He had to get her and Amy out of there and to a neutral corner. Getting in was possible. It was getting back out again that presented the problem. He smiled, remembering that the power of the press and the power of vanity could accomplish great things.

He pushed open the car door, forcing it against the flow of the crowd. He squeezed out, quickly scrabbling atop the Chevy's hood, then its roof.

"Ladies and gentlemen!" he called out through cupped hands. "Ladies and gentlemen!"

People began to turn toward him, some of them pointing, his name rifling quickly through those gathered near the house.

"You will all have your chance to visit with Tawny Kyle!" he called. "But first, we must have order! Please! Let me pass so I can enter Ms. Kyle's home. Then, I promise you that you'll all have your turns and I'll put you on television!"

There were shouts of affirmation, the crowd backing up slowly, forming a human pathway leading up to the trailer steps. He quickly jumped off the car, feeling like Moses parting the Red Sea, but then he thought about Frank's remark of the night before about having to run the gauntlet and it sobered him. There was death in crowds this size, trouble in such determination.

"Thank you!" he kept yelling as he made his way to the door. "Thank you! You'll all get your turn!"

He took the rickety three steps up to the trailer door, knocking loudly. "Tawny!" he called urgently, lest the fickle crowd change its mind. "Tawny Kyle. It's Denny Stiller! I've come to help!"

After several minutes, the door opened a crack, the woman peering out, her face white with fear. "M-mr. Stiller?"

"It's okay, Tawny," he said. "Let me in. It'll be all right."

She opened the door a little more, just enough for him to squeeze through. The crowd cheered loudly as he entered. All sorts of furniture were piled up by the door from the inside; Tawny immediately pushed it back into place.

The trailer was filthy inside and smelled of rot. What furniture there was was broken down and bleeding stuffing. Ashtrays and paper cups full of cigarette butts were scattered everywhere. The place could have been a makeshift skid row shack, except that it was hidden in a metal box that no one could see in. Tawny and her daughter were destitute.

He turned to the woman. She was dressed in a housecoat, her beehive hairdo falling down around her ears. Without makeup, she looked old and sickly and dissipated. He wanted to feel sorry for her, but couldn't hold down his revulsion. A cigarette bobbed obscenely between her lips.

"What's goin' on out there, Mr. Stiller?" she said, her eyes dull, listless. "What'd Ah do to all them people?"

"Are you okay?" he asked.

She smiled. "Nothing wrong that a little drink wouldn't cure. Ah don't guess you . . ."

"No, I don't," he replied. "Have you got a phone in here?"

"Course Ah got a phone," she said indignantly, drawing herself up. "Got a TV, too. Ah even watch *you* sometime."

"Where's Amy?" he asked, listening to pounding footsteps on the flat roof.

The woman's eyes narrowed. "She's fine," Tawny said sharply. "Don't you pay her no mind."

"First the phone," he said. "Have you thought to call the police?"

Her eyes opened wide in surprise. "Cops!" she said. "Cops ain't here for people like me."

"Where's the phone?"

"Right through heah," she said, leading him down the length of the forty-foot home toward the bedroom. "Sorry Ah ain't had a chance to clean up yet."

From the looks of the debris strewn around the trailer, the place hadn't been cleaned in years. Everywhere he looked were faces; the windows surrounding the place were filled with faces peering in shamelessly, like the gawkers at the freak show. The trailer rocked slightly from bodies outside shoving on it. If he didn't get something done quickly, they'd try and get in. And they'd succeed.

He feared what would happen if they did get in. He feared they'd love Tawny Kyle to death.

They moved into a bedroom cramped with trash and dirty clothes and storage boxes. Amy sat in the middle of the filthy, single bed staring impassively at her hand, her concentration absolute, her world totally her own. A small black and white TV sitting on a beat-up dresser blared Denny's voice loudly, his feature being rerun.

"Phone's on the night table," the woman said, pointing.

"Great," Denny said, moving to pick up the receiver. "You turn down the TV?"

He sat on the edge of the bed and dialed the Irving police number. Amy, who paid no attention to him until this time, quickly scooted all the way to the opposite corner of the mattress.

The police answered on the tenth ring. "This is Denny Stiller," he said. "WCN news. I want to report a riot in progress."

"A what?" the man on the other end said.

"The Happy Times Mobile Home Park," Denny said, "on the Old Post Road."

"I know the place."

"There's a massive riot in progress," Denny said. "Get here quick!"

To emphasize the point, he hung up immediately, looking up at the woman, who was staring at her silent picture on the television. She turned and met his eyes.

"It makes me look old," she said, and Denny hated to tell her that the picture on TV was far younger looking than the genuine article.

"I think we should have some relief soon," Denny told her, "but as soon as we get a break, we're going to have to get you out of here."

The woman jerked the cigarette out of her mouth, ashes scattering everywhere. "What do you mean?" she said loudly. "Go where?"

"I'll think of something."

"This is mah home, Mr. Stiller," she said, lighting another cigarette off the butt of the one she was smoking. "Ah don't have the money to go no place else."

"I have a proposition to offer you," he said.

She angrily stubbed the butt out on top of the dresser. "Ah don't do that no more," she said. "Ah ain't since the child's been born. At least . . . not less Ah had to."

Denny stared hard at her, stifling a smile. Suddenly, the trailer rocked violently, the lights and TV flickering, then dying.

"Damn," Denny said, jumping to his feet to push aside the bedroom curtain. There had to be a thousand people out there, jamming tighter and tighter against the sides of the mobile home. This couldn't hold up much longer. He turned back to the woman.

"Look," he said. "I want you to come work for me."

"What kinda work?" she replied. "Ah got a pretty bad back and—"

"No," Denny said. "The kind of work you've been doing . . . you know, with Amy."

"Now listen. Amy don't have nothin' to do with this."

"Good. Then we won't need her around when you do it."

The woman tightened her lips around her cigarette and just stared at him for a moment. Soft light filtered through the closed curtains. The end of her cigarette glowed brightly when she drew on it. Then she said, "Why would Ah need to come to work fer you? Looks like them people out there's jes dyin' to meet me. Ah kin just dip out there in the folks and make all the money Ah need.

"And how many could you see in a day?" he replied. "Fifty? A hundred?"

"Maybe."

"Well at fifteen dollars a crack that comes out to fifteen hundred dollars," he said smoothly. "Then tomorrow, after this is all blown over, you're back down to nothing."

"Suppose it don't blow over?"

He smiled at her feeble attempts at negotiation. "You're just a freak Tawny. Tomorrow somebody reinvents the Hula-Hoop and everybody goes and buys one of those instead."

"A hula what?"

"Never mind," he said, reaching into his jacket pocket and pulling out the envelope stuffed there. "I'm prepared to offer you ten times what you could make in that crowd out there just as a bonus for signing a personal service contract with me."

She snorted loudly. "Big talk," she said. "Where'd you go gettin' that kinda money to give to me?"

He tossed the envelope on the bed, exactly half his bank account. "Count it," he said. "Fifteen thousand dollars."

She gave him a sideways look, then moved up beside her daughter, the girl still staring at her hand. When she picked up the envelope and opened it, her cigarette fell out of her mouth.

"Gawd damn," she whispered, the trailer quaking violently again. "There must be—"

"Fifteen thousand," he said again. "Count it."

She drew the large wad of hundreds out of the envelope and tossed them to fan out on the bed. "And what do you git in return?" she asked, but the words came weakly, her eyes locked in wonder at the stack of green paper that worked its own kind of miracles.

Denny heard sirens blaring loudly in the background and

worked hard stifling his smile. "You'll be under contract to me for the next five years," he said. "I'll be your business manager and get you jobs that befit your . . . talents. I'll take twenty percent of everything you make during that time. I'll handle everything. All you have to do is keep on doing what you were doing last night."

Tawny looked at the money, then looked at Amy. "Mah little girl . . ." she said sadly.

"We'll get her the best treatment that money can buy," he replied.

The woman walked around the side of the bed, moving within inches of Denny. She smelled of alcohol. "She's so puny, Mr. Stiller. And the people with the State . . . they want me to lock her up someplace. Ah ain't gonna do that to mah baby, you understand?"

"I won't let anything happen to Amy," he replied.

The woman looked at Amy again, then at the money, her lips trembling slightly. "And Ah wouldn't want nothin' . . . Ah mean, Ah don't want no people laughin' at her or makin' fun . . ."

"I promise you that you'll make enough money working with me that you won't have to fear the State or anybody else for that matter."

She looked up at him, her eyes filled with tears. "It's jes that folks . . . they don't understand her problem. Ah took her to the doctors once and they . . . they wanted to beat her to make her be like everybody else. Ah'm sceared that if we . . . if we . . ."

He took her by the shoulders, looking down at his ticket out, his heart going out to her despite himself. "You're not being completely honest with me, are you?" he asked.

Tawny Kyle slowly shook her head. "It's Amy," she said, her eyes fearful. "It's Amy's got the power. Ah jes take it from her. It don't hurt her none . . . she ain't got nothin' to do with it herself. I-is that wrong, Mr. Stiller?"

Denny looked at the girl. She had picked up a stack of the bills and was waving them in front of her face. He'd known it was her, known it from the first minute he'd seen her at Billy Bob's. He walked to stand before her, his pulse racing wildly. This was it—God in Texas in the form of a mentally retarded thirteen-year-old, a beautiful, crystal figurine ready to shatter with a glance, with only an alcoholic social outcast standing between her and the unfeeling mobs, between her and infinity.

He heard windows breaking at the side of the house, even as the police bullhorns worked to disperse the crowds outside. His call had been just in time. Another few minutes and they'd have been swamped. The girl stared, unseeing, at the stack of bills waving wildly in front of her, while Tawny peered anxiously out the window.

"Does she . . . know anything that goes on around her?" he asked.

The woman sat heavily on the bed, finally relieved of her burden. "Ah don't know what she knows. She kin feed herself and use the bathroom. She kin dress herself if'n she wants to . . . but she never wants to. She never really lets me know if Ah'm doin' all right or not. It's kinda like havin' one of them real fancy baby dolls, you know?"

He knelt down in front of the girl, at eye level with her, but she wouldn't focus on him. "But you obviously communicate with her somehow."

"She knows Ah do for her," the woman answered, and the trailer had stopped rocking as the crowd dispersed. "She calls fer her mama when she's sceared. She knows how to say no, that's fer sure. And when she's hungry, she asks fer meedle."

"Meedle?"

"Uh-huh. Ah think she could learn other words, 'ceptin' she don't want to. She's . . . happy with the way things is, Ah guess. Sometimes Ah do what she does, and Ah think it make some difference."

Denny reached into his pocket and withdrew the contract that he had written up with his lawyer the night before. He tossed it on the bed near the woman. "Sign this," he said. "As soon as the crowd is gone we'll get you to safety."

"You promise you won't hurt Amy none?" she asked, digging through her night table for a pen.

He couldn't take his eyes from her face. All the innocence and all the knowledge of the world was contained in that smooth, impassive countenance. It was as if he could almost feel the power that generated from her. "I promise," he said, and, reaching out, took a stack of bills in his own hand, waving them in front of his face the way Amy was doing.

They both waved frantically, the money blurring into unreality. He stared hard the whole time, trying desperately to communicate nonthreatening mental waves to her. And then, for just a second, it happened. Amy came in from whatever mental room she inhabited just long enough to look at him before retreating back into the safety of her own mind. She couldn't have looked for more than half a second, but the contact jerked Denny's body, nearly knocking him off his knees.

"She looked at me," he said softly, the contact jolting him like an electric shock.

"No she didn't," the woman answered harshly. "Amy don't look at nobody."

She slid across the bed and handed him the contract with one hand, while reaching out to take the wad of bills from his other hand. "Guess we ought to buy us a bottle to celebrate our partnership," she said, smiling through crooked teeth.

Denny rose slowly, shaking his head to clear it. "I tell you she . . ."

"You jes worry about gittin' us some jobs," Tawny said, standing and taking him by the arm to lead him away from Amy. "The child's *my* responsibility."

Denny nodded absently, walking to the window to peer around the side of the curtain. The crowd was, indeed, dispersing—but not easily. Eight police cars, two ambulances, and a paddy wagon all sat on the circular road with their lights going. There were a number of people being led away in handcuffs, a larger number being treated by the ambulance drivers for exposure to the canisters of tear gas that had been lobbed into the crowd to finally get them out of there. Smoke drifted idly in the misty air—smoke like clouds, smoke like dreams, as the riot police in their gas masks and medieval-looking gear hustled the last of the people and their desires out of the park.

To want is a great and terrible thing, and this was just the beginning. For the first time Denny began to realize just how complicated this whole thing was going to be.

But now it was too late. There was no turning back.

Scene 4

(later that day)

DAY—INT—THE WHITE HOUSE OVAL OFFICE. We see the PRESIDENT OF THE UNITED STATES sitting on a French provincial living-room couch, the small table before him holding a sterling silver tea service and two cups. Leaning forward in an easy chair set at an angle to the president, we see Denny Stiller asking questions to the chief executive.

<u>DENNY</u>

But, sir, How do you respond to critics who say that there are other ways to stem the communist threat to our hemisphere other than the proliferation of arms and the support of right-wing military forces in those areas?

<u>THE PRESIDENT</u>

Communism is a godless evil walking in the guise of men. The avowed purpose of the regime in Moscow is a communist-controlled world. That sounds like a direct threat to me. What would you have us do, let every neighboring country in the Americas be crushed under the boot of Soviet domination?

<u>DENNY</u>

History shows that, traditionally, communist revolutions in Third World countries are generated through the people of those countries . . . not by Russian troops, and that poverty and malnutrition are the major reasons for the rise of communism in our century. So, I ask you again, sir: would it not be better to send food to Mexico than arms to Nicaragua?

                    THE PRESIDENT
                  (flustered somewhat)
That's . . . not our way, Mr. Stiller.

                       DENNY
                    (persistent)
Humanitarian aid isn't our way?

                    THE PRESIDENT
That's not what I meant—

                       DENNY
But that's what you said. Perhaps if I ask the question again—

                    THE PRESIDENT
You've asked the question a sufficient number of
times, Mr. Stiller, and I must say that the situation
isn't nearly as simplistic as you make it out to be.

                       DENNY
Perhaps if you could . . . explain to me where I'm
wrong . . .

We PULL BACK to reveal a television studio. The previous
exchange has been taking place on a screen placed between
two men who are sitting on easy chairs and drinking coffee.
Above the screen is a logo of individual letters that reads THE
NEWSMAKERS. The two men are named BOB and RICH-
ARD. Bob speaks while Richard sips from a coffee cup bearing
his name.

                        BOB
Most network insiders regard Denny Stiller's tough
interview with the president last November as the
turning point in his career.

                      RICHARD
That's right, Bob. Stiller had been the top hard newsman at WCN until this interview. In his five years
with Ted Gayler's news division, he had risen like

cream to the top, commanding the highest salary in
the organization, plus a freedom from editorial control unheard of in the industry. But within days of
the broadcast of the presidential interview, he was
demoted unceremoniously to regional features where
he's languished ever since. Many people feel that
Gayler's personal friendship with the president had
much to do with the move. Others feel that Stiller's
badgering of the chief executive was tasteless and in
bad form and had to be dealt with harshly.

BOB

Well, languished is hardly the word, Richard. With
the Tawny Kyle story, Stiller has put himself back in
the public eye and returned with fanfare to the top of
the heap . . . and where the bad boy of television
journalism goes from here is anybody's guess . . .

We PULL BACK again to reveal the GREEN ROOM at Dr.
Connover's Church of the Savior. Connover and another man,
LARRY GATES, have been watching the previous news show
on television. In the background we can hear muffled choir
singing. Connover is dressed in vestments. Gates is tall and
suave, darkly handsome, and dressed in a blue suit. Other
people move in and out of the room: singers in vestments,
stagehands, and "witnesses." Several young girls dressed in
white flowing gowns giggle together nervously in the corner of
the room. Connover reaches for the television and CHANGES
THE CHANNEL, the music we've heard in the background
now loud as the service being broadcast from the church is
playing on the screen.

LARRY

Just exactly how deep a coverage are you talking,
Doctor?

CONNOVER

Let's get it straight, Larry. I want full service—taps,
surveillance, interviews, the works.

LARRY

That kind of blanket on the woman *and* Stiller is go-

ing to take a lot of manpower. You sure this whole
thing's a fake? What I saw on the tube—

CONNOVER

Of course it's a fake. There can't be any questions
about it. God wouldn't let Denny Stiller within a
hundred miles of His saving Grace. (he laughs) No,
Larry. There's no chance of this nonsense being on
the level. And I don't care what it costs, *you're* going
to prove that it's a fraud.

ANGLE—THE DOORWAY. A stagehand sticks his head in
the door space.

STAGEHAND

Dr. Connover, you're on in three minutes.

ANGLE—CONNOVER AND GATES.

CONNOVER

Thank you, Mr. Brunner. (he turns back to Gates)
Now tell me what you're going to do for me.

LARRY

I've been authorized five full-time people a day.

CONNOVER
(angrily)

I told you I want full service.

LARRY
(calm)

Perhaps you'll get more later if you need them.

CONNOVER

That's crazy. How can I hope to shut this bastard
down with five people? Are you sure you told—

LARRY

They understand. I won't second guess my superiors.

The two men share a long, knowing look, Connover then

straightening his robes and walking to the Green Room door.
He turns to Larry.

                          CONNOVER
                       (from the doorway)
You take those five people and work their legs off.
The important thing is that you keep me separated
from the hard stuff. I don't mind being out front, but
I've got a reputation. (he starts out the door, then
turns back around) We'll deal in person, of course.

                          LARRY (os)
Of course.

                          CONNOVER
And Larry . . . nothing in writing, okay?

Connover walks out the door. In the background, we can hear
him being introduced to a large, enthusiastic audience.
CUT TO:
THE GREEN ROOM TV. We see Connover walk onto the
magnificent pulpit of the Church of the Savior, the pulpit looks
like a heavenly chariot being borne by the images of angels
into the clouds. A huge audience cheers loudly as he takes his
place before them.
FADE to BLACK. FADE OUT.

"Look, I forgot my badge, okay?" Denny said, glancing up
at the security guard who stood, rain dripping from his clear
plastic poncho, beside the car. "I've never needed it to get in
here before, anyway."
    I don't know anything about that," the man responded in a
monotone not dissimilar to the parking valet's at Billy Bob's.
"All I know is that nobody gets in without a badge."
    A horn honked loudly, Denny turning to see the driver of
the pickup truck behind him gesturing with his hand for them
to hurry. There were several cars lined up behind him. Funny,
he didn't think it was payday.
    "What's the big deal all of a sudden?" Denny asked. "Did
we get a bomb threat?"
    The man's eyes widened, his hand going to the gun at his

side, resting on its butt. "What do you mean by that?" he asked.

"Look, Sherlock," Denny said, reaching into his back pocket and coming out with his wallet. "My name's Denny Stiller and I work here. And if you haven't noticed, I'm driving a company car." He opened the wallet and held it up. "Here's my driver's license. Now you must have some sort of master list you can check me off of."

"Yeah," the man said, narrowing his gaze. "I recognize you." He ran an uncertain hand through his wet, slick hair. "I guess it wouldn't hurt any to let you go on in."

"Right."

Denny rolled up the water-spotted window and gunned the Ford through the standing puddles that were the result of the Dallas–Fort Worth metroplex sky perhaps trying to come down to earth and visit the Galleria. The WCN building, only five years old, was long and low to the ground. Windowless, like a blockhouse, its very simplicity was an imposition on the North Stemmons Freeway carnival of mirrored asymmetrical wet dreams that was Dallas architecture. Management called the building utilitarian. To those who worked there it was known as "the rock."

Denny pulled into a reserved slot in the fenced-in security parking area and sat watching the windshield wipers clear the rain for a moment before shutting off the engine. He'd gotten Tawny and Amy registered in a motel under a different name. When he'd returned home, his machine was full of messages from Dick Horton, WCN's executive producer telling him in no uncertain terms to be at the station by one P.M. for a meeting with Mr. Gayler.

He would like to have gotten some sleep first; he'd need his priorities totally under control to negotiate with the big man. Gayler was one of the new breed of superrich, a communications entrepreneur who'd made his fortune controlling legislation through controlling what people see, hear, and read. In a world that no longer seemed to understand the meaning of the Taft-Hartley Labor Act, he owned newspapers in ten states, local TV stations in fifteen, and seemed to hold the note on the entire state of Tennessee through control of its country and western entertainment outlets, that state's most exportable asset. Denny wasn't kidding himself, Ted Gayler ate up and spat out people like him on an hourly basis. He'd have to tread water like a madman just to keep his head above;

but right now he had something he was sure Gayler wanted, and if he just kept that in mind, he might survive—with class.

He took several deep breaths and tried to clear his mind away from the reality of exhaustion. Then he shut down the Ford and climbed out into the rain.

The sky rolled heavily above, blue-gray clouds reflecting in the surrounding mirrored, neon-rich buildings. Before entering, he passed another security guard he didn't recognize and had to get out his driver's license one more time. He finally entered the security door, soaked and disheveled, still wearing the same tan sport jacket he's had on at Billy Bob's and it was still wet.

Floyd at the check-in desk gave him the once-over as he bent to sign in. "Looks like you've had a rough one, Mr. Stiller."

"What the hell's going on with all the security?" Denny asked. "Bozo the Clown coming in or what?"

"You oughta know," Floyd said, his old, weathered face settled into a posture of constant amusement. "People have been trying to get in here since that story of yours ran about the miracle woman. We had to bring in extra help to turn 'em away at the gate. This whole damn place has been under siege."

Denny smiled. "Really?" he said, thinking about how much easier things move if you've got a lever.

The man pointed over his shoulder. "You don't believe me, just take a look in the lobby."

Denny moved up to the glass doors that led into the reception area. Four receptionists instead of the usual two were working full-time at the boards. He pushed the door open slightly, listening to what was apparently the official response.

"Good afternoon, WCN. . . . No, sir, the miracle woman is not here at the studios. . . . No, sir, we don't know how to reach her. . . . Yes, sir, just keep watching."

That message, or one most similar, was being repeated over and over by all the receptionists as often as they could pick up a call. Good. Let Gayler try and deal with him on this.

Denny looked at his watch. It was one-fifteen. He was late, but only enough to make them think of him. He turned to Floyd. "Is Mr. Gayler at the station?"

The man nodded broadly, the tiny smile never leaving his

lips. "He came breezing through about thirty minutes ago."
The man chuckled. "He asked about you, too."

"Good," Denny said, and pushed through the glass doors
that led past the lobby to the office suites. Gayler had been
early for a meeting with him. That showed something right
there.

He walked casually through the lobby, calling, "Hello,
ladies," to the receptionists, only to be bombarded by insults
and shaking fists in return. This was working out far better
than he could have anticipated.

The lobby squeezed into a well-carpeted hall that led past
the advertising and layout departments to the executive offices
beyond. He walked a hallway filled with framed awards and
photos of famous people and knocked briskly on a solid oak
door with the words Executive Producer stenciled on it in
black. He always found it interesting to note that no name was
ever painted below the title, a reminder of the impermanence
of success in television journalism.

"It's open," growled Horton's voice from the other side,
and from his tone, Denny deduced that the producer was
going to play bad cop to Gayler's good cop this time around.

He opened the door and moved into the large, junked
office, surprised to see not only Horton and Gayler there, but
Molly Hartwell and Frank Hargrave also.

"Well, the gang's all here," he said, looking for a seat.

Horton was a man who believed in hominess, his office
cluttered with knickknacks and plants and pictures of and by
his children. The man sat behind his spacious, paper-filled
desk, a large frown on his smooth face. His bald head glistened
with humid sweat and his black-frame glasses were pushed up
high on his forehead. He was a man who took everything
seriously, especially his job—especially trouble connected
with his job. His phone wasn't ringing, so it must have been
trouble. His ceiling leaked slowly, an occasional drop plum-
meting from the water spot to land in the World's Greatest
Dad coffee cup shoved up under it.

"You're late," he snapped, as Denny cleared a stack of *The
New York Times* from a folding chair and sat down. Molly sat,
looking sleepy, on a folding chair near Denny's while Frank
Hargrave stood, walking—apparently still trying out his new
leg. Mr. Gayler sat, small and quiet, in a high-backed leather
chair set behind and to the side of Horton's massive desk.

"I got here as quick as I could," he said. "I had to save Tawny from a mob at her trailer park."

He looked around for reaction, but everyone was watching *him*.

"I'd like to congratulate you on your story," Gayler said softly, his voice barely more than a hoarse whisper. The man was old and seemed deceptively frail. Nothing about him gave the hint of money or authority—certainly not his clothes at any rate. The man's wrinkled suit was done up in a chocolate brown and seemed a wide-lapeled product of the late sixties. When Gayler came to the station, it was usually on the bus, and he always, *always* brought his lunch in a brown paper sack. His eyes though—they were something else again. His eyes shone bright with intelligence and were as cold and hard as his body was soft and gone to decay. "You've managed to set the world on its ear."

"Thank you, sir," Denny said.

"The phones have been ringing off the wall," Horton said, as he shuffled papers around on the desk. "The nets have been demanding access to the Kyle woman. They want you on *Nightline* tonight . . ."

"*Nightline*," Denny said, raising his eyebrows.

"Yeah," Horton said. "We'll decide on that later. There's a couple of points I'd like to clarify first. I've already told your producer and now I'm going to tell you."

Denny shot a look at Molly, who shrugged sadly with her eyes.

"You intimated in your story that you, personally, would be covering the Tawny Kyle story," Horton said, finally finding the paper he wanted from his stack and reading from it. "I quote, 'I will continue to study Tawny Kyle, continue to explore her power.' "

"What about it?" Denny said

"Who covers this story is not your determination to make, Denny. You know that. It seems as if one of our science editors would be better qualified—"

"No," Denny said simply.

Horton calmly put down the script he'd been reading and stared across the desk, his long face prepared for the worst.

"This is my story," Denny elaborated. "You don't take a reporter's story away from him."

"But, Mr. Stiller," Gayler said quietly. "This is *my* station. Don't I have the right to do anything I want?"

"People are going nuts over this story, Mr. Gayler," Denny said, "and you know it. And it's *my* story. *I* brought it in. *I* wrote it. You've taken stories away from me before, but you're not going to take this one away from me. It's not fair and it's not right and I'm simply not going to allow it this time."

"Regardless," Horton said, his voice tightening, "we're doing it anyway."

"Then I quit," Denny said.

Frank snorted loudly, then stifled a laugh as everyone turned to him. He shrugged and walked around some more.

"Denny," Horton said. "Think about what you just said. You've got a good job here. Hell, you're making twice my salary. This is just another story—"

"Just another story?" Denny said, incredulous. "Molly warned me of the possible impact of this thing last night, but I didn't believe her. But now, that just-a-story crap won't wash. I was nearly crushed by a mob today—a huge, destructive wave of mindless power—and they wanted nothing more than to talk to the woman who could redesign a man's body with a touch." He pointed to Frank. "For fifteen dollars she did for Frank what all the combined knowledge and talent and resources on the planet could never accomplish. This isn't just a story, Dick, it's the biggest thing since Jesus Christ."

"You said it wasn't religious," Molly said.

"It's not," Denny replied. "But you're the one who told me that people would think it was."

"Why should that matter to you?" Gayler asked.

"It matters because this thing is exploitable in a lot of different directions," Denny said angrily. "And I'm not going to sit here and let myself get kicked off the gravy train."

Gayler reached into his suit coat pocket and withdrew a small vial of pills. "I can appreciate your . . . enterprising attitude," he said, opening the vial and popping a small yellow pill into his mouth. "But you're hardly in any position to do anything about it."

"You've got all the answers, don't you?" Denny said.

"No, sir, I do not," Gayler said. "I just know the difference between the superior and inferior position, Mr. Stiller. And it seems to me that in this day and age with all the economic problems and so forth, that a man is pretty lucky just to have a job at all, if you know what I mean."

"Is there an implied threat here?" Denny asked.

"No, sir," Gayler said. "Just advice."

"So, you're still quits?" Horton asked.

"In spades," Denny said, rising. "And I'll get in touch with the *Nightline* people myself."

Horton stood with him, turned to Gayler, then back to Denny. "You're a good newsman. I don't want you to quit, damnit. Can't we work this out?"

Denny responded, looking at Gayler the entire time. "I worked hard to be the best hard newsman on this or any other staff," he said. "Then, after a string of exceptional stories, you people blew me off without a word, demoting me to the shit detail. Now you want to do it again. You may not want me to quit, Dick, but I have a feeling that it's the best news Mr. Gayler's had in quite some time."

"I could have fired you anytime, Mr. Stiller," Gayler replied calmly. "But I chose—"

"To keep me around and humiliate me," Denny interrupted. "Don't play coy. You didn't fire me because I would have taken you to court for breach of contract and made you say the reasons. That's the one thing you haven't wanted to do."

The old man took a deep breath. "I suppose if you want to go, we can't stand in your way."

Denny walked to the door, then turned back around—smiling. "It's hard for me to understand, though," he said, shaking his head, "how a couple of smart guys like you would let the Tawny Kyle story get away from you this easily."

Horton closed his eyes, as if the surf were pounding against him, and sat down heavily. "What do you mean?" he asked.

Denny snapped his fingers and pointed. "Oh, that's right," he said. "I forgot to tell you. Tawny Kyle signed a personal service contract with me this morning. If you want to do anything with my client, you'll have to work through me."

"What!" Horton said, his eyes flying open wide.

"I didn't stutter," Denny said.

The old man laughed, a dry, humorless cackle. "Very good, Mr. Stiller," he said. "Very resourceful . . . but not very smart."

"It seemed like a good idea to me," Denny said.

"You can't put someone under personal contract to you while you were interviewing her on our nickel," Gayler said.

"I didn't, though," Denny said, opening the door. "I did it this morning, on my own time."

The old man shook his head slowly. "That's a simple

justification of unethical behavior, Mr. Stiller. It will never hold up in court."

Denny put a hand behind him and opened the door. "Ethics have absolutely nothing to do with what we're talking about here. Tawny Kyle has no 'news' value in the truest sense of the word. You people are sitting here trying to figure out how many ways you can use her to make a buck. Well, she is mine." He jammed an index finger into his chest. "And she's going to stay mine. I've got a pat hand and I'll be damned if I'm going to be bluffed out of it. I will be gracious in victory, however, which is more than you'd do with me. I'll give you guys first crack at making a deal for exclusive rights. Think big, though . . . and fast. I open this up for bids in the morning."

He turned and started out the door, but turned back when Gayler called his name.

"Do you really want to play this game with me, Mr. Stiller?" he asked. "I have unlimited resources at my command—"

"And I've got the girl."

"What will you settle for?"

"Make me an offer."

The old man slowly folded his hands in front of his face as if he were praying. "I'm offering you your livelihood. I'm offering you your ass—intact. It's a most generous offer. Most generous."

Denny stared hard at him, nearly backing down in the face of the cold steel that was Gayler's look. "I'm going for an exclusive contract. If you want the woman, you'll join the bidding or make me a realistic offer." He looked at Frank, the man smiling in return. "Talk to me later. I have a deal for you."

With that, he turned and walked back down the hall, his stomach turning like a pinwheel. It was harder than he'd hoped, but about like he'd thought. Gayler would get over it. The man just didn't like the idea of getting pushed around a little. He'd get used to it. Everyone does.

He'd nearly reached the lobby when he heard his name being called. He turned to see Molly hurrying to catch up with him.

"Hi," she said sheepishly when she got abreast of him.

"Hi, yourself," he replied. Taking in the circles under her eyes, he said, "You look like you got about as much sleep as I did last night."

"I was worried," she said, "that something like what just

happened might happen. On top of that, my horse kicked down the fence last night and ran off."

"I guess it's all a little strange right now," he said. "But, I can't let Gayler steamroll me again."

She put a hand on his arm. "I know," she said. "I guess I just wanted to tell you that I wasn't a part of what went on in there. I was called in same as you."

He put an arm around her shoulder and hugged her briefly. "Thanks, Moll. I'm sorry you had to get caught in the middle."

They walked into the bright lights of the lobby, Denny self-consciously dropping his arm from her shoulder.

"I'm not in the middle," she said. "I'm on your side."

He stopped walking, turning to face her. "Don't make commitments you won't be able to keep," he said. "This isn't going to go down easy."

Her eyes searched his. "Denny, I—"

All at once, there was a commotion at the checkpoint, people yelling, the sound of glass breaking. They turned in time to see a man with wild eyes break away from two security guards and come crashing through the glass doors at full speed only to stop, transfixed, at the sight of Denny.

"M-mr. Stiller," the man said, almost reverently.

Denny just stared at him, the guards now coming through the door. The man threw himself at Denny, going to the floor five feet before him and crawling as Floyd and the outside guard jumped him.

"Please, Mr. Stiller," the man yelled as the guards pulled him roughly to his feet. "You've got to help me."

"Me?" Denny said.

Floyd roughly pulled the man's hands behind his back, handcuffing him. "Come on, you bastard."

"It's my little boy," the man cried. "He's dying an inch at a time." Tears streamed down the man's face.

"Police are on the way," the third guard yelled from outside the glass door. "The son of a bitch must have climbed the fence."

"They say he needs a heart–lung transplant," the man said, his words tumbling through sputtering lips. "But there aren't any . . . any donors. Please God, we can't stand it anymore. My wife, his mother, she . . . she . . . "

"Come on, we'll cool him off outside," Floyd said, the two guards dragging him backward by the arms. The man stopped walking and let himself go, making then drag him.

"Please God!" he screamed loudly. "You and the miracle woman—can't you save my little boy? Can't you? We're all dying . . . all of us a little more each day. Please . . . please."

Denny stood silently, watching them drag the pitiful man out, kicking and screaming. He was a newsman, an observer. It was his job to focus on others' lives, his own always staying in the background. The demand for activity jolted him—and scared him a little.

"Mr. Stiller," one of the receptionists said.

He turned and stared at the woman.

"We've just gotten a call," the woman said. "Dr. Connover of the Church of the Savior is talking about you on his program right now."

Denny turned without thought and moved to the lobby television that was always tuned to WCN. His hand shaking from the confrontation with the intruder, he turned to channel 37, Connover's niche. He knew the station well, had watched it many times in preparation for an investigative report he'd been doing on the man's financial dealings months ago, a report that had gotten shelved with all his other reports when he'd been kicked downstairs following his interview with the president.

The station came in, Connover installed in his gaudy chariot pulpit, taming the fears of death of his congregants, looking for all the world like somebody's kindly rich philanthropist uncle on a tear.

He felt a hand on his shoulder, then Molly's voice. "Denny . . ."

"A minute," he said, turning up the sound.

Connover was intense, his gentle voice full of deadly portent. "And wasn't it Jesus Christ himself who said, the way to the Father is through me. The way to the Father is through me! He didn't say salvation came through some TV newsman, or some painted woman who has a magic show."

He chuckled softly, shaking his head, the audience picking it up and intensifying it. "Oh my friends," he continued with an easy drawl. "Satan's ways in this world are myriad. And the Devil, he's a smart old bird. He doesn't show us sin in all its rotted, wasting ugliness. No indeed. He wraps it in the beauty of this world, and he holds out hopes and false promises to lure us away from the light and salvation of Jesus Christ!"

Connover straightened, the crowd responding with loud amens.

"We all know this spawn of Satan, don't we friends? This demon in the clothes of Man who calls himself Dennis Stiller has been seen lurking around these premises before!" He paused while everyone laughed. "He's tried to bring shame to this ministry . . . but he failed! And now he comes forward with his false prophet and his camera tricks and tries to get us to fall for his Devil's lure. He tries to tell us that for fifteen dollars . . . fifteen dollars my friends . . . he can heal the sick and cure the infirm, when all of us know that the only hope for mankind is to get down on our knees and beg God's forgiveness and to accept Jesus Christ as our personal Lord and Savior!"

More amens rang through the cathedral, Connover staring straight at the camera as it came in close on his face.

"My friends, I am here to tell you that Dennis Stiller is the disciple of the Lord of the Underworld. His prophet is a false prophet . . . his hopes—false hopes. Don't be taken by his Devil's promises! The price tag isn't fifteen dollars. The cost is your immortal soul! Shun this Devil! Shun him with your last ounce of strength!"

Denny grunted and turned the channel back to WCN, his feature running again, Frank once more trying out his new leg for the world to see. He straightened, looking at Molly. "But there's nothing religious about this."

She just shook her head. "Denny," was all she could say. "Oh, Denny."

ACT TWO

Scene 1

(later that evening)

DAY—EST—THE COLOMBIAN JUNGLE. We see the rolling gray clouds heavy with rain as they charge across the tops of the lush green rain forest. We see the sky, then the trees, then we look lower to see American National Guardsmen moving in disarray from the loading bay door of a camouflage-painted C–130 aircraft that is sitting on a pitted, deserted airstrip deep in the jungle.

> NARRATOR (os)
>
> . . . near Mitú, Colombia, on the Vaupés River, as the Guardsmen continue to offer assistance in what is being termed the largest manhunt in history. They are searching for this man . . .

CUT TO:
A PHOTO. The picture is of a handsome, young latin-looking man with long, tangled hair and a cold stare.

> NARRATOR (cont, os)
>
> . . . Jesus Marin Cardera, who is already living under three death sentences in his native land for murder, and who is allegedly the world's largest supplier of illegal cocaine to the United States. Cardera,

wanted in this country on thirty separate counts of distribution and conspiracy to distribute a controlled substance, was recently the subject of an itense investigation by the Drug Enforcement Agency working in cooperation with the Colombian government. The investigation ended last week in a small hut in Miraflores, where Colombian authorities found the remains of fourteen DEA investigators.

CUT TO:
NEWSREEL FOOTAGE. We are watching an underlit scene inside a hut. A large number of bodies are piled there, all of them lying facedown on the floor with their hands tied behind them.

NARRATOR (cont, os)

The agents were killed execution style, the largest masacre of DEA investigators in U.S. history, prompting an angry message from the president to the Colombian government, which responded by inviting the United States to participate in the hunt for Cardera. So far, no leads have turned up as to the location of the convicted murderer. (pause) On the national front . . .

CUT TO:
EXT—DAY—FRONT STEPS OF THE DALLAS COUNTY COURTHOUSE. A short, dark balding man with a salt-and-pepper beard and glasses is shown talking to reporters. He is CHARLES KORNFELD, Denny's lawyer.

NARRATOR (cont, os)

A lawyer representing newsman, Dennis Stiller, who shocked the world with his pictures of a miracle in action, held a news conference today to explain that his client has gone into seclusion with Tawny Kyle, the self-styled Texas God.

KORNFELD
(smiling and bemused)
Mr. Stiller just wanted me to let all of you know that, because of all the publicity surrounding his stories

about Tawny Kyle, he is going into hiding for a while
to work with the woman and will be back in touch
when he has more to report. Everything's fine, and
he appreciates everyone's concern, but he asks that
you not try and find him. He wants to do the story
right, and can't without the proper distance.

REPORTER

Is there any substance to the rumor that Stiller and
Tawny Kyle are planning to start a new religion?

KORNFELD
(rolling his eyes)

Absolutely not. There is nothing religious about any
of this. Denny has simply discovered a phenomenon
and wants to test it in peace. Please, there is no
more story today. That's it.

REPORTER

Any thought on the remarks made by Dr. Connover
about Stiller on his program this morning?

KORNFELD

Besides the obviously slanderous nature of the doctor's harangue, I feel that Connover says very little
worthy of comment.

CUT TO:
CLOSE-UP—THE FACE OF AMY KYLE. We are looking
at the face of an angel, a pristine spinning of delicate, fragile
crystal. We are drawn to her eyes for they are a reflection of
absolutes—innocence, purity, all the brightness of childhood
that tarnishes in the adult—but something more is present; an
overwhelming righteousness of the purity bleeds out to us, an
almost intellectual righteousness that comes from the scholar's
distance from the subject—an alienness. Amy Kyle *could* be
God, so unlike is she to our understanding, to our *struggle*.
We can almost resent her position. In her eyes we also see the
reflection of her mother, who sits before her patiently trying to
feed her from a jar of baby food. We PULL BACK slowly to
reveal Tawny and Amy sitting in a motel bathroom.

TAWNY

Come on, baby. Eat it up.

AMY
(loudly)

No!

TAWNY

You always liked the strained peas best of all. Now we kin afford all we want.

AMY

No! No!

The light is bright in there, reflected off shiny white tiles and walls. Amy sits on the closed-up toilet, Tawny on the edge of the tub. A glass full of amber liquid sits at Tawny's feet. Tawny's lips tighten into a hard line as the girl keeps dodging, moving her head away from the spoon, finally hitting the spoon, green glop slinging against the shower curtain. In the bg, we can hear the same newscast that we've been watching.

TAWNY
(pleading)

Please eat, darlin'. You and your mama done hit the gravy train. We don't wanna be messin' nothin' up, do we?

Amy sticks her tongue out, making a disagreeable sound and SPITTING FOOD everywhere. Tawny, cursing softly, sets down the jar of strained peas and picks up her glass, drinking it down in one swallow. We continue to PULL BACK, moving out of the bathroom and into a large, motel bedroom, a Holiday Inn. From another room we can hear the continuing newscast, plus male voices just below our range of understanding. We move through the bedroom, seeing a paper bag full of clothes belonging to Tawny and Amy. A carton of unfiltered cigarettes lays torn open on the still-made bed, cigarette packages strewn across the bedspread. We move through the room and out the bedroom door to find ourselves in a large living area—we're in a suite. We glide slowly past a wet bar that has been in serious use, with one empty and one half-empty bourbon bottle sitting atop it. One wall is a sliding glass door that leads to a balcony overlooking the pool, one floor below. At the far side of the room we can just make out Denny Stiller and Charles Kornfeld sitting on a sofa, dressed casually, watching Kornfeld on television just as we had been doing. We move through the papier-mâché elegance of the room toward them, just picking up their conversation.

DENNY

. . . don't see how they have any right to stop me from entering into an agreement with whomever I choose.

KORNFELD

Shit, Denny. This isn't the courtroom. You don't have to play innocent with me on this. I've been on the phone all day with Gayler's attorneys, and their position is simple: you contracted while under exclusive contract to them. In fact, you contracted while doing contract work for them. Being bound to them, you weren't free to enter any other agreement.

DENNY

Can they make that stick?

KORNFELD

Anything can happen in court, Denny. You know that, but *I* wouldn't mind having their side of the argument. They could make a great de facto case here about your intentions to defraud, since you will undoubtedly make a substantial profit from this, perhaps even from WCN.

Denny rose from the couch and moved to turn off the television. "Looks like you could use a hairpiece, Counselor," he said, pointing to the man's thin hair on the screen before shutting off the set.

Kornfeld smiled tiredly at him. "My wife says that bald is sexy," he replied, leaning forward to take a sip from the bourbon and water that sat before him.

"Your wife is trying to make the best of a bad thing." He

pulled a high-backed easy chair near the coffee table, sitting across from the lawyer. Charlie was a good man. He'd stayed up all night with Denny working on Tawny's contract, then gone to work and spent the entire day trying to keep Gayler's mad dogs from Crowe and Donlevy from nipping him to pieces. Denny sat, leaning down to pick up and take a sip from his own drink. "So, is there a way out of this?" he asked, bringing the cold glass up to rest on his forehead.

"There's a way out of everything," Kornfeld said. "The law isn't a rigid instrument."

"Which means that whoever has the best lawyer, wins the most cases."

Kornfeld smiled wide. "And I think I'm as good as Gayler's fuckers any day. I've been thinking a lot about this, and it seems to me that our first approach was far too narrow—"

There was a knock on the door, Frank Hargrave's voice following directly. "Denny! Open up, you sorry sack of dog shit!"

Denny stood, putting down his glass. "The cavalry," he said, moving toward the door. He'd need Hargrave on this. The man was an exposed emotional nerve, a condition that he felt would come in handy when dealing with the girl. He pulled open the door to see Hargrave balancing his equipment and a six-pack of beer.

"Brought my gear," the man said, stepping into the room and putting his equipment on the floor. "Where's the bathroom?"

Denny closed the door behind him, locking it with the chain. "Tawny's back there right now," he said. "You can—"

"No, Ah ain't," Tawny said, walking in from the bedroom to stop at the bar. "We're all through." She looked at Hargrave while pouring herself another drink. "How's the leg, sweet thang?"

"Good as new," Hargrave said, walking toward the woman to get to the bathroom.

Denny looked at Tawny. She was weaving, slightly drunk, and he realized that he was going to have to keep her under better control. He walked to the bar, just able to see Amy through the doorway sitting on the bed, wagging her head back and forth. "Maybe you've had enough for now," he said, taking the glass away from her and setting it back on the bar. "We've got a show to put on."

"You ain't mah daddy and you ain't mah husband," Tawny

said, her bleary eyes flashing for just a second. "What Ah do
with mah life ain't any bi'ness of yours."

She reached for the glass, but Denny pulled it out of her
reach. "When we're through tonight you can drink yourself
into a stupor, but right now you stay straight." He took the
bottle and stuck it under his arm.

She moved up close to him, her face softening and Denny
realized she was trying to vamp him. "Ah'll just finish this
teeny one," she said in a little girl voice, her hand reaching for
the glass he held at arm's length.

"Not even if pigs had wings, honey," he said in the same
seductive voice she'd used. "If you want the drink, do a good
job tonight." He pulled back from her, face hardening.

He expected anger from her, but instead was greeted by
nearly embarrassing subservience. "Yes, sir," she said, head
lowered, and he began to get a feel for just what kind of life
she'd led until now.

There was another knock on the door, Denny turning
quickly to look at Kornfeld, who was shrugging widely. "I
didn't tell anybody," the lawyer said from the couch.

"Did anybody order room service?" Denny said.

The knock came again, followed by Hargrave walking back
in from the bedroom area. "No," the man replied. "But it
sounds like a helluvan idea."

Denny hurried across the carpeted floor, peering through
the head-level peephole. He saw Molly peering back, her face
distorted in the fish eye, her fingers pulling her lips apart as
she stuck her tongue out at him.

Setting the bourbon bottle on the floor, he pulled the chain
loose and threw the door open. "How did you find us?" he said.

"Now is that any way to greet the love of your life?" she
asked, and walked past him into the large room. She smiled at
Kornfeld. "Howdy, Charlie," she said. "Isn't this cozy?"

Kornfeld held up his drink. "You're looking lovely tonight,
Molly," he said.

She shook her head. "Why are all the good ones married?"
Then she caught sight of Tawny Kyle, the woman leaning
forlornly against the off-limits bar.

"Molly—" Denny began.

"Not now," she said, ignoring him and walking up to the
Kyle woman, extending her hand. "I'm so pleased to meet
you."

The woman looked surprised. "You are?" She put out a tentative hand for Molly to shake.

"Come on," Denny said from across the room. "What gives?"

Molly turned to face him. "You know, I feel really hurt that I wasn't included in your little meeting of the minds here."

"You still work for WCN," Denny said. "I didn't want to put you in any . . . untenable positions."

She pointed at Hargrave, who was leaning against the bedroom door frame, smiling stupidly. "What about him, then?"

"I'm hoping that Frank will leave Gayler and come to work for me," he said.

"All right!" Frank said loudly.

Denny finally realized why Molly had come in so close on Frank's heels. "You followed him, didn't you?" he asked her.

"I've got some information for you," she said, "and didn't know how to reach you. I asked Frank . . ."

"But I didn't tell her anything," Hargrave said.

Molly smiled. "He acted so strangely that I took the chance and followed."

Denny looked around the room, not entirely unhappy that Hartwell had shown up. Perhaps it was time to put their thoughts together, including Molly's. So far, she'd seemed a hundred eighty degrees opposed to him on this issue and he wanted her hard-edged cynicism to test his ideas. "Let's talk about it," he said. "We've got to formulate some plans."

They gathered in the living room, Denny's mind moving in multiple directions as he tried, above all, to figure out exactly what it was he *wanted* from Tawny Kyle. The woman had brought Amy in, the girl looking ghostly in a long, white nightgown. She'd been given a chair to sit on, but opted to walk around it instead, round and round, in a continuous, never-ending circle while humming tunelessly. Frank sat on the edge of the sofa, assembling his camera equipment as if it was as natural to him as breathing air.

"I'll be honest with you," Denny said, as they all stared at him expectantly. "I'm not sure why any of us are sitting here right now. Twenty-four hours ago I'd have told you that I was a thirty-eight-year-old career newsman who believes in nothing but hard work, the drive to succeed and a basic adherence to the maxim The truth shall set you free. A day later, I've quit my job, spent my savings, and am the business manager of a faith healer."

Everyone laughed, except Tawny Kyle. "Ah'm afraid Ah have to tell you somethin'," the woman said, her eyes fearful.

"What's the problem?" Denny asked suspiciously.

"Ah didn't say it before, but . . . now that Ah work fer you, Ah . . ."

"Just say it," Denny urged, watching Amy make her unending rounds out of the corner of his eye. "Please. We're going to talk about a lot of things before this is over."

Tawny Kyle looked at each of them in turn, confusion and shame evident on her face. "Ah'm not much of a . . . God fearin' woman, Ah guess you'd say. Don't git me wrong, Ah believe in Jesus and all that, but Ah jes never got around to goin' to church or nothin' like that. Ah g-guess that the way Ah've lived . . . Ah didn't much think that God would want to see me in his house, is all."

"What's that got to do with anything?" Denny asked.

"Well," the woman said, still fearful. "Mah . . . faith healin' ain't really any kinda healin' at all. Ah don't pray or git no visions or nothin' like that. Ah jes thought that maybe folks . . . Ah don't know . . . *want* to hear about God when healin's goin' on, so . . . that's jes what Ah told them."

Denny smiled triumphantly at Molly. "That probably makes you just about the same as most faith healers," he told the woman. "Don't worry about it."

Molly turned in her chair to stare at the small woman on the sofa. "What happens then . . . how do you make it work?"

"It started with babies," Tawny said. "Ah kin close mah eyes and touch a pregnant woman's belly, then Ah jes pitcher mahself walkin' into a nursery and starin' down into the crib. Then Ah pull back the covers and see whether it's a boy or a girl. Ah jes picture thangs, that's all. When Ah touched Mr. Hargrave's leg, Ah jes pictured it all healed up and that's what happened."

"Don't feel bad," Denny said. "We're going to work together no matter where the power comes from, okay?"

The woman smiled wide. "Fine with me," she said happily.

"So what happens now?" Denny asked. "Why have I done what I've done already?" He stood up, thinking as he talked, trying to find his own sense of truth in his thoughts. "There are two feelings driving me right now. The first is selfish—I want to get rich off Tawny and Amy. I want them to get rich, too. I want all of us to get rich. It's the mark of success in America and we all deserve it."

"I'll drink to that!" Hargrave said, holding up a bottle of beer, Tawny staring at it with open desire.

"I think that getting even with WCN probably fits in there somewhere, too," Molly said.

"I think beyond that, though," Denny continued, "is something more fundamental. I don't believe in anything beyond myself, nothing greater, anyway. Most people do. I don't; I . . . can't. But a wonder has fallen into my hands, a gem untouched by conditioning and genetic fears and hatred and thought patterns. What we have here is power and innocence going hand in hand, terms that are usually mutually exclusive. I've discovered raw power in its purest form, the kind of power that everyone holds in reserve for God. As Molly told me last night, no one is going to look at what we do as simply an interesting scientific experiment, and she's right. It was proven to me this morning when I was nearly trampled at Tawny's trailer park. They all wanted something from her. God, they were nearly insane with want."

"You're already ruining your 'scientific experiment,'" Molly said. "By saying the power *doesn't* spring from God you are already categorizing it."

"No," Denny said. "The difference between you and me, Molly, is that I'm not trying to prove anything here. You see what you consider supernatural power and begin looking for supernatural explanations. I have no axes to grind. I don't hate or love God because God, whatever God is, has played no part in my life. Therefore, I believe I'm the perfect person to examine this phenomenon in a totally objective light. The Truth, whatever it may be, won't hurt me one way or the other. If it turns out that Tawny or Amy is actually God, then I'll be the first one to line up and make a donation. But, it's going to have to be proven. That's what I'm here for, to find Truth, whatever that truth may be."

"Dangerous ground, buddy," Kornfeld said, smiling boyishly. "People who go around looking for truth usually end up in alleyways with knives sticking in their backs."

"What's that supposed to mean?" Denny said. "You're a working lawyer, you look for truth every day."

"For such a smart guy you sure are dumb," Kornfeld replied, shaking his head. "The law isn't aimed at finding truth. Its purpose is greater; we maintain the status quo, and consequently, the life of society. All lawyers protect the fantasy of self-determination. Nietzsche said, 'the will to truth is merely the longing for a stable world.'"

"He's right," Molly said. "It's stability people want, security not truth."

Denny looked from one of them to the other. "I don't relate to any of this," he said. "My life is very simple: I dig for facts, then present them in the most unbiased manner possible. Truth must be the ideal, and it's the truth of Tawny and Amy Kyle that I intend to dig out."

"Your problem is that you're unwilling to accept any responsibility for your actions in this," Molly said.

"That's what I've been trying to tell you," Denny said. "My responsibility is clear and pure. I'm to dig out the facts. Everything else will take care of itself."

"But what happens," Hargrave asked, standing and screwing the camera onto the tripod, "if you somehow prove that these people don't got nothin' to do with God? What are all those religious folks goin' to say about it?"

Denny shrugged. "I don't guess they'll say anything about it," he replied. He knew what they were leading up to. He just couldn't or wouldn't believe that it would make that much difference.

"Mind if I smoke?" Tawny asked, reaching into her beat-up handbag.

"It probably doesn't matter anyway," Molly said. "I hate to burst your balloon, but I overheard Horton on the phone with Gayler earlier. His lawyers are going to hit you with a breach of contract suit in the morning and ask for a restraining order against you to keep you from utilizing Tawny Kyle, at least until after a hearing. That's what I came to tell you."

Kornfeld sank down in the sofa, sighing deeply. "I was afraid of that," he said.

Denny turned to him. "Charlie?" he said, drawing out the last syllable.

"Where do you want me to set up the gear?" Hargrave asked.

"We'll use the sofa," Denny said. "I want good, direct cross lighting. No shadows please. I don't want any dark corners."

"If you leave things as they are," Kornfeld said. "I'm afraid they can get their restraining order."

"You said, 'if,'" Denny replied.

Kornfeld looked at Molly. "By coming here," he said, "you've put yourself, your career, and Denny in jeopardy. If you listen to what I have to tell him, you'll be complicating things even more."

Hartwell stared at Denny, a kind of desperate longing in her eyes that he couldn't identify. "What do *you* want me to do," she asked. "Job or no, I want to be with you on this."

"Why?" Denny asked.

"Somebody needs to keep you out of trouble," she said without conviction, her expression becoming pained.

Denny took a breath. "You're here," he said. "Let's roll with it. But you have to promise not to say anything to anybody at WCN."

"Great," Kornfeld said. "We'll all make a friendship pact and learn the secret handshake. Damnit, this is the big time you're talking about. Gayler plays with a loaded gun and if you're not as smart as him, your brains are going to end up splattered on the sidewalk."

"I'll have to hand it to you, Charlie," Denny said. "You sure go for the violent imagery."

"I'm not talking imagery," Kornfeld said. "But since you're determined to go on with this thing, who am I to tell you no. Just remember you've made your own decisions."

"Okay," Denny said. "What do we do about Tawny?"

"Get her another carton of cigarettes," Tawny said, sticking the last from a pack between her lips. She crumpled up the empty package and dropped it on the floor.

"We were so tied up in trying to get Tawny's 'talents' under contract," Kornfeld said, leaning over to light the woman's cigarette, "that we failed to consider her life."

"What do you mean?" Denny asked, sitting again, leaning forward, idly watching Frank move around the room positioning light poles.

"Power of attorney," the lawyer said. "You can get the form from any office supply. It's simple and covers everything. As her guardian under the power of attorney, all decisions have to be made by you anyway."

"In other words," Denny said, "we could tear up the personal service contract between her and me and let anybody come on."

"They'd have to come to you," Kornfeld said. "And no court of law is going to overrule a power of attorney made with the consent of all parties. They could still try and come at you from

the fraud angle, but the restraining order would probably not
be a viable possibility for them, since they'd have to prove why
you weren't fit to administer Tawny Kyle's affairs."

Denny looked at the Kyle woman. "Would that be all
right?" he asked.

"What?" the woman said, blowing out a long plume of
smoke.

"Would you sign a paper that lets me handle all your affairs,
all your business?" Denny asked.

Tawny laughed. "Oh, honey," she said loudly. "Y'all takin'
good care of me and Amy already. Ah'll sign anythin' you say."

Denny looked at Kornfeld with raised eyebrows, the man
shrugging in return. "Okay. Let's go with it."

Hargrave plugged the lights in, the room suddenly alive,
sparkling like a diamond in the intense light. Amy screamed,
running wildly around the room, knocking over an end table.

"Ah'll git her," Tawny said, dropping her cigarette on the
floor and running after the girl, who had disappeared into the
bedroom. Molly got up and retrieved the cigarette, depositing
it in the nearest ashtray.

Hargrave moved to the end table beside the sofa, removing
the shade from the big lamp that sat on it. "You're all ready to
roll tape," he said.

But nobody needed to tell Denny that. From the moment
the lights came up he'd felt his energy levels begin to build.
Stories to Denny were like morning coffee to most people. A
charge, a wake-up. When Denny was involved in a story,
nothing else mattered. He lived it and breathed it and no clock
could hold its time. He was like some automaton in a pulp
fiction book who only came to life when news was breaking. It
was air to him, and food, and love.

All previous debate on the subject had been mere
formality—he knew that now. Any discussion aimed at him
walking away from the Tawny Kyle story was worse than futile.
The bottom line for him was that this was the story of his
lifetime. He was going to make the most out of it, personally
and professionally, that he possibly could.

He walked over to join Hargrave at the camera, the man
intently peering into the viewfinder, at the small screen hiding
there. "Take a look," the man said. "Think I got your lighting
set."

Hargrave moved away from the camera, Denny bending
slightly to look. The viewfinder was set on Kornfeld, bright
light hitting him from all sides, leaving his face smooth,

unwrinkled, and unpitted. It was the clinical look and feel that Denny had wanted, coupled with the homey furnishings of the suite to keep it from feeling too cold.

"See anything you like?" Kornfeld said, making a monkey face at the camera.

"Can't tell," Denny said, straightening. "I keep getting this blinding glare from the top of your head. We might need to powder that bald spot."

"Fuck you, Stiller," Kornfeld said, smiling, as he leaned back to pick up his drink off the coffee table.

Denny turned to look at Hargrave, the man staring down at him already. "You know why I want you," he said.

Hargrave nodded. "It's that little girl," he said. "You want me to feel her feelings with the camera."

"I'll pay you more than you're making now," Denny said.

"Shit, buddy," Hargrave said. "You know that don't mean diddly-squat to me. If you hadn't stood up for me with Horton I'd have been out on the streets long time ago. I owe you, Denny."

"Then you'll do it?"

"I'd do it for nothin'."

Denny put his hand on the man's arm, nodding. "Not for nothing," Denny said. "But I appreciate it. When we start rolling tape, don't stop for anything. I want honesty, and we'll have to begin with ourselves, with our own approach to the filming."

Hargrave nodded. "Gotcha."

Denny heard a gutteral, animal sound behind him and turned to see Tawny attempting to carry her squirming daughter into the room, the girl every bit as large as her mother.

"She'll be fine," Tawny said, weaving as she walked, Denny running to her side. "She's jes scared of the lights, that's all."

Amy was shaking as if she were having a seizure, the sounds coming from her throat like nothing human Denny had ever heard. Her eyes were rolled up in her head, the lids fluttering madly.

"Let me take her for you," Denny said, reaching out his arms.

"Ah kin do it!" the woman snapped angrily, then lost her balance, going to the floor, Denny impulsively reaching out and grabbing Amy before she, too, fell.

The girl stiffened in his arms, going completely rigid. Her shaking had stopped, along with the animal sounds.

"Ah told you to leave the child alone!" Tawny yelled, jumping back to her feet, face contorted in anger. She reached clawing fingers for Amy.

Denny, remembering their previous conversation, stared fire at the woman. "Stop it!" he said with authority, the sound of it shocking Tawny, holding her back. "Now go sit on the sofa and shut up!"

The woman's eyes softened immediately, her body slumping in submission. Without a word, she shuffled to the couch and sat down. Denny, still holding the girl, looked up to see Molly staring at him in bewilderment and maybe just a touch of anger.

He turned his gaze to Amy. Her body was relaxing in his grasp, her eyes rolling back down to stare past him as he carried her into the bright egg of light. He set her gently beside her mother, who was watching Denny fearfully. The woman put her arm protectively around her daughter.

"Ain't nobody ever been able to touch her before 'cept for me," she said.

"Does she always react this way to bright light?" he asked.

Tawny shrugged. "Don't guess she's never been around none before. Course, she don't much like goin' out in the sun, neither."

Denny stared at the girl's impassive face, a strange, electriclike tingle running through his arms and chest where her body had been touching him. "Do you think she's okay now?" he asked Tawny.

"Amy ain't never been okay, Mr. Stiller," the woman said, and she seemed deeply troubled.

"Do you think it will be all right to make another tape now?"

"Yeah," the woman said. "Let's go on and git it over with."

Kornfeld rose and moved away from the couch, Denny looking at Molly. "Any thoughts before I start?" he asked her.

"If you've got to go ahead," she said thoughtfully, "do it as you said you wanted to—honestly, without bias. I'm scared to death of this, Denny. Walk carefully."

He nodded, then looked at Kornfeld.

"Same here," the man said. "Just don't libel anybody."

Denny moved to stand beside Hargrave, the man hunched over the viewfinder again. Hargrave straightened and looked deeply at Denny, an unspoken understanding passing between them. Denny bent to the viewfinder once more, knowing that it would be Amy Kyle's face he'd see there.

He stared at the black-and-white image of her face in the viewfinder, staring the way he could never do in real life. He idly reached a hand to the lens to sharpen the focus. She was so distant, so beautiful, so . . . otherworldly. His arms still tingled where he had held her. He forced himself away from the machine, then nodded curtly at Hargrave.

"Tight on me first," he said, dragging a chair to butt up against the sofa. "We'll just use the camera mike." Tawny slid down to the end of the couch right next to him, dragging Amy with her.

"Got it," Hargrave said, his head up tight against the unblinking eye of the camera.

"You're on your own," Denny said, trusting the man to handle it. "Go ahead and roll."

Hargrave nodded and, a second later, pointed a finger to let Denny know they were taping.

Denny took a breath and stared down the one-eyed monster. "This is Dennis Stiller reporting from a motel room somewhere in downtown Dallas, Texas. This is my second report on the truly amazing powers of Tawny Kyle, and I don't mind telling you that I'm nervous. I'm going to try a few experiments today that will begin to test the extent and the limits of the power I saw exhibited last night at Billy Bob's.

"I want to stress to you that nothing has been rehearsed. In fact, I haven't even thought up the experiments yet. The reason that I sit here unprepared is that I want the process of discovery to be one that we experience together. Wherever it takes us, we will go. I want to start small, then build until we find the limitations of Tawny's ability. It should be a fascinating journey.

"For the record, I've quit my job, my life currently devoted to the successful recording of this story. There will be those who will accuse me of trickery, as has already occurred. To those people, I have nothing to say. They can believe as they will. To those of you who have an open mind, I think you are about to be dazzled and amazed." He smiled sheepishly. "At least I *hope* so. Again I repeat, nothing has been arranged or rehearsed in advance. You are watching literal history as it unfolds. We will discover together."

He sat back in his chair, watching Hargrave's lens ZOOM

OUT to take in the three of them. He was excited, shaking inside and out, his mind frantically turning to try and figure out what was going to happen next. He loved journalism, being there as things happened, taking them off the cuff, and ad libbing.

"This is Tawny Kyle," he said with a gesture toward the woman, "and her daughter, Amy." Tawny sat stiffly, as if she were holding still for a photograph and her eyes showed the unmistakable blank stare of stage fright.

Denny smiled. This didn't hurt at all. He wanted humanness—polish would kill the whole thing. "Are you nervous?" he asked her.

"Yes, sir," she answered.

"You're among friends here, Tawny," he said warmly, then reached out and took her bony, livered hand, the woman relaxing somewhat. "It's going to be all right."

The woman smiled, rolling her eyes childishly. "Aw, Ah know that," she said. "Ah guess it's that damn camera thingy."

"Well Frank Hargrave's running the camera and he's a friend." Denny was loving this. It was real, down-home stuff. "He'll make sure you look good on the tape."

The woman nodded, still smiling, and he could feel her hand relax in his. "Are you ready to try a few things?" he asked.

"Ah'll try," Tawny said, her hand now squeezing his tightly.

Denny stared around him. He was an open conduit, accepting all the visual data that flooded into his brain, searching for just the right bell to ring. He stopped on Frank Hargrave, his eyes traveling to the Buck knife the man wore on his belt.

"Frank," he said. "Give me your knife."

The man took the knife out of the leather holster, unfolded the blade, and carried it to Denny without question or hesitation. Denny then held it up for the camera, twisting the blade to catch the highlights under the glare of the spots. "We've watched Tawny heal an old injury," he said. "Let's see what she does with something more recent. Frank. Can you come up tight on my hand?"

As Frank tightened, Denny held his left hand out in front of him, bringing the blade up next to the skin. "I'm going to cut myself," he said casually, "then see what happens. Wish me luck. Here goes."

Denny would have never intentionally cut himself under any other circumstances, but once the camera was rolling he was capable of anything, as if the unreality of life on tape somehow made the actions performed in that state unreal also. He watched, detached, as the blade sank into the back of his hand, then drew a line three inches long across it. He could hear Molly moan loudly from behind the camera. The cut burned, then began seeping blood along its length, the liquid bright red, still heavily oxygenated for its trip through the circulatory system. He made a fist, the blood flow increasing until it slicked the entire back of his hand.

"Now, Tawny," Denny said, "Describe for me what you must do to heal my hand."

"Ah have to touch you," the woman said. "Ah have to touch yo hand."

Denny held his hand out and she held it, the camera PULLING BACK to take in all three of them.

"I noticed you're holding Amy's hand, too," Denny said, treading on the one dishonest area of the newscast. Tawny absolutely refused to put her daughter fully in the limelight. They'd have to brush past it.

"It's the way Ah always done it," she said. "Gimme yo hand."

Denny gave her his hand. "I'm in pain," he said, chuckling softly. "I'm wishing at the moment that I hadn't cut myself quite so badly. Miracles are one thing, but hurting myself in order to experience one is asinine."

The woman put her hand on his and shut her eyes.

"What are you doing now?" he asked her.

"If'n you'll ever shut up," she said, "Ah'm gonna think about yo hand. Ah'm gonna pitcher it healed up."

"And that should do it?"

"If it ain't," the woman said, "yer gonna need some stitches."

Denny shut up and watched Tawny. The woman had closed her eyes tightly. This time she didn't add any phony preaching to the mix.

He jerked, the burning numbness of an electric charge jolting through him. "I feel something," he said, voice rising, "something flowing through me."

He jerked his hand away from her, so intense was the charge. "Ahhh!" he yelled, grabbing his wrist, the hand shaking uncontrollably in front of his face. "Intense pain is charging through my hand. I'm already bathed in sweat. I-it's like . . . e-electric shocks . . . and . . . and . . ."

All at once, he sagged with relief, falling back in his chair, breathing heavily. "The pain," he said weakly. "The pain is gone with no residual. I feel dragged out, but strength is returning quickly. I . . . I . . ."

He stopped talking and looked at his hand, holding it up for the camera. "It's still covered with blood, as you can see," he said. "But I don't know about the cut. It feels fine, I . . . wait."

He brought the fingertips of his right hand to his mouth and licked, then used the wet fingers to wipe at the blood on his hand, clearing it. Denny laughed, wiping away more.

"Amazing," he said, shaking his head, overwhelmed. The camera came TIGHT on the back of his now smooth hand. "The cut is not only completely healed, but it's as if it had never been there at all. Absolutely incredible."

He sat back, staring at the hand in awe. "Tawny," he said idly, his eyes still fixed on his hand, "could we do a little more?"

"Why not," the woman said, obliviously free of wonder of the power that wasn't hers to begin with.

"Okay," Denny said, mind racing, trying to get back on track. He looked up, past the camera, to see Charlie Kornfeld drinking the rest of his bourbon. Kismet. "Charlie. Come over here."

Kornfeld drew in his brows and pointed to himself. "Me?" he mouthed silently.

"Come over here in camera range," Denny said. "Ladies and gentlemen, this is my attorney, Charles Kornfeld, who is going to give us a hand with our next little experiment."

Kornfeld moved into the scene and stared down at Denny in perplexity. Denny rose, making Kornfeld sit in his place. He stood beside the chair, his hand on the lawyer's shoulder.

"You may have noticed that my friend, Charlie suffers from an ailment we all know as male pattern baldness—"

"Denny!" Kornfeld said indignantly.

"It's hereditary, isn't it?" Denny asked.

Kornfeld drew himself up in the chair, mustering as much dignity as was possible under the circumstances. "I think so," he muttered.

"Tawny," Denny said. "Let's see if we can 'cure' Mr. Kornfeld's hair problem."

"This is ridiculous," Kornfeld said, trying to rise, Denny using the hand on his shoulder to push him back down again. "My hair is . . ."

"Put your hand on his head," Denny told the Kyle woman,

"before he squirms away. You must have been hell at the barber shop when you were a kid, Counselor."

Kornfeld burned slowly, lips tight. "This will all be reflected in my bill, Stiller," he said, Denny scrunching up his nose and shaking his head at the camera.

"Tawny Kyle knelt on the couch, Kornfeld not bending to help her get at him. She put a hand to his head, the other reaching back to hold onto Amy. The woman closed her eyes.

"Whoa . . ." the man said softly. "There's a tingling, a . . ."

He jumped from his chair, screaming, his hands going to his head. "It b-burns!" he yelled. "My head is on fire, it's . . . burning!"

He bent at the waist, groaning deep down in his throat, his hands on his head. Then silence.

The man straightened slowly, face quizzical. "Something," he said, quietly, removing his hands, a luxuriant growth of curly black hair covering his entire head.

"Ah went ahead on and got rid of the gray, too," Tawny Kyle said. "Hope that's okay."

"Mirror," Kornfeld said, like a junky needing a fix. "Get me a mirror!"

"Here," Tawny Kyle said, rummaging through her purse and coming out with a small compact. "Try this."

He grabbed the round compact, opening it with trembling hands, Denny marveling at the hairline a sixteen-year-old would have been proud of.

"My God," the man said, moving the mirror back and forth around his head. "My God . . . my God!"

"This is no fake either," Denny said, moving up to grab a handful of the new hair and tug at it.

"Hey . . . ouch!" Kornfeld said, pulling away.

Denny turned and smiled at the camera as Kornfeld moved out of the frame, still looking in the compact mirror. "Just as last night," Denny said, "we're looking at a total destruction of our concept of physical laws. You begin to wonder just where this ends. Could she make a million dollars appear out of nowhere? Could she change us all into eagles so we could swoop through the skies? W-we've got to proceed carefully here . . . slowly. I don't want to try too much. Maybe one more thing. Something simple."

He looked up at Molly. She'd said she was in. Well, this would ice it. "My producer, Molly Hartwell, is also here," he said. "Molly . . . come out here in front of the camera for a change."

Her face fell, darkening immediately, and he wondered if she'd really meant what she'd said about wanting to see this through with him. She shook her head, and he became uncompromising in his reporter's way.

"Come on," he said playfully. "It's your chance to see life on the business end of the camera."

She showed him empty palms and whispered to try and keep her remarks off the tape. "I'm not sick," she rasped, "or cut or bald."

"Come on," he said again, moving out of camera range to approach her. "It'll be fun."

He got right up on her, her eyes flashing angrily. "I said no, Denny."

He took her wrist and pulled. She tried to jerk away, but he held fast, half-dragging her into the picture, where she stood stiffly, looking unhappy and mad.

"Now," Denny said, hurrying to move things along. "What would you like Tawny's help with, Molly?"

"I'm not sick," she repeated for the audience. "I'm not hurt or broke or unhappy. This is silly, Denny, I don't—"

"There must be something," Denny persisted, ignoring her obvious embarrassment. "Maybe something you'd like to know."

She tightened her lips and gazed at the floor. "Really, there's nothing I . . ." She cocked her head, looking at the camera, thinking.

"You've thought of something," Denny said.

"Not really," she replied. "You know I live on five acres in Grapevine. It's just that my horse, Oater, kicked down the fence and got out of the yard last night. I'd sure like to know where he is, what happened to him."

Denny turned and looked at Tawny. "Can you do something like that?"

"Ah find lost thangs all the time," the woman answered. "Easy as pie."

"Then this should be a simple enough test to end today's session," Denny said, returning to his chair. "Just tell Molly what you want her to do."

"Jes think about the horse," Tawny said, "and let me take your hand."

"Okay," Molly said, relaxing somewhat, Denny moving his

chair a bit away from the couch so that Molly could stand beside Tawny and not block her from the camera. The woman took a breath and closed her eyes, reaching out a hand to Tawny.

They held hands, both of them closing their eyes. Denny watched as Molly shivered a touch, her face becoming harder, more angular, furrows deepening with internal pain.

"Nooo," she whispered from down deep inside. Then she jerked again, violently, pulling away from Tawny to wrap her arms around herself, eyes still closed.

And then it happened.

"No!" she screamed, a plea. "No!" She shook violently, pitching sideways like an off-balance drunk, animal sounds groaning through her lips. She banged into the television, careening back from the contact to fall to the floor, Denny jumping to her aid.

The television suddenly came on loudly, Molly springing up to a sitting position, her eyes wide open, intense with fear.

"Molly," Denny said bending to help her. "Are you . . . "

"Denny," Hargrave said.

Stiller looked up at the camera. "Keep rolling!"

"The television," Molly said, pointing. "The television!"

Denny looked up at the screen as Kornfeld bent to the controls

"Turn it off," Denny said.

"It *is* off!" Kornfeld said.

Denny looked at the screen. It appeared to be a poorly lit movie, a point of view shot from within the front seat of a car driving overland across a pasture at night. Through the windshield and just ahead of the car, a chestnut-colored horse was galloping full speed.

"It's Oater!" Molly yelled. "Oh, God, shut it off!"

"Why?" Denny said, pulling her to her feet. "Why?"

"Please . . ." she begged.

"Get a picture of the screen!" Denny yelled at Hargrave, who scrambled to comply.

"Whooo cowboy!" came a voice through the TV. "Round 'em up!"

Molly began crying uncontrollably, her face buried in her hands. Denny found himself glued to the television, watching the screen with perverse fascination.

The point of view in the movie on the television was from the driver of the speeding, bouncing car. A teenage boy sat beside the driver, a cigarette hanging out of his mouth. He smiled at the screen as he pulled a .45 automatic from beneath the seat.

"Now, let's do some huntin'," he said.

Molly wailed loudly, making Amy cry, too, Tawny wrapping the girl in her spindly arms.

"I'm unplugging the damned thing!" Kornfeld said.

"Don't touch it!" Denny yelled. "Keep rolling tape!"

Kornfeld ignored him and jerked the electric cord out of the wall, holding it up.

The TV kept playing loudly, a gunshot distorting through its speaker. On the screen, the punk in the passenger side was shooting through his window at the sweating, running horse.

"Yip! Yip!" he yelled. "Bring her in closer!"

"Oafer," Molly whined, her hands on the side of her tear streaked face, her eyes inescapably rivetted to the screen. "Oh, baby."

The car ANGLES CLOSER, coming within fifteen feet of the horse. We can see its mouth, foaming, the unreasoning fright that fills its wide eyes.

> PUNK
>
> Eat lead, you four-footed son of a bitch!

He FIRES again, the horse rearing as blood spurts out of its neck. He FIRES at the animal's shank and it pitches forward, collapsing in a heap, as the still-moving car distances it.

> PUNK
> (laughing)
>
> All right! Let's finish it off.

The car circles, coming back for the kill.
ANGLE—MOLLY. Her eyes hollow, distant.

> MOLLY
> (a whisper)
>
> Please don't. Oh, please . . .

ANGLE—TV. We're looking down at the horse from outside the car as its jerks spasmodically, its lungs wheezing in and out. The punk with the gun looks directly at us, holding the weapon out for us to take.

<u>PUNK</u>
See how many times you can shoot it before it dies.

ANGLE—MOLLY. She breaks from her reverie, her eyes
hard and glassy.

<u>MOLLY</u>
(hard)
No you won't! No you won't!

She turns and grabs the chair that Denny had been sitting on
and heaves it up over her shoulder, charging the TV, GUN-
SHOTS loud in the background. She SMASHES the screen
with the chair, the television crashing to the floor, sparks
flying, Molly staggering backward into Denny's arms.
ANGLE—TAWNY. Her face like a hunted animal's, her
daughter tucked against her.

<u>TAWNY</u>
(in a small voice)
Careful what you do, Miss Hartwell. The first three
months is the most dangerous time.

ANGLE—MOLLY AND DENNY. They freeze, looking at the
woman.

<u>DENNY</u>
What? The first three . . .

ANGLE—TAWNY. Hope lights her face.

<u>TAWNY</u>
It's a boy, Miss Hartwell. A boy!

<u>HARGRAVE</u> (os)
Somebody's on the balcony!

ANGLE—BALCONY. Through the sliding glass door we can
just make out a shadowy figure with a video camera raised to
its face, photographing us!
ANGLE—DENNY'S POV. We charge the sliding door, the
figure on the other side scurrying to get away. We get the door

open just as the man climbs over the second floor railing and jumps.
CUT TO:
A TV SCREEN. Taken from the balcony at the Holiday Inn, we watch from a distance as Molly crashes against the TV and falls, pandemonium ensuing. From without it is a jumble of people and movement and muffled yelling, culminating with Molly putting her chair through the screen and Denny Stiller charging right at us.
ANGLE—DR. CONNOVER. He is staring straight ahead. He is sitting in a leather chair, dressed in a suit, a steaming cup of coffee poised at his lips. We can see the running television reflected in the wire-rim glasses he wears. We hold for several beats, the man's face remaining totally impassive. Finally he takes a small sip of coffee.
FADE to BLACK—FADE OUT.

Scene 2

(four A.M. the next morning)

Denny sat beside Molly in the old Ford station wagon, staring through the dirt-spattered windshield at the corral. It wasn't so much a corral as a large pen attached to the barn, surrounded by a homemade fence of white pine that glowed under the harsh, artificial glare of the car's headlights.

"I just assumed that Oater had kicked down the fence," she said, "because who would have thought—"

"Yeah," Denny said, staring at the slats that had been pulled out of the fence posts and dropped to the ground. "Well, let's see if we can find anything else . . . if you're up to it."

She turned to him, her face gently radiant in the dash lights, her eyes glistening. "I *have* to," she said. "The thought of Oater lying out there, I . . ."

She closed her eyes tightly, leaning her forehead against the steering wheel and fighting back the tears. "Oh Denny," she said, "why would anybody want to hurt such a gentle creature?"

"We don't know that anybody has yet," he said.

She turned to him, face strained. "But the image in my mind . . . and the picture on the television . . ."

He reached out and touched her shoulder, Molly leaning her head to the side so it would touch his hand. "Look," he said quietly, "I understand that somehow Any Kyle passed energy to and through you, the television proved that, but whether or not that's the truth of the matter, we don't know."

"What do you mean?"

"What is Truth?" he said. "Everyone defines it differently, sees it differently."

She restarted the car. "What you're telling me is that what appeared on the screen could simply be a manifestation of my own fears."

"I don't know," Denny said. "That's what we have to find out. Drive a distance out into the pasture. Tire tracks shouldn't be too hard to find on this wet ground."

She backed up, then turned the car around, heading away from the old plasterboard-and-shingle farmhouse where she'd grown up and that she'd inherited after the death of her parents. Molly had an apartment in the University Park area of Dallas, but spent most of her weekends here in the interior lowland country of Grapevine, Texas. It was her weekend retreat, a quiet place with a party line phone and spring onions growing in the red prairie clay heavy with accumulating lime. This was grassland country, with more than five hundred varieties growing wild. Denny had come out here with her a number of times for intimate weekends over the last two years, and though he'd enjoyed an amount of the solitude that seemed so important to her, he was always itching to get back to the action in town long before the weekends were over.

"Great," she said. "It's beginning to get foggy."

"This shouldn't take long," he said. "Try the outside spotlight."

Fog was beginning to come thickly from the south, washing in on the trailing edge of the storm system that had moved along the jet stream to the northeast. Molly had turned on the adjustable beam, but it wasn't doing much good except to illuminate the fog, make it burn with a life all its own.

"Maybe we should switch everything off and ride with the parking lights," he suggested, as they found themselves quickly enveloped in a dreamlike haze that knew neither time nor place.

She shut down the high beams leaving only the amber glow of the parking lights, immediately folding the darkness in on them. But at least the dark was familiar and accountable.

"I don't see anything yet," she said, staring hard over the wheel, trying to get up high on the windshield for the amber lights to do her some good visually.

"Just drive a circuit back and forth," he said. "God, there's not much out here."

"We butt up to a big conglomerate," she said, "that gets paid by the government for not planting here. Probably got two or three thousand acres of nothing out in front of us."

"There!" Denny said, pointing. The tracks were set a good two inches in the ground, the wild buffalo and wheat grasses flattened down where the vehicle had driven over them. "You can see where they parked, then where they turned around to chase the horse."

"Now what?" she asked. "Follow the tracks?"

"What else?" Denny said. He could hear the tension in her voice, feel it in the atmosphere of the car. There'd been a great deal unspoken between them since the session with Tawny and Amy, volumes left unthought until the truth of this particular episode could be sorted out.

"Still think I may have created it in my own mind?" she asked, voice tight, high pitched.

He shook his head. "Let's just follow the tracks," he replied, his mind turning involuntarily to the rest of Tawny's message.

They drove slowly, pushing into the bleak Texas night, fog batting against them in thick patches, taking their world away only to return it seconds later.

He watched her as she drove, eyes glued to the windshield and the tire tracks outside. She was relentlessly driving a path that would lead her to unhappiness, for both of them knew already that Tawny had been right. They were simply playing out the inevitable, a thought whose consequences Denny couldn't hold in any longer.

"Is it true?" he asked her, watching her jaw muscles tighten in the dim light.

"What?" she said, turning to stare briefly at him, her face pleading silently.

Denny ignored her look. "Tawny said you were pregnant," he replied. "Is it true?"

"Not now, Denny," she said in a small voice. "Please?"

"I just want to know if it's true or not, that's all," he said.

She closed her eyes and took a breath. "Possibly," she said. "I missed a period, but I don't—"

He stared hard at her in the pale light of the dash. "I don't understand," he said. "I thought you were on the pill."

"I am . . ." she said, shaking her head. "I was. Do you remember when we covered the Shuttle flight last month at Canaveral?"

"Sure."

She just glanced at him, her eyes misty. "I just . . . forgot to pack the pills," she said in a tiny voice. "We were sharing a room and . . . I guess I just hoped for the best. I started taking them again as soon as I got back." She laughed dryly. "I even took the ones I'd missed."

"Wow," he said low, and turned to look out the windshield at the indented tracks leading into the fog. He'd always lived his life on the easy slope, on the safe edge of responsibility. But a child was something real, something substantial. The thought of it scared him to death. "I wish we could have talked about it before."

"I didn't do it on purpose," she said. "It was a mistake and now I'm going to have to live with it."

"No," he replied, harsher than he'd intended. "We *both* have to live with it."

He watched her profile tighten for just a second, then relax, tears now glistening on her cheek. "Listen to me," she rasped, lower lip trembling. "I'm not trying to c-catch you or anything. I made the mistake . . . me. I've loved my independence for years. I'd never try and destroy yours because I made a mistake."

"You do have options, you know," Denny replied, feeling relieved to be off the hook, then guilty for feeling relieved.

She nodded, smiling sadly. "It's funny," she said from far away. "Maybe subconsciously I wanted this to happen. It's like I'm a refugee of the love generation. I bought the whole package: career, freedom, life on my own terms. It's been great, except lately I wake up in the morning wishing I was somebody else, anybody else. All my friends from the old days, even the diehards, eventually drifted off into marriages and parenting while I stayed free—and alone. Somebody once said that, without children, a person might as well be dead. Well, when I look in the mirror anymore, I see a zombie."

She turned and looked at him. "Does any of this make any sense?"

He nodded, afraid to tell her that commitment was like death to him.

"I don't want to die alone," she said. "I want companionship; I want someone to love me and care about what happens to me. I don't want to spend the last half of my life the way I spent the first."

"I wish," he said softly, "that I felt that way."

"Yeah," she replied. "Me, too."

"Molly . . ."

"Don't worry," she laughed. "I'm not going to put you back on the hot seat. You've never misrepresented yourself. I know what your are, and I ended up in a relationship with you at my own peril. I love you, Denny, but for the life of me I don't know if it's really love or simply desperation that drove me your way. At my age, you're the best thing out there, and *that's* scary."

"I suppose that's one way of putting it."

"It's just that—"

They hit something, Molly screaming, the impact throwing Denny up out of his seat to bang the windshield, cracking it like a spiderweb with his elbow.

"Aaahh," he fell back hard in the seat, grabbing his arm.

"Are you all right?" Molly asked, her hands locked on the wheel, her eyes wide and frightened.

"God, what did we hit?" he said, twisting in his seat to unlatch the door. Pain shot through his forearm, making his whole body weak. He half-tumbled out of the car, the fog totally encompassing.

He heard Molly getting out of the driver's side as he stumbled around to the front of the car to confront the carcass of Oater, the horse's eye still wide with fear in death. Bullet holes pocked the once-beautiful body, and it appeared that they'd hit it with the car also.

Molly cried deep in her throat. He turned to look at her as she stared down at the carcass, her eyes retreating, her mind desperately searching for some distant place where young punks couldn't shatter the calm of life in a violent, hostile outburst.

He wanted to put professional distance between himself

and the scene, but Molly, by her involvement, made it impossible. Childhood memories long buried forced themselves into his mind— the police coming to get him from the baby-sitter's when his parents burned in the car crash; his seeing the wreckage of the car in the newspapers, their covered bodies on the highway next to the accident; the foster homes who only wanted him for the state money they could collect.

He moved to her, knowing that he was expected to help. "I'm so sorry," he whispered, putting an arm loosely around her shoulder.

She stood stiffly in his grasp for a moment without acknowledging his presence, then slowly, like a music-box ballerina winding down, turned to him and buried her face in his chest. She cried.

"There," he said. "There." And he put his arms around her, pulling her closer to him as she wept gently, like a soft, cleansing rain. And he thought about how much luckier she was than him. At least she had something she cared about enough to cry over.

CUT TO:
DAY—EXT—A YOUNG MAN RIDING A BICYCLE. We see him winding through a large traffic jam, a small leather ZIPPER CASE under his arm, the fog from the night before nearly dissipated. We PULL BACK to see that the jam-up leads to the main gate of WCN, as tempers flare and horns HONK. The boy takes his package through the traffic and all the way up to the . . .
MAIN GATE. We watch as the boy hands his package to the same guard who'd given Denny a hard time in Act I, Scene 4.

BOY
This is from Mr. Dennis Stiller.

The guard NODS and carries the package away. We follow the package as the guard takes it inside and hands it to Floyd, the inside security man.

GUARD
It's from that Stiller character.

> FLOYD
> (smiling)

Thanks.

We follow Floyd as he carries the package through the glass
doors and HANDS IT to one of the busy receptionists.

> FLOYD

It's from Denny.

> RECEPTIONIST
>
> Oh my. I'd better call Mr. Horton. (she punches up
> her switchboard and waits a beat) Is he in? . . . Oh
> dear . . . well, I have a package from Mr.
> Stiller. . . . Yes. . . . yes. . . . Thanks, Annie.

ANGLE—HALLWAY. We see an OFFICE BOY hurry out of
one of the executive offices and run down the hallway toward
us. He passes us and we follow as he moves into the reception
area and snatches the package off the high counter, not losing
a step as he hurries through reception, passing Floyd on his
way back to his position, and moves through the doorway and
into the production end of the building. He jogs down the
hallway past the studios and enters a closed door. We move up
the hallway behind him, but he enters the room and CLOSES
THE DOOR in our face. The word NEWSROOM is printed
on the door. Beneath it hangs a sign that reads

> REMEMBER, THE VAST MAJORITY OF OUR VIEWERS
> HOLD BLUE COLLAR JOBS. THE VAST MAJORITY OF OUR
> VIEWERS NEVER WENT TO COLLEGE. THE VAST
> MAJORITY OF OUR VIEWERS HAVE NEVER BEEN ON AN
> AIRPLANE. THE VAST MAJORITY OF OUR VIEWERS HAVE
> NEVER SEEN A COPY OF THE NEW YORK TIMES. THE
> MAJORITY OF OUR VIEWERS DO NOT READ THE SAME
> BOOKS AND MAGAZINES THAT YOU READ . . . IN FACT
> MANY OF THEM NEVER READ ANYTHING. THE MAJORITY
> OF THE VIEWERS IN THIS TELEVISION MARKET
> CURRENTLY IGNORE TV NEWS.

CUT TO:
INT—THE NEWSROOM. Dick Horton is sitting on the edge
of a desk, a cup of coffee in his hand, talking with HANK

GREEN, WCN sports director, who is watching a baseball game on the screen of a TV on his desk, taking notes on the activity. The room is large and full of desks, many of them occupied with reporters and scriptwriters busily rewriting wire copy as tape editors pull features and hard news items off network, bureau, and local feeds. We also see the "Twinkies," the on-camera readers, sitting at their all-but-empty desks, fixing their hair or chatting with others of their kind. In the extreme bg, across the room , we see the office boy enter with the zipper case and hold it up.

OFFICE BOY

Mr. Horton! A delivery from Denny Stiller!

HORTON
(waving him over)

Oh boy. Here we go.

GREEN

Hope you got your life insurance paid up, buddy.
This one looks like a killer.

HORTON
(frowning)

I can't die, Hank. It would put the antacid people
out of business.

Horton takes the zipper case from the office boy and slowly opens it, reaching inside. He extracts a videocassette, holding it delicately with thumb and index finger at arm's length. He GRIMACES.

HORTON

Is this a dagger I see before me?

GREEN
(reaching for the tape)

C'mon, Macbeth. I want to see it.

Green takes the tape from Horton and slips it into a tape machine connected to the TV on his desk.

<u>GREEN</u> (cont)

Everybody! Over here! Dirty Denny's sent a tape!

As the people in the newsroom gather, Green reaches out and
PUSHES A BUTTON on the tape machine.
ANGLE—TV SCREEN. A picture juices to life. It is Denny
Stiller sitting on a sofa, smiling broadly.

<u>DENNY</u>

Good morning, Dick, and whoever else happens to
be sitting there. I'm sure you've all been waiting pa-
tiontly to hear from me . . .

<u>HORTON</u> (os)

Screw you, Stiller.

<u>DENNY</u>

True to my word, I've made another tape with Tawny
Kyle, and what a tape it is, too. We've go liquid dy-
namite in our hands, Dick. And just to show you that
I'm a nice guy, I'm going to share my good fortune
with you.
    Now there are terms connected to my cooperation,
but I'll wait until after you've seen last night's interview before I go into them, and I understand my
lawyer has set up a meeting with your lawyers for
later today. So, sit back and enjoy. By the way, Frank
Hargrave has asked that I tender his resignation for
him. I think that Molly is going to resign, but she
wants to talk with you herself. In the meantime,
think about the enclosed, and try not to think of my
terms as . . .

CUT TO:
CLOSE UP—DICK HORTON.

<u>HORTON</u>
(wild eyed)

Preposterous!

PULL BACK to reveal a WCN conference room. Dick Horton
sits at the head of a long table, surrounded by three fancy
lawyers in silk suits. Behind him, the visage of Ted Gayler
glares malevolently down at them from the screen of a

twenty-five-inch monitor, a television linkup with his main office on the other side of town. At the end of the table sit Denny and Charlie Kornfeld, Charlie SCRIBBLING NOTES on one of the yellow legal pads that sit before everyone at the table, while Denny idly plays with a pencil and slumps down in his chair.

<u>HORTON</u> (cont)

You're asking for things that are just unbelievable. Look at this! (he holds up a sheet of white paper) You're asking for a thirty-minute live feed every week to be broadcast from some unknown location with unknown content and without commercials. How can you expect us to produce something like that?

<u>DENNY</u>

We're not asking you to produce it, Dick. I'm going to produce it myself. All I want you to do is schedule the time slot and pay us for the finished product.

<u>HORTON</u>

(exasperated)

Yeah, at a million bucks an episode. And then you have the gall to tell us how much we can roll it over to the nets for!

Denny hated this part of it—the negotiations, they called it. The lawyers sat like leeches, not caring about outcomes but about their share of the continually running meter. Talking to them costs money; advice from them costs money; action and litigation cost even more money, and when whatever airtight case they've got falls apart at the seams, the client takes the lumps—and eats the expenses.

So, they sat here and negotiated whether or not he was going to get to live as a free human being and talk to Tawny Kyle, or whether they could come up with or make up some rule or other that would say he had to do what they told him to do. Denny'd been in court before and knew the fright of having his life in the hands of incompetent, insignificant others who spoke their own language and had their own system of priorities. Whenever he heard people get angry and threaten to sue someone, he always assumed that they'd never really been to court before—or they'd know better.

"There is nothing inherently undignified about our monetary requests," Kornfeld said, his new head of hair curled in tight ringlets against his forehead. "We have set up a system whereby we can make decent money and you can make even better money. We've established a ceiling of fifteen million dollars on your cash intake per episode because my client, Mr. Stiller, feels that this is a historically significant news event that will better serve the public if it is presented in a noncommercial way."

One of the WCN lawyers clapped loudly and shook his head. "Very egalitarian of you, counselor, but our stance is still nonnegotiable: Mr. Stiller is operating in breach of contract by employing Tawny Kyle."

Denny looked at his watch and wondered what Tawny and Amy were doing right now. He'd managed to get another motel under another assumed name, but he feared it was only a matter of time before they were discovered again.

"If the points were truly nonnegotiable, Mr. Belvet," Kornfeld said, "you wouldn't be sitting here right now. And we all know that your breach of contract suit went out the window the minute Denny tore up that contract with Tawny Kyle."

"We can still make a case for intent to defraud," Belvet said.

"Maybe," Kornfeld said. "And maybe by the time we got to court with something like that, our interests in Tawny Kyle would have run their course. The difference, of course, is that some other network would have gotten the contract. Gentlemen, it seems to me that Mr. Stiller is being quite kind to a production facility that has treated him unfairly in the past. If you want to break it off right now, that's fine. I can think of several major production companies that would jump at Mr. Stiller's generous offer."

Denny was getting itchy to return to the motel. Now that Tawny was beginning to get a real glimpse of the power she had so stupidly used, he was afraid to leave her alone with her daughter, afraid she'd realize that she didn't need him anymore. He'd given her two quarts of bourbon before leaving today, hoping she'd get sloshed enough not to worry about Amy and her power.

"This is stupid!" Horton said, wearily pulling his glasses down off his bald head to quickly scan the proposal again. After a few seconds, he pulled off the glasses and set them on the table. "Denny," he said, rubbing his eyes with the heels of his hands. "Can't we throw this fucking thing out the window?

You're a journalist, not a sideshow barker. You've always behaved with integrity before. Come on back into the fold. I've been authorized to give you the go-ahead to cover the story yourself if that's what you really want. You're a newsman. Behave with a little professionalism. We want you back."

Denny smiled at him. "I can always count on you, Dick old buddy, to put me on the straight and narrow. You talk to me about integrity after the way you pulled me off an important assignment and busted me down? You call news read by mannequins who couldn't find their butts with both hands professional? Hell, every year when the circus comes to town, one of us has to ride the damn elephants into the city. Now *that's* reporting. The news has become a show geared to the lowest common denominator just so people will watch it, Dick, and I for one don't see a thing wrong with Denny Stiller playing theatrical entrepeneur just a little bit to cop the ratings. Hell, you'd do the same if you were me."

Horton looked straight at him. "No, I wouldn't," he said.

"You'd eat worms out of the ground if your boss told you to," Denny replied, then looked up at the silent Ted Gayler on the monitor. "How about you, Ted. You don't mind if I call you, Ted? You know the value of the property I control. Do you think I'm a little shit for walking out on my responsibilities?"

"I do," Gayler said, then smiled thinly, "but I don't blame you for it. Actually, Mr. Kornfelds's absolutely right. Your offer is most generous considering our past . . . shall we say, differences of opinion? And I believe that we should accept your offer as written, at the risk of rousing the ire of my attorneys, who at the moment seem unable to grasp the larger view. In fact, I find the situation much more palatable this way—it makes WCN merely an agent for bringing this news into the home and not the instigator. It lets us off the hook, Mr. Stiller, and always leaves the ball firmly in your court."

Denny watched the screen in disbelief. The old man was smiling slightly. Something was wrong here, terribly wrong. Charlie leaned toward him.

"You won," he whispered.

"Then why does *he* seem happy?"

The man shrugged. "Shit, who cares? Let's just take the moncy and run."

"Yesterday, he was ready to fight me tooth and nail," Denny said low. "But today . . ."

Kornfeld just patted his arm and stood. "At Mr. Gayler's

recommendation, I ask that we dispense with the rest of the discussion of obligation and move right to the contract wording—"

"You write it up," Gayler said. "We'll sign it. I trust your wording."

Belvet turned to the screen. "But, Mr. Gayler, it's only good practice to negotiate the contract language, I—"

"Enough," Gayler said wearily. "Mr. Stiller isn't trying to cheat us, he just wants to use us as an outlet. He could take it to the larger markets, but he knows that their way of doing business is even more rigid than ours. The only thing I ask is that we try and set a time every week for the show and stick to it. This is more for the watchers' peace of mind than my own."

"Done," Kornfeld said, but nothing allayed Denny's suspicions as he recalled his conversation with Gayler the day before.

"Wait a minute," Denny said, pointing a finger at the screen. "What's on your mind? Why are you giving in so easily?"

"It's very simple," the old man said, "but it's nothing you will believe."

"Try me," Denny replied.

"All right," Gayler said. "What you've performed here is the journalistic equivalent of winning the Irish Sweepstakes. You're starting out with all the marbles gripped tightly in your sweaty hand. But, when you've got all the marbles, you've nothing to do but start losing them. Do you know, for example, that an overwhelming majority of poor people who've won major lotteries are right back where they started within three years of their good fortune?"

"What has that got to do with me?" Denny asked.

The old man's face turned dark and he leaned up closer to the screen. "You've climbed the mountains of power, son," he said, voice low, "a position you neither made nor deserve. You cannot survive at the pinnacle, for you come unprepared. Nothing but tragedy awaits you, and I don't want myself or my company in a position to fall with you when you misstep."

"You *do* understand what I've got hold of," Denny said with satisfaction.

"Far better than you," Gayler replied. "We'll provide you with the equipment you need to set up your studio."

"But its location remains my secret," Denny said.

"As you wish," Gayler said, eyes intense. "I suppose it's

foolish to warn you that you're standing in water far over your head."

Denny stood up and pointed at the screen. "I've been treading water my whole life, Ted, I—"

But Gayler had cut off from his end, the monitor screen going blank.

"Well, gents," Kornfeld said, standing and running a hand through his full head of hair, "like the man said, we'll write it up and you'll sign it." He looked at Horton. "And Dick," he said, bending slightly and tugging on his hair, "it's the real thing. You should try it sometime."

Horton looked at him blankly, then moved to turn off the monitor and operating camera just above it. "Try and decide on an air time and a method of payment," he said over his shoulder. "And Denny, you and the others need to do exit interviews to straighten out your profit sharing and insurance cutoffs."

"This is going to work out all right, Dick," Denny said, as he watched Gayler's lawyers filling their expensive briefcases with the paperwork they'd use as the basis for their big retainer. "It's going to be good for all of us."

Horton turned and looked thoughtfully at him. "I honestly hope you're right," he said. "You're a good man, Denny, a good newsman. But this whole thing . . . I don't know, it seems wrong somehow . . . dangerous."

"You're just a nervous Nelly."

The man smiled sadly. "I guess that's what they pay me for."

Kornfeld tugged on the sleeve of Denny's sport jacket. "I need to talk to you out in the hall," he said low.

Denny nodded in return. "Sure," he said, looking at his watch. "Problems?"

"We'll talk," he said.

The WCN lawyers filed dutifully out of the room, Horton playing host, holding the door for everyone to leave. Denny and Kornfeld followed the others out, Denny stopping to stare at his former boss.

"I know we haven't always gotten along," he said, putting out a hand, "but I want you to know that I've always respected you."

The man shook his hand. "Same here," he said.

Denny glanced around to make sure nobody else was listening. "Now that it's all over and I'm quits here," he said, "tell me why you guys pulled me off the Washington beat. Was it that interview with the president?"

Horton looked Denny in the eye. "The order came down from Gayler," he said. "He never said why and refused to discuss it, even when I reminded him of the implications to you and your career and your future here."

"One more question. Did you send a cameraman out to follow us last night?"

The man shook his head. "I don't know what you're talking about."

Denny nodded. "Thanks," he said, and walked into the hallway to find Kornfeld waiting for him a respectable distance from the conference room.

"That was the easiest negotiation I've ever gone through," he said. "I feel guilty about charging you for this one."

"But you will," Denny replied.

Kornfeld smiled. "Of course. But maybe I'll knock a little bit off the top for the . . . 'hair treatment.'"

"Off the top?" Denny said, frowning. "Stick to law, buddy. A comedian you're not. Let me ask you a question. Why do you think Gayler really gave in so easily?"

"We showed him miracles, Denny," the man said. "It's tough to argue with that."

"Let's call them, wonders, instead of miracles, okay?"

"Gotcha."

"What did you want to talk about?"

Kornfeld looked up and down the hall. "Let's walk," he said, and they moved off together, Denny quietly saying good-bye to five years of his life.

"I've waited until I could confirm this," Kornfeld said as they walked. "But I got a call from Europe this morning and everything's copacetic. I've got you another place to house Tawny and Amy."

"Is it private?" Denny asked.

"Pretty much," the man replied, as they arrived at the lobby, lowering their voices automatically. "A client of mine who lives in Turtle Creek is spending the entire summer overseas. We're caretaking his place for him. It's a huge house that sits on several acres of hillside. There's only one other house within blocks of it. I spoke with the owner this morning and he gave me the go-ahead to move you guys in there until he returns."

They walked out of the lobby and past the guard station to

the parking lot. The fog had all burned away, the day bright and muggy, Denny skinning out of his jacket. "We've got to be totally secretive about this," he said. "After last night's fiasco, we're not taking any chances."

"I agree. Before we go out there, we need to make sure no one is ever following. The Turtle Creek location is perfect for that, too, because it's all rolling hills and snaky roads. Nobody could follow you up there without your getting suspicious."

Denny nodded. They arrived at Kornfeld's Mercedes, the lawyer unlocking the car door and climbing in. He started the engine and powered down the window to talk to Denny. "Do you want to go out there with me now?"

"No," Denny replied, looking past the car to the congestion still evident at the front gate. "I'm going to meet Frank out here so we can get all the equipment we need. If you can, I want you to get Tawny and Amy out to the house this afternoon. Give me the address and Frank and I will meet you there this evening. Is there a covered garage? We'll probably be driving a mobile remote."

"There's a garage," Kornfeld said. "What about Molly? She's at the motel with the Kyles right now."

Denny leaned down into the window space. "Things are confusing with Molly right now," Denny said, thinking about their earlier conversation. "Talk to her. Try and get her out there with you, and I'll straighten everything out with her when I come tonight. They're running our second tape as an independent feature tonight at eight. I'll be in before that."

Kornfeld pursed his lips, writing on a notepad that was lying on the passenger side. He tore off a piece of paper and handed it to Denny. "Here's the address. Memorize it and then tear it up. I've already pulled reference to the place from our files at the office."

Denny did as he was told, ripping the paper into little shreds that he gave to the southern Texas breeze, warmed from the Gulf of Mexico. "How about your secretary?" Denny asked.

Kornfeld turned on his radio, the antenna rising from its berth in the front fender. An Eric Satie piano composition drifted gently from the innards of the car. "I handled everything myself," he said, and looked at his watch. "I have to be in court at two. I'll take care of the move after that."

Denny straightened, taking a long breath. "It's kind of a strange feeling, isn't it?"

"What?"

Denny looked hard at him. "Paranoia," he said.

"Yeah," Kornfeld replied and, powering up the window, he drove quickly out of the parking lot, Denny watching carefully to see if anyone drove out after him.

CUT TO:

NIGHT—EST—AN AIRPORT. We see an ultramodern airport amid a jungle setting, huge, dark hills rising in the bg, making us feel small and trapped by the will of nature. A sign on the airport entrance reads

BOGOTÁ INTERNATIONAL AIRPORT

CUT TO:

A HANGAR. From a distance, we see a busy hangar set somewhat apart from the rest of the airport. Frantic activity is taking place within the bright area of light that defines the hangar bay. A KC–135 Stratolifter is being loaded by Colombian Army personnel using hoists and forklifts. A convoy of covered army trucks is lined up outside the hangar, the vehicles with their lights on. Large wooden crates are loaded in the trucks. On the side of the huge, cargo jet are written the words AIR WESTERN.

CUT TO:

A SECURITY GATE. We sit on a single-lane road behind the lowered gate. A guard shack sits to our right, two sloppily dressed enlisted men playing cards on the floor. A jeep is DRIVING TOWARD US and STOPS when it reaches the gate, one of the guards getting up from the floor and walking to the jeep. While the jeep's driver speaks low in Spanish with the guard and shows him papers, the passenger, an Army captain, stands in his seat and looks out over the top of the dirty windshield toward the hangar. The captain is wearing sunglasses.

CAPTAIN

¿Qué hora es?

DRIVER
(looks at watch)

Dos y diez.

<u>CAPTAIN</u>

¡Apurate!

The guard hands back the papers and salutes, the guard within the shack raising the gate with a mechanical hum.
CUT TO:
KC–135 CARGO BAY. We are looking out from within the side bay of the plane as a crate is lifted by forklift and dragged into the plane by Americans dressed in jeans and T-shirts. A man in a suit is directing the activity. Beyond the line of forklifts we can see, in the distance, the jeep carrying the captain driving toward the hangar.

<u>MAN IN SUIT</u>

C'mon! Keep it moving!

ANGLE—CRATES. We see an American prying the top off one of the crates with a crowbar, while another is busy setting up a spray-painting gun. The man PRIES OFF THE LID and reaches within the confines of the crate, coming out with . . .
CLOSE-UP—A PLASTIC BAG FULL OF WHITE POW-DER.
ANGLE—LOOKING OUT THE BAY DOORS. We see the captain's jeep drive up to the plane, the captain climbing out. The man in the suit leans out the bay, waving to the captain.

<u>MAN IN SUIT</u>
(pointing to the forklift)

Come on up!

The captain climbs onto the forks along with a crate and is LIFTED up to our vantage point in the bay and fills our line of vision. In the extreme darkness of the bay, he removes his sunglasses and we can see that the captain is actually JESUS CARDERA, the man wanted for the deaths of the DEA agents.

<u>CARDERA</u>
(unsmiling)

Buenas noches, Mr. Trent.

Cardera and Trent, the man in the suit, shake hands, Trent leading Cardera farther back in the plane where we see the pried-open crate and the man with the crowbar, who has opened the package and is using a small spoon to put an amount of the white powder into a test tube that he vigorously shakes. Beyond him, the man with the spray-painting gear is busily holding a stencil up to the side of a crate.

TRENT

We're getting everything squared away right now.

ANGLE—CRATE. We see the man with the test tube nodding thoughtfully at what he sees, then he dips his little finger into the bag of white powder and rubs some powder on his upper gums. He winks and gives the THUMBS-UP sign, pulling a large aluminum suitcase out from behind the crate. Trent pulls a flashlight out from within his suit, he and Cardera bending to the suitcase. Cardera slowly (he does everything slowly) opens the case, Trent shining the flashlight into it. ANGLE—SUITCASE. The suitcase is full of microchips.

CARDERA (os)

Bueno. (he reaches in and grabs a handful of chips, letting them overspill his hand) *Bueno*.

TRENT (os)

Plenty more where these came from.

CARDERA (os)

Very good. It is always a pleasure doing business with the United States of America.

We hear a loud HISSING SOUND. We PAN UP to see a man spray painting over his hand-held stencil right onto one of the crates, but we can't read anything. We hold for several beats, then . . .
CLOSE-UP—CRATE. The man pulls the stencil off the crate and we can read the words printed there.

PROJECT BUMPER
TOP SECRET

Scene 3

(Turtle Creek—that evening)

Denny sat in the van with Frank's camera up to his face, his eye glued to the image in the viewfinder. Thanks to the spring rains, the lawns were deep green, the trees and thickets and high hedges lush emerald against the dying glow of the pink-stained sky. He gently fingered the juice, rolling a bit of establishing tape to make the whole place seem real to him. Wet greens photographed well— deep, vibrant and mysterious—bursting with life. He lowered his focus to the house across the street from them, zooming in on a cocker spaniel twirling and jumping, trying to catch the butterfly that alternately dipped and soared on the wide front lawn in sweet, blissful oblivion. They sat off the side of the road in a WCN remote, waiting for the sky to darken a bit more before continuing around the snaking blacktop to the hideout Charlie Kornfeld had provided them. The van was semidisguised, Denny covering the logo on the side with sheets of taped cardboard and wrapping a blanket around the microwave antenna on top.

"I had a dog like that when I was a kid," Denny said, smiling as the champagne-colored animal went high into the air in his viewfinder, only to come down off balance and fall to roll on the lawn. "I really loved that thing. His name was Mr. Brown."

"It's about fifteen till eight," Frank said, looking at his watch. "We ought to git on over there if we want to catch the show."

"Yeah," Denny said, turning the camera to look in the long side-view mirror, seeing nothing but trees and twisting road behind. The Turtle Creek area sat right on the edge of Dallas proper, in an area called Highland Park. It was preserved and private, and as he sat amid its planned pastoral elegance, it was difficult to believe there was anything else beyond the trees and enchanted-forest atmosphere. It was as if the rich people had created a never-never land of contemplative peace, an alternate universe unknown to the less fortunate city dwellers. "We've been here nearly twenty minutes and I haven't even seen another car."

"Leastways we know we haven't been followed," Frank said, picking his beer up off the floor and taking a long drink from the bottle. "Lookee yonder."

Denny, tape still rolling, shot through the windshield, toward the three-story, turreted palace that the champagne spaniel called home. A woman appearing to be in her fifties had come out the front door, dressed in frilly white blouse and toreador pants. The dog immediately forgot about the butterfly and, yipping madly, charged the woman, playfully jumping all around her as she walked out to turn off a sprinkler that had been watering her flower beds.

"She doesn't seem to see us," Denny replied. "Once she goes in we'll head on."

"What ever happened to that dog of yours?" Frank asked.

Denny frowned, sorry he'd brought it up. He focused on the woman, but the image was too hazy in the poor light. "When my folks died in that car wreck I couldn't keep Mr. Brown in the foster homes I went to. They had to give him to the pound. I guess they put him in one of those chambers that sucks all the air out to suffocate them." He took a breath, wondering what it would be like to suffocate and watching the dog as it barked at the woman's heels for attention. "He wasn't a bad dog, you know? But I guess that doesn't guarantee anyone staying alive."

"Everythin' dies," Hargrave said, and Denny felt the man welling deep emotional pain.

The woman moved around the front of the house wearing gardening gloves. Apparently on a weed hunt, she'd dive occasionally into the bed bright with daffodils, coming out triumphantly seconds later clutching something she'd drop on a nearby pile. It was getting just dark enough that Denny couldn't tell what she held, even when he zoomed all the way in. "I'm ready to move on now," he said, shutting down the camera and trying to focus on his own watch in the growing darkness inside the van.

"Did you spend any time thinkin'," Hargrave said after a moment, "about whether or not it's a good idea to do all this stuff with Amy and her mom publicly?"

Denny turned to stare at the man who sat, beer bottle poised close to his mouth, his leathery face wallowing in thoughtful wrinkles. "I'm not sure I understand what you're trying to say, Frank."

"Well, you know I understand what you're tryin' to do and all," the man said, turning to just touch Denny with runny blue eyes, "and I admire it, but I don't know how clearly you're thinkin' about just who could get hurt."

"I'm willing to take my chances," Denny said. "I've really got nothing to lose."

"Damnit, I'm not talkin' about you," the man returned, tightening his lips. "I'm talkin' about that little girl. Whatever comes out of this, you're makin' her out to be a freak in front of, God knows, the whole world. Anythin' we fuck up is gettin' fucked up in front of maybe billions of people."

Denny handed Frank the camera. "She *is* a freak though, isn't she? I mean, by this point, if I don't exploit it, somebody else, somebody even less sensitive, will."

"She is no freak," Hargrave said low. "I don't see a whit's worth a difference between her and me, is all. I went off to war and *saw* with my eyes what kind of animals we all are and walked away from it, from life. Amy . . . she just knew all the time, that's all."

Denny silently watched the man until he turned in the darkness and stared again. "Don't you understand, Frank?" he asked. "I mean, don't you really understand? The Truth is the Truth, that's all. Sometimes it hurts people and sometimes it helps, but in the long run, we must have it."

"Why?"

"Because something has to matter. Life has to have some sort of purpose in order for us to want to live through it. I live for the story, the truth of the story. Amy Kyle is a story that may profoundly affect the way people think, and I feel that my mission in life is to get this story out in as straightforward a way as possible regardless of who gets hurt for the short term."

"She's gone in," Frank said, pointing to the house where the dog had been playing.

Denny started the engine and pulled out quietly, without the headlights. "If I was capable of feeling any different," he continued, "I'd undoubtedly be in some other line of work. I'm a lot more worried about making people mad than I am in making a fool out of Amy."

"What do you mean?"

Denny shook it off, some of Molly's fears of shaking the viewers' philosophical trees rubbing off on him. "Nothing," he said, watching the road as they passed the cocker's house and followed a small curve that fronted another lawn, another palace. "I think this is it. I can't read an address, but it fits the description."

"I haven't been in anythin' so fancy since the American Embassy in Saigon back in '73," Hargrave said.

Denny turned into the long, paved driveway, a mailbox beside the drive providing an address that matched the one he'd committed to memory. Charlie hadn't been kidding about the place. It was huge. Two towering stories of gray brick, set off by antebellum columns in front, and large dormer windows at the attic level that alluded to a third floor. The house was set back off the roadway by a good two hundred feet and, as Charlie had said, the house with the cocker spaniel was the only other place within a mile in either direction. He couldn't shake the feeling that he was going off to a vacation resort.

He drove past the house to the four-car garage out back, Kornfeld running out of a back door to greet them. Denny climbed out of the van before pulling into the garage to make sure the dish antenna could pass safely beneath the eaves.

"How's it going?" Denny asked as he stood on the step-up and tried to gauge the clearance by sight.

"Great," Kornfeld said. "Amy is screaming, Tawny is falling down drunk, Molly is locked in her room and won't talk and I think my wife's decided that I've deserted her and she's run off with the pool boy."

"Sounds like you've got everything under control," Denny replied absently, deciding that the antenna would just clear the overhang. He climbed back into the truck and drove into the darkness of the garage.

He shut down the engine and turned to Frank in the darkness. "Find the best place inside to set yourself up a little studio, preferably someplace without much distraction. Tawny says that too much activity distracts Amy and messes up her head."

"Denny . . ."

"Just a minute," Denny said. "Set up your studio, but leave the coaxials in the garage. We'll only tote them out when we're ready to use them."

"Can I talk?" Frank said.

"We'd better hurry," Denny replied. "The newscast—"

"I want you to promise me that you won't let anything happen to that little girl or her mother," Frank said, voice tense.

"How can I promise that?" Denny said. "I can't predict the future."

Frank's skeletal hand snaked out and grabbed Denny by the wrist. "Promise me!" he said hoarsely.

"All right!" Denny snapped, pulling his wrist away. "As long as I am able, I'll protect them both."

"With your life?" Frank said.

"What the hell . . ."

"Say it!"

"I'll protect them with my life," Denny said. "Satisfied?"

"Yes," Frank said, opening his door, light coming on in the van.

Denny got out on the driver's side, wondering just how much store Frank Hargrave set in promises, and how he could expect Denny to live up to the one he'd just made. *Artists,* Denny thought. *Children.*

He joined Kornfeld outside of the garage. "Any news?" he asked, as they walked toward the back gate to the house.

"Not much," Kornfeld said. "True to Gayler's word, all preliminary lawsuits regarding Tawny Kyle or breach of contract have been dropped."

"Good," Denny said, pushing through the redwood gate. They walked into a fancy cabana overlooking a huge swimming pool shaped like the state of Texas. "This must be quite a landmark from the air."

"Thought you'd be amused," Kornfeld said. "We've also had a great many calls from media all over the world at my office, everyone wanting an interview. The people at *Nightline* are getting pretty persistent."

"Put off everybody else but *Nightline*," Denny said, as they walked through the cabana and opened the glass back door to the house itself. "I'll do them tomorrow night . . . but just me. They can't have Tawny. I'll have Frank work out the broadcast so that we can do it from here."

The inside of the house was an exercise in conspicuous consumption with wide-open prairielike rooms and high ceilings and furniture stuffed to bursting. The incredible amounts of wall space were filled with paintings with the emphasis on French impressionists. Denny was surprised to find that he recognized several of the hung works.

"Does this guy own the mint or what?" Denny asked, then charged across the thick carpeted floor to throw himself on a sofa.

Kornfeld laughed, walking to join him. "Better," he said. "He's one of Texas's new indispensables, a bankruptcy lawyer."

"Well, howdy darlin'!" yelled Tawny Kyle from the wide sweeping stairway to the second floor. "How about all this fancy do!"

The woman had a drink in her hand and was dressed in cutoffs and a tank top that looked ridiculous on someone her age. She tried to walk and fell, coming down hard on her back three steps from the ground and sliding the rest of the way to the living room.

Denny was up, running to the woman, Kornfeld walking slowly behind. He reached her only to find her chuckling, lying on her back at the foot of the stairs.

"You okay?" Denny asked, peering down at her glassy eyes.

"Hell," she said. "Ah done all mah best work from this position." She struggled to her knees, holding up her glass. "Perfessionalism. Look. Didn't spill a drop."

Denny helped her to her feet, Kornfeld moving up beside him. "That's not the first time today," he said softly. "I've never seen anybody drink like her."

Denny nodded at the man, wondering if there was any implied criticism of him and his methods in Charlie's tone. He couldn't worry about that now. Time was running short.

"How's Amy?" he asked the woman.

"Whiny," she responded and took a drink. "Always gits that way when Ah'm havin' a good time. It ain't no deal, okay?"

"Okay," Denny said, turning to Kornfeld. "Where's Molly?"

Kornfeld let his eyes ascend toward the second floor. "She took the master bedroom," he said, then looked at his watch. "You've only got a few minutes until showtime."

Denny nodded, looking at Tawny. "You just take it easy," he said. He put a finger on the rim of her glass. "We're not trying to retire the national debt here."

"Sure, darlin'," she said, wandering off, and no one in the room believed that either Tawny or Denny had meant what they said.

Denny started up the stairs, Kornfeld stopping him with a hand on his arm.

"I think I'm going to go on home," he said, "and see if my wife has changed the locks."

Denny nodded. "Thanks for setting all this up. I couldn't have done anything without you."

The man shook it off. "It was my job and my pleasure," he returned. "Just make sure you do a good job, that'll be thanks enough . . . that, and my fee, of course."

Denny laughed as the man turned to go. "Tell Wendy that I'm sorry for keeping you away from home so long."

The man waved over his shoulder. "Call me in the morning."

"And Charlie," Denny called, the man stopping and turning to face him. "You're the only one outside of this house who knows where we are. We've got to keep it that way. I don't want any repeats of last night."

"Don't worry," Kornfeld said. "On my new hair I swear the secret's safe with me."

Denny watched him move across the wide expanse of a living room they could have played field hockey in. The man passed Frank coming in with an armful of equipment, the cameraman totally oblivious to everything save the spatial relationships and shadows of the house as he gazed around with a professional eye. Work was Frank's only connection to humanity and, thank God, he kept that sense working all the time.

Denny walked up the stairs, everything unfamiliar, everything alien, all of it somehow appropriate to the atmosphere that had enveloped him. Everything was new to Denny at this point. All ground was uncharted in every aspect of his life. It was scary and exhilarating.

The upper hallway was white with beige carpet, Modigliani originals lining the walls, liquid assets for a man who had no faith left in the American dream. As Central Americans trafficked in jewelry and Asians in pearls, so this man used cracked oil paint as a substitute for money in the bank.

The sound of muffled wailing greeted his entry into the hall. He followed it to a closed door of off-white edged in antique gold. It was a tiny, high pitched sound, like a siren from very far away. Without hesitation he reached out and turned the knob, opening the door.

Amy sat cross-legged on a bed in a room so antiseptic it could only be the guest room. Her hands were on the sides of her head, her mouth open wide, the tiny sound wheezing from her with every breath, as if it were something terrible she was having to let out from inside.

She was naked, her skin the smooth pale marble of a statue, Denny looking involuntarily, his throat constricting as he forced himself to close the door while chastising himself for not closing it sooner, feeling he had somehow taken advantage of the girl. And as he was shutting the door, the sound stopped. He opened it again, looking only at her face.

Amy had lowered her hands, her face now placid. She didn't look at him, but seemed to be staring at something right beside him. Then, for just a second, she turned her eyes to him. He felt a jolt inside, a connection of some kind, and he somehow knew that she recognized him and that the recognition calmed her. He felt a numbness, a tingling in his fingertips not unlike an electric shock. He moved to get into her line of vision again, but she simply turned it elsewhere. He fought back the urge to go to her and turn her face forcibly to his, but, realizing the awkwardness of his position, he turned and walked out the door instead, closing it solidly behind him.

He continued down the hall. His legs had gotten weak and he was sweating. He felt nervous, on edge, and fought the feeling back as he approached the closed door at the end of the hall, afraid to handle a delicate conversation with Molly in the mood that had come upon him.

He stood at the door and took several deep breaths, finally reaching out to knock lightly. "Molly?" he called. "It's me, Denny."

"It's open," she said from the other side.

He wiped sweaty palms on his pants legs and opened the door. Molly sat in the center of a water bed, cross-legged, just like Amy. She wore jeans and an old T-shirt. The room was a man's room, the room of a man who lived alone, with stocky, rough-finished furniture and several western paintings by Charles Russell on the walls. The place smelled like men's cologne and just this side of sweat. The woman looked totally out of place there.

"You've been crying," he said, noticing red eyes and near the bed a small trash basket filled with tissues.

"A little," she said defensively. "Women do that from time to time. It comes with the territory. But, then, you wouldn't know about that, would you?"

"Molly, I . . ."

She put up a hand. "I'm sorry," she said. "Peace. I'm not trying to give you a hard time. Really."

"It would be okay if you wanted to give me a hard time," he said, walking into the room and shutting the door. "I guess I really never have held up my end of the relationship very well."

She smiled thinly and held her arms out to him. "Come here," she said. "Let's make up."

He moved to the bed and sat beside her, leaning toward her for a kiss. When their lips touched, a massive charge of static electricity jumped from him, Molly jerking back with wide eyes, a hand going to her mouth.

"God!" she said loudly, covering her mouth in pain. "Did you shuffle across the carpet coming up here or what?"

"Sorry," he said, a finger going to his own lip.

She laughed painfully. "I-I think I got burned!"

He reached for her again, touching her quickly on the leg to make sure the charge had dissipated. What in the world had happened? This was far stronger than any normal static charge. He gently pulled her hand from her mouth. A small charred circle was burnt into her lower lip where his lips had touched her. "You *are* burned," he said, incredulous. "Guess I didn't know my own strength."

"Do things like this happen?" she asked loudly.

"I've never seen anything like it," he said.

"Wait till my analyst hears about this," she said, tenderly touching the spot again.

"About this morning—"

Once again she stopped him. "No, wait," she said. "I've got something I want to say first. I wasn't kidding this morning when I said I wasn't sure why I went off the pill . . ."

"But," he helped.

She smiled, then grimaced with lip pain. "No jokes tonight, okay?" she said, then continued, her eyes drifting to the bedspread. "I s-suppose that somewhere in the back of my mind I thought about you and me and . . . you know, a family and all that. But I know, really know, that you never shared that kind of fantasy."

"I'm sorry," he said, and meant it. "Relationships have never been something I've handled well."

She looked at him, put a hand on his arm. "Look, Denny. You've never lied to me about anything. You've been out front and real with me the whole trip. I was the one who put conditions on it, and I'm the one who disappointed myself, not you."

"That doesn't make me any nicer, though, does it?"

She sighed. "Listen. At my age, a girl takes what she can get. No offense. I just happen to love a man incapable of returning that love."

"I wish I were different," he replied. "I want to give; I've just never known how." He let himself fall back on the bed, staring at a pebbly, sparkly ceiling, the kind he always associated with motels. "I'm not crass enough to not feel bad. I asked Charlie to get you over here, hoping I could . . . I don't know, make it up to you somehow.

"What have you got in mind?" she said, moving up close to him and staring down.

"I want to work with you on this project," he said. "I really need your levelheaded professional insights. I can pay you more than you make at WCN . . ."

"How about maternity benefits?" she asked, only half-smiling.

He sat up and looked at her. "You know I'll take care of everything," he said. "Whatever you want to do with the baby, don't worry about the cost. If you decide to have it— "

"I'm going to have it," she said without hesitation.

"Okay," he said. "Then we'll work out support payments or something."

"No," she said. "I'm responsible for this child. I want any maternity benefits written into my contract with you, but at that point your obligation ends. I won't lock you into any kind of relationship with me."

He hoped the relief wouldn't show on his face. He'd tried to do the right thing, but it was refused. "However you want it," he said.

"I want you to know something else, too," she said. "I'm here for the project, not for you. Somebody needs to make sure you present a balanced viewpoint on this thing."

He smiled. "The old professional curiosity kicking in?" he asked, not believing her for a minute.

"Something like that," she returned, leaning over to kiss him quickly, no shocks this time. "While we're on the subject of the project, I think you allow Tawny Kyle far too much to drink. Have you seen her?"

"Tawny's *my* responsibility," he said, standing. "I'm not doing anything without a reason."

"I'll accept that for now," she said.

"Hey!" came a small voice from the bottom of the stairs. It was Frank. "The show's started!"

"We'd better get downstairs," he said, then thought about the girl. "Would you see to Amy for me? Make sure she's . . . all right." He was too embarrassed to tell her that he'd seen Amy naked. That was stupid. What was wrong with him?

"Sure," she said to his back as he moved to the doorway. "And Denny?"

He turned to her. "Yes?"

"It's a big bed," she said, "too big for one."

He looked at her, his feelings in conflict. "I'll remember that," he said and walked out of the room. Molly was confused, her offer to him merely a mirror of her own fears. That he would take her up on the offer was a function of his own selfishness and lack of ethics in relationships, but Denny had discovered long ago that the only kind of feelings that could hurt you were the ones you dwelt on.

He walked back down the hall, stopping for just a second in front of Amy's door before moving on. Frank was waiting for him at the bottom of the stairs.

"You ought to *see* this place," the man said. "They got a fuckin' bowlin' alley in the basement and a Jacuzzi as big as my pickup. And I found a big old steam room that we'll use for a studio."

"Where's the TV?" Denny asked.

"In here," the man said, pointing a thumb over his shoulder. "There's a den off the kitchen."

He followed Frank back through an elegant dining room with a low-hanging crystal chandelier and into a modern kitchen with lots of stainless steel and chopping blocks scattered around. Tawny stood at a kitchen counter mixing herself a drink, which at this point meant pouring bourbon into a glass full of ice.

"Showtime!" Denny called to her as he passed, the woman looking up as if she didn't recognize him at first, then smiling wide through crooked teeth.

"You sure do know how to look after a woman," she said, raising her glass.

Frank moved to her, taking the drink away. "Isn't it about time for you to be thinkin' about a little sleep?" he said, walking to the stainless-steel sink and pouring the drink into it.

"You've got to give them whiskey companies time to make some more."

Her eyes got hard and she flared around to Denny. "You cain't let him push me 'round this way, sugar. You tell him."

Denny looked at Frank, the man's face set firm. "I think Frank might be right this time, Tawny," he said. "Why don't you—"

"Ah know what Ah'm doin'!" she said and made a sweeping gesture with her arm that knocked the bottle of Jack Daniel's off the counter to shatter loudly on the checkerboard vinyl floor. She stared at the shattered bottle for several seconds then burst out crying.

Frank moved to her, pulling her to his chest where she sobbed into his shirt. "It's goin' to be all right," he said. "You've just seen too many bottle bottoms tonight, that's all." He turned to Denny. "Go on in. I'll git her up to her room."

Denny nodded and moved through the opening to the den. This was the most comfortable-looking room in the house, perhaps the only room where the owner actually spent time. The furniture looked homey and lived in, the knotty pine walls and red throw rugs on hardwood floor were inviting. Magazines and newspapers were stacked in holders and under tables and, perhaps most noteworthy, not one valuable oil painting hung on the walls. A big-screen TV sat at the far end of the room, already turned on to WCN.

He laughed when he saw who was on the screen. It was Gloria Talifero, a Twinkie newsreader who'd originally been hired because she had naturally red hair and pronounced all her rs as if she were a revving engine. She looked serious up there, bigger than life, wearing the kind of face usually reserved for assassinations, school bus accidents, and state funerals.

". . . as our own Dennis Stiller continues to probe the deepening mystery of Tawny Kyle, WCN has committed itself to a policy unheard of in television broadcasting. Beginning in just a few days, we will be bringing live, unedited reports to you from Mr. Stiller. He will be broadcasting from a location that is being kept a secret not only from our viewers, but from us as well. Mr. Stiller feels, and we agree, that the amount of publicity this story is bound to generate could only hurt the experiments by exposure. As a matter of policy and public responsibility, the management of WCN is limiting the amount of revenue profit that it can make from these broadcasts, and no commercial time will be sold."

"A bunch of altruistic bastards all right," Molly said from the doorway.

"You're just in time," Denny said, taking a seat on a flower-printed couch and patting the space beside him. "Gayler's explaining to the world what a humanitarian he is."

"My God, it's Gloria!" she said, walking to the couch.

"Yeah," Denny replied. "They must be letting her practice two-syllable words tonight."

Molly sat beside Denny. "And look, she's not even drooling."

She kittened up beside him on the couch, Denny's arm going around her shoulder. The closeness stirred him and he was glad for all the wrong reasons that he had asked her to stay at the house with them.

"I tried to dress Amy, but she wouldn't let me near her," Molly said. "But I passed Frank with Tawny on the way up. Will it be all right to leave her with her mother?"

"They've survived this way for a great many years," Denny said. "I assume they'll figure out some way to survive us, too."

"Still . . ."

On the screen, after suitable warnings and fanfares, Denny's tape had begun to run. He saw himself sitting next to the woman in the motel, talking as he tried to figure out what to do next.

"I didn't teach Tawny how to drink, Molly," he said, tired of having that particular bundle dropped into his lap. "She's a free, grown woman who is spending her paycheck on something that makes life tolerable for her. She can flush it down the toilet for all I care." He turned to stare hard at Molly. "It's her business, not mine. And it's not yours either." Why did they continually try and make him take responsibility for a news story?

"I just don't want to . . . see anything happen while she's with us, that's all," the woman said, hurt evident in her voice.

"I don't either," he replied, stopping short of telling her that he allowed Tawny to stay drunk in order to limit her control. Molly wouldn't understand that a sober Tawny could be a dangerous Tawny. "I'll look in on her in a little bit, to make sure they're okay. Fair enough?"

She nodded, snuggling up closer. On the screen Denny saw his hand in close-up, watched the knife as it dug into his skin. The sight made him shiver, pain shooting through the place he had cut. He couldn't help but look down at it, marveling at the smooth skin he encountered.

But he also remembered the pain, the deep wracking pain that must have compressed the whole spectrum of healing into several seconds of unbearable agony. He shivered involuntarily, his neck hairs bristling.

As the blood flowed down Denny's hand on the screen, Molly turned and buried her face in his shoulder. "I don't know if I can watch this," she said.

"You want me to turn down the sound?" he asked.

She shook her head against his arm. "You go ahead and listen I . . ."

The scream came from the TV, Denny looking up to see his own face contorted inhumanly, his anguish ripping unbidden from his throat. Molly dug in harder, her hands locked in a death grip on his arm.

And then the screaming stopped, Denny staring in fascination as his face, fifty-inches wide, relaxed out of the strain, color coming slowly back.

"That one'll never fly," Frank said from the doorway, a fresh Budweiser in his hand. "It looks just like the blood pellets they use on TV rasslin', fact, not as good." He laughed dryly. "I seen special effects that worked better than that."

Denny smiled. Frank was right. The genuine article didn't look nearly as real as the stuff they used in the movies. "You get Tawny up okay?"

The man nodded and walked in to join them on the sofa. "Got her to the door anyhow," he said, leaning forward to set his bottle on the coffee table. "Don't know what kind of luck she had after that."

"Thanks, pard," Denny said, watching himself wiping the too rusty-looking blood from the back of his hand. The "effect" may have looked phony, but his performance had been of academy award caliber, his image on the screen still shaking with the residue of pain.

"I know why you set the lights up that way," Frank said, "but it don't work right. It all looks too harsh, like mug shots that way."

"How would you do it?" Denny asked, as his screen ego tried to talk Kornfeld in front of the camera.

"Diffuse the light," Hargrave said, his eyes glued to the screen. "Make it look natural, pastoral. I might even filter it down an f-stop or two. We won't have no shadows, but we won't have no carny show neither. The camera needs to love that little girl."

"That's what I hired you for," Denny said. "You handle it any way you want." He turned to Molly. She had pulled some tissue out of her jeans pocket and was stuffing a wad of it in each ear. She looked up at him sheepishly. He smiled. "I'll go look in on Tawny."

She nodded happily, patting his leg, so Denny rose and walked out of the room, ready to put on his concerned act to placate Molly. He moved back through the kitchen and dining room to the stairs. It wasn't that he bore Tawny any ill feelings, it had just simply looked to him from the first that she was the barrier he'd have to overcome in order to get to Amy. Actually, the compassion shown by his colleagues toward the woman surprised him and made him want to show them that he was compassionate, too.

He took the stairs two at a time, surprised that it was so easy for him to walk out on the broadcast. Seeing his own pain had knocked the interest right out of him, and he determined that if he were to handle this whole thing objectively he'd have to concentrate on keeping the substance of the experiments away from himself.

The door to Tawny's room was closed. He walked up quietly and listened for any sounds without success. Light spilled from beneath the door. He reached out and knocked lightly, then turned and began walking away. Then he stopped again. He'd told Molly that he'd look in on them. He went back to the door and knocked again without answer. He reached for the knob only to find his hand shaking like before. What the hell was going on?

Mad at himself now, he opened the door and walked into the room. Amy lay on her back in the bed, her fingers tracing rapid, angry, cryptic patterns in the air. Her mother lay beside her, passed out, flat on her stomach, arms and legs splayed. She'd obviously tried to undress, but had gotten no farther than pulling her cutoffs halfway off before succumbing to the darkness and falling where she'd stood. A lit cigarette was clamped between her fingers, already smoldering against the bedclothes. Denny leaned across the bed and removed it, stubbing it out in an ashtray.

He walked up on Tawny's side of the bed, staring down at her. Just the edge of some sort of tattoo poked out from under her panties near the hip. Unable to resist, he reached out and pulled her underwear down just far enough to see the Harley Davidson logo emblazoned on her right ass cheek. He smiled. Figures.

He turned to go, getting to the door before realizing that he'd subconsciously avoided looking at Amy, almost as if he were afraid of her. He turned and stared hard, watching those tireless fingers blurring the air.

He walked right up to her, looking down and then, impulsively, reached out a hand to touch her shoulder. Her motions stopped immediately, body going rigid, and instead of taking his hand away, he left it there.

It struck him that the supposition had always been that Amy had to perform her wonders through the medium of Tawny, but that Tawny always touched the people to be helped, almost as if she were simply an electrical conduit through which the power was passed. Amy didn't allow many people close to her, but she allowed *him* close enough to touch.

"Do you know me?" he asked gently. "Do you know who I am and why I'm here? Do you understand anything that's going on around you?"

"Mama?" Amy said loudly, her head turning back and forth. "Mama?"

He got down on his knees, watching her face, fascinated by the inscrutable. "I want to get inside of your head," he whispered, his hand idly stroking her long, dark hair. "I want to see all of you. I want to know what it is you know and keep locked up in there."

The girl relaxed somewhat on the bed and began wiggling her fingers in front of her face again. Remembering what Tawny had told him, he duplicated the process, entering her world. "Would you talk to me like you talk to your mama?" he said. "Would you let me in there with you?"

He was filled with excitement and a deep sense of longing. Taking his eyes from her face, he looked at Tawny. The woman was sleeping deeply, snoring.

He stood, bending over the girl. "Let's me and you take a little walk," he said. "Just for a few minutes." He slipped his arms beneath her and picked her up, cradling her gently, lovingly.

Once she was in his arms, he straightened and walked quickly across the room and out the door, Amy staring past

him, as oblivious to the world around her as the butterfly he'd
seen on the neighbor's lawn.

He hurried down the stairs with his bundle, moving
through the house until he reached the den. There was
screaming on the TV, Molly's segment running. The real Molly
sat stiffly on the sofa, eyes closed to the visuals, hands over her
ears. Frank looked up at him as he entered.

"What the hell you doin' with her?" he asked.

"Get your camera," he said. "Hurry."

Molly had become aware of his presence and stared at him
in confusion as Frank hurried out of the room. "I-is everything
all right?" she asked.

"Tawny's passed out cold," he said. "I'm going to find out
how necessary she is to the project."

"What do you mean?"

"It's not difficult to figure out," he said, sitting on the edge
of an easy chair, resting his burden. "I'm going to try and
contact Amy myself."

"You can't," she said, rising from the couch to walk near
them. "You have no right . . ."

He glared her to silence. "For God's sake, I'm not going to
operate on her; I'm only trying to say hello."

"Tawny would never allow it."

He searched her face until he found her eyes. "Fuck
Tawny . . . and the horse she rode in on."

Frank came back into the room, carrying camera, already
mounted on tripod, over his shoulder. "What do you need?" he
said.

"Just turn it on," he said. "I want a record and I want to do
this quick. No big deal, just contact."

Frank had the tripod opened in seconds, his head bent to
the viewfinder. "I'm on battery pack," he said. "We're rolling
now."

"Okay," he said, trying to tame his racing mind. With the
girl still on his lap, he took one of her hands in his and could
physically find a pulse beat of energy flowing through him. He
felt his face flush, then a pounding and receding of emotion, in
and out, like waves.

"Denny?" Molly said softly.

"Shh," he whispered, closing his eyes, riding a crest of
pure, undirected feeling like he'd never known. It was a
butterfly high, like the second your stomach drops out from
under you on the big hill of a roller coaster. No wonder Tawny

wanted to keep it to herself. He forced his mind to focus beyond the feelings. "What to do," he said. "What . . ."

Then it came unbidden, the image of the dog with the butterfly, the image of Mr. Brown. A dog . . . a dog . . . every house needs a dog. He concentrated on that need, a totally incongruous, off-the-wall thought.

"What are you doing?" Molly asked.

"Shh."

"You said you were just making contact."

He clarified the image, his lock on the viewfinder of his mind as the brain-photographed cocker spaniel jumped and twirled in the warm sunshine of life and love, a big, furry dog bringing happiness and no pain, a dog just like Mr. Brown, a dog to give unselfish love . . .

"What the hell?" Frank said loudly, breaking the spell, Denny pulling out to hear a monstrous, rending sound from outside.

He looked at the others, their faces frozen in confusion as the sound grew in intensity. It was almost alive, the sound, like the amplified, dying screams of a rogue elephant. Then came the horrible sounds of crashing glass and destruction.

Denny was on his feet without realizing it, putting Amy on the chair as Frank shut down the camera.

"Bring it!" Denny yelled as he ran for the door. "Molly, watch Amy!"

He flew through the house, his mind disconnected from the action as he tried unsuccessfully to put a reason to the horrible sounds.

The front door was locked, his hands fumbling stupidly on the lock as he tried, too fast, to open it. Frank had caught him by the time he jerked it open and ran onto the wide front lawn.

The sight that greeted him was incredible. Across the street, the palatial house was self-destructing. Without seeming reason, it was twisting against itself and its moorings, shaking violently as if the hand of God had come down to destroy it. He watched in rapt fascination as one of the turreted windows fell, crashing loudly to the driveway.

"Jesus . . . Jesus," Frank kept saying from beside him as he ground out tape in the almost total darkness.

With a loud, unearthly groan, the roof and third floor collapsed in an implosion of dust and shingles, a chimney falling in a single piece to explode in brick shards at ground level. The walls of the massive structure were buckling inward, wheezing like a concertina until the left side went in, taking the second floor with it, the whole of the structure vibrating precariously for just a second before collapsing in on itself with a deep, rumbling roar, a massive cloud of dust enveloping the entire area. Before the sound even died out there was another explosion as the gas line went on a spark, an orange fireball rising majestically above the dust cloud to light the area to daylight.

"This is freakin' nuts!" Frank said too loud, panning up to get the plume of smoke shooting out of the ruins. "What the hell is goin' on here!"

And the dust cloud rolled ominously toward them, enveloping everything in dirty haze as it made its way across the big front lawn.

Denny strained his eyes into the dust, picking up movement, a shadow flitting, jumping in the dirty fog. The shadow got closer, running, charging in his direction and before he could react, it leapt at him!

He yelled, falling back, only to find the cocker spaniel in his arms, madly licking his face, the dog from across the street, his fantasy dog.

"How did that damn thing get out of that mess?" Frank said, turning the camera to film Denny holding the animal.

Denny Stiller just stood there, frozen in fear and bewilderment, holding the squirming dog that seemed to love him as much as Mr. Brown had.

He wondered if he had just committed murder with his mind.

CUT TO:

A MIDDLE-CLASS TAVERN—NITE. The place is decorated in a sports motif, with football paraphernalia adorning the walls. It could be any blue-collar hangout in any city. Two men sit at the bar, drinking draft beer out of pilsner glasses and watching Denny's broadcast on the big-screen TV usually reserved for the sports station. Their names are RALPH and MORT. Every other patron in the bar has stopped what he's doing and stands, watching the broadcast.

RALPH

Bunch of bullshit if you ask me. (he takes a drink) I mean, you know, if that woman could already do all that shit, she'd be president or something already.

MORT
Maybe she just likes helping people, I don't know.

RALPH
Right, asshole. If you haven't figgered it out, this
world is a grab for bucks and a grab for glory; and I
damn well guarantee you, if that power was real and
I had it, I'da been runnin' the world a long time ago.
Besides . . . shit like this just don't happen. Look at
that fool cuttin' his hand. Does that look real? Does
it?

MORT
(indignant)
It could be real . . .

RALPH
(laughing)
Then I got some swampland in Florida you might
want to buy from me.

MORT
Just for the sake of argument—what if it *is* real?

RALPH
(he looks at the TV, watching Denny wipe the blood
off his hand, then turns back to Mort) Things like this
just don't exist.

MORT
You believe in God, Ralph? Do you believe that God
could work miracles if he wanted to?

RALPH
(frowning deeply)
You know I don't.

MORT
Right.

He physically TURNS from Ralph and in so doing is able to

give his entire concentration to the television, which he watches, his face transfixed.

CUT TO:

SPLIT SCREEN. We are watching both sides of a telephone conversation. On the left is Ted Gayler, dressed in tuxedo, on a pay phone. In the bg we can see a formal banquet in progress. On the right is the president, whom we recognize from the earlier newsreel. He's dressed in striped pajamas and is sitting in his bedroom at the White House watching Denny's broadcast, a cup of cocoa in the hand not occupied by the phone. In the bg we can see his wife moving in and out of our vision, undressing, getting ready for bed.

GAYLER

. . . because the son of a bitch was craftier than I gave him credit for. He had the woman tied up before we could get control.

PRESIDENT

And you don't know where he is now?

GAYLER

That's only a temporary inconvenience. We've got Gates and Bumper people on it. At worst it could only be the matter of a few days.

PRESIDENT

And then what? Is there any truth to what I'm seeing on the screen? Is it possible to have this kind of power?

GAYLER

So far it looks absolutely on the up-and-up. That's why I pursued it to begin with. To my mind, the only question now is how encompassing the power is.

PRESIDENT

Ted, do you have any idea of what you're saying?

GAYLER

I'm saying that it's possible that we're sitting on an unknown force of untapped, perhaps unbelievable,

potential that seems directable at will and that so far
has shown no indication of limitation. Tawny Kyle is,
at least so far, an entirely new kind of animal, a kind
we've never seen before.

PRESIDENT

If we don't get hold of her, somebody else is going
to. I'll be honest, Ted. The reality of this is really
more than I can comprehend.

GAYLER

I understand that.

PRESIDENT

And if we can't control her . . .

GAYLER

I know, we'll have to stop her. I'm staying on top of
it. So far, everything's under control.

PRESIDENT

God, let's keep it that way. I have enough trouble
sleeping at night as it is. Corral in that little prick,
Stiller, and sit on him. This thing has *got* to be kept
under our control.

GAYLER

I know.

The president HANGS UP, the split screen DISAPPEAR-
ING, leaving only Gayler, who slowly HANGS UP, then
reaches into his breast pocket. He comes out with his small vial
of yellow pills, taking one out and looking at it thoughtfully
before popping it into his mouth.
CUT TO:
INT—NITE—A SMALL FRAME HOUSE. A family sits in
the living room of a tiny, obviously lower-class house. The
lights are turned out, the flickering light from the TV the only
illumination in the room as it plays on their faces. There are six
people present, parents and four children under ten years old.
We can't see the television, but we can hear the sound of
Denny's broadcast in the bg. Everyone is crowded up on the

sofa or on the floor in front of it. The parents appear to be in their mid-thirties. The father wears a moustache. His T-shirt is torn and dirty, unchanged from work that day. They seem transfixed by the pictures on the screen. They are all touching one another.

OLDEST CHILD (a girl)

My teacher says there ain't no miracles and no miracle woman.

FATHER

Ain't everybody gonna believe in the power of God on Earth. But it won't matter soon. There can't be any denying the truth of our eyes.

MOTHER

(she takes hold of her husband's arm, laying her head on his shoulder) Oh, Jerry. She seems so sad.

FATHER

I think she's bearin' the weight of sin on her shoulders. She's takin' on all our pain . . . just like Jesus did. She ain't no fancy preacher, either. She ain't asked for dollar one.

GIRL

Then what is she, papa?

FATHER

I was talking to George Ord at work today. His daddy's a preacher over in Fairfield and says that she might be the lamb from Revelations come to cleanse sin from the world.

WIFE
(whispering)
Would that mean the Second Coming's here?

We PULL TIGHT on the father's face as we hear Charlie Kornfeld screaming on the television in the bg as his new hair grows. On the man's face we see wonder and a little fear, but behind it is a bedrock of deep and abiding faith, a justification of himself and the Truth he's believed for so long. He is a man mystically triumphant.

FATHER
Yeah. I guess it would.

Scene 4

EXT—DAY—A HIGHWAY. We are staring down the length of an impossibly straight deserted highway that travels relentlessly toward the barren, absolutely flat horizon far in the distance. Clouds roll ominously overhead, high clouds, wall clouds dangling small tornados, all of it speeding by. But there is no wind. In the distance, black smoke rises into the clouds. We begin moving down the highway in the direction of the smoke, going faster and faster as we realize just how far ahead of us the smoke is. Ahead we see a FIGURE WALKING in the same direction we're going. As we approach the figure we see it is a NAKED MAN. We CATCH UP with the man and PACE HIM. He turns to us and we see that it is DENNY STILLER. He holds a cigar up close to his mouth and SPEAKS INTO IT as if it were a microphone.

DENNY
(radio voice)
This is Dennis Stiller, WCN news, reporting live from the scene of a massive accident on the southbound lane of Highway 101, occurring just moments ago.

ANGLE—DENNY. He walks up to the billowing smoke, moving into it. It's thick and roiling, like a large fogbank. All around Denny we see the twisted wreckage of cars and several trucks. Ambulance attendants run through the wreckage, yelling to one another as they hustle the dead and dying onto wheeled stretchers. The fire department is there, putting out car fires and using chain saws to cut people from the wreckage.

There must be as many as fifteen cars involved in the collision.

> DENNY (cont)
> (hushed tones)
> The devastation is unbelievable, the magnitude of the carnage here barely comprehendable. We'll try and find out some details.

He moves to a still-burning car just off to the side of the confusion. It's the wreck of an old Lincoln Continental, the metal now twisted and black. Beside the fire lay two bodies covered in bright white sheets, a policeman standing beside the car with a flashlight, trying to direct unseen traffic around the area. Denny walks up to the cop and sticks his cigar up near the man's mouth.

> DENNY (cont)
> Excuse me, Officer. The people at home are wanting details of the accident.

> COP
> (voice strained)
> What sort of details, Mr. Stiller?

> DENNY
> (casual)
> Just the usual . . . how many cars involved, how many deaths, how much pain, how long before the roadway is open for use again. The folks at home have the right to know all the details.

> COP
> Why?

> DENNY
> You can't ask me that question. You are a public servant and have the duty to answer me. I'm a representative of the news media and have a right to ask. The people at home . . . they have the right to know. It's the way of things.

COP
(shaking his head sadly)
This has been a horrible tragedy, Mr. Stiller. The
price in pain and life has been immense. Isn't that
enough?

DENNY
No, sir! The public has a right to the details.

COP
(somewhat angry)
You want details? All right, I'll give you some. You
see those people under the sheets?

ANGLE—BODIES. Smoke drifting out from under the un-
moving sheets.

DENNY (os)
Yes.

ANGLE—COP.

COP
Those are your own folks, Mr. Stiller. They died horribly, screaming and burning. Gasoline makes for a
hot fire. But even at that, it took your mother nearly
ten minutes to die. You sure you want me to go into
this?

ANGLE—DENNY. We watch him work all emotion out of his
face until he becomes an empty, smiling mask.

DENNY
(smoothly)
It's my job. This is news. What can I do? The viewers have a right to know and I have the responsibility
of telling them.

COP
But it's not right. You have to grieve.

DENNY
It's business, that's all.

The cop, his face set in anger, bends down to one of the sheets and whips it off, exposing a charred corpse, still smoking, looking almost like a blackened twig.

COP

You call this, business?

CLOSE-UP—DENNY. His face is set like wax, a human mask and nothing more. Still he smiles.

DENNY

Mind if I get an interview?

ANGLE—THE CORPSES. Denny bends to the remains, sticking the cigar near the smoldering head.

DENNY (cont)

Why did you allow this to happen to yourself?

The corpse doesn't answer. Denny waits several beats, then begins talking again.

DENNY (cont)

You know you left a child all alone to raise himself?
The folks at home want to know all the painful details. Can you give us some of those? What's wrong,
cat got your tongue? Come on. Time is money. Why
won't you give the people what they want? This is
my job, damnit! We've got time slots to fill!

COP

(bending into frame)

What's wrong with you? These are your folks?

DENNY

No! They're news . . . that's all! Don't you understand? I have no parents. I'm a newsman!

All at once, the corpse, still covered, SITS UP. The sheet slowly slides down to reveal AMY KYLE, unburned. She sits relaxed, staring into space. Denny is looking at the girl nervously. He shakes visibly, his naked body bathed in sweat.

DENNY
(nearly frantic)
What are you doing here? What do you want? Why
won't you look at me?

The girl begins HUMMING TUNELESSLY, wagging her
fingers in front of her face. The cop leans toward Denny,
holding out a CIGARETTE LIGHTER.

COP
She's news, too, isn't she? Here, take the lighter.
Maybe you want to burn her, too.

Denny ignores him, instead moving to the girl and shaking
her, her head still turned away.

DENNY
(screaming)
Why won't you look at me!

CLOSE-UP—AMY. she turns and LOOKS DIRECTLY AT
US and FIRE IS BLAZING FROM HER EYES. It encom-
passes us.
ANGLE—DENNY. He is BURNING, beautiful orange-red
fire consuming his body as he twirls wildly, almost a dance, as
the cop laughs loudly in the background. His laughter louder
and louder . . .
CUT TO:

Denny jerked up, a scream choking in his throat, the
darkness of an unfamiliar room closing him in. He was gasping,
still trying to push the dream from his mind, its reality nearly
overpowering, not like any dream he'd ever had.
He reached beside him and turned on the bedside lamp,
its light the only thing dispelling the fears that had come upon
him.
"Jesus," he said, laughing at his shaking hands. He sat on
the edge of the bed, shivering, his body cold with sweat. His
heart was pounding and he had to take deep, calm breaths for
several minutes before returning to normal.
His watch lay on the nightstand. He picked it up and

looked at the time. It was after four A.M. He thought about trying to go back to sleep, but he seemed more wide awake than he'd ever been in his life. The images of the dream were still strong in his mind, still dominating his thoughts. He shivered, feeling the burning pain from the fire that had consumed him in the dream.

He got up and took a shower in the antiseptic-smelling bath that connected up to his bedroom full of bamboo furniture, tropical plants, and Paul Gauguin paintings. He was able to wash the smell of fear from his body, but not the feel of it from his soul. And he knew why.

He came back in the bedroom, still wet, and slipped into boxer shorts from his suitcase, then put on the dress shirt he'd worn that day without buttoning it. He had never truly appreciated Amy Kyle's power before tonight, had never even conceived of the idea that its application could be as dangerous as it was benevolent. He'd been so wrapped up in his own drive for control of the girl, he'd never even considered the consequences of his actions. If he was to continue with this, he'd have to begin practicing more caution with his approach, perhaps even by consulting with experts—but experts in what? Science, metaphysics, philosophy? He was truly beginning to appreciate that he had hold of something completely unique in the history of humankind, perhaps even the link between man and a higher consciousness. He shook his head. He was beginning to sound like Molly.

He moved to the door and opened it quietly. The dog from across the street lay right in front of it, the animal jumping up excitedly when Denny entered the hall and running around his legs.

"Shh," Denny said, trying to calm the spaniel. The upper hallway was completely dark, everyone but him asleep. He glanced at the door at the other end of the hall, Molly's room, then hurried to the padded stairs and down.

The dog panting happily at his heels, he silently pulled open the front door on well oiled hinges and stepped into the night.

The still air reeked of charred wood as he gazed out over the wide front lawn. He leaned against one of the columns for a moment, smelling the odor of destruction and idly petting the dog that had jumped up to balance its front paws on his leg. They had called the fire department and police anonymously following the destruction, then had hidden like children with the lights out when the authorities had finally arrived to deal with the remnants of the minor holocaust. Later, when they'd watched it on the news, it was confirmed that a widow, Mrs. Sandra Beasley, had died in the fire, and they'd watched films of her body being taken out zipped up tight in a black, plastic bag.

Had he been responsible? Had his simple wish for a dog like this one been the reason for the death of the Beasley woman? As near as he could figure, the only way to answer that question realistically would be in determining the nature of Amy Kyle's power. Did Amy, in fact, have something to do with the destruction of the Beasley house, or did she simply provide the energy—for lack of a better word—while his own mind directed it in the most simple, straightforward means possible. He'd never wished for anyone's death, and Amy seemed incapable of it, yet for all his profound ability to rationalize, it seemed nearly impossible to look at what had happened as a coincidental, unrelated occurence. And even understanding that he never would have meant anyone any harm simply didn't relieve him of the guilt that had kept him awake for hours and had probably given him the dream that had awakened him again.

"A penny for your thoughts?"

He turned, startled, to see Molly standing in the doorway, a Japanese blue silk robe wrapped around her.

"Couldn't sleep," he said quickly, feeling caught.

She walked out onto the porch to join him. "Me either," she replied. "Too much excitement, I guess."

"I was getting ready to walk across the street. Want to join me?"

"Sure."

They moved down the three steps to the yard, then walked slowly across it, the grass wet and velvety on his bare feet. The dog hurried after, yipping playfully as it charged around them in a wide circle.

"That dog sure thinks the world of you," Molly said. "What's your secret?"

He smiled. "Just a lady's man, I guess."

"Oh? Is the dog a girl?"

"I have no idea." He stared over at her. She looked incredibly sexy in the slick silk, her body undulating beneath the robe as she moved. The wrap had pulled open at the top, part of one large breast exposed to the pale moonlight. He began to feel himself get excited, amazed that such an intense feeling could charge through him considering his state of mind. He forced himself to look away.

"Tell me something," he said. "You've seen Amy in action. How would you describe her abilities?"

"Do you really want to know?" she asked.

They reached the end of the lawn, the still smoking ruins of the mansion across the way now visible. They started to cross the street, the dog crying loudly, then charging back across the lawn to sit on the porch.

"I respect your opinion," he said, "in fact more all the time. I'm open to anything right now."

The asphalt street was hard on their feet, Molly stopping to lean against him as she brushed a rock from her heel. The contact was electric, almost like fire, a flush of desire for her bolting through him. He put an arm around her shoulder, letting it slide to her hip, naked under the robe, and he had to force himself away from her to keep from grabbing her in his arms right there.

"I believe that Amy has a power that no human being has ever had before," Molly said as they continued walking. "Her power, if not supernatural, is certainly *preter*natural. Now, where does it come from and why? I believe in God, a force for good, that somehow observes if not directs our actions. If Amy Kyle is as powerful as she seems to be, then I must believe that she can, perhaps, change the course of life on this planet. I mean, if she can generate hair on Charlie Kornfeld's head, I wonder how difficult it would be for her to . . . say, bring peace to the world. Both actions entail revising the laws of nature. At this point the difference seems only one of magnitude."

"So basically," he replied, "what you're getting at is that Amy Kyle can, perhaps, alter the way the world lives by altering the game rules with her new power, and, given that, such alteration must come from God as the universal source for good."

"Nicely put," she said.

They arrived at the other house, walking up on its lawn, crossing slowly toward the ruins. Smoke drifted from the rubble, the bright, gemlike glow of still-smoldering chars making the whole place look like some monstrous treasure chest of glittering diamonds and rubies. The air was rank, the heavily wooded surroundings dreary and darkly ominous as smoke swirled slowly through branches and thicket. Denny had never felt so detached from reality as he stood before his perverse handiwork dressed in his boxer shorts.

"You've made an assumption," Denny said, "and it negates, at least temporarily, your theory."

"What's that?"

"You assume that Amy's power is a force for good."

"We've seen it do good," she said. "My theory extrapolates from that until further notice."

Denny stared at the burned out pile of boards and masonry, his mind returning to the unbelievable sight of that huge, interrelated structure of inanimate objects tearing itself to pieces, literally killing itself. On the television news they had simply assumed, as the fireman had, that the house had burned down. Only he and Frank had witnessed the true nature of its death, and with Frank, Denny could never be sure if the man ever really related intellectually to anything he saw.

"I'm thinking of consulting with experts," he said, "proceeding very slowly."

"The audience isn't going to want slow progress," she replied without hesitation. "Neither is Gayler. You've buried yourself in this thing and you're making a million bucks a shot with the eyes of the world on you. Experts are one thing, but you've got ratings to worry about."

"I just wonder now if I'm . . . equal to the task."

She looked at him, shaking her head. "You should have thought about that the night you were so fired up to get that first broadcast on the air. You're committed, lover. You've signed on to perform miracles and now you're going to have to deliver."

He looked at the ruins again, knowing now that the Truth could certainly set him free . . . and kill him in the bargain. This was not an intellectual discussion where absolutes were only what you said they were. Amy Kyle was, herself, absolute gut-busting Truth—power without ethics, a wind bringing not only rain, but destruction, too. Maybe. He'd said often that he believed in Truth, but that was because he'd never thought of the truth as deadly to him. If his quest was a quest for Truth and he intended to continue it, he'd have to get used to the fact that he might not survive the truth he'd find. Amy Kyle had ceased to be a game between him and Gayler or between him and the "wrong thinkers" of the world. Amy Kyle was not a story he could remain removed and aloof from. The search was his, the truth, his. He had spent his entire life on the outside. Now, like it or not, *he* had become the news, *he* was the ant under the microscope. In truth, he had *become* Amy Kyle, and she, him.

"Why did this have to happen?" he said, and realized he was talking about his involvement and not the Beasley woman's house.

He could feel her eyes upon him, accusing in the darkness. Then she said in a small voice, "Is there something about this fire you're not telling me?"

Yes! he screamed inside. *My mind has killed! My thoughts are poison!* But instead, he merely looked at the ground. "No. I guess it just shook me up, that's all." His secret was his for now. And maybe somehow he'd find a way to make up for it.

"You've changed," she said. "Something— "

"You're right," he said, arching a menacing eyebrow. "I have changed"—he stooped over slightly, letting his arms dangle like a gorilla's, his face twisting into a snarl—"into, the Monster!"

He growled, lunging playfully at her, Molly laughing and fighting him off. He grabbed her robe, the material pulling off her right shoulder, leaving her half exposed to the night.

"Denny!" she squealed, pulling the robe back around her, her head darting to make sure there was no one to see.

"More," he groaned low, and lunged for her again, only this time there was an edge to it that he couldn't seem to control.

Molly, still laughing, slapped at him, then turned and started running back toward the house.

And Denny was after her, his instincts primal, his desire nearly out of control. He wanted her. He wanted her so much that his body was no longer his to command. As he loped in his gorilla posture back across the road, some small part of him was screaming to stop. Yet passion was his brain, the monster his soul, and as he gained ground on the protesting, giggling woman, he'd never wanted anything in his life so much as he wanted to possess this creature.

He caught her at the edge of the lawn, his hand reaching up to grab her by the collar and pull her back, the material ripping in his hands as she tumbled back into his arms.

His hands were all over her as he held her from behind, puling the remnants of the robe from her white, luminescent body.

"Whoa, Tarzan," she gasped, groaning down deep in her throat as her own hands reached behind her to caress his enflamed manhood. "What if somebody comes by. L-let's go back in the h-house."

He whirled her around, unable to snap his face back out of its snarl, unable to totally stand erect. She stood before him naked, pendulous breasts swaying with her gasping, hips wide, inviting. "Nooo," he growled, and pulled her hard against him.

The dog ran down from the porch, growling and circling, yipping fearfully, the sound driving his brain into a frenzy.

She bent back, her face confused as he desperately tried to regain control of his own actions. But the *feel* of her was overpowering, his want painfully tightening his belly as his mind popped white-hot light.

"Oh, Denny," she moaned as he took her to the ground, her hips bucking slightly as he spread her thighs and fell upon her out there on the wet grass with the dog going crazy and his mind lost in a fiery maze that sought release at any cost.

"Oh God!" she cried, her own excitement mounting with his. She reached out and took him in her hand, bringing her hips up to meet his thrust.

At that moment, any semblance of control left him. He hunched her like an animal, his only sounds gutteral growls and frenzied wails as he pounded her with quick, jackhammer jerks, her own screams mixing with his as she, too, sought relief.

Rationality left him. His mind saw neither Molly, nor their surroundings. Even her own sounds disappeared as his mind spun into a dizzying pattern of selfish, animal need punctuated by mental images of Amy Kyle—her face, her body. He fought for control, unsuccessfully, cried out with shame and grief, then exploded over some kind of emotional edge, his mind and vision burning violent white, then fuzzy brown, then black.

There was a time of darkness then, consciousness coming back slowly. He opened his eyes to the stars and moon. He still lay on the grass, his boxer shorts hooked around an ankle, his spent penis, the measure of his shame, laying small against his stomach. The dog was licking him on the face.

"Are you all right?" Molly asked from beside him.

He turned his head, reaching up to push the dog away. Molly sat next to him on the grass, what was left of her robe wrapped tightly around her. He sat up, a bit dizzy.

"Did I hurt you?" he asked.

She narrowed her eyes. "No, of course not," she said. "Though I'll have to say that you've never been so—"

"Animalistic?" he helped.

She smiled. "I was going to say, aggressive. Those noises you made— "

"I'm sorry," he said, standing and pulling up his shorts. He felt like some sort of freak or maniac. God, what if he had wanted to kill instead of screw? Or, what if it were some woman besides Molly? He was out of control—the most frightening feeling a human being can experience.

"Why are you sorry?" she said, but he could tell that she was looking at him differently than she ever had before.

"Nothing," he said. "Let's just forget about it."

"Look. There was nothing— "

"I say, let's drop it," he said harshly, feeling bad and stupid immediately as she bit her lower lip and stared at the ground.

What was happening to him? He had to somehow get himself together. He looked at her sheepishly. "We'd better go in," he said.

They walked back toward the house, but when Molly tried to get up close to him, he pretended to be playing with the dog and avoided her, afraid of what he'd do. They reached the porch and she stopped him at the door.

"Want to spend the rest of the night at my place?" she asked, wiggling her eyebrows. "The neighbors won't mind."

"No," he said, too quickly. But when he looked into her face he saw relief rather than hurt at his rejection.

She moved to him and kissed him quickly on the cheek. "Well, I'm going back in to bed then. G'night, apeman."

"Yeah . . . good night."

She moved into the house, her last look at him one that people usually reserved for paraplegics in public rest rooms.

He moved back to sit on the stairs, the dog, *his* dog, curling up in a protective ball beside him. Something was happening to him, something terrible, and he felt that there was nothing to do except ride it out.

He lowered his head then and did something he hadn't done since he was six years old—cry.

CUT TO:

A RINGING COKE BOTTLE. We are looking at a full bottle of Coca-Cola that is ringing gently, like chirping birds, in a semidark room. A HAND reaches into our vision and grabs the bottle. PULL BACK to reveal Charles Kornfeld in bed, his new head of hair disheveled, his eyes heavy lidded. Beside him, his third wife, Wendy, sleeps heavily, her peroxided hair fixed in tiny, bent-up spikes. She is obviously naked under the sheets. Kornfeld pulls the coke bottle to his face.

> KORNFELD
> (groggily)
> This'd better be damn important.

> VOICE
>
> What the hell you got going over there?

> KORNFELD
>
> W-What?

He sits up straight, shaking his head and reaches for the bedside clock.

> VOICE
>
> If you don't take care of it right now I'm calling the cops!

The caller hangs up, Kornfeld pulling the phone away from his ear and staring blankly at it. He pulls the clock up to his face. ANGLE—CLOCK. It reads 6:17. ANGLE—THE ROOM. Charlie cocks his head, listening. In the bg he, and we, can hear muffled crowd sounds. He pulls back the covers and stands. He's dressed in red bikini shorts, his body muscled and wiry, a man who works out. His chest is covered with gray, curly hair. He moves to a shuttered bedroom window and peeks between the slats. ANGLE—THROUGH WINDOW. We are looking down from the second floor at Kornfeld's front lawn in a new-money, country-club neighborhood. It is covered with people, perhaps a thousand, all milling around on the well-kept lawn. The streets are jammed with parked cars, with a far greater number driving up and down the streets. Many people are carrying signs reading FREE TAWNY KYLE. A large group near the front door is kneeling in prayer, facing the house.

<u>KORNFELD</u> (os)

Sons of bitches.

ANGLE—THE ROOM. He moves away from the window, back to the bed. He leans across it, slapping his wife on the ass.

<u>KORNFELD</u> (cont)

You'd better wake up, babe.

<u>WENDY</u>
(groggy)

Huh?

<u>KORNFELD</u>

Get up! Take a look out the window!

Wendy rolls heavily out of bed, her naked body tanned all over. She plods half-asleep to the window as Kornfeld grabs a terry cloth robe from the closet and slips it on, angrily tying the sash. Wendy peeks through a slat on her window, jumping back, her arms coming up to cover her naked breasts.

<u>WENDY</u>

Charlie! What's going on?

<u>KORNFELD</u>

Just get dressed! I'm going to try and get rid of them.

Kornfeld hurries out the door, turning on a portable television as he exits.
ANGLE—LIVING ROOM. We are looking, at an angle, at Charlie's front door, the stairs to the second floor in the bg, a pair of tennis rackets leaning against the wall near the door in fg. We hear Charlie before actually seeing him as he curses and fumes all the way down the stairs, finally coming into our line of vision and THROWING OPEN THE DOOR.
ANGLE—CHARLIE. He stands framed in the doorway, his face contorted in anger.

<u>KORNFELD</u>
(enraged)

What's wrong with you people? Get the hell out of here! This is my home! I can't do anything for you!

ANGLE—THE CROWD. We watch them as they catch sight
of Charlie, their eyes widening in hope, his name rifling
through their ranks as they point to him, to his new hair. His
words fall on them like rain on rocks as they begin moving
toward him. Many of them cripples. There are old people in
walkers, and people in wheelchairs and on crutches. There are
even a number of bald people.

ANGLE—CHARLIE. Fear comes to his face as he watches
them closing in on him and he realizes they won't be talked
away. He reaches around the door frame, coming out with a
tennis racket, which he brandishes above his head like a
sword.

KORNFELD

Get out! I told you I can't help you. Now get out!

He backs into the house as the crowd comes up the steps to the
front door, a nightmare vision of desperate people clinging to
a desperate hope as they drag stainless steel equipment up
with them.

ANGLE—LIVING ROOM. Kornfeld closes the front door
against them, shoving a crutch out of the door in order to get
the thing closed. He locks it tight, leans against it for a second,
then charges out of our vision.

ANGLE—BEDROOM. Wendy is dressed in shorts and halter
top. She is moving back and forth between the window and the
TV screen as Charlie rushes in.

KORNFELD
(out of breath)

Quick . . . pack a bag. We're going to have to get
you out of her.

WENDY

What do they all want?

KORNFELD

They want me to tell them where Denny and Tawny
are. God, I should have figured this to happen.

He reaches into the closet and pulls out a suitcase, then
another, throwing them on the bed. Then he hurries across the

room to his dresser and begins pulling out his clothes. Wendy begins to do the same.

WENDY
Look at the TV.

ANGLE—PORTABLE TELEVISION. We are watching a helicopter shot of Stemmons Freeway, the WCN building far below us. Traffic is at an absolute standstill as many thousands jam the highway and surround the property as police move through the crowds trying to disperse them.

ANNOUNCER (os)
. . . as people from all over the country congregate in Dallas, hoping for an audience with self-proclaimed faith healer, Tawny Kyle, who has apparently gone into hiding along with WCN newscaster, Dennis Stiller. All hotels in the Dallas area are reporting one hundred percent occupancy, and the campgrounds within a fifty-mile radius are having to turn people away because of overcrowding. There is a news conference scheduled for noon today in which the mayor and chief of police are reportedly going to plead for people to stay away from a city that is beginning to burst at the seams. And through it all the question remains—where is Tawny Kyle and what is the nature of her amazing power?

ANGLE—BEDROOM. Charlie and Wendy continue packing, as we hear the sound of glass breaking downstairs. The crowd outside is much louder.

KORNFELD
I called the police from downstairs. They should be here any minute. I'll take you right to the airport. You're going to your mother's until this thing cools down.

WENDY
What about you?

KORNFELD
I can't leave with this thing going. I'll find another place . . . a hotel or something.

Kornfeld straightens, listening, as we hear the sound of a police siren in the distance, getting closer.

KORNFELD

Hurry.

ANGLE—OUTSIDE. From the lawn, we see the crowds still moving up against the house. Then, in the distance, we see the approach of a black and white, with the light bar blazing atop it. It intrudes our vision, bouncing up onto the lawn, people scattering, hurrying their wheelchairs, as the police car DRIVES UP TO THE HOUSE, stopping just in front of us. Two policemen get out, one of them holding his handset up to his mouth, engaging the loudspeaker.

COP
(amplified)

Please disburse immediately. You are congregating illegally and are liable to arrest. I repeat, please disburse immediately.

CUT TO:

ANGLE—WITHIN A CAR. We are sitting in the passenger seat of a car parked across the street from the disturbance, watching the policeman trying to keep back the shouting crowds, as another cop clears the steps up to the house. We are sitting next to the driver, a man in a meticulous suit who is turned from us, watching the action out his side window, chuckling softly. The man takes a cigarette out of his suit coat pocket and puts it in his mouth, turning to push in the dash lighter. We see that it is LARRY GATES, Connover's man. As he lights his cigarette we see, through the window, Charlie and Wendy hurry out of the house with their suitcases and into the police car, which, once again, turns on its siren before peeling out across the lawn. The crowd scatters, hurrying toward their own vehicles to try and follow the speeding police cruiser.

REVERSE ANGLE—THE CAR. We are watching Gates from without, cigarette in his mouth, as he tracks the departing car with a hand closed to look like a gun, his thumb the hammer. He tracks it a distance, then stops, dropping his thumb.

GATES

Bang.

We FREEZE-FRAME on Gates, pulling in tighter and tighter on his unlined face, finally stopping tight on eyes that are hard and amoral, eyes that reflect no humanity, only obligation.

ACT THREE

Scene 1

(late the following night)

ANGLE—TELEVISION. We are watching *Nightline*, a late-night news program, already in progress. The host of the show is sitting behind a desk, a monitor containing the live image of Denny Stiller is situated beside and behind him, the announcer turning in his chair to face the monitor as if that's where Denny really is sitting.

> ANNOUNCER
>
> . . . logical question, of course, is why are you handling this issue the way you are?

> DENNY
> (laughs)
>
> You act as if I had a choice. The reaction of the American people toward my experiments has forced me to take the steps that I've taken. It has nothing to do with personal choice.

> ANNOUNCER
>
> That position certainly seems to make an amount of sense. I'm sitting here looking at a story we pulled off the wire that says your former employer, WCN, is being swamped, not only by people, but . . .

DENNY
They tell me that employees are having to be flown in and out by helicopter just to be able to get to their jobs.

ANNOUNCER
Also, an incredible amount of mail for you and Tawny Kyle is arriving at the station. From our reports, it seems that a lot of that mail contains money in the form of donations . . . yet you continue to deny that there are religious overtones to your work with the Kyle woman?

DENNY
Absolutely. And this is as good a time as any to address this issue. First off, leave the poor people at WCN alone. They have no more idea of where we're hiding than anyone else. They can't, and won't, help you in that regard. All money being received is being put in escrow by the station. I will have no part of it. I'm being well paid for my work with Tawny Kyle. We are *not* starting a religion and positively *do not* need or want any donations of any kind. All monies received will be given to an appropriate charity. I also hear that there is some sort of large-scale manhunt going on for us in and around the Dallas area. I want to say, please folks, stay home.

ANNOUNCER
Yet, you do admit that Tawny Kyle does have the power to heal the sick or crippled?

DENNY
The tape doesn't lie.

ANNOUNCER
Well, accepting that as a given, how could you expect people to behave otherwise?

DENNY
I'm not sure what you mean.

ANNOUNCER

I think you understand, Mr. Stiller. You're offering
hope to the hopeless, aid to those who are beyond
aid. If I were desperate enough, a trip to Dallas and
a chance to see Tawny Kyle wouldn't seem such a
farfetched possibility.

DENNY

Is that a question?

ANNOUNCER

Perhaps it would be appropriate at this time to introduce our other guests tonight.

The picture switches to a MULTIPLE SCREEN containing
four images. Denny is in the bottom right fourth of the screen.
Next to him is DR. CONNOVER. Above is a scruffy-looking
man dressed in a blue-jean jacket, and a gray-haired, severe-
looking woman.

ANNOUNCER (cont, os)

Beside Mr. Stiller on your screen, is Dr. James Connover, well-known theologian and founder of the
Church of the Savior, who is said to have over twenty
million followers worldwide. Good evening, Dr. Connover. Is that figure correct, twenty million?

CONNOVER
(smiling, fatherly)
Give or take a million. We like to believe that the
whole world is our flock.

ANNOUNCER

Above Dr. Connover on your screen is Hollywood
special effects expert, Murray "Shorty" Greenberg,
who's had a hand in the technical end of nearly every
major film in the last decade. Shorty rushed over to
our Hollywood studios from the set of his latest film
for this program and we really appreciate it.

SHORTY

My pleasure.

ANNOUNCER

And next to him, Dr. Sheila Rayner, head of the
Physics Department at Brandeis University, formerly
with the National Aeronautics and Space Administration and best-selling author of *The Frontiers of Man*.
We welcome you, Dr. Rayner.

RAYNER
(stoic)

Good evening.

ANNOUNCER

It seems to me that the case of Tawny Kyle presents
a great many questions of significant proportion to
the body politic of humanity if . . . and I stress the
word *if*, the events we are witnessing are in fact true
events. And I must believe investigating the truth of
the matter should be our main concern here tonight.
Since you are the closest to this phenomenon, Mr.
Stiller, I present the question to you first—is Tawny
Kyle for real? Are the things we are seeing on television true and accurate portrayals of her abilities?

DENNY
(smiles)

To begin with, I've only known Tawny Kyle for four
days myself. It's amazing how rapidly things have
happened, but I just suppose that's the nature of our
modern world. I have simply acted as a reporter on
this thing, questioning and filming events as they
have occurred. I'm absolutely convinced beyond any
possibility of doubt that what you're seeing on your
TV screen is pure, untampered, and unadulterated
truth. I have no idea of what your other guests are
going to say, but I can assure you that, whatever they
say, they will be unable to offer proof of fraud on the
part of Tawny Kyle or myself. Such proof does not
exist. Ms. Kyle is absolutely genuine.

ANNOUNCER

Dr. Rayner, you're a scientist of international standing. You've had the opportunity to study all available tape on the Tawny Kyle phenomenon. What is your estimation of her legitimacy?

RAYNER

Mr. Stiller's claims are absolutely and patently ridiculous.

ANNOUNCER

How so?

RAYNER

Quite simply, the supposed "miracles" are impossible and fly in the face of all physical laws of the universe. Take the example of the healing of the leg. We are being asked to believe that by the power of one woman's mind, bones reform and make new cells reminiscent of their old genetic pattern. Kind of like growing back a new arm if one was cut off. A healing pattern wasn't helped along or encouraged, it was created from scratch. It's unthinkable.

ANNOUNCER

You don't believe in the possibility of miracles?

RAYNER

As Mr. Stiller himself pointed out in one of his broadcasts, a real miracle has never been documented. So we have to assume that, whatever a person's religious leanings, that person must look even at miracles as things working within the physical laws. This can be nothing but some cheap, theatrical stunt.

DENNY

On surface, I must agree with everything Dr. Rayner said with the exception of the line about cheap, theatrical stunts. I would like to ask the good doctor a question, though. Would you explain to the viewers what a quark is, Doctor?

RAYNER

It's a theoretical term we use to describe the smallest particle in existence, the building block, as it were, from which everything else is made.

DENNY

Has as anyone ever *seen* a quark?

RAYNER

No . . . I said it was theoretical. The point is, according to our knowledge of physics and the physical laws, it must exist.

DENNY

But you don't know for sure. How about black holes in space. Has anyone ever seen one of those buggers?

RAYNER

There is a world of difference between extrapolating from known, empirical science and reinventing science for your own ends.

DENNY

How about Einstein? Would you say that Einstein, what was your word, reinvented science when he came up with his theory of relativity?

CONNOVER
(laughing)

Gentlemen . . . and lady. The possibility of miracles is not on trial here. Every God-fearing man, woman, and child in your audience believes that God can do whatever he likes with the physical laws that He invented. The question is, would God work through someone like this woman.

DENNY

If He works through you, He'd work through anybody!

ANNOUNCER

So, Dr. Rayner asserts that what Tawny Kyle is doing
must indeed be fake, since such activities are literally
impossible. I'd like to turn this issue over to Shorty
Greenberg for just a moment. Shorty, you also have
had a chance to study the tapes. Strictly from a technical point of view, could they have been faked?

SHORTY

Absolutely. The second broadcast is especially interesting in that all of the special effects work could
have been done without any camera cuts. The dam-
aged hand, for instance. . . .

He holds his hand up for the camera, a knife in his other hand.

SHORTY

I have applied a simple, prosthetic device to the back
of my hand, so that when the knife blade is
applied . . .

He draws the knife across the back of the hand, a line of blood,
then a rush of it appearing.

SHORTY (cont)

. . . it appears that the hand has been cut. Then you
simply wipe off the hand, and the device with it, revealing the unhurt hand beneath. The newly grown
hair would also be a simple matter to fake. The actor
wears a false skullcap with thinning hair. During the
supposedly painful process of regeneration, when he's
bending over, he pulls the cap off and palms it, revealing his real head of hair beneath. As for the "miracle" of the televised murder of the horse, that would
simply take an advance filming for dramatic effect,
the prerecorded tape being played at the appropriate
moment. The TV's power cord appeared to be pulled
from the wall, but that could simply have been a
dummy cord arranged in advance. I don't want to
degrade the quality of the special effects, however.
Whoever thought them up and executed them has
got a job with me whenever he wants to move to
L.A.

DENNY

How about the healing of the leg? You haven't mentioned that.

SHORTY

The leg was quite convincing. It would take a prosthetic device of extreme complexity to make that one work. I studied it and couldn't find the seams anywhere, even in extreme close-up. I assume it was a device because, upon studying the tape, I found no evidence of cutting or duping.

DENNY

Could you duplicate that stunt?

SHORTY

Give me a million dollars and about six months and I could probably get pretty close. That leg was *damn* good. Oops. Pardon my mouth.

DENNY

What would it take for you to believe what you're seeing. I mean, after all, in the movies today, you can create nearly any effect you want to.

SHORTY

Here's what it would take for me to believe: first, the freedom to study the tape for edits; second, the creation of something out of nothing, a materialization; third, a big clock with a sweep second hand that is visible at all times on the tape. That would make tampering impossible.

DENNY

My next broadcast will contain all of those elements.

SHORTY

If you can produce a miracle under those circumstances, brother *I'll* join your religion.

DENNY

There's no religion involved here.

ANNOUNCER

What *is* it then?

CONNOVER

It's *anti*religion! Don't you people understand what
this man is doing? He's trying to make himself rich
by undermining the religious faith of this great country. Denny Stiller is no God-fearing man. He's a radi
cal humanist who has tried, and failed, in the past to
destroy *my* ministry. Through his access to media and
his professional camera tricks he is attempting to use
the faith of simple people against them. It's a disgust-
ing ploy for money from a truly faithless man. My
own experts have studied his tape and have found it
to be fraudulent in all respects.

DENNY

For the record, I'd like to say a word about my at-
tempted "destruction" of Dr. Connover's evangelical
empire. Over six months ago, I was involved in a series of reports stemming from an IRS investigation of
Dr. Connover's finances in which it was revealed that
nearly a hundred percent of the money that went
into financing his satellite systems and stations overseas did not come from donations. It was all drawn
on a Swiss account that showed up merely as a nota-
tion in his records under the heading of "Bumper."
The investigation was abruptly canceled by the IRS
for unnamed reasons and I was assigned to other du-
ties, also for unnamed reasons. I was never trying to
get Dr. Connover. To my way of thinking, people can
spend their money on anything they want, *including*
the good doctor's ministry—as long as it's legal. As to
the doctor's "experts," I say, let's trot them out and
question them in this forum. I have the right in this
country to face my accusers.

CONNOVER

I don't need to prove anything to you. People
know—

DENNY

And I don't have to prove anything to you. But I will remind you, Dr. Connover, that we do have slander laws in this country and the videotape of this conversation would serve well as evidence in a court of law. I ask you again, sir—where are your experts? You accused me of fraud. You have your chance here on national television to prove it.

CONNOVER
(unruffled)

You are an evil man. Venom drips from your words as from the fangs of the serpent . . .

ANNOUNCER

For the sake of fairness, Dr. Connover, if you have evidence to present, you should bring it out at this time.

CONNOVER
(smiling)

I *do* have evidence, but I will present it when the time is right.

DENNY

And by the way, two teenagers were arrested today in the killing of my producer's horse. They were recognized by viewers who saw the videotape. They've already admitted their guilt.

CONNOVER

In return for a suspended sentence, no doubt. I'm sure their confession was more than worth their while.

DENNY

And what would it take for you to believe me, Doctor?

CONNOVER

My life has been spent in the study of and commun-

ion with my lord and savior, Jesus Christ. I know my
God and I know my place in the Divine Plan. There
is nothing you could show me that would make me
fall for your ruse. I know the Truth when I see
it . . . just as I know lies.

DENNY

In other words, I could take the sun from the sky and
it wouldn't be enough to convince you.

CONNOVER

Don't compound your indecency with blasphemy.

DENNY

And don't compound your stupidity with libel.

ANNOUNCER

Gentlemen. I'm afraid we've moved away from the
original issues here and into personal matters. But let
me ask a question here—Mr. Stiller, we've heard
from Mr. Greenberg on what you would have to do
to convince him that your claims are real; would you
be willing to come back sometime soon and try to
satisfy his requirements in front of the nation.

DENNY

It would be a pleasure. I have nothing to hide. Just
like you, I'm a newsman trying to do his job.

ANNOUNCER

I'd like to leave us with two thoughts. The first is the
result of a Gallup poll released this afternoon that
stated that twenty-five percent of the American people believed in Tawny Kyle's power, thirty percent
believed it was a fake or publicity stunt, and fully
forty-five percent undecided, which tells me that the
world is still waiting to see the proof positive with an
open mind. Second, I'd like to pass on something a
bit more ominous. In an interview with the Russian
ambassador this morning, a reporter asked if the ambassador had heard about the controversy. The ambassador said he believed it was a complete hoax, but

added that if it were true, it could be a dangerous
complication of the balance of power—adding that
Tawny Kyle should be turned over for study to a
team of scientists representing all the major powers—
not an American newsman. For all the *Nightline* staff,
I want to wish you a good night and a pleasant tomorrow.

ROLL CREDITS, BRING UP MUSIC.
CUT TO:
INT—MOBILE UNIT. We are inside the mobile broadcast
studio given to Denny by WCN. Frank sits at the control
board in dim lighting. The booth is cramped with only enough
room for one technician. Before him sits a small black and
white monitor juicing the same broadcast we've been watching. Beside that is another monitor showing only Denny, the
picture that Frank has been sending to WCN for network feed.
Frank is speaking over a headset, his hand up to the earpiece.

<u>FRANK</u>
Yeah, basecom . . . this is Hargrave in Mobile One.
I am cutting transmission . . .

He reaches out to the control board and FLICKS a toggle
switch.

<u>FRANK</u> (cont)
. . . now. See you clowns in the funny papers. Out.

Frank leans back in his chair, pulling his headset off, then
reaching back to the panel to shut down the system. All the
lights go off one by one, finally leaving Frank bathed in a deep
red emergency light over the back door of the van. He picks up
a bottle of beer from the floor and takes a long drink, then
stood, stooped over in the confined space, and moves to the
door. He OPENS the door.
ANGLE—DOORWAY. We are looking out. A STRANGE
MAN is standing on the driveway, staring into the open door
space.

<u>MAN</u>
Hello.

"That's it," Molly said, cutting off the kliegs, Denny sagging with relief the second he was free of live air.

"How was it?" he asked, leaning his head back against the highly varnished redwood walls of the steam room.

"All right . . ." she replied, looking at him one more time through the camera's viewfinder before shutting it down, "considering. You held your own, but it's a shame no one else was willing to take your viewpoint."

He shrugged. "What do you expect them to do? Everything that's happened so far with Amy defies five thousand years of collective, civilized logic."

Denny stood, surprised at just how exhausted he was. Behind the camera, through the open doorway, he could still see the announcer's massive face peeking in at them from the screen of the big TV. They'd had to roll it to the steam room door because it was the only television in the house, and his only way of communicating with New York. Life was so strange, people speaking from different parts of the world, their images brought together in one place to once again be disseminated to the world in the form of electromagnetic waves. No wonder people didn't believe in things anymore. There was nothing real to believe in. Least of all the riddle of Amy Kyle.

It was maddening. He'd found a wellspring of power in the girl, yet wasn't sure he could use it. Power, like the rest of life, doesn't exist in a vacuum. All deeds have consequences. The unpredictability of such cause and effect frightened him. The responsibility of making decisions knowing those decisions might have broader repercussions numbed him almost as much as his own loss of mental control.

"You look awful," she said, moving up to put a hand to his forehead.

He clenched his fists, suffering her hand on him while his brain concentrated on images of ugliness and hatred, so afraid of himself was he after his performance with her the night before. For her own sake, he couldn't let Molly get close to him, not until he was sure of his own ability to hold himself in check.

"You feel a little warm. When's the last time you got a night's sleep?"

"About five days ago," he said, turning from her, hoping that she wouldn't notice his tension. He'd stayed away from her the whole day, just as he'd stayed away from Amy. And he never, never let his thoughts drift in sexual directions, directions so close to violence.

"Well I prescribe a good night's sleep," she said. "I think you're suffering from exhaustion."

"I second that," Charlie Kornfeld said from the doorway. "You look like death warmed over, pal."

Charlie was running around with shorts and no shirt, his body glistening with sweat from exercise, a headband holding back his new curly hair. He'd been jogging. It was his obsession.

"Easy to say," Denny told them, "but there's still so much to be done. Charlie, I want a big clock with a sweep second hand installed in here so that it will always be in camera range. And I need—"

"Tomorrow," Charlie said, walking up to Denny and taking his face in his hands. He forced Denny's eyes to his, Denny fearing the man would be able to look beneath the surface. "We're not on any deadline, here. It'll work itself out."

"We've got to stay on top of this thing," Denny said, breaking from him and walking to the door, a commercial shoving a huge pizza at the TV screen, trying to make him hungry. "We don't want to let it get out of our hands. There's so much to try to understand, I—"

"Stop it!" Molly said, and he turned to see genuine concern on her face. "You're not going to be able to do anything from a hospital bed."

He nodded then, letting out a long breath. He knew they were right. He was being ridiculous. What was happening? Where was his judgment?

"Okay," he said, smiling. "We'll back off for a day or two and rest up."

"Not yet we won't," came a voice from behind. Frank.

Denny turned to him. "What is it?"

The man's face was stoic as he brought the beer to his lips, then held it. "Got somebody I want you to meet. He's waitin' in the livin' room."

"Here!" Kornfeld said. "You brought somebody *here*?"

"Nope," the man replied. "He brought himself."

"Shit!" Denny said, trying to force his tired mind to capacity. "Why didn't you—"

"Look," Frank said. "He walked up to me in the drive when I was gittin' ready to put the van back in the garage. He recognized me right away. I figured that keepin' him here was the best thing for now. I sure as hell didn't think you wanted me to let loose of him."

Denny turned to the others. "We can't let him out of here. What if he gives us away?"

"What are you suggesting?" Charlie asked. "Kidnap the man?"

Denny brought his hands to his face, his mind spinning. The more he tried for control, the more it leaked away. A thought was forming in the back of his brain, but he forced it away. He pulled his hands down and stared at Frank. "Was he looking for us or what?"

The man shrugged. "Says he's some kind of insurance investigator or somethin'."

"Well," Denny said, turning to Kornfeld and Molly, "I guess all we can do at the moment is go and see what the man wants."

"You can let me handle it," Charlie said.

Denny shook his head, then reached out and took Frank's beer. "This is my problem," he said, taking a drink and handing the bottle back. "We'll straighten this out and then rest."

He moved around the bulk of the huge television and headed down the hallway leading to the kitchen and the den, the walls here covered with Rembrandt engravings. He had no idea of what he was going to do, but after the events of the last several days it would be disastrous to put his charges in the hands of the mob.

The kitchen was a mess of paper cups, beer bottles and fast-food wrappers as he entered it, turning to see the others trooping behind. "Frank," he said. "Get the camera."

"Why?" Molly asked. "What's the point?"

"I want everything on tape," he replied. "There's truth here somewhere, and if nothing else, that truth must be served."

"But this—" Kornfeld began.

"Just humor me," Denny snapped, regretting it immediately. "We're not going to be able to depend on our own recollections here. Everything must be verifiable."

"What are you getting at?" Kornfeld asked, his brows drawn in suspicion.

"Just get the camera," Denny said, and walked into the dining room to avoid an answer. How could he tell the man that he feared for the state of his own mind and didn't trust himself anymore?

He moved quickly through the dining room and into the wide open living area. An old man in a worn brown suit and bow tie rose to greet him from the other side of the long room. He was small and mousy, but his gaze was steady, dependable. He carried a battered briefcase and a long-handled flashlight.

"Sorry to keep you waiting," Denny said in his sincere TV voice as he approached the man. He put out his hand. "I'm Dennis Stiller."

"Recognize you anywhere," the man said in a firm voice as he shook Denny's hand. He had an eastern accent, probably Pennsylvania. He looked wiry, his eyes clear. This was a man who would live to be a hundred and never get sick or retire. "My name's Roy Geist. Sorry to barge in this time of the night."

Denny smiled and sat on an overstuffed white couch, motioning the man into an easy chair across from him. He never could get comfortable on this furniture; it never really felt as if it belonged in the room, as if it were simply stuck in to block off the soccer game that should be going on in there. Bleacher seating would've been more appropriate. Out of the corner of his eye, he saw Molly and Kornfeld approaching, Geist standing again when Molly joined them.

"These are my associates—" Denny began, the man interrupting him.

"Hell, I know who they are," he said, nodding to them. "Everybody does."

Denny looked at Kornfeld, who was still staring at him in concern. "Mr. Geist was just getting ready to tell me the nature of his business here," he said, then turned back to the man.

Geist sat on the edge of the chair, obviously as uncomfortable in it as Denny was in his. He reached up and ran a hand through thinning hair. "Well, it's kinda strange," he said, pulling the briefcase up onto his lap and withdrawing a notepad from inside. "I represent Mid Continent Life, which has the insurance on that home across the street . . . the one that burned down?"

"I understand," Denny replied. "Go on."

"Well, it's our policy to send someone around after a claim to . . . you know, poke around to see if the local inspectors are doing their jobs. You know, nobody's going to protect your money the way you are yourself."

Denny smiled. "So, you were investigating across the street. Wasn't it pretty dark for that?"

The man shook his head. "It was still light when I started." He laughed. "I had a list of places and a couple days to get to them. I guess at my age, you feel you have to prove to yourself that you can still get the job done as good as the kids they hire. So, I figured I could get all of it out of the way tonight, but it didn't work out that way."

"What do you mean?" Kornfeld asked.

The man glanced down at his notepad. "Well, the fire marshal placed the cause of the blaze as a boiler explosion in the basement . . . it was an old house, you know."

"But . . ." Denny helped.

"But it didn't line out that way when I checked it."

Molly came and sat beside Denny, the lawyer opting to stand.

"See," the man continued, "when a boiler explodes, especially a big one, it blows things out—windows, doors, loose bricks, insulation. I should have found debris spread out over a good hundred-yard area. But it wasn't. It was all neatly piled around the house itself. The next thing, is that the fire would have started there in the basement, done its damage there, then moved up the walls. The stuff closer to the ground would have been charred up totally. But in this one, it looked like the stuff from the roof was on the bottom and was no more scorched than anything else."

"Are you saying the boiler didn't explode?" Denny asked.

"Oh, it exploded all right," the man replied. "No doubt about that. But I'm thinkin' that it exploded after."

"After what?"

"That's the strange part," Geist said. "I spent a good part of the evening digging myself down to the foundation, trying to get a line on things. I found something I haven't seen before. The foundation was torn apart in four equal sections, almost as if an earthquake had occurred right beneath it, pulling the foundation forcibly against itself, literally tearing the house to pieces. But when I checked the grounds, there was no evidence of any major upheavals in the area."

Frank had moved up near the sofa, his camera set on the tripod. Denny glanced briefly, then turned to Geist. "Do you mind if we run some tape?"

The man shrugged. "It's none of my lookout."

Denny nodded to Frank. "What, exactly, are you trying to tell us, Mr. Geist?"

"I'm not trying to tell you anything," he answered. "I'm just saying that I think the house collapsed before it burned, and I don't know why."

"What's this got to do with us?" Molly asked.

"Nothing, probably," he said. "I was just finishing up over there and was driving back to the motel, when I saw the lights on here and that van out in the drive with the motor running and the lights on. I thought I'd take a chance and stop to see if you saw or heard anything suspicious last night. Sure was a surprise to see that man from the television getting out of the van."

"We weren't here last night," Denny said.

There was muffled barking from upstairs.

"Sounds like a dog," Geist said.

"Yeah," Denny said. "He's mine. I've got him closed up in the room. He's always underfoot."

"Strange," the man replied. "The woman across the street had a dog, too, but they never found it."

"Probably ran off," Denny said.

"Yeah," Geist said. "Probably. Though that's not like a dog." He shook his head. "Sure is something to stumble across you people out here. There's folks combing this whole big city looking for you and here I just walk right up on you."

"You know," Denny said, "that we're trying to stay hidden here. I hope that you . . ."

Geist waved him off. "Hell, it's nothing to me," he said. "I haven't got a reason to tell anybody. Don't you worry. I'll keep your secret."

"Great," Denny said, smiling. "Say, how about a quick drink before we send you back out into the night."

Geist cocked his head, smiling. "Couldn't refuse a short one. No, sir, my dad taught me that back in the coal fields. Be hospitable, he'd say. Life's too short."

Denny stared hard at the man. There was no way in hell he'd keep his mouth shut. It was too good a secret to keep to himself. Denny had wrested a lot tougher information from a lot tougher men during his time. There was only one way he was going to make this work. Amy. The thought of her chilled him. "While you're here," he heard himself say, "how would you like to meet the Kyles?"

The man sat back finally, smiling like the Cheshire cat. "Now that would be a pure pleasure," he said.

"Hang on for a couple of minutes," Denny said. "Relax." He looked at Molly. "Come up and give me a hand, will you?"

They stood. "We won't be but a minute," Denny told Geist. "Why don't you chat with Frank while Mr. Kornfeld fixes us all a drink."

"Fine, fine," Geist said, gaping at all the expense hanging on the walls. "Nothing sweet though. I'm not too fond of lady's drinks . . . excuse me, ma'am."

"Quite all right," Molly smiled.

Denny turned and moved quickly across the room, Molly right behind him. Kornfeld hurried after, catching them at the bottom of the stairs.

"What are you going to do?" he asked low, taking Denny by the arm.

"I'm not sure yet," Denny said. "I'm going to bring down Amy and then play it by ear."

"He's promised to keep his mouth shut," Molly said.

"Do you agree, Counselor?" Denny asked.

Kornfeld grimaced. "I give him from here to the nearest pay phone," he said. "Maybe we should offer him money."

"I just can't trust that," Denny said. "Besides, he's got an insurance report to rectify."

"Yeah," Molly said. "What was all that about the house across the street?"

Denny looked her straight in the eye. "I have no idea," he said, then turned and started up the stairs.

He started quickly, then slowed down halfway upstairs. It was almost as if he could feel the atmosphere thicken the closer he got to Amy. He felt an odd surge of excitement inside, a racing of his pulse. He deliberately slowed. He'd be damned if he'd run to her.

Molly was beside him when they reached the landing. He had asked her to help him because he wanted her there when dealing with Amy, hoping that the presence of someone else would dampen the strange sensations that went through him when around her. In other words, protection. He couldn't believe how much he'd changed in the last four days.

At the end of the hall, the dog was scratching at Denny's door and whining at its base. It had been so adamantly attached to him during the day that they'd finally had to lock it up. The others had begun calling the dog Teddy, in honor of

Gayler, but Denny wouldn't call it anything. It was the measure of his failure and his stupidity and it was all he could do to keep from going to Amy and wishing it away.

"Why didn't you tell Mr. Geist that we have the dog from across the street?" she asked as they turned down the hall and moved toward Amy's door.

"I didn't want to complicate things," he replied. "We told him we weren't here last night and I didn't want anything to contradict that."

They reached the door, small Amy sounds drifting, muffled, back to them. Denny's hand was shaking when he raised it and knocked on the door. "Tawny," he said. "It's me, Denny. Can we come in?"

"Go away!" the woman screeched from inside. "Ah don't wanna see you!"

He shared a look with Molly. They'd never heard the woman sound like this before. "Tawny," he said. "Open up!"

"Ah'm not dressed! Go away!"

"Do you think something's wrong?" Molly asked.

"You bet I do," Denny said, knocking again. "I'm sending Molly in."

"No!"

He tried the door. Locked. He bent to the knob. It was a push button lock. "You got a bobby pin?" he asked Molly.

"Sure." She ran a hand through her long hair, coming out with a bobby pin. Denny straightened it then pushed it through the hole on his side of the knob, the lock springing immediately.

He stood. "You go in first," he said, not wanting to embarrass Tawny if she was, indeed, not dressed.

"Sure," Molly said, opening the door and slipping through, closing it behind her. There was a pause for several seconds, then, "Oh my God . . . Denny!"

Denny rushed through the door, his heart pounding. The first thing he saw was Amy, sitting in the middle of the bed, stuffing handfuls of potato chips into her mouth from a pile in front of her, the torn up bag thrown aside. Then he turned to the side of the room and saw it.

Molly had grabbed Tawny, the women struggling. The dresser had been cleared of knickknacks and a large plastic bag full of white powder set in its center. Long lines of the powder had been carefully laid out all across the dresser, and Denny could only think of one thing—cocaine.

He ran to the women, grabbing Tawny by the arms and staring into her face. Her eyes were wild, darting things, her mouth twisted into a sneer. Residual powder clung to her nose and upper lip. "What the hell have you done to yourself?" he said loudly.

"Fuck you!" the woman spat viciously. "Fuck you and your little bitch. Leave me and mah baby alone! We don't want you anymore. We don't need you! Get out!"

Amy was moaning loudly, her hands to her ears, as if she were trying to shut out the disharmony.

Denny pulled Tawny from Molly's grasp, throwing her violently on the bed. "You make me sick!" he yelled back. "God . . . can't you control yourself at all?"

"Fuck you!" she yelled again, her mood inflamed by the coke and booze. "And you stay away from mah little girl, too. Ah know what you want her fer. Ah know what you wanna do to her!"

"Stop it!" he yelled, involuntarily cocking a fist.

Amy rolled off the bed, her hands still clamped over her ears as she convulsed on the floor.

"Yeah, hit me! Go ahead! You wanna! You'd love to!"

Molly was at his arm. He swung around, fist still up. "What!"

She backed off, fear in her eyes. "The closet," she said. "Look in the closet."

He looked at her face, then at his shaking fist. What was happening? He forced calm, forced his hand to his side. "I'm sorry," he whispered quickly, rushing past her to the closet.

He looked into the closet in disbelief. It was full of bourbon, bottle after bottle, piled up from the floor in pyramids. There must have been a hundred bottles of Jack Daniels.

Molly was at the door. "Are you all right?"

"I'm sorry," he said again, and wanted to shout that nothing was all right.

"Where did all this come from?" she asked. "Have you—"

"No!" he said sharply. "It wasn't me."

He turned back to the room, moving deliberately to the dresser. Wetting a finger, he dipped it in a line of the powder, then brought it to his lips, touching his tongue. The numbing sensation worked into his tongue immediately. It was cocaine all right. With his arm, he shoved all the lines off the dresser, then grabbed the bag itself and walked into the bathroom.

"That's mine!" Tawny yelled from the bedroom. "You leave it alone!"

Denny raised the lid on the toilet, dumping the bag into the blue tinted water.

"Where did she get it?" Molly asked from the doorway.

Denny flushed the toilet and turned to her. "She made it," he said. "She fucking made it."

"What . . ." the woman began, then stopped herself, thinking. "You mean Amy?"

He nodded. Shutting the seat on the toilet, he sat down and, leaning his arms on the white porcelain sink, buried his face in his arms. "Jesus," he said softly. "She's figured it out."

"Figured what out?" Molly asked.

"She's figured out that she can ask Amy for anything in this goddamn world that she wants, and that Amy can get it for her."

"What do you mean—anything?" Molly asked. "I don't understand."

He looked up at her. "You were the one who warned me," he said. "And now it's happening. That woman in there has just realized that she can do anything her imagination can invent." He stood up abruptly. "God, we've left them alone together!"

He rushed out of the bathroom, Tawny in the process of crawling across the bed toward her daughter on the floor beside.

"Get away from her!" Denny said, diving at the bed.

He came down hard on Tawny, the air going out of her in a grunt, her scrawny arm reaching, reaching for the girl.

"Get . . . off me!" she wheezed, bucking violently beneath him, her inflamed mind giving her strength.

Amy began yelling, "No! No! No!" She swung her head back and forth wildly, long hair whipping around her face as she bounced up and down on the floor with the motions of the fight.

Denny rolled over, pulling Tawny with him, taking her away from Amy. The woman struggled wildly, limbs flailing as Molly stood helplessly looking on.

"What are you doing?" she said loudly. "Denny. Denny!"

They rolled off the other side of the bed, Denny coming down atop Tawny again. She groaned loudly as she slammed the floor, the fight going out of her.

Amy jumped up, running into the bathroom screaming.

"You mother fucker," Tawny strained through teeth

clenched in pain. "You jes want mah little girl. You wanna fuck mah little baby!"

"No," Denny said. "No I don't!" He looked up at Molly. "Get Frank up here. Quick!"

"Why? Why Frank?"

"Damnit!" he yelled. "We can't let her near Amy. God knows what she'll do! Frank can talk to her, maybe calm her down when I take Amy away."

"Away?"

"Do it!" he yelled. "Get Frank!"

Molly ran out of the room, Denny grabbing Tawny by her checkered shirt and dragging her to her feet. "You asshole," she rasped, wrapping arms around her sore ribs.

Denny dropped her back on the bed, Tawny rolling into the fetal position immediately.

"You used her to make the dope and the booze, didn't you?" he said. "You thought it up and she did it."

Tawny rolled to face him, a sick smile on her face. "So what? She's mah kid. Ah kin do anythin' Ah want to her. At least Ah ain't tryin' to fuck her!"

Denny tensed again, forced it down again. "You can't do that anymore," he said.

"Ah'm through with you and with all this bullshit," she said. "Me and Amy's gettin' out of heah tonight. You kin have all yo damn money back and yo damn contrak."

"No," he said.

"Mah ass!" She sat up painfully and started off the bed.

"I said no!" Denny said, grabbing her by the arms. "I'm not letting you within ten feet of that girl."

"You cain't keep me heah," she said, struggling again. "You ain't got no right."

"Listen to me," he said, shaking her, feeling the anger rise again. "Your daughter has an incredible power that you're not capable of controlling."

"Ah did all right afore you came along."

"That's because you're an idiot," he said. "Your head's so full of animal energy that you never thought beyond instant gratification. It never occurred to you that she was capable of anything more than finding lost wallets."

"Ah've always protected mah little girl," she said. "We was doin' all right, jes her and me. Jes like it's gonna be agin."

He shook his head. "No," he said. "She's mine now. I can't trust you with her."

Behind the wild eyes, a note of understanding began to creep in. "No," she whispered. "You caint. You cain't take mah baby from me. Oh please, Mr. Stiller. Don't take mah baby girl from me."

Denny turned his head from her, but didn't let her go. How could he let Tawny near Amy after what had happened? God only knew what wishes, what dreams could come out of her head and be made flesh. God, indeed.

"What's wrong?" Frank said from the doorway.

"Come here," Denny said, then looked hard at the man when he was standing beside him. "I've got to take Amy for a while—"

"No!" Tawny screamed. "Gawd, don't let him!"

"What do you mean?" Frank said, confused.

"Please," Denny said. "Just listen to me. Trust me. Watch Tawny for a while. Talk to her while I take Amy downstairs . . ."

The woman screamed again, struggling wildly. "Amy!" she yelled. "Amy honey! Come heah to mama!"

"Stop it!" Denny said.

"What are you doing?" Frank said, putting a hand on his arm.

"I'll explain later."

"You'll explain now."

The man's face had gotten hard. Denny looked toward the doorway. Molly was standing there, her hands up to her face, her eyes wide.

"Please," Denny said. "Wait outside for a minute."

"Denny . . ."

"Please!"

Without a word, Molly went out the door, slamming it behind her. Denny looked frantically at Frank while the woman squirmed in his grasp.

"You remember last night?" Denny said. "The woman's house?"

"I don't really want to know anythin' about that," Frank said. "It's none of my affair. I just want to make sure you're not hurtin' that girl."

"You signed on for the whole megillah, buddy," Denny said, angry that everything fell to him. "I haven't got the time to be sensitive to your problems right now."

"I just take pictures . . . that's all." Frank stared at the ground, his lips working silently.

"You can't close your eyes to this," Denny said. "Listen to me. That house last night tore itself apart because I wanted a dog. A simple thought, a simple wish. I pictured in my mind the dog that's going nuts in my room right now. I pictured it and a woman died so that I could have it."

Frank kept shaking his head. "No . . . that can't be right. No. . . ."

"Frank, for God's sake," Denny said. "If you don't believe me just humor me! I have *got* to keep that girl and her mother apart until we get this thing ferreted out. She's just had Amy fill the fucking closet with booze and cocaine. Go look if you don't believe me."

Frank turned and walked to the closet.

"Amy, honey!" Tawny called. "They's keepin' yo mama from you, baby!"

"Stop it," Denny said, voice hard as nails. "Stop it or I'll break your fucking arm."

Her eyes met his, animal eyes, darting, looking for escape. If scaring her was the only way to shut her up, so be it.

"I mean it," he said, and jerked her arm hard behind her back to make the point. "I'll take you apart, bitch."

Frank walked back, staring at Denny. He nodded imperceptibly, his large hand coming out to take Tawny by the arm.

Denny took a long breath. "Thanks," he whispered, and turned toward the bathroom.

"We'll talk later," Frank replied.

Denny moved into the bathroom and closed the door behind him. Amy was all but hysterical, tears streaming from her eyes as she walked around the bathroom, fast walking, banging into things then turning the other way like a mechanical toy.

"It's all right," Denny said quietly, his eyes, as always, drawn to her pristine face, his pulse beating faster. "I won't let anything happen to you."

He moved up to her, stopping her movements with his hands, her touch sending electric tingles through his system. He gathered her to him, feeling the tension in her delicate body.

"Don't be afraid," he whispered, wrapping his arms around her. "Denny will take care of you."

He could feel her relaxing, feel her taking him into her mental universe and he wanted desperately to understand her, to end her loneliness and fear. And as with other times, he felt an overpowering wave of sensation roll through him, sensation that must be the sum total of Amy's secret world and he fought for all he was worth to keep his head above the wave, to not let it power him away from himself.

He picked her up, cradling her like a baby or like a new bride, and carried her out of the bathroom, whispering encouragement to her the whole time.

Tawny was lying on the bed, crying out an artery of self-pity as Frank sat beside her stroking her gently. "Now, don't you be worryin'," he said. "Denny and them others are just a bunch of old shits, that's all. Frank's right here and he ain't goin' to let nothin' happen to you or your little girl."

Denny moved quietly to the door, Frank looking up once to stare inscrutably before going back to talking Tawny down. Denny balanced Amy with his right arm, using his left to open the door. Molly was sitting on the floor in the hall, her face drained of all color. She stood the moment Denny came out the door.

"I'm going nuts with this thing," she said, as he walked toward the stairs, struggling to maintain his own composure amid the chaos.

"Not now," he replied. "One thing at a time."

"You tell me that this . . . retarded girl has got nothing short of godlike power and can do anything she wants, and then . . ."

"She's not retarded," Denny said. "Not even a little bit. She's *chosen* her lifestyle."

"What are you saying?"

They'd reached the top of the stairs, Denny stopping to look at her. "I don't know what I'm saying, okay? All I know is that we all made the mistake of assuming her power to be some sort of healing gift. But healing was merely the vehicle that introduced us to her." He stared hard into the frightened woman's eyes. "I think she can do anything, *anything* she wants."

"And we're in charge," she replied, low.

"Kind of like having your finger on the atomic bomb button, isn't it?" he said, and started down the stairs.

She followed, tugging on his shoulder. "We can't be responsible for this," she said, her tones making it sound like a pronouncement.

"It's out now," he said. "Who do you trust with the responsibility?"

He kept walking, leaving her, without an answer, in the middle of the staircase. He walked into the living room, Kornfeld and Geist sitting at the distant furniture grouping, the camera still sitting on its tripod, taping away. And Denny could almost think of the camera as a living member of their group.

He started across the floor, images flashing through his mind, images of crowds, their faces white with pain and anger. Something . . . he pushed the images away forcibly, urging his mind back to the present.

"Sorry to be so long," he said, walking up to the man. Kornfeld had removed his headband and put a shirt on. "Tawny was asleep, so she won't be joining us. But her lovely daughter, Amy, has come down in her place."

"Yeah," the man said, eyes narrowing. "There's something wrong with her, retarded or something, right?"

"She's autistic," Denny said, "not retarded. She'd like to shake hands with you."

The man smiled awkwardly, standing and transferring his highball to his left hand and putting out his right.

"Denny . . ." Kornfeld said, Stiller ignoring him, his mind turning wildly against itself, his fear of doing the wrong thing doing battle with the necessity of protecting their anonymity.

He moved Amy up close to Geist, Molly coming up beside him. "Run the camera, would you Molly?" he asked.

Her lips tightened, but she did as she was told, moving behind the machine, then PANNING up to take in the meeting between Geist and Amy.

The girl shrank from Geist, pulling harder against Denny and turning away as his mind spun crazily, like a whirlpool. He pulled one of her arm's from around his neck and held it out, the old man gingerly taking her hand in his while Denny filled his mind with forgetfulness, deep and abiding.

"Ouch!" the man said, pulling back from the touch. He shook his hand around, a deep frown set on his face. "Like a damned electric charge."

Denny's heart was pounding. "Now why did you say you came by, Mr. Geist?" he asked.

The man looked at him, smiling stupidly. "I—I'm not exactly sure, I . . ." He scratched his head, obviously lost in confusion.

Denny looked at Kornfeld, the man's eyes dark.

"Wasn't it about the fire at that house across the street?" Denny asked.

The man thought for a minute, then smiled broadly. "That's right!" he said, triumphant. "I came about that house across the street."

"Well all I can tell you," Denny said, "is that it burned down because the boiler exploded, but we weren't here to see it."

The man nodded in understanding. "Burned down," he said. "That's right. Pretty simple if you ask me, Mr— "

"Jones," Denny said. "Mortimer Jones."

"Let me write that down," the man said, picking his pad up off the easy chair, "just in case they want to follow up. They probably won't though."

"And these are my children," Denny said, feeling a surge of confidence, "Huey, Dewey, and Louie."

Geist wrote quickly, taking it all down. "And that house just burned down," he said.

"Correct."

"But you didn't see it, Mr. Jones."

"I did not see it."

Denny moved to sit beside Kornfeld on the couch, putting Amy next to him. He bent to pick a drink up off the floor. "Is this for me?" he asked.

The lawyer was just staring at him, shaking his head slightly in disbelief. Denny took a long drink, bourbon, of course.

Geist finished writing, settling a period with a flourish. He looked at them. "Open and shut," he said. "Looks like a boiler explosion."

"Bet there's a lot of those dangerous boilers around in these old houses," Denny said, sitting back, relaxing in his power.

The man bent down for his briefcase, sticking the notebook back into it. "People don't understand how dangerous those old systems are," he said. "All it takes is one pressure valve to stick and . . . flooey!" He imitated an explosion with his hands.

"I know what you mean," Denny said, standing to lead Geist gently by the arm toward the front door, steering the men right past his already forgotten briefcase. "People never notice problems until they're ready to blow up in their faces."

"That's what my dad used to say," Geist returned. "Yes,

sir . . . my old dad . . ." The man stopped, putting a hand to his head. He laughed strangely.

"What is it?" Denny asked, still trying to edge the man the last ten feet to the door.

"Funny," he said. "I . . . can't remember . . ."

"Remember what?" Denny asked.

The man looked at him, his face drawn in fearful confusion. "His name. I can't remember . . . my father's name."

Denny half-dragged him the rest of the way. "Geist," Denny said. "Same name as yours." He opened the door, pushing the man toward the outside.

"Geist," the man said, as if he were trying the name on for size. "Geist." He looked at Denny from the darkness of the porch, a lost child look. "I don't understand."

"Just go back to the motel and get a good night's sleep," Denny said. "Everything will look better in the morning."

"Motel," the man said, his eyes unfocused. "How did I get here?"

"Your car is parked at the end of the drive," Denny said, pointing. "Good luck."

"Thank you, Mr. Jones."

Denny stood for a second, watching the confused Mr. Geist walk aimlessly out across the lawn, leaving his briefcase behind. He hoped the man would be able to keep his mind together long enough to drive off the block. He pushed on the heavy door, watching it close behind its own weight.

He turned, both Kornfeld and Molly standing before him.

"What did you do to him?" Kornfeld asked.

"I made him forget," Denny said. "I didn't know what else to do."

The lawyer ran a hand through his hair, his face a war of conflicting emotions. "You've got that kind of power through Amy?"

Denny nodded.

"This is too weird," Kornfeld said with finality. "It's gotten completely out of hand."

"No it hasn't," Denny said. "This thing tonight . . . it won't happen anymore. We're free now to carry on our experiments."

"Can you control this power?" the man demanded loudly. "Can you pinpoint it accurately?"

"Not yet," Denny said.

"How can you experiment with something this dangerous?"

Molly said. "God only knows what kind of damage you did to that poor man."

"I didn't 'damage' him," Denny said. "I just made him forget."

"His own father!" Kornfeld said. "His own name! Jesus. This is too deep. I've got to get out of here."

He turned and moved toward the stairs.

"You can't leave!" Denny said.

"Watch me," Kornfeld replied, starting up the stairs.

"If they get you," Denny said, "you'll tell where we are."

The man flared around to him. "So . . . will you make *me* forget too?"

"I'm just trying to protect the girl," Denny said. "You tell me, Counselor. After our demonstration of power, whose hands would you trust her in?"

The man just looked at him blankly. Finally, he spoke. "I'm just a lawyer, Denny," he said softly. "My world is a very closed, structured one. I'm not ashamed to admit that I'm way over my head here, just like you are. I don't know who you could trust with this, but that's not my problem. I know that I can't deal with it anymore. I'm taking myself off this one. I won't tell anyone where you are."

"What if they try and force it out of you?"

Kornfeld held tightly to the banister, leaning down closer to Denny. "I'm history, buddy," he said. "Out of here. This is your baby, not mine. You're not the Army; I'm not bound to your representation."

"How can you leave me with this?" Denny asked.

The man laughed dryly. "I can't tell you how easy it's going to be," he said. "I'm scared to death, of Amy . . . and you."

He turned then, hurrying upstairs to get his belongings from Frank's room.

"You're a son of a bitch!" Denny called angrily up the stairs. He looked at Molly, who was staring sadly at him. "Well, what the hell's *your* problem?"

"Charlie's right," she said. "None of us are capable of controlling this sort of power. It's already begun to get to you. You've got to pull out now before it takes you down."

"You don't get it, do you?" he replied, turning to move back into the living room where he'd left Amy. "I can't think of anybody *better* than me to handle this. I'm unbiased, with no axes to grind beyond getting to the truth. Anybody else gets Amy, and they're going to have a program they want to put into effect. I've never had a program, Molly. For the first time in my life, my emotional ennui is going to come in real handy."

"But what can you gain by this?" she asked his back as he moved across the floor.

He turned to her, holding his hands out in frustration. "Maybe I can find a way out of it," he said, voice strained. "God, I'm desperate to find a way out."

He turned again, walking quickly to the couch. Amy had slid onto the floor and was studiously twirling Geist's flashlight around and around in her hands, touching the ribbed contours of the aluminum tool and holding it close to her face as if she were trying to memorize the thing.

Of course he felt bad about Geist, but there wasn't anything else to be done. Denny had thought a lot about this, certainly more than the others had, and he was absolutely convinced that the girl couldn't be turned over to anyone. The potential for abuse was too great.

He moved idly to the camera. It was still running, pointing at nothing. He turned it to Molly who moved slowly closer, obviously lost in thought. He heard Kornfeld coming down the stairs, the man hurrying into the living room, a suitcase in his hand, a sport jacket slung around his shoulders in counterpoint to his gym shorts and tennis shoes.

Kornfeld came into camera view, Denny ZOOMING IN for a CLOSE-UP of his confused face. "Denny, you and I have been friends for a long time," he said. "You've got to listen to me. You've gone overboard with this thing. I don't believe that you're thinking clearly . . ."

"Are you saying that I'm incompetent?" Denny asked, relating to the man only through the viewfinder.

"I'm saying you're confused," Kornfeld replied, his jaw muscles tightened from having to deal with Denny through the camera only. "If you weren't, you'd have enough sense to realize that this thing is too dangerous for you to tackle alone. It won't hurt you if you go on the air and say you're turning it over to the government—"

"And what if someone in the government decides that it would be a good thing if there weren't any more Russians around?" Denny asked.

"Nobody would—"

"Or let's forget that and take something simple," Denny interrupted. "Suppose a Republican president simply decided that it would be nice if everyone voted the way he did and believed the way he did. Nothing fancy, just destruction of the reasoning ability of every human in the country. It would be just as easy for someone to do that as if was for me to make Mr. Geist forget."

"You could 'what if' until the end of time," Kornfeld said, "and it wouldn't alter the fact that *you* can't handle it either. God knows, maybe Amy Kyle should be locked up, or . . . something."

"Killed?" Denny asked. "Were you going to say maybe she should be killed?"

The man stared coldly at Denny, taking his measure directly through the lens of the camera. "I've heard worse ideas," he said. "And you can quote me on that."

The man turned then. "I can find my way out," he said over his shoulder. "And don't worry. I won't be the one to turn you in. All I want to do is forget about this— " He suddenly flared around and pointed a finger. "But I'll do my own forgetting, thank you very much."

With that he strode resolutely to the door, pulling it open and slamming it loudly on his way out. Denny shut down the camera and straightened.

"I've known that man for twenty years," he said.

Molly just stared at him. "You've changed, Denny," she said softly.

"Of course I've changed," he said. "I've been forced to join the parade. I've finally developed a little of the sense of responsibility that everyone's been bugging me about for years. So, what's the damned problem?"

She just looked at him, her eyes wet with unshed tears. "I'm going to bed," she said slowly. "I'm all tired out."

She turned then, looking old, as if in the space of one day she went from being young to being middle aged.

"Molly!" he called after her, but she didn't turn around. "Molly!"

She reached the end of the room and started up the stairs. Denny took three steps after her, then turned and saw Amy on the floor, the girl's energy bringing him back. He sat down on the floor with her, fascinated at the total concentration she was giving the flashlight, even though she looked at it peripherally.

"What am I going to do with you?" he asked, then realized that the question might very well be what was she going to do with him. It was getting increasingly difficult to separate his own sense of self from the images and feelings that he felt were feeding back from Amy's overactive brain. It was somehow electrical—he was sure of that, and he knew that the brain was basically electrical in origin. But beyond that thought, he had no idea of what was going on. He needed a way to get some professional help in this area as he proceeded. Some sort of explanations would have to be forthcoming.

He felt a jolt in the pit of his stomach and looked at the girl again. She had taken the long-handled flashlight and placed it between her legs, her hand moving up and down on the shaft of the thing.

"What are you doing?" he said loudly, and felt his own sexual tensions building. His hands began shaking uncontrollably as he felt an erection pushing resolutely against his tight pants.

"Stop it!" he said, grabbing the flashlight away from her and throwing it aside.

The girl let herself go backward on the floor, eyes closed, squirming slightly as waves of unfulfilled need pushed through Denny's brain like fire. He was almost out of control. He felt as if he hadn't had sex for years, and he couldn't look at the girl on the floor without the feelings heightening, pushing him to the brink.

"No!" he yelled, jumping to his feet. "Leave me alone!"

He backed away from her, the desires undiminished, his body in complete turmoil. He stumbled toward the door, his vision jacked up, the lines and colors of the house vivid and pulsating, the altered realities of the French impressionists on the walls jumping from the pictures alive and hungry. He had entered another world.

Desperately he fought back, filling his mind with counterthoughts. He remembered his parents's death and their pictures in the newspapers. He remembered the sadness, dwelled on the sadness, trying to let it overpower him and push the other feelings away.

He made the door, his hand missing the knob several times before he actually got the thing open. Conscious thoughts were all but gone as he stumbled onto the porch, falling down the front stairs to the lawn.

His hands were clenched as he fought for control of his mind. He got himself on all fours, crawling without thought, trying to distance her power as he opened all the floodgates of sorrow that he'd kept closed for so long, and still the tensions increased. He'd never known such desire. It was worse than

last night, worse than he thought possible, and he'd gone
beyond the sorrow and was doubling numbers in his head,
doing math to turn his mind and still he couldn't shut her out
as the desires became finally overpowering.

He fell heavily onto his side, an orgasm raking him like the
worst of the d. t.'s, his body heaving and shaking, animal noises
tearing involuntarily from his throat. And when it was done,
he lay exhausted on the grass, humiliated and ashamed.

He was lost.

Scene 2

(the next day)

DAY—INT—A TV STUDIO SET. We are watching the
syndicated television program, *God's Day*, a staple of Dr.
James Connover's televangelical empire. The talk set is
cheery, with a round coffee table in the fg flanked by a number
of pastel-colored Leatherette swivel chairs. Between each seat
is a large bouquet of brightly colored flowers and in the bg we
can see the program's logo in flashing neon, a large pair of
hands holding a globe with the words God's Day scrawled in
script within the globe. There are five chairs, three of them
occupied. In the center spots are JERRY MILK, *God's Day*
host, a rotund man with a jolly face, and besides him his cohost
and announcer, PAUL WASHINGTON, a black man who
reminds one of an undertaker. The other inner seat is taken by
JOHNNY BARNELLI, a tall, boyish man with close-cropped
sandy hair. He's a quarterback for the Cincinnati Bengals and
a national representative for the Fellowship of Christian
Athletes. All three men are applauding and smiling, with
audience applause evident in the bg.

MILK
(friendly, casual)

That was the lovely Miss Ginger Lynn, singing "Jesus
is My Witness," and what a wonderful voice our Lord

has given her, too. Come over and join us,
Ginger . . .

The applause RISES, a young woman with a bouffant hairdo
and a sequined gown walks onto the set, the spotlights
glittering in brilliant sabers from her gown. She nods sheepishly to the crowd and takes a seat next to the quarterback as
the applause dies.

MILK

Oh, I tell you, friends. What a wonderful day it is
when we can wake up in Jesus' saving grace and listen to the voice of an angel.

GINGER
(demurely)
You're too kind, Mr. Milk. My singing's just my way
of praising God and trying to bring His word to the
people of this great country.

BARNELLI
(loudly)

Amen!

A chorus of amens rifles through the hosts and the audience.

MILK

You know, we all give praise every day by using our
talents to the best of our God-given abilities. This is
the idea behind the Fellowship of Christian Athletes,
isn't it Johnny?

BARNELLI

Right you are. We believe that by developing our
bodies through athletic competition, we can praise
God and avoid the pitfalls of pride and selfishness
that can characterize the professional athlete.

MILK
Are you referring to the so-called jock mentality?

BARNELLI
Not exactly . . . I was thinking more along the lines
of girls and drugs, stuff like that. Jesus has taught me
that you should always respect the girl you're going
out with, especially if it's the first time—which of
course happens a lot if you're an athelete. And if Len
Bias had prayed to Jesus instead of snorting that evil
stuff up his nose, he'd probably be alive today.

WASHINGTON
(nodding knowingly)
Amen. The world moves so fast today and has so
many opportunities for straying from the path. . . .

MILK
And speaking of the pitfalls of modern life . . . you
know, there's something going on in this city right
now that shakes me with anger all the way down to
my very soul. You all know what I'm talking about.
This assault on Christianity from the liberal press in
the form of Dennis Stiller and his camera tricks is
enough to make any true Christian just shake his
head in disbelief at the sin and evil that runs rampant
in our modern age. You know, at the top of the program I told you we had a special surprise for you and
I think this would be the perfect time to bring it on.
There's going to be an important announcement here
on *God's Day*, and here to tell us about it is our
founder and spiritual head, my boss . . . you know
who I'm talking about . . . let's welcome Dr. James
Connover.

The applause is loud, as the guests rise to their feet for a
standing ovation. Connover, looking fatherly and imposing in
a gray suit walks purposefully onto the set, waving and smiling
to the crowd. He then greets the hosts, hugging Milk and
shaking hands with the others before Washington vacates his
center seat and moves to the end of the line.

MILK
(when applause dies)
Well, Dr. Connover. Through the magic of television
and God's grace, we're here together again, sharing

fellowship with our extended family all over the world.

CONNOVER
(genial)
Good to be on your show, Jerry. (he looks around) I see all the equipment's still in relatively good shape.

MILK
(laughing)
You bet it is! Old Satan hasn't run us out yet!

There are shouted amens and applause from the audience and guests.

MILK
(becoming serious)
While we're always happy to have our spiritual leader on the show, I guess you wouldn't exactly call today's visit a social call, would you Dr. Connover?

CONNOVER
(intense)
No . . . no I wouldn't, Jerry. As all of you well know, I have taken the lead in the condemnation of the viper that has come into our midst. This problem of Dennis Stiller is not new to Christians . . . we've had to fight against Satan's evil in one form or another for thousands of years. But this one, dear friends, has been particularly nasty and distasteful. You see, the problem is, television is looked upon by many as a vehicle of Truth. Surely, it is so with us . . . with this program. But, unfortunately, many people tend to believe *everything* they see on the screen, saying—if they put it on TV, it must be real. And that frightens me like a cold hand gripping my heart for there are many people of a base and distrustful nature more than willing to do the Devil's work in order to make a dollar. Why is sin so out of control in our society? Why are we plagued by sexual and mental diseases in ever increasing numbers? It's television . . . it's television. Television legitimizes

promiscuity on every level. I suppose it's little wonder that it would finally enter the domain of God.

MILK

Living here in Dallas, Dr. Connover, I guess we're
getting a dose of it firsthand. And it's frankly scary, as
anyone who has to drive on the freeway in the morning can tell you. These poor misguided people are
everywhere, all of them looking for something that
doesn't exist. You just want to grab them and shake
the fear of God into them!

BARNELLI

Amen!

CONNOVER

This entire episode has troubled me deeply in my
heart, Jerry. On one hand, I want to reach out to pity
all those who have hurt themselves and their immortal souls by chasing Satan-created rainbows, and on
the other hand, I want to take Satan's emissary, Dennis Stiller, and personally cast him into the fires of
eternal damnation for the harm he's done to his fellow man.

CLOSE-UP—CONNOVER. He reaches into his suit coat and
comes out with reading glasses and a piece of paper, which he
unfolds.

CONNOVER (cont)

In the interests of truth and the public good, I have
been conducting inquiries into the background of the
self-styled "healer" Tawny Kyle. When I received the
findings, I was frankly surprised, not by what I had
found, but by the fact that Dennis Stiller had so little
respect for his audience that he thought it would be
this easy to pull the wool over their eyes. Let me tell
you about the "new" God: (he reads) 1954—Tawny
Kyle arrested for breaking and entering and
sentenced to term in juvenile facility; 1956—arrested
for offering to engage in a lewd act, convicted and
sentenced to thirty days in Dallas county jail; 1959—

arrested and released: prostitution; 1961—*four* prostitution arrests in Houston, serving a total of one
hundred and ten days in jail; between '61 and '85 are
a total of nine other arrests for crimes ranging from
shoplifting to vagrancy to possession of narcotics. (he
removes his glasses, staring) In the parlance of the
underworld, friends, Tawny Kyle has a rap sheet as
long as your arm. This is the healer. This is the miracle worker . . . a habitual offender, a hardened
criminal out to bilk the public with the help of the
Devil's agent on the face of this Earth. Dennis
Stiller. This doesn't surprise me, friends, nor should
it you. I have preached against this man and his her-
esies, and I will say now what I've said from the first:
Tawny Kyle and Dennis Stiller are frauds and fakes
out to con the good, God-fearing people of this country. (he holds up the paper) Here's the proof for all to
see. I have sent copies of this woman's past criminal
record to all of the television stations and newspapers
in the Dallas area; also I've been in touch with the
county prosecuter's office with an eye to the possibility of filing criminal charges against this woman and
her accomplice. Perhaps now, we can put the Tawny
Kyle issue to rest and get on with preaching the gospel of Jesus Christ—what we should have been doing
all along.

WE PULL BACK to find that we have been watching the
preceeding on television, the sound becoming more distant
and tinny as we slowly pull away. It is the big-screen TV at
Denny's hideaway.
ANGLE—TAWNY KYLE. She's sitting in the room with the
television on an old rocking chair. She's TIED to the chair, a
GAG on her mouth, rocking slowly, a lit cigarette dangling
from beneath the gag, Connover's voice small in the bg. Amy
lays on the floor near her mother, seemingly oblivious to her
presence as she studiously concentrates on a set of keys that
has somehow come into her possession.
ANGLE—THE KITCHEN. Denny Stiller, slovenly and un-
shaved, paces back and forth around the kitchen, a cup of
coffee in his hand, dark circles under his puffy, troubled eyes.
His free hand holds a cordless telephone up to his right ear.

DENNY
(voice shaky)

Of course I heard it. Why do you think I called you?
I don't see what you're so upset about . . . what
difference does it make whether she's been arrested
or not? . . . Damnit, I never said it was religious.
It's all the rest of you fuckers who keep saying that.

Denny took another sip of Frank's coffee and tried to
concentrate on Horton's words, his mind so dark and confused
that it was difficult to hold onto any line of thought for too long.

"Religious or not," Horton was saying, "people expect a
certain type of behavior from the people they elevate to moral
positions."

"It's not my problem," Denny said. "I never checked
Tawny Kyle's background because I felt it had no real bearing
on my experiments into her power."

"It damn well *is* your problem, hotshot," Horton said. "The
implication has been raised that you and the woman are
charlatans because of her long arrest record. It seems a fair
allegation to me, one that you're going to have to answer to not
only the public's satisfaction, but mine, Denny. So help me
God, if there's some kind of scam going on here. . . ."

"There's no scam, Dick," Denny replied, moving to stare
out the kitchen window to the backyard. Frank was out there,
puttering around with something near the pool. "I want you to
check the rap sheet yourself, but I have no reason to doubt that
it's authentic. It simply is immaterial. You don't have to be
godlike to have power."

"A lot of people think otherwise."

"A lot of people eat dog food, too, for God's sake," Denny
said angrily, "but that doesn't mean I'm taking out stock in the
Alpo company."

"Let me make this as plain as I know how," Horton said.
"I've got Mr. Gayler on the other line and he agrees. Your
integrity has been put in question by your associating with a
convicted felon in a business deal. Our asses, plus our
operating license, are also on the line because we are involved
with contractually producing this for the viewers, and if it
turns out to be a scam we lose everything."

"It's not a—"

"That's not good enough, Denny! Listen to me. Unless you go public . . . and soon about this whole affair and clear it up to everyone's satisfaction, we're going to have to pull you off the air. Have I made myself clear enough?"

"I'll go on live tonight," Denny said quietly.

"What?"

"I said I'll go on live tonight," Denny repeated. "And I guarantee you, that all the questions about Tawny Kyle will be answered, and when we're through, everyone will understand and be satisfied. How's that?"

"Almost good enough," Horton replied.

Denny took a breath, waiting for the other shoe to drop. He had gotten himself into a bad bargaining position and was now going to have to pay the consequences. "What else?" he asked quietly.

"Mr. Gayler wants a public meeting between you and whatever representatives of the scientific and religious communities he chooses to bring along. The meeting will be televised and your protégé tested. . . ."

"It's not that easy," Denny said.

"It'll have to be." The man's voice was harsh and uncompromising. "You've got to go public with whatever you know about Tawny Kyle, and she's got to be tested in a public forum by experts of our choosing. This thing has gotten too big, Denny. The station's practically under siege, and if your deal proves to be a fraud, we're screwed big time."

"It's not—"

"You've already told me that. Now you're going to have to prove it. What time do you want tonight?"

Denny closed his eyes, trying to bring his mind back from the fog. There was so much to do. So much . . .

"Denny!" Horton said impatiently.

"I don't know . . . ten o'clock," Denny said.

"Good. We'll start advertising right away."

"Give me a little time on the other thing . . . the testing. Okay?"

"We don't have a lot of other time," Horton said. "Think about it today. We'll set something up tomorrow. Can't you give me your phone number so we can keep in necessary contact?"

"Absolutely not," Denny said, hearing the dog loudly barking nearby. Within seconds it came charging into the kitchen, skidding across the tile floor to bang into Denny's legs, then jump up at him happily. "Phones can be traced, lines tapped. With the crowds on the streets the way they are, I'm not sure what would happen if anyone knew where we were."

"We'll have to work something out," Horton said, not at all sympathetically. "This whole thing is more trouble than it's worth."

"Bullshit, Dick," Denny said. "This is a gold mine and you know it."

"Not if you don't get your shit together. Remember, ten tonight."

The man hung up, Denny looking at the receiver in disgust before setting it on the window sill. The dog was jumping up at him, wagging his tail and panting heavily. Someone must have let him out. Almost involuntarily, he reached out and patted the dog on the had, the animal whining pathetically, then rolling over on its back, its legs quivering, its liquid brown eyes pleading with him for love.

He hated the animal for what it was and what it stood for. It was his symbol of failure, deadly failure. Every time he looked at it he saw the mirror of his own stupidity. Horton had said it: hotshot, he had called him. Denny Stiller, willing to blunder into anything newsworthy and damn the consequences. He shook his head, realizing how hollow his viewpoint had always been simply because it had never affected him directly. How easy to stand above everything and judge, like the statisticians who predict how many people a year will die in car wrecks or of AIDS without the figure meaning any more to them than satisfactorily completed mathematics. But he wasn't above it now. He was a part of the statistics, a victim of his own self-image. Like the little Dutch boy, he had put his finger in the dike and couldn't pull it out without destroying himself and everyone else around him.

He moved away from the window and refilled his mug from the Mr. Coffee. It was the consistency of old crankcase oil and probably didn't taste as good, but right then it was a miracle of the highest order if it could help to clear his head from the night before. He had fallen asleep on the lawn last night, then woken up and stumbled into the house sometime in the early morning. He'd covered Amy, who'd fallen asleep on the living-room floor, then thrown himself on a sofa and slept the rest of the night.

He'd awoken to a stiff neck and overpowering guilt.

Although he hadn't actually touched the girl, he'd apparently
had sex with her. He couldn't quite put his finger on it, and
even trying brought on the guilt again, but something was
happening to his mind, something well beyond his control. He
was afraid of the girl and drawn to her at the same time. He felt
at once violated and aggressive. The situation as it stood was
impossible for him to walk away from. He had painted himself
into a corner and had no idea of how to escape the predicament
other than to flow with things and hope for the best. If his head
just wasn't so fuzzy. He looked at the dog, which was now at
his feet staring lovingly up at him, and fought back the urge to
kick it away from him.

"You look like hell," came Molly's voice from the entryway.

He looked up at her. Uncombed hair and dark circles
under her eyes tempted him to return the compliment, but he
swallowed it down with another sip of Frank's coffee. "Once
you taste this," he said, holding up the cup, "you'll know why."

She moved through the breakfast area to stand near him,
her kimono held together with her right hand. She leaned
forward to sniff the coffee, crinkling up her nose and pulling
away. "If I was tempted by your recommendation, my round of
throwing up this morning would probably keep me away
anyhow."

He moved, casually he hoped, several paces away from
her, still frightened by his own out-of-control sexuality. "Are
you sick?" he asked, pretending to look out the window at
Frank again.

"I guess you'd call it a good kind of sick," she told his back.

He turned to her, confused. "What do you mean?"

She smiled and shook her head. "Morning sickness," she
said. "It happens to all pregnant ladies."

He nodded, feeling stupid again. Where was his head?
"A-are you okay now?" he asked, not knowing what else to say.

"Sure," she answered, a questioning tone in her voice. He
sought her eyes for just a second and found her studying him.
He turned back to the window. "I let Teddy out of your room,
he was—"

He flared around to her. "Teddy?"

She frowned at the dog. "I know you don't like me calling
him that, but we've got to name him something."

"No." He shook his head violently. "I don't want to name
the dog. It's not ours. We can't give it a name."

"What's wrong with you?" she asked, moving up to take him by the arms. "Why are you acting so strangely?"

He jerked away from her, searching desperately for something to say. "It's Tawny," he said finally. "Connover's released information that she's got a prison record and Horton's about to have a cat over it. I'm going on the air tonight to refute it."

"How will you do that?" she asked.

He looked toward the doorway leading to the den where Tawny was tied up to keep her from contact with her daughter. "Maybe it's time," he said, "to take Tawny Kyle out of the process entirely."

"And replace her with whom?" Molly asked, voice high pitched.

"Maybe me," he replied softly.

He watched a wave of horror cross her face as she shook her head. "You can't do that," she said. "You've got to remain apart from this. You've got to stay objective."

He held his breath and took a long drink of the coffee. "I've got to remain in control of this situation," he said. "And I can't do it with Tawny at the forefront anymore. She isn't the power, and I've got to let people know that or we're shot."

"What do you mean, 'we're shot'?" She asked. "This is just a story. You either do it or you don't. If nobody's interested, it's not much of a story."

"You sound like Kornfeld now," he said, finishing the cup and pouring another. "Just cut the ties and walk away."

"Why not?"

"And what happens then?" he demanded. "If you care one iota about what's happened so far, you've got to ask yourself that."

"I've got other concerns," she replied. " I have a baby to worry about."

He had no answer for that, none at all. He'd been foolish to ask her to come here to begin with. "Let's go out and talk to Frank," he said. "Maybe it's time we settled our feelings on this once and for all."

She met his eyes, but he found no answers there. "All right," she said. "I'm going to dress. I'll meet you out there."

"I'll get Amy." The dog nipping at his heels, Denny set down his coffee and walked to the den, looking in. Amy lay on the floor, playing with the keys. Fear rose in his throat, fear and a certain excitement.

He moved past Tawny, her eyes wide and accusing above

the gag in her mouth. Denny considered speaking to her, but instead he flicked the barrel of ash off her cigarette and moved past. They'd have to let her loose soon. The dog, sensing Amy's presence, stayed out of the room. He would never be in the same place at the same time with her.

The girl was still dressed in her white nightgown as he knelt beside her. "Come on Amy," he said. "Let's go outside for a while."

She ignored him as she held one of the keys up in front of her face, her finger tracing the ridges over and over, moving rapidly, almost a blur. Why did she do it? What was the fascination? Once again, he realized the need for professional help with this.

Unable to get her attention, he reached out and picked her up, his senses jolting immediately. She was a life flowing into him, like jets refueling in the air. His ragged brain cleared, his mind alive with thoughts not his own. As had happened last night, the colors brightened and sharpened in the room, sound becoming an imposing force, as if all his senses had increased in power exponentially. When he held her he *felt* powerful.

Cradling the girl, he stood and walked past Tawny, large tears rolling down her cheeks from the corners of her eyes.

"We'll untie you soon," he said, but was unable to look at her face, hurrying past and into the kitchen.

"Meedle!" Amy said loudly as he walked through the kitchen. "Meedle! Meedle!"

He looked around for something to eat, finally settling for an already opened loaf of bread. He gave Amy a piece, the girl grabbing it with both hands and tearing into it like an animal. They'd have to find a way of stocking some food in.

He moved to the patio door off the breakfast area, sliding the door with one hand while balancing Amy on his free arm. When they walked out into the sunshine, Amy screamed, dropping her bread and burying her face in his shoulder. Tawny hadn't been lying when she'd said the girl hated sunshine.

The large veranda was covered and afforded an amount of shade. Moving under the cover of the cabana, he set Amy on the ground, the girl covering her eyes with her hands, then eventually lowering them. "Meedle!" she yelled.

Denny went back and retrieved the bread from the ground, handing it to Amy without thought. She scooted farther back in the shadows and sat happily munching on the dirty bread.

As soon as Denny had turned loose of her, he felt his spirits sink once more, as if some measure of his confidence rested in Amy's touch. It made no sense. He shook it off, trying to wake himself up again, and walked to where Frank had knelt down behind a small fence at the edge of the lawn.

Denny peered over the fence. Frank was working on a motor of some kind with tools he had acquired from God knows where.

"You need to put a warning label on that coffee of yours," Denny said. "You're going to kill someone with it one day."

"I drink it to git awake," Frank said as he tightened a bolt on the side of the motor. "No use goin' halfway."

"I want to thank you for keeping control of Tawny last night."

The man stopped working and squinted up into the sunshine rising over Denny's left shoulder. "She was up most of the night," he said, putting up a hand to shade his eyes. "Done a shitload of talkin'. She ain't had no easy time, Denny."

"I'm sure," Denny replied.

"And that little girl's her whole life." He turned to the motor, reaching out a finger to twirl the cooling fan blade. "Don't seem right that we got her trussed up like we do."

"If you can tell me how to keep them separated," Denny said, "I'll cut her loose right now."

"We don't got the right to keep her away from that girl."

"I don't think we've got the right to do anything else," Denny answered. "What are you working on?"

Frank stood, uncoiling his lean frame like a rearing cobra. "The pool filter motor had froze up," he said. "I was just puttin' it back in order."

"I think sometimes that you like machines more than you do people." He turned and looked back at the house, wondering if it was worth the trouble to go back in and get his abandoned coffee.

"Machines are dependable," Frank said, walking over to the Texas-shaped pool and staring down into the dark, greenish water. "Their motivations are right out there in front, their needs limited and predictable. A fellow can git to know a machine." He turned to Denny. "Is it safe to leave Amy out here around the pool?"

"She won't go into the sun," he replied. "No problem."

The man nodded gravely. "People are somethin' else again," he said. "They think one thin' and say another, or they git all worked up about stuff that don't matter. How can you figure that?"

Denny walked over to stand beside him, looking down at his own shimmering reflection in the dank water. "If you're trying to tell me that the world's fucked up you can save your breath. We make our living from the craziness, remember?"

"Yeah . . . maybe," Frank said. He coughed, then spit loudly into the pool, ripples extending across their reflections, breaking their images into thousands of pieces. Both men stared silently for a time before Frank spoke again.

"When I was with CBS," he said, "they sent me to Nam when Walter Cronkite went over in '68. We seen some stuff that really shook us up. Guess that was when Walter went on back to New York and told America that they was crazy for supportin' the war and everybody stopped . . . just like that. Even Johnson said that if he'd lost Cronkite, he'd lost America and pulled himself out of the '68 race. Anyhow, I stayed behind to take pictures, you know?"

Denny nodded, afraid to break the mood. He'd never heard Hargrave talk about the war before.

"Well, I shot so much film—we used film in them days— that it just got to be a kind of overkill. How much film do you roll before you realize that war's not for shit? Anyhow, I got to where I wasn't relatin' to any of it. I was just an eye on the lens, and that ain't the way for nobody to be.

"I finally went and got myself caught in a firefight up near Chu Lai. It went on for three days and by the time it was done, nobody wanted the footage cause it was too gross for prime time and the shit that wasn't gross looked like all their file footage, so I put down the camera and helped them fill body bags with the meat from both sides. We filled body bags till our arms were numb and our backs were stooped and we were covered all over with other people's guts. We filled body bags so long that I started in to hatin' the meat we was shovin' in the plastic, and I hated them so much I wished I could bring them all back to life so I could kill them again." He stopped talking and looked Denny in the eye. "Ain't that a hell of a note?"

"You became desensitized," Denny answered. "You did it to keep from going crazy."

"That ain't the point!" Frank said loudly, then calmed. "The point is we shouldn't do that to ourselves or nobody else. We're human bein's for God's sake. We don't have to act like animals."

"You're telling me this for a reason," Denny said.

"I am indeed," Frank said. On impulse, the man sat at the edge of the pool and laboriously pulled off his cowboy boots and socks. Then he rolled up his jeans, slipping his legs over the edge of the Texas panhandle to dangle in the shallow end. "I walked away from it all in Nam, Denny, and started lettin' the camera be my heart and soul. It's easy you know; that big old unblinkin' eye is its own kind of life, its own viewpoint. Things on tape aren't like things in real life. It's purer somehow. It stands alone from the craziness."

Denny squatted beside him, hoping this wasn't the pre-amble to a walkaway. He needed Frank. He really needed Frank. "I don't know if I can do this without you," he said. "Without you, I don't know what will happen to those women."

"I already figured that," the man replied, "and I already figured that if I had to come back, you're the only one I'd do it for, but God, Denny, you don't know what you're askin'. Comin' back's one thing . . . but a situation like this . . ."

"You're doing fine," Denny said glibly. "Really."

The man turned and stared at him. "We been too close for you to hype me, pardner."

"I'm sorry," Denny said. "I'm just that desperate to keep you here with me. I'm literally afraid of what will happen if I have to turn loose of the Kyles."

"CBS let me go cause they said I was crazy," Frank said. "I spent time in Bellevue and I spent time in Parkland and I spent time in an Air Force hospital in Guam—all of it in the psycho ward. Sometimes I dream at night that I'm bein' eaten alive and that I'm nothin' but a giant eyeball. You still want me?"

"It's not a question of wants, Frank," Denny said.

"What is it a question of?" Molly asked. Denny turned to her. She'd changed into a loose and attractive sundress, but still hadn't done anything with her hair. Something was odd about her, but not odd enough to be able to get a fix on it.

"Let's get out of the sun," Denny said, straightening on stiff knees. He walked back toward the veranda; Teddy the dog was inside the house, jumping at the patio door. Amy had seated herself primly on a redwood chair and was rubbing what was left of her meedle all over her as if it were a washrag. Denny took a chair fifteen feet from her, as close as he could get without feeling at least a tingle of vibration.

Molly pulled up a chair near Denny, Frank opting for a

cross-woven recliner on an aluminum frame. The man stretched out, putting his arms behind his head and crossing his bootless feet at the ankles.

"Pretend this is a production meeting," Denny said. "I don't know any other way to approach it as quickly as we need to."

"Well, as your producer," Molly said, "I urge you to drop this before you lose your objectivity. This process may be cost effective and timely, but it's sensationalism, not news. It's not worth your stepping over the line journalistically. If we're voting . . . I say we cut and run."

Who and what do you think Amy Kyle is?" he asked her.

The woman folded her arms thoughtfully and searched for a real answer. "I think it's possible that she's God," Molly said after a moment.

"The discovery of God isn't newsworthy?" Denny asked.

"Not in this world, Denny," she replied. "Nobody here wants to see God."

"Are you serious?" he asked loudly. "*Everybody* wants to see her."

"They just think they do. They don't . . . not really."

"You think she's got power?" he asked.

"Beyond measure."

"What happens if we turn loose of her, then?"

"It's not our problem."

Denny turned to Hargrave. "How about you, Frank? What do you think?"

"I think Molly's scared, but not scared enough," the man said. "I think that if Molly was as scared as me, then she'd be a lot more worried about what happens to Amy and her mom after we're done with them. We may not've asked for this, but we're stuck with it now and I'm just hopin' that we figure out somethin' to do with them girls before we're discovered. She's a wish stone, Denny, but they ain't no good wishes, not a one."

Denny turned directly toward Molly. "I can't look at it any other way than Frank does," he said. "I note your objections . . . I don't even say you're wrong, but I'm scared shitless over the thought of somebody else getting control of those women. Hell, I'm even scared of Tawny anymore."

"Maybe we should just kill them and be done with it like Charlie suggested," Molly said quietly.

"What!" Denny said.

The woman sat stiffly in her chair, her face strained. "You

think I don't understand the implications," she said. "You're wrong. And I am afraid. I'm afraid for us and I'm afraid . . . for the baby. I've never been so afraid before. It's just like in the movies: we're in a car with no brakes speeding out of control down a mountain road. The outcome is inevitable, it's simply a question of how many turns we can survive."

"I don't accept that," Denny said. "We're alive, we've got brains, we're clever . . . we can think of something."

Molly stood and walked over to stare at Amy. She reached out as if she were going to touch the child, but recoiled at the last second. She turned back to Denny. "Has the thought occurred to you that this might somehow be . . . destined to happen? That we may be playing out some . . . I don't know, karmic manifestation."

"No it hasn't," Denny said. "And it's not going to. You may think that Amy's God, and the whole rest of the world might think it, but to me she's just a little girl with a big problem. Don't go getting all New Age on me, sweetheart. We don't need that right now."

"You have the answers for everything, don't you," she said bitterly.

"This is gettin' us nowhere," Frank said. "Fact is, we got to decide right now whether or not we're goin' to fly with this thin', and for the life of me, I don't see what choices we got."

"Me either," Denny said, looking at Molly the whole time. "I'm in up to my elbows."

"What do you want me to say?" she asked.

"Stay or go," Denny said. "In or out. It's simple. I can use you and I want you here, but you need to follow your own conscience. Take a walk now if that's how you're disposed. I'll see to it that you have the cash to get away from here for a while. Otherwise, we lay battle plans."

Molly moved to him, kneeling beside his chair. She gripped his arm tightly with trembling hands. "Last week," she said, "I thought I understood you . . . and us and our relationship. Today I'm scared and confused. Let's put all the bullshit aside. Denny, I love you and I want to be with you. I understand the importance of this and I have a serious professional interest in it, but God, for the last three nights I've been dreaming about death—"

"You, too?" Denny asked.

Her face drained of color. "Isn't there any way out of this?" she pleaded softly.

Denny's fist was clenched tightly on the arm she held. He

fought to ignore her touch and the pulsating waves of negative energy he sensed coming from Amy. He shook his head. "Not for me," he said. "Charlie walked away, but I don't believe that's going to be as easy as he thinks. We're screwed, Molly. We've got the power, but it may be like trying to control one of Frank's tornadoes. If you want out, I'll understand and make it as easy for you as possible."

"Would you forgive me if I left?" she asked.

He looked hard at her. "Probably not," he said.

She stood and returned to her seat, her face set in resignation. "Let's try and handle this as intelligently as we possibly can," she said.

"The first problem is in settin' Tawny free," Frank said. "I take it you want me to keep her occupied, but we're goin' to have to let her go soon for me to be able to."

"What if we built something at the top of the stairs that would keep her from getting down?" Molly asked. "That way, she could have the upstairs and Amy the down."

The man nodded. "I seen some stuff in the garage," he said. "Maybe I can whip up somethin'."

"Good," Denny said. "Look. I don't know how else to say this, but I think we're all going to have to resign ourselves to a long stay here. Obviously we'll have to get out sometime, but we'll have to handle that carefully. A good deal of outside contact might have to be handled by you, Molly. You've been the least seen on the air and are the least recognized. Maybe a different hairstyle and makeup will help you if you have to go on the streets for food or whatever."

"I need to make a doctor's appointment," she said. "I'll have to—"

"No," Denny said. "We can't have you in one place that long. We'll work something out later. I'll make a list for you in a bit. We'll send you out on a foray in disguise and try to stock up everything we need to stay holed up. As near as I can figure, there's a massive manhunt going on for us right now, and I'm afraid of what will happen if we're discovered. Not everyone is happy with us, you know."

"How long will this go on?" Molly asked.

Denny scratched his head. "I can't imagine," he said. "We might know better after tonight's broadcast."

"Are you still intent on replacing Tawny as Amy's channel?" Molly asked.

"We can't use Tawny anymore," Denny said, standing to

walk over to the girl. "Amy responds to me. What choice do we have?"

"This might kill Tawny," Frank said. "You sure you want to go through with this?"

"I don't want Tawny within ten feet of her daughter," Denny said. "A second touching her could be too long." He stared at the girl. She was dirty, her face smeared with grime and food crumbs. He turned back to Molly. "Can you bathe Amy?"

The woman's eyes were hollow. "I won't touch her, Denny," she said, embarrassed, then looking down. "I—I can't."

"Why not?"

"Number one, she may not let me. Number two, I just . . . can't."

"That's not an answer," he snapped.

She took a long breath, idly smoothing her skirt as she searched for the right words. "You're not a believer in anything except yourself," she said. "From your viewpoint this is all simple and straightforward. I wish I could be like you, but I can't. I guess my free-thinking independence isn't all it's cracked up to be. My life is all wound up with notions of God and Heaven . . . it's all probably very silly to you, but to me, I've got to have some reassurance that this isn't the end of things, this . . . thing we call life." Her eyes traveled nervously from Amy to Denny and back again. "That girl's power is a Divine thing to me, but I haven't figured out whether she's God or . . . or . . ."

"This isn't religious," Denny said.

"Denny, I love you," she said, "but your point of view isn't any more informed than mine, or than Jim Connover's for that matter."

"She's right," Frank said. "The smoke you're blowin' out your ass ain't any whiter than ours."

"We've got to proceed without notions, though," Denny said. "This is a search for Truth. We've go to keep it that way. If Amy Kyle turns out to be God, I'll be the first one to slaughter a calf and tell her how wrong I was. In the meantime, we treat this as much as possible as a scientific experiment. Frank, your job is to record everything the girl does and try and keep her mother out of trouble. Molly, you'll handle everything mechanical to do with this, everything logistical, plus running the camera when Frank's in the mobile unit."

"What's your job?" Frank asked.

"Working with Amy," Denny answered, "and trying to figure out ways to test her power that won't backfire on us or anybody else. I'll be happy to switch with anyone else if you like."

As Denny expected, there were no takers. They adjourned after that, Frank hurrying to the garage to try and find the means of making a more comfortable prison for Tawny. Denny felt badly about the woman, but he felt badly for all of them. They were all trapped in a bad situation with only their wits and their sense of decency to sustain them. Tawny, without self-control of any kind, was about the most dangerous exponent he could imagine in his little controlled environment, and prison seemed almost too good for her at this point. He wished he could trust her, but she had the kind of egocentric and addictive personality that made it totally impossible. If he could think beyond the next couple of hours, he'd probably wonder about how Amy and her mother could *ever* get together again. But at this point, his only thoughts revolved around immediate survival.

He carried Amy back into the house, and found himself fighting sexual yearnings again. To escape her, he practically ran through the kitchen, dropping her back in the den with her mother, his thoughts dwelling hard on the images of body bags that Frank had conjured for him.

No sooner than he'd left the girl, the dog was all over him again. It was insane with passion for him, and though he tried to ignore the animal, he felt that it would be literally impossible for him to ever love it enough. It lived to be near him, like some kind of monstrous joke revolving around love potions and excesses. He moved toward the phone, the dog jumping at him the whole time. Finally he picked it up and set it out back, the cocker immediately throwing himself against the patio door, trying to break through it to get to Denny.

He found a phone book in a small kitchen desk, and turned it to the yellow pages under doctors. He picked a name at random and dialed the number. A woman answered on the fourth ring.

"Dr. Moreland, please," he said.

"I'm sorry," the receptionist said. "The doctor is with a patient right now. Can I help you?"

"I must speak with the doctor immediately. Will you please tell him it is a matter of the most extreme urgency."

"I'll need more information than that," the woman replied in a no-nonsense voice. "Perhaps if you told me a little, Mr.—"

"I can't give you my name," Denny said. "I'm well known and I must have total secrecy. Please. It's really important."

"Let me speak with the doctor," the receptionist answered, then put him on hold, a solid dose of elevator music drifting through his handset. Within three minutes a gruff voice cut through the music.

"You are taking away from someone's time, sir," a man said. "This had better be good."

"I want you to make a house call," Denny said.

"I'm hanging up in ten seconds," Moreland said.

"My name is Denny Stiller. I picked you at random from the phone book and need your help desperately."

"You're *the* Dennis Stiller?"

"I am, and I need you to examine someone."

"Is it possibly the same someone who has been on television recently?"

"Yes, sir, it is. I'm giving you the opportunity to psychoanalyze God. It isn't a joke; it isn't a prank. I need to pick you up tonight and take you to a secret location. Believe me this is the real thing. Can you do it?"

"What do you expect of me?"

"Simply an evaluation, something you can give me in a couple of hours."

"I can't give you much of anything in a couple of hours. Psychiatry is precise—"

"Noted. We'll just have to work with what we have. Are you in?"

"I'll have to cancel my group tonight . . ."

"Are you in, doctor?"

"Only a fool would say no. What time?"

"Be at your office at seven P.M.," Denny said, looking at his watch. They had so much to do before the broadcast. "Someone will pick you up. This is the last message you'll receive from me. Tell no one what you're doing."

He hung up, not having the time to become embroiled in a long-winded conversation with the man. Denny moved into the kitchen, just glancing out the window. Molly was still out there. She seemed to be kneeling by the pool, her head bent in . . . prayer? In all the time he'd known her, she'd shown absolutely no religious leanings until the discovery of Amy Kyle.

He walked away from the window, not sure of what to think, and poked his head in the den. The TV was still on, Miller Stetts, the daytime anchor, gravely reading the news. He moved in and turned up the sound, totally ignoring Tawny, as Amy lay on the floor by her chair, rocking it wildly with a hand on the runner.

". . . is the top story this hour," Stetts was saying. "Texas Governor Clements has ordered the mobilization of the Texas National Guard and says he is ready to call them in if the situation doesn't improve rapidly in the Dallas area. The incredible influx of people joining the search for Tawny Kyle has sorely taxed all of Dallas County, the mayor establishing a curfew for people on foot after dark. The next step will be the declaration of martial law. The crowds have been large and unruly, as these scenes will show."

The picture switched to a montage of shots, Denny watching them with a sickening feeling in the pit of his stomach. He recognized Tawny's trailer as huge orange flames licked out of the windows of the thing, the metal buckling under the incredible heat. Then he saw his own apartment, ransacked, totally gutted, then Molly's apartment torn to pieces. Next came Charlie's house and even shots of riot police trying to keep a huge mob away from his law offices. Everyone was going nuts.

Stett's voice droned above the scenes that seemed straight out of a wartime nightmare. "Mobs descended upon the residences of all the people involved with Tawny Kyle, a combination of the curious, the devout, and the opposition. They either took or destroyed, all of them looking for evidence, the anonymity of the crowd, and its power, making destruction casual and justified. The studios of WCN have been under a virtual state of siege for the last few days now, the crowds outside growing to incredible numbers."

Denny watched, spellbound, as an ariel shot showed many thousands of people jamming up to the WCN gates, more people than he could have believed possible. The scene switched to a handheld camera shot panning the crowds from close-up. They carried banners and prayed together. They were poor people, people inflicted with illness and deformity, people beyond all hope. And there were others—stoic-faced people with sunburns and Ku Klux Klan robes and banners condemning, always condemning. They screamed at those gathered, shaking their fists, here and there fights breaking out as self-styled preachers of the religion of Tawny moved through the crowds, preaching her salvation over the jeers and the ballpark cants of the food vendors who worked their way through it all, the bridge between the scoffers and the believers. Denny could only shake his head.

The picture switched once again to Stetts, the man smiling grimly. "And I'd like to announce again," he said, "that our own Dennis Stiller will go on the air live tonight at ten P.M. Central Daylight Time to answer the charges of fraud leveled at him by World Ministries Chief Executive Officer, Dr. James Connover. Mr. Stiller promises that all charges will be dealt with beyond a shadow of a doubt. And that shadow, right now, looms large."

Denny watched more airborne pictures of the crowds around WCN, the impressive size of the mob backfeeding legitimacy and scope to the entire operation, taking it out of place and time and making it larger that itself, larger than life. He remembered something that Edward R. Murrow had said years before about stories told on the medium of television. "What seemed to concern television was not the horror of the atomic bomb," he'd remarked, "but the unique picture it makes."

The crowds on the screen were large and beautiful—and deadly.

Scene 3

(later that evening)

CLOSE UP—IDENTICAL MALE TWIN FACES. The twins
are singing a country and western song, "Act Naturally," the
twangy accompaniment loud in the bg. They are all smiles and
TV plastic hair and dressed in checkered shirts with fake
mother-of-pearl buttons as they hold opposite hands up to
their headphones and strain toward the sock-covered, hanging
mikes.

GAYLER (os)

Limit the multiplexes and cut three musicians from
the rest of the tracks.

TECHNICIAN (os)

The number of musicians is set in the McClain's contract. Ben's gonna raise holy hell over it.

GAYLER (os)

Their last album barely earned out its recording
costs. Tell them to sue me if they don't like it.

ANGLE—INSIDE A RECORDING BOOTH. We are looking
out a large picture window at the McClain Brothers recording.
The sound of the music is considerably lower in the booth.
Although a great many instruments are strewn around the
studio, the twins are the only ones present. Watching from our
vantage point are TED GAYLER and JAMES CONNOVER, a
technician sits before a large control board, monitoring sound
levels.

GAYLER (cont)

Limit to three rerecords, too. Tell them to rehearse

199

on their own time. If they can't sell records by this point, they need to be learning a trade anyway.

The song ends, the McClains laughing and slapping each other on the back. Gayler walks to the control board and leans down to a mike, switching it on.

GAYLER (cont)

Great boys! Hope you've got a lot of space on your walls for gold records.

The McClains smile and wave, one of them giving the thumbs-up sign. The technician takes the mike as Gayler walks away from it.

TECHNICIAN

Great guys . . . let's go once more from the top, harmony only.

The music starts up again, Gayler leading Connover through a doorway in the back of the booth.
ANGLE—OFFICE. A man in a sharkskin suit sits at a cluttered desk, talking on the telephone and drinking coffee from a Styrofoam cup. He is STAN MEIRS, the McClains' agent. The office is piled high with junk. Album covers and promotional material cover the walls, but no gold records. As he talks, GAYLER and CONNOVER enter the room.

MEIRS

No, no . . . I want adjoining rooms, double beds in each, that's the way we laid out the frigging contract. . . . Because Wesley and Wesley can't stand each other offstage and if you don't keep them apart they're going to get blood all over your stage, ruin the rest of the frigging run and save me about eighty headaches next year. . . . Yeah . . . (he looks up and sees Gayler and Connover enter) Look, I gotta go. . . . Yeah. (he hangs up phone) Aren't they sounding incredible out there? I tell you Mr. Gayler, I think they've really got it together this time. The boys have been working their hearts out and I think are beginning to hit their stride.

GAYLER
(cold)
That's what I'm afraid of.

MEIRS
(undaunted)
I think that when we negotiate the new contract, we
should go for the full orchestra effect, you know? A
lot of artists made it big when they started using the
big sound. I've got some ideas—

GAYLER
I need the office, Mr. Meirs. Do you mind?

MEIRS
(standing) No, no, sir. I know you're a busy man.
We'll just chat later.

The man grabs his coffee and exits into the studio, Gayler
moving behind the desk immediately and sitting down. Connover sits in a straight-backed chair near the desk.

GAYLER
(sternly)
Now, Jim. You know that we decided not to meet
during the working out of this Stiller deal. What's so
important that you had to see me?

CONNOVER
I'm really sorry, but I just don't understand what's
going on. I sent to your station this morning unignor-
able evidence that Stiller and that woman were committing fraud, yet you still insist on letting them go
on the air tonight.

GAYLER
You sent me evidence that Tawny Kyle has a prison
record . . . not evidence of fraud.

CONNOVER
(angrily)
It's the same thing! That woman's a common tramp
and you know it. How can you let her go on acting as
if she's under orders from God Almighty?

GAYLER
No one has said this has anything to do with religion.

CONNOVER
These people claim miracles . . . the source of all
miracles is Jesus Christ. This entire episode is blasphemy of the highest order. I'm surprised at you.

GAYLER
(smiling)
Is it cutting into your donations, Jim?

CONNOVER
That's not the point. You are using a national forum
to promote fraud and it's going to come home to
roost. Why do you persist?

GAYLER
I'm not so sure it's a fraud, is why. I put Stiller on it
so he could tear it apart and now he's selling it. I put
you on it to rouse national ire and dig up the dirt,
but all you've done is focus more interest. I'm not
going to turn loose of this thing, Jim. If I'm
convinced beyond doubt that the power is genuine,
then I'm going to be in a position to control it.

CONNOVER
But, it can't be real. Things like this just don't happen. God would never allow it.

GAYLER
You speak for God, Jim?

CONNOVER
Yes, I do.

GAYLER

You'll excuse me if I just apply that statement to your ratings book and make my own decisions about the future of Tawny Kyle. God is as God does. I do have one bit of information that may perk your day up, though. I've maneuvered Stiller into making an appearance with the woman where her powers can be tested on TV by experts.

CONNOVER

Are you going to include me?

GAYLER

Most certainly. How is Larry coming with locating our wayward boy?

CONNOVER

He thinks he may have results tonight. He's dogging that Jew lawyer, what's his name . . . Kornfeld.

GAYLER

Good. I can't stress enough the importance of getting these people under our thumb. In other matters, I spoke to our man in Bogotá yesterday.

CONNOVER
(brightening noticeably)
Did everything go all right?

GAYLER

Exchange went well, and things are set at point of delivery for tonight. The president is happy, and quarterly earnings should be rolling into the Bumper fund in a few days.

CONNOVER

Thank God. I always sweat these things.

GAYLER

Now . . . if only Larry would have some luck. . . .

CUT TO:
ANGLE—LARRY GATES. He's dressed in a three-piece gray suit and wears dark glasses and doeskin black gloves. He's leaning against the driver's door of a late-model Ford, talking to a swarthy-looking man behind the wheel. The car is parked in front of a run-down bar called the RED RACE LOUNGE. We're in the homosexual-hippie-Mexican-Indian run-down section of Dallas called Oak Lawn. Despite Larry's sunglasses, dusk has descended, the sky streaky, pastel pink and dark blue. The streets are full of people, most of them looking for a way to get off the streets before the rapidly approaching curfew arrives. Gates is LEANING DOWN to speak to the man, but isn't facing him. His attention is drawn by an innocuous Buick parked beside the Ford.

LARRY

You sure this is the car?

MAN

I double-checked it through the rental agency. He used his credit card and left his Mercedes parked at the lot. You want me to go in with you?

LARRY

Naw. You stay out here and keep an eye on things. I won't be long.

CUT TO:
ANGLE—PAY PHONE IN BAR. We see CHARLES KORN-FELD talking on the phone attached to the wall, which is covered with penciled-in numbers and obscenities. Smoky darkness fills the bg as he covers his free ear to try and keep down the loud, heavy metal music that pounds through the place.

KORNFELD

Good God, Myron. Give me a break . . . just for tonight. The hotels are all full of these freaks. I had to sleep in my fucking car last night! . . . Yes . . . I saw what they did to my house. . . . Look I'm at my wit's end right now. I just need a place to sleep for tonight. I promise there won't be any problems . . . Great. . . . Thanks, Myron, and thank Jan, too. Promise her I'll make

sure I'm not followed. I came to you because nobody
would connect it. Thanks.

Shaking his head, Kornfeld HANGS UP. He turns toward the
bar area, then turns back around and heads through a door
marked MEN.

ANGLE—MEN'S ROOM. Kornfeld walks in, grimacing in
disgust at the filth and the smell. There is one urinal full of
cigarette butts and a stall beside it with the door ripped off. He
moves quickly to the dirty porcelain sink with the cracked
mirror and begins WASHING HIS HANDS.

VOICE (os)
(a whisper)
Welcome to hell, Counselor.

ANGLE—MIRROR. Kornfeld looks into the mirror and sees
the reflection of Gates behind him. The man is HOLDING A
GUN.

KORNFELD
You must have me confused with someone else.

Gates walks up behind him and JAMS the gun in his back.

GATES
(menacing)
You and I are going to take a little ride, Counselor.
You're going to show me where your friend, Denny,
lives.

Kornfeld turns to him, arms outstretched, face expansive.

KORNFELD
(exasperated)
Now isn't this silly? Come on, fella. This whole thing
has really gotten blown way out of propor—

Gates SLAMS Charlie viciously in the midsection with the
barrel of the gun, doubling him over, Charlie GAGGING
loudly.

GATES

The hard way or the easy way. It makes no difference
to me. Now come on.

He grabs Charlie by the arm and begins jerking him up. At
that moment, the door bangs open and two men in jeans and
flannel shirts and ball caps walk in. One is Mexican, the other
a Navaho Indian. Gates hides the gun under his suit coat as the
men, obviously drunk, smile broadly at him and Charlie.

NAVAHO

Hey, don't mind us. We don't give a shit what you're
doin' in here.

Kornfeld straightens, thinking quickly and knowing this is his
chance to escape.

KORNFELD
(solicitously)
Don't you guys recognize me? I'm Charlie Kornfeld,
you know, the miracle guy.

MEXICAN

Wait . . . you *are* him. Did that woman really put
that new hair on your head? (he pulls off his ball cap
to thinning hair) I could really use a little of that myself.

KORNFELD
(tugging at his hair)
She sure did. How about you guys letting me buy
you a drink?

NAVAHO
(drunkenly)
You bet, man . . . hey . . . how about lettin' us
take you outside to meet some of our friends. They
ain't gonna believe us if you don't. Man the whole
city's lookin' for you and here you are in this crappy
pisser.

They all laugh, except for Gates, who has backed up against the wall, his hand in his jacket, a terrible darkness settled upon his face. Kornfeld WINKS at him and heads for the door.

> ### KORNFELD
> Let's go right now.

> ### MEXICAN
> Hey, man. I gotta piss.

> ### KORNFELD
> Hold it a minute.

He walks out the door, his new friends right behind, Gates following closely, his hand still in his coat. The strange entourage moves through the dingy bar and out the red door to the streets.

ANGLE—FORD. Gates's man, frowning, climbs out of the car when he sees Kornfeld and the others.
ANGLE—KORNFELD AND FRIENDS. Charlie is studiously looking for a way out.

> ### MEXICAN
> Look what we found! Tomas! Russell!

A crowd quickly gathers, everyone talking excitedly, more coming all the time. Gates and his man try to edge up, but can't make their way through the excited crowd. People are yelling, asking for things, Charlie trying to explain it to them.

> ### KORNFELD
> Hey, I'm nobody! I've got no power.

> ### MEXICAN
> But where are your friends, man?

> ### KORNFELD
> I can't tell you where they are. Give me a break!

> ### NAVAHO
> You want to keep it all for yourself, white asshole

lawyer. Aren't we good enough to get your white
man's miracles?

The crowd roars its agreement. Many of them have come from
far away to find Denny Stiller and Tawny Kyle.

MEXICAN
(angry)

My family *needs* miracles. Why don't you have some
for us. Why do you need miracles for? Come on, tell
us where to find the woman . . . we won't tell nobody else, right?

A crowd of over a hundred roars its agreement, all of them
pressing in close, reaching for Charlie, grabbing his clothes,
grabbing his hair. Charlie looks around frantically. He can
smell their need, nearly taste their desires. This is the closest
any of them have ever been to realizing a dream and they're
not about to let him get away. He only has one chance and
knows it.

KORNFELD

All right . . . all right. Let me get the address out
of my car.

The crowd still roaring around him, he walks the small path
they have allowed him to get to the car. He moves in the
narrow alley between his rented Buick and the car belonging
to Gates's man and wishes he were wearing his running shoes.
He takes out the keys and unlocks the door, then SWINGS it
wide, BANGING the man right behind him. Without a
backward look, he RUNS.

The crowd gives chase as Charlie hits the middle of the
street, heading for Inman Road, two blocks away. They are
charging, yelling, a terrible commotion. Charlie is practiced,
faster, but more people keep joining the hunt from the crowds
on the streets.

ANGLE—INMAN ROAD. From the middle of the street, we
are watching Charlie a block and a half away making his
desperate bid for freedom. He is charging right toward us,
then entire street behind him filled with screaming people. As

he gets closer, the crowds fill our vision. They are no longer
humans. They are the living embodiment of the mob, a single,
intense organism, pulsating with its own kind of life and we,
long before Charlie, realize that his flight is destined to fail. As
he approaches we see the fear on his face, our entire line of
vision now filled with running people. A huge black man
breaks from the crowd and closes in on Charlie. The man
towers over him, his long, loping strides quickly closing the
distance, and just as Charlie is about to reach us, the man puts
out a long arm and GRABS HIM BY THE HAIR..
FREEZE-FRAME. Charlie being jerked back by the hair, his
face contorted in fear and pain. Hold for several beats.
CUT TO:
CLOSE-UP—MOLLY. Her eyes are wide in shock, a trembling hand held to her mouth.

> ### TV ANNOUNCER (os)
> . . . was then apparently trampled to death by the
> large crowd of spectators. Mr. Kornfeld, a well-
> known and flamboyant attorney here in the Dallas
> area was pronounced dead at the scene. In a grisly
> aside, Kornfeld was apparently scalped by the crowd,
> pieces of his hair and scalp then sold to onlookers as
> souveniers.

Molly listens silently, face transfixed. A single tear edges out of
the corner of her eye and slides gracefully down her right
cheek.

Denny Stiller sat at the scoring table in front of the single
bowling lane that graced the far end of the converted basement. He stared across the carpeted floor to the bright area of
light fifty feet distant that defined the exercise section. Amy
Kyle and Dr. Moreland, the psychiatrist, sat on the floor in the
midst of the shiny stainless steel equipment and harsh lights
playing with blocks. The rec room was comfortable and
inviting. Its walls were warmly paneled, its pool and Ping-
Pong tables active and accessible. There was a wet bar, a
storage freezer, and even a mechanical bull covered with
cobwebs, a holdover from urban cowboy days.
Amy screamed loudly in exasperation and threw a handful
of the blocks, Lincoln Logs, across the carpet, the doctor

calmly gathering them up and bringing them back to her. What good any of this did, Denny couldn't imagine, but he looked forward to Moreland's input and help. It gave him the illusion of not taking on the world all by himself.

For his part, Stiller was scared and confused. He was getting ready to put himself smack in the middle of the controversy, a move from which there'd be no escape. By pushing Tawny Kyle out of the picture he was pushing himself in—for keeps—and that was frightening. For he didn't see any simple wind-down to this story.

He looked at his watch. It was twenty minutes before airtime. He'd have to stop the examination. The doctor was unhappy at having to diagnose in such a short period of time, but that couldn't be helped. A small 8-mm video camera sat on a tripod filming Moreland's examination. Perhaps reference to it could help in the future.

As he stood, he saw light spill down the stairway from upstairs, Molly walking vacantly down, her face a bloodless mask. Something was wrong.

He hurried to the woman, intercepting her at the bottom of the stairs. "Molly?" he asked quietly.

Her eyes looked at, but through, him. "Charlie's dead," she said.

He felt the blow fall on him, but he absorbed it. He was surprised at his own inner defenses, surprised at his lack of feelings. "What happened?" he asked.

"A mob got hold of him," she said in a monotone. "They trampled him, they . . . scalped him."

The floodgates broke then. Molly, sobbing loudly, threw herself into Denny's arms, the man looking at his watch over her shoulder. His heart was breaking for Charlie, but he simply couldn't give his emotions over now. They didn't have time for this.

He pulled her slightly away from him, finding her eyes. "Did he give us away?" he asked.

Her eyes narrowed and she jerked out of his grasp. "He's *dead* Denny! Didn't you hear me? They've killed Charlie and they're going to kill us!"

"Not if they can't find us," Denny said. "Now, do you know if Charlie gave them any information before he died."

She began crying again. "I don't know," she said. "I-I don't think so."

"Okay." He paced quickly, Molly sitting on the bottom step

and staring straight ahead, at nothing. It was horrible about
Charlie, but the man had brought it on himself by not taking
the whole thing seriously enough. In a sense, Denny was
almost relieved. Now he wouldn't have to worry about Charlie
giving them away. The whole affair just convinced him anew
that he was right for maintaining total secrecy. He looked
down at Molly. He had not time for a breakdown from her,
either.

"Get yourself together," he told her. "Go up to the studio
and make sure everything's set."

"Denny—" she began, but he cut her off.

"We've got an airtime to meet," he said. "Pretend it's a war.
Pretend the stock market's crashed. We've got to get out a
report and I need you coherent."

She looked at him blankly, then stood and reclimbed the
steps.

"That's enough, doctor!" Denny called across the room to
Moreland. "We've got to put this on the air in fifteen minutes."
He moved toward them, ready to speed them along. But it
wasn't necessary. The doctor was already gathering his notes
and equipment together.

"Will I at least get to talk to her mother?" Moreland asked.
"There is so much . . ."

"No," Denny said. "This is it, all there is. Are you willing
to go on the air and tell what you've discovered?"

The small man stared for a moment, thoughtfully stroking
his salt-and-pepper beard. His eyes were alive and dancing
beneath a stoic, soft skinned face. "Are you the girl's legal
guardian?" he asked.

"I have power of attorney over all of her affairs," Denny
replied.

"And you give me permission to disregard the doctor-
patient relationship and release this information to the world?"

"Yes, sir."

The man smiled. "Well, the notoriety can hardly do me any
professional harm if you will let me explain fully my thoughts
and if you let me begin with a disclaimer saying I didn't have
the proper time or facilities to conduct an in-depth examination."

"You've got it," Denny replied. "Now let's get upstairs. You
and I will talk on the air. We'll discover together."

As the man moved toward the steps, Denny walked to
Amy, who sat between a pair of Nautilus arms, her hands

moving rapidly up and down the reflective steel as if she were grabbing for her distorted image. He picked her up gently, feeling the sting of contact immediately. Once, in college, he had tried heroin just to see what it was like. The rush of sensation experienced as the drug ran through the blood-stream was not unlike the sensation of touching Amy. What bothered him more was that, like with an addictive drug, her touch was something that he looked forward to. The exhilarating rush of sensation was something he found himself missing and wanting more of. He was like a cigarette smoker trying to quit, promising himself only one after dinner.

He carried her quickly upstairs, wanting her out of his hands before she began manipulating the sensations. As he carried her, she put her arms around his neck, holding tight. It was the first time she'd ever done it, the first time she had ever related to him physically.

The basement stairs exited into the hallway leading to the steam room-studio. He carried her into the room, quickly setting her on the redwood bench that wound around the inside of the thing. Dr. Moreland sat a little farther down the bench, looking slightly nervous as his hands came up to tug on his red bow tie.

It looked like a real studio now. Frank had earlier put on a punk disguise complete with pink, spiked hair and had made a foray out into the world against Denny's better judgment, returning with a great deal of equipment and enough food to last them for a month. He had set up a number of low intensity spots that pointed toward the studio ceiling, diffusing the light and softening it for the camera to make Amy look angelic. A small boom mike hung over the center of the room. A real monitor sat beside the camera, showing a picture of the floor, where the camera was presently pointed. Frank had somehow managed to acquire a large clock with a sweep second hand. It looked like a giant pocket watch complete with gold chain dangling, its face Roman numerals. It was mounted directly onto the knotty pine walls in camera range.

Molly fiddled with the camera, bending to the viewfinder. She was doing Frank's job while he handled transmission. She'd ignored Denny when he'd come in. He didn't have the time or the inclination to deal with anything complicated from her at the moment. As long as she ran the camera effectively, everything would be fine.

A small makeup mirror on a vanity was set up just out of

camera range. Denny moved to it and applied light makeup.
As he powdered, he caught Moreland's reflection in the glass.
"Don't worry about it, Doc," he said. "It'll be just fine."

"When do I go on?" the man asked.

"Pretty near the top," Denny said. "I have a small announcement to make, then we'll talk to you right away. Okay?
I appreciate you coming right up here, by the way, and not
trying to get a look outside."

The man shrugged. "I'm treating this entire episode in a
confidential manner," he said. "If I don't know anything, I
can't tell anything."

There was a commotion at the steam room door, Teddy, the
dog, charging in. The animal ran happily to Denny, then stopped,
seeing Amy on the bench. He whined loudly, backing toward the
door, his tail curled between his back legs.

"Who let him in here?" Denny asked angrily.

"Sorry," Hargrave said, poking his head in the door, his
hair still done up in little pink spikes. "He followed me in the
back door. It's time to juice things up. I'm gittin' ready to make
contact with the station."

"Did you get Tawny taken care of?"

The man nodded sadly. "She don't like it none, but I got us
a door installed up the top of the steps. It's enough of a drop
that I don't think she'll try and git out a window. I give her a
bottle to keep her quiet. That okay?"

Denny shrugged. "Sure. Whatever you think. We're about
ready in here." He put the powder down and turned to Frank.
"This is the big one, buddy. Let's give 'em a show."

"We always do," Frank said, and winked.

"And take that goddamn dog out of here."

Frank, smiling, picked up Teddy, the spaniel twisting and
squirming in his arms as it tried to lick his face. "Break a leg,"
he said, walking away rapidly.

Denny turned to Molly, her face still pained. "Are you
going to make it?" he asked.

Her eyes were hard when she looked at him. "I can look
out for myself," she said.

Denny ignored her tone and continued. "For the first part
of this, I want you tight on my face, understand?"

She nodded absently as she angled the camera up and
tightened down the lugs on the tripod.

"After I've made my announcement, pull back and take in

the whole set. We've got some ground to cover tonight. Once we get rolling, spend a lot of time close on Amy."

He looked at the big clock. They were jingling live air in five minutes. He wasn't scared now, though. The studio gave him familiarity and confidence. This was his life, his profession. He could handle it. In fact, he was going to blow everyone's socks off tonight. Now that he was exposing the real power, his march toward the truth of Amy Kyle would be relentless. He would know the nature of her power. And when he knew, the world would know.

"Let's check the setup," he said, moving a few steps closer to the camera and looking in the monitor. Molly sharpened the focus. He looked good. He had debated whether or not to wear a suit and decided to go with a sport shirt and slacks instead. It was the ordinary people he was trying to reach here. He didn't want to come on stuffy and, more than anything, he didn't want to be mistaken for a preacher.

Molly bent and put on the headset, shaking somewhat out of her funk. Nothing like work to opiate the mind.

"Take it back just a touch," Denny said. "Give me shoulders, too."

Molly pointed at him, then rolled back several inches until he was satisfied with the picture on the monitor. This was going to do it. He'd reestablish credibility and solidify Amy's power all at once. The fact that he wasn't sure exactly how to do it didn't bother him. He had spent the day trying to think of the safest courses of action that would still show the girl's power, but had given up when he realized there was simply no way of knowing what was going to occur no matter what he asked. So he decided to simply go with the feelings. Once the camera came up, so did the inspiration. He was making magic at that point. The consequences would take care of themselves.

"One minute," Molly announced. "Anybody needs to cough, do it now."

Dutifully, Dr. Moreland coughed loudly, clearing his throat.

"There's a pitcher of water over there out of camera range, Doctor," Denny said.

The man put up a pudgy hand. "I'm fine," he said.

"Thirty seconds," Molly announced, Denny turning to the monitor and watching his sincere expression, the kind of man anyone would be proud to buy a used car from.

"Ready," Molly said.

He was never readier. If there was a God, it was him at that moment, controlling the eyes, ears, and brains of uncounted millions who'd be hanging on his every word.

Molly put up five fingers, Denny taking a breath. Then she pointed at him, the red light coming on beside the camera.

"My friend Charlie Kornfeld died tonight," he began, hoping to rouse sympathy immediately. "He was killed by a crowd who wanted to get to me . . . and to the Kyles, a crowd that had given over its collective mind to dreams and fantasies even as others condemned us as false gods. Why? Because all of us are seeing here what we want to see, all of us wanting without measure or sense or reality. All of us wrong. From the hellfire spitting of Jim Connover to the people who brutalized the body of my friend, all of us are refusing to look at this situation for what it is. Tonight I hope to clarify all of that. Bear with me."

He glanced at Molly once, her tear-filled eyes bent to the viewfinder. "Dr. Connover says that I'm a fraud because Tawny Kyle has a record. He says I'm a false God. Well, he's right there. I'm no God at all. I'm just a news reporter with a story, nothing more or less. Have you ever noticed how people blame others for things that they, themselves, are guilty of? Perhaps, Jim, you should look a little closer to home for your demons. As for me, the story continues, the insights growing with every hour.

"Dr. Connover is worried about Tawny Kyle's record and her possible fraud setup. As many of you have recalled, neither Tawny nor I have put forward any kind of religion. We haven't accepted any money for this series of stories except from WCN, who have agreed to resell it to local stations at a reduced rate. We have accepted no personal contributions, nor will we accept any in future. For those of you still worried about the fact that Tawny Kyle has a prison record, I will set your mind at ease. It isn't Tawny who has the power. It is her daughter, Amy. I have engaged a psychiatrist from the Dallas area to speak with all of us about the condition from which Amy suffers. Tawny merely channels Amy's power, which seems to me to be electrical in origin. I have discovered that I, also, have the ability to channel Amy's power, and will be handling that end of things myself from tonight onward.

"We won't be seeing Tawny Kyle on camera anymore. She has . . . retired from this end of it and I wish her well. And if prison records still bother you, I can assure all of you that neither Amy nor I have records." He smiled, looking genuine. "Amy and I will try to work together to bring you the truth of the admittedly awesome power she possesses, but please . . . please keep this thing in perspective. A man has died today for no reason. Please. Don't look for me. You won't find me. Don't go to WCN; they don't know where I am either. They are simply pulling my signals in blind. And most of all, please don't let the ramblings of idiots like Connover affect your thinking in any way. He's a professional money raiser and can bullshit with the best of them.

"Listen to me . . . please. We're not trying to change your world. Don't you see that? Amy Kyle doesn't fit with your attitudes, so you're trying to make her fit by squeezing her into places where she doesn't belong. Forget your attitudes, forget your notions. All we ask is that you keep an open mind. Accept what we do on face value. Nothing more. Honest appraisal—is that too much to ask? In a sense, Amy is reinventing the wheel. It's different, but it's nothing to be afraid of. You all know me. Believe what I'm saying."

Denny stepped back to the bench where Amy sat. He moved her over so that she was just beneath the clock, then motioned for the doctor to also move into the frame.

"This is Dr. Abel Moreland, Dallas area psychiatrist. Would you like to explain to the viewers just how you came to be here today Dr. Moreland?"

The doctor cleared his throat again, then looked nervously at Denny. "You called me this morning at random, I assume, picking my name from the phone book and asked if I would examine the woman we'd seen on television. I accepted and was brought here blindfolded earlier this evening. I thought I was going to interview the girl's mother, but I was wrong. I haven't even seen the girl's mother."

"Was that a problem?" Denny asked in his professional voice.

"Somewhat," the doctor responded, his nervousness gone. He reached into his pocket and came out with a cellophane-wrapped cigar, sticking the thing in his mouth without lighting it or taking off the wrapper. "You see, the girl's a special case. Luckily I had some of my testing equipment in my briefcase."

"What do you mean . . . special case?" Denny asked.

"Well, you see, children like Amy exist in a kind of nether-world that is situated somewhere between the real world, the world we know, and the world of her mind, her world of control."

"Could you elaborate on that please?"

"Certainly," Moreland said, shifting the cigar to the other side of his mouth. "I'd noticed her on the television before and made a snap diagnosis. I believe I confirmed it today, even though time constraints kept me from doing as complete an examination as I would have liked. But basically, Amy Kyle manifests all the signs of classical Infantile Autism."

"What exactly does that mean?" Denny asked, soaking up everything Moreland said like a sponge.

"In layman's terms," Moreland said, "it means that for some reason unknown to us, Amy lives in a world apart from the rest of humanity. It's a small, sad world, one in which the afflicted reduces his life to a series of repetitive movements and closed-in places. The autistic child withdraws to this world, determined to control every aspect of it. The repetitive actions are merely a means of control, of understanding."

"What causes the condition?" Denny asked, looking down at the girl, who sat quietly between them, twirling her hair around her finger over and over.

The man removed his cigar and thought. "Physical or psychogenic," he said after a moment. "No one knows. The current theory going around is that it could be brought on by overstimulation. In other words, the activities of normal life are simply too frenetic, too energetic. The autistic child simply surrounds himself with an invisible shield that keeps everything out."

"What can be done about it?" Denny asked, fascinated.

"Sometimes isolation helps," Moreland said, chewing on his cigar again. "Control the amount of stimulation. Sometimes it helps the child to seek out that outside stimulation. The trick, of course, is to penetrate the shield and gain the child's confidence."

"You keep saying, 'child,'" Denny replied.

"Most autistic children either come out of it or die before adulthood," Moreland said. "There's a real burnout going on here. Plus the danger of repetitive activities can lead to self-mutilation simply through the repetition. Amy is a full-blown case. What I did mostly was observe her at play this evening. She was laying out Lincoln Logs in even, perfectly straight rows. But at some point she decided to build a gate of some sort that would go up and down. She didn't have the proper blocks for that and the gate kept falling down. It incensed her. She'd angrily throw the toys away, then get them back and begin all over again, getting hung up at the same point. The control of her environment was all important. It dictated her every action. She expended a great deal of energy in these tasks, too, another sign of the autistic. It's a way of structuring time."

"Amy's not retarded, then?" Denny asked.

The man shook his head. "Not in the clinical sense. Most autistic children are highly intelligent, many of them inordinately so. It's important to note here that many researchers believe that a child *chooses* autism. It isn't something thrust upon them. In the profession, we tend to regard autistics as pseudoretarded."

"Is there a chance that she can be helped?"

"There's a chance for everyone to be helped, Mr. Stiller," Moreland said smiling. "Even us. I believe that with Amy, even though her autism is profound, with proper therapy she can return to the normal world. This is a difficult task, however. The autistic is caught between two exaggerated extremes, alienation and fusion. The alienated Amy is quite literally the God of her world, in total control of everything around her and in need of nothing from without. The other pole is fusion, becoming totally one with the environment. Each pole attracts and repels the other. The answer, of course, is in the middle ground. For the therapist, the job becomes one of trying to reach a fusion stage with the patient, then pushing back just enough to let the patient rediscover the real world, a world not of extremes, but of compromises. It's not an easy task emotionally, but this approach has had an amount of success. People have been able to begin entering the world of the autistic by mimicking their actions, literally sharing the alienated world with the patient."

Denny nodded. This is basically what Tawny had spent years doing with Amy as a means of establishing some sort of communication with her. Unfortunately, Tawny was herself so disassociated that her actions never represented reality in any form. A great many things were beginning to make sense to Denny. "Did you notice anything else unusual about Amy upon examination?" he asked.

For the first time, Moreland looked disturbed. "I-I wasn't able to touch her at all," he said. "Whenever I tried, I received a staggering jolt of static electricity."

"Let me try something hypothetical with you, Doctor," Denny said. "Do you think that the power Amy appears to generate could be electrical? And do you think it's somehow connected to her illness?"

"I would be worse than a fool to speculate into such matters, Mr. Stiller, " the doctor replied. "That's your job and a job for physicists. I will say, that if she does have the power you suggest, her godlike stature is certainly something beyond ethics or morality. Be careful in its application."

Denny looked beyond the camera to see Molly staring hard at him. He wished that the doctor hadn't used the term *God* so much, but there was nothing he could do about it now. Perhaps diffusion was possible. "Doctor Moreland," he said. "Just for the record, did Amy Kyle exhibit any powers, and . . . preternatural abilities of mind or body during your examination of her this evening?"

"I'm glad you asked me that," Moreland replied. "Outside of the electrical jolts that I've already mentioned, Amy seemed to be the typical autistic child, though her illness is, indeed, of a profound variety."

Denny stared straight at the camera. "I'd first like to thank Dr. Moreland for coming here tonight. The doctor was right when he said that I picked him at random. That was, indeed, the case. The doctor was blindfolded when brought here and has no idea of where he is at this moment. I tell you these things in the hopes that Dr. Moreland will be left alone. One needless death has already occurred in connection with our experiments. Charlie Kornfeld was a good and true friend. I'll miss him more than I can say. Please believe me when I tell you that Dr. Moreland knows nothing about our whereabouts. We even drove him around for a long time before bringing him here to keep him from being able to judge the distance from his office to our studio."

Denny felt the excitement building within himself and knew that it was time to move on with the experiments. He turned to Moreland. "I want to thank you again," he said, directing the man out of frame. "You've performed a great service here tonight."

The man nodded, smiling at him and moved behind Molly, who was bent to the camera, ZOOMING slowly on Amy. "The face of Amy Kyle," Denny said, looking at her in the monitor. "Frightened, indrawn, inscrutable. What is the nature of her unique abilities? I don't know. Perhaps no one can. But I do have theories. I certainly believe that Amy's power is some-how electrical, though I'm not sure if the electrical power is the source or simply the form that her power chooses to take. Obviously to create or change in the face of the laws of nature, an expenditure of energy would most certainly have to take place. Perhaps the electricity is simply a bleed-off valve of some sort for this built-up . . . for lack of a better word, phantom energy."

He turned to Amy, putting an arm protectively around her shoulder, feeling the power and being reassured. "She doesn't seem to perform the actions herself. In fact, I wonder, given the nature of her closed world, if she even knows what she's doing? I doubt it. She seems to need a channel, someone who can take the raw energy that is Amy Kyle and direct it toward a goal. I've never known Amy to perform on her own. And I've never known her to relate in any sense to the tasks she performs. Let's try something and see what happens."

He picked Amy up, setting her on his lap. The studio was bright, busy, and distracting. He hoped that the stimulation, or in Moreland's lexicon, overstimulation, would occupy her and keep her from inside his head, at least long enough to perform.

He turned to the wall and pointed to the clock. "A special effects man on *Nightline* told me he'd believed me if I could materialize something from thin air while a sweep second hand on a clock ran in the background. Tonight I will try and accomplish that and put to rest the notions that I'm performing some sort of special effects wizardry."

He had wanted to hold back, to build the dramatic tensions enough that his miracle would have the ultimate impact. But he found he couldn't. With the power in his hands, he simply couldn't wait to use it. He'd been holding himself back ever since he'd put Amy in front of the camera.

"I have to be careful in what I ask for," Denny said, the first time he admitted it publicly. "The form that things take can be unpredictable, so bear with me. I'll ask the cameraman to please keep the clock within the frame at all times."

He stared at the camera, so excited he felt he was vib-rating. "I want food," he said. "I want food here, prepared and ready to eat. Food from all over the world. Foods of many nations."

He closed his eyes and took Amy's hands, squeezing tightly, his mind all centered on his desire. He felt the current rush through him, not painful this time, just jolting—small jolts, over and over, jerking him like a seizure. And then he heard Molly gasp loudly.

He opened his eyes to a wonderment. The room was full of food, steaming hot, a million smells blending together like a free-form bouquet. It was everywhere—hamburgers and steaks; steaming rice in bowls with chopsticks; an entire Arab lamb on a platter with rice, head and all; chicken soup in a huge pot; candies and sweetmeats; chili with beans; fish and chips; brautwurst; fish heads and octopus; yak butter; Scotch eggs—thousands of dishes buried under other dishes. It was on plates and in pans and pots, barbeque pork ribs still sizzling on a small grill, cheese on boards and shit-on-a-shingle served Army-style.

Denny was exuberant. He'd done it and done it big. They were on live and there was no way it could have been faked. He set Amy on the seat and rose, laughing loudly.

"Oh wow!" he said, bending to pick up a fried chicken leg to take a bite. He waved the leg round, his mouth full of dark meat. "And good, too!"

He pointed to the clock. "Did you see it?" he asked the unseen audience. "Did you? Look at all this! Molly . . . Dr. Moreland. Come on over here and get a bite."

The others joined him in front of the camera, walking, giggling through the small mountains of food piled four feet high all around them, sampling as they went.

"This is significant," Denny said, deciding that the chicken leg was too unprofessional and setting it aside. "It's the first time we've tried Amy out on things beyond her range of touch. It's . . . incredible. I felt the energy flow through me. Then I suppose it moves into my brain, my own subconscious controlling the direction of the energy. This is practically beyond belief." He shook his head. "Perhaps it's time to think not of the range of Amy's powers, but of their limitations. What in the world can she *not* do?"

He regretted those words almost immediately. All he needed was to stir up things even more. But the whole concept was just so enervating. He fought to get himself under control as his mind conjured up visions of Aladdin's lamp. He could have anything, *anything* he wanted. No, he mustn't think of it that way. He had to remember the house across the street. He had to remember the man with no memory. Fire was at once the greatest discovery and the greatest curse to befall mankind. He had to balance his feelings, but success was so hard to argue with.

Moreland was back out of camera range, happily munching on a huge taco. Molly was still moving through the piles of food, tasting small bites of many things. He got her attention and motioned her out of the frame. It was time to move on.

He stared at the camera, sitting beside Amy again. The girl was shaking her arms around, her face drawn, agitated, and Denny thought about Moreland's words about overstimulation. "As I have already mentioned," he said. "I have no idea of how this kind of power works, though I am convinced that it is simply an extension of our understanding of physics, not metaphysics. I must repeat. Amy Kyle is not God, though Dr. Moreland called her a God in her own universe. She's just a young lady with a very strange problem."

He took her hand, accessing the power. "Perhaps it's time to stop showing off and send this stuff back where it came from," he said, returning to a serious posture. "I'm going to ask Amy to get rid of all this food."

He took a long breath and squeezed tightly, wishing the food away. A painful, burning sensation tore through his system and he yelled in agony. Suddenly, all the food in the studio burst into flame, smoke quickly choking up the small room.

He sat frozen amid the blistering inferno that surrounded him, his mind locked in instinctive fear as Amy began screaming beside him, Molly backing away from the camera, moving away from the searing heat. Was this the result of his wayward thought about the nature of fire? He drew a breath, getting choking smoke and went gagging to the floor as the fire roared in triumph, reducing the food to carbon ash.

He could hear Molly yelling for him to get out as Amy, also choking, fell atop him on the floor. Panic filled his mind as he fought his brain for consciousness. The room was a dark fog, a dreamlike haze as his hand found Amy's and with his last bit of self-control he wished the fire away.

The steam room slammed shut, all the smoke sucking through the room's vents in a loud hiss, Denny calming as the killing smoke disappeared rapidly. He struggled to a sitting position, Molly and Moreland backed against the door in stark terror. He tried to smile and wave to the camera as the fire all around him winked out, leaving rubble. Then he tried to stand and found himself dizzy, falling once more to the floor. He drew an impossibly long, hard breath and watched Molly fall to the floor, her hands at her chest.

Little brown flashbulbs, like old-style reporters' cameras, began exploding brightly in his head, and he realized that the fire had died for a reason—the power had simply sucked all the air out of the room, killing the oxygen that fed the flames.

He slipped down again, praying for air as he lost consciousness, spiraling ever downward into a darkness that knew neither fear nor hope.

The minute he lay there was an eternity, and as he slowly regained consciousness, he looked across the room to see the doctor helping Molly to her feet. His head was pounding, his heart still beating rapidly with encompassing fear. He could hear Amy coughing beside him, her eyes fluttering open, the fear still strong on her face, also.

Still sitting on the floor, he looked at the camera, the red running light still glowing on its side. "Ladies and gentlemen," he said weakly. "As you can see, the application of this kind of power is not an easy thing to manage. You will . . . excuse us if we go off the air . . . for now and regroup. This is Denny Stiller for WCN news."

The red light went out, the on-air status controlled by Frank out in the truck. Denny stood slowly, the pain in his head nearly blinding as bodily tissues starved of oxygen repaid in kind. He bent and picked up Amy, the girl sobbing in his arms as she glued herself to him.

"It's okay," he said gently. "It's all over now."

"It's not over until I get out of this crazy place," Moreland said from across the room. The man stood, supporting Molly who leaned heavily upon him. His eyes were wide, his bow tie pulled apart and hanging. Both he and Molly were sweating and smeared with soot, and it began to sink in just how close to death they all had come.

The steam room door was standing open now. They were all free. "I'm sorry," Denny said.

"Just let me go home," the man replied. "Please. Just let me go home. You're playing a dangerous game here. I don't want to have anything more to do with you people."

Denny nodded as Frank came charging in. "Everybody all right?" the man asked, nodding as he saw them on their feet. "God, you should of seen it on the tube. It was amazin'. Not nobody goin' to doubt you now, Denny."

Stiller put the girl on the bench and moved to Molly as

Frank walked up to the camera and sprayed the lens with cleaner. "You okay?" he asked, putting an arm around her shoulder.

"Nooo," she said weakly. "Please don't touch me. Please."

He looked in her eyes and saw nothing but darkness and fear. He moved away from her.

"I want out right now!" Moreland said. "Out!"

"It's all over now, Doctor," Denny said.

"I can't deal with this," Moreland said. "You must let me go. You must . . ."

"All right," Denny said, putting up a hand in surrender. "Frank, could you please see to it that Dr. Moreland gets home?"

The man nodded, looking gravely at all of them, his eyes finally settling on Denny. "You *are* all right?" he said.

Denny nodded, the pain in his head subsiding by degrees. "I'll walk you out," he said, then turned to Molly. "Could you keep an eye on Amy?" he asked, the woman not answering. She just stood, slumped over somewhat, staring at nothing.

Denny moved out of the room and down the hallway with them, his mind gradually moving back to business. "Did everything show all right?" he asked Frank as they headed through the kitchen and toward the back door. "We have visual all the time?"

"We lost a little to the smoke," Frank replied, "but it was real dramatic."

Denny suddenly realized that he'd left Moreland unblind-folded. "Do you mind?" he asked, pulling the long black scarf out of his back pocket.

The man stared at him. "Do what you have to," he said, and stood quietly as Denny covered his eyes and tied the scarf around the back of his head. Then Denny took Moreland gently by the arm and guided him to the back door.

As he moved to pull the door open, Denny could hear muffled screaming and pounding from upstairs. Tawny must have seen the broadcast.

"What's that?" Moreland asked, cocking an ear.

"Nothing," Denny said, half-shoving the man through the open door space. "Let's go."

A stiff breeze was blowing outside, cooling off the night somewhat. Denny took several deep breaths, coughing up some dark mucus and spitting it out.

"About your fee," Denny said, reaching into his pocket as

they approached the black Lincoln that had been left by the house's owner in the garage. Frank had already pulled the mobile unit back into seclusion.

"I don't want anything from you," the man said, feeling his way into the passenger side. "I think I've made a terrible mistake in coming here."

"Doctor . . ."

"No," Moreland said. "This is going to be nothing but trouble for everyone. I let my ego get in the way of my better judgment. Just get me out of here."

Frank, looking ridiculous in his spiked hair, opened the driver's door and spoke to Denny over the roof. "I'll git back quick as I can, pard."

Denny nodded, closing Moreland's door. "Drive him around a little first, though," he said.

Frank gave the thumbs-up sign and climbed into the car, Denny turning immediately to walk away. Frank gunned the engine and jerked into reverse. Just then the dog caught sight of Denny from around the other side of the garage and ran happily toward him.

Frank wasn't going fast, but Teddy never saw him. The dog was tagged by the bumper, then fell under the back wheel, his cry as loud as a siren wail, then abruptly cut off as the car thumped over him.

Frank stopped immediately and jumped out of the car, racing around to look. Denny had already run to the animal, who lay under the car between the front and back wheels, his insides spewed all over the pavement.

"Aw no," Frank said, shaking his head. "Aw, damnit, no!"

"It wasn't your fault," Denny said.

"Please," Moreland called from the car. "Please. What's going on? Can I take off the—"

"No!" Denny shouted, his exasperation releasing itself in furious anger. "Goddamnit it, Frank. Get that son of a bitch out of here now!"

Frank frowned. "I'll help you drag the body out from under," he said.

Denny took a breath, the two of them pulling the carcass out from the bite of the wheels, the innards dragging along with it. The dogs eyes were frozen wide with delight at seeing Denny, its large tongue hanging out, wet with blood. Why did everything have to express itself in pain?

"Now go on," he told Frank. "I'll take care of all this. We've got to get the shrink out of here before he goes nuts on us."

Frank straightened and Denny could tell that his mind was on body bags. Without a word he turned and headed back around to the driver's seat. He climbed in and sped away.

The night blew cool around Denny, the dark neighborhood throbbing with the sounds of the unseen. The dog's guts were shimmering in pale moonlight, its eyes still wide and alive. He stood, listening to his own breathing and condemning the directions of his own mind—for an idea had occurred to him.

The dog was dead. That was none of his doing. But now that it was dead, its death surely shouldn't go to waste. On the air, he had spoken of finding Amy's limitations. Here, surely, was one.

Even as he mulled the idea over, his hands were working the buttons on his shirt. It was off and in his hands before he realized what he was doing.

He *had* to do this. It was part of the responsibility he had taken upon himself. He bent, grimacing, to the still warm body. Spreading out the shirt, tentative hands reached for the body, dragging it onto his shirt. He clenched his teeth and held his breath, scooping the animal's entrails onto the shirt with the body.

Then he wrapped the shirt around the body and hoisted the whole thing into his arms. He stood slowly, turning his mind in all other possible directions as he carried the bloody carcass into the house.

He moved like a zombie toward the studio, not thinking, reacting automatically. He took the long hall, then walked into the studio, Amy lying on the bench, Molly still standing leadenly in the center of the room.

"Don't freak out," he said stupidly, Molly turning to look at him, her face contorting in horror and disbelief when she saw him and his gristly bundle.

"My God!" she screamed. "What are you doing? What's that! Oh Jesus, Jesus!"

"Molly . . ." he said, but she kept babbling, hands to her face, lips trembling wildly.

He carried the body into the studio, putting it on the floor near Amy. He walked back to the woman, his shirtless chest and arms covered with blood. She moved away from him until she ran into wall. Then she cowered, lips sputtering.

"I need you to run the camera," he said.

"W-what?" she rasped. "The c-camera? I d-don't under— "

"Just run the fucking camera!" he yelled, taking her by the arm and pulling her toward the thing. "Just do it!"

Her fear of him greater than her fear of the body, she stood dutifully behind the camera as Denny moved around to its front, using lens cleaner and a rag to wipe any smoke residue off that Frank had missed.

"Just stay tight on the body," he said, turning to Amy. "Go ahead and roll tape."

He knelt beside the carcass, unwrapping it gently, Molly crying out when she saw what it was. He looked up at the camera, catching sight of himself covered with streaking soot, sweat and gore in the monitor. He looked inhuman, his face strained in animal passion. The red light was on.

"We're going to test Amy's powers," he said quietly, his voice hoarse from the smoke. "We're going to find out just how far they go." He reached out and laid a hand on the dog's face, touching Amy with his free hand.

He took a long breath, his thoughts frozen in his head. The room was charred, residual smoke drifting from the piles of cauterized food. He was an alien mind trapped in an alien environment. He went with it. "I'm going to wish this dog alive again," he said.

"Nooo!" Molly screamed and ran from the room.

He stared hard at the animal, willing life and health back into its broken body. "Live," he whispered. "Damn you, live!"

And he felt his body growing colder, a darkness descending upon his eyes and his mind as he went numb. His heart felt like a block of ice in his chest. He struggled to draw breath and knew the gentle touch of the hand of Death.

Then, as he sank to the floor, his spirit at the point of flight from his body, his hands warmed, gradually, toward normal, then beyond. His hands began to heat up as if he were holding them above a candle and slowly, slowly, he watched the dog's shimmering entrails crawl back into the body, the body itself closing over the wound. The animal began to shake wildly, Denny shaking with it.

And then it calmed, like an ocean storm quickly passing. Denny gingerly removed his hand from the still inert animal and watched it in perverse fascination as a low whine twisted through still bloody teeth. Suddenly, it jerked, jumping to its feet, and turned to stare at him with dark, soulless eyes.

Denny fell back off his haunches, his whole body tingling. He turned and stared at the now-sleeping girl, then back to the stoic dog.

He had done it. He had raised the dead.

ACT FOUR

Scene 1

The nighttime road was dark and twisting, two lanes of unmarked blacktop made treacherous by the occasional patches of fog that drifted ethereally across it, escapees from the brief stretches of pasture land that interspersed the changing pattern of hillsides through which the road was hewn.

Denny Stiller sweated the road, his eyes scanning constantly ahead as he tried to keep the fourteen wheeler he was highballing from leaving the asphalt and making its own trail down the California mountains. He was going too fast, the steering wheel lethargic in his hands, unresponsive. He had to fight it on every turn, using all his strength just to hold the road as his feet tapped the brakes without much success. There was trouble coming and he knew it.

He almost missed the first flare. It was a mere glow, a diffused ray of sunshine peeking fuzzy red through the fog curtain. Denny saw it, abstractly appreciating its cheery addition to his sensibilities before realizing, too late, its dire implications. He jammed the brakes with both feet, coming up off the rig's seat cushions to stand, his hands fighting the steering wheel as the rig threatened to jackknife right off the mountain.

The truck was skidding wildly as it entered the fogbank, Denny's mind scattered like a wild animal's in a forest fire. He heard his own screams loud in his ears as he skidded past the first flare and bore down on two others. He hit the next flare and the next, but felt the truck begin to come back under his control. Falling back onto the seat, he took his foot off the brakes that he had locked up, then began tapping them furiously, trying to stop the thing. It worked. The whining tires finally caught about ten feet before the fourth flare, the truck jerking to a full stop, throwing Denny up against the steering wheel, then back to the seat again.

He sat for a minute, breathing heavily, laughing as he felt the cold weight of the sweat-drenched shirt he was wearing. It was the laughter of relief.

"Better see what the trouble is," he said to no one and pushed open the truck door, climbing down into the now-thick fog.

He walked to the flare, then past it, finding nothing except another flare in the distance. He walked the twenty yards to the next flare, but found nothing there either except the glow of another flare far in the distance. He glanced back toward the truck, the weak, twin glow of its headlights the only thing visible in the drifting fog. And still he couldn't shake the feeling that something was wrong.

He walked to the next flare, but saw nothing but another flare farther ahead. He turned back to the truck, but its lights were no longer visible. He decided to walk back, reassured when he saw the headlights dim glow again after traveling several yards.

Then came the sound, screeching tires heard from the outside, loud, chilling, the call of human need that causes bolts of fear and compassion to charge through the listener. The crash was next, tearing metal and exploding glass, and he knew that someone had hit the truck.

His legs moved without thought and he found himself running, charging back the way he had come, the number of flares on the road seemingly doubled, tripled. But the headlights grew in intensity with each step and he eventually reached the wreck.

The car, a pink Cadillac, had run up beneath the truck back, the impact peeling off the passenger compartment like the skin off a grape. Thick smoke bled from under the crumpled hood, the smell of radiator water mixing with the heavy aroma of wet grass and leaking gasoline.

He looked dumbly at the car, knowing there were, or had been, people inside of the metal eggshell that had opened and let all the live stuff out. Small dogs ran around his feet, yipping madly. They were miniature poodles, dyed pink and groomed, tiny lavender ribbons fixed in their hair.

He kicked at the dogs, then ran back to the cab of the truck. He had to see what had happened to the passengers, and the only way to do that was to move the semi. His hands were shaking on the wheel, but in excitement, not horror. They were on a slight downgrade. Rather than restart the truck, he merely kicked it out of gear and let off the emergency brake.

The truck moved slowly, pulling loudly away from the twisted metal of the Caddie, the scraping loud, grating, like the creaking of a monstrous mansion door on rusty hinges. Once the sound ceased, he stopped the truck again and jumped out of the cab.

He hurried back to the wreck, grabbing a flashlight as he went, nearly slipping in large pools of internal car fluids and blood that covered the road. The driver's compartment of the Cadillac was now open and exposed under the glare of the flashlight, the fate of the passengers no longer a matter of conjecture.

The driver, a man, still sat in place, hands firmly locked on the steering wheel. His chest and face were scraped off, like rain off a windshield. The cavities still existed—half a brain, several teeth in the remnants of jaw, a spinal column—but the rest was somewhere in the trunk with the spare tire now. The bodies of several of the small dogs also lay scattered around the inside of the car. Between the living ones and the dead, there must have been ten animals. Denny looked with professional detachment, wishing he had a camera to record it all. And in the back of his mind, something seemed familiar about the whole thing.

He played the light from the driver to the passenger. It had been a woman. She wore a white evening gown and was sitting up somewhat in the seat, her legs spread apart. She had no head. It had been a clean sever, the head nowhere to be seen. There wasn't even much blood. Not a drop was on her white white gown. He stared at her, at her body, and found himself getting sexually excited as the little dogs continued to bark and run around his feet.

He reached out a tentative hand and touched the woman's arm. He fondled the arm, the body squirming slightly in the seat. Moving slowly, he slid the straps of the gown from the headless shoulders and pulled it down, exposing the woman's large breast. He was shaking again, unable to believe how excited he was. He put the flashlight down on what was left of the dash and put his hands on the dead woman's breasts, squeezing softly, the body moving up and down on the seat now.

He pulled away, grabbing the flashlight and shining it all around the interior of the car looking for the head. It wasn't there. Frantically, he played the light around on the ground near the car until he found it by nearly tripping over it.

The head lay on the ground, platinum blond, smiling up at him. He reached down and picked it up by the hair, holding it in front of his face and shining the light on it. He recognized it now, recognized the situation. It was the movie star, Jayne Mansfield, who'd been killed in a car wreck when he'd been a teenager. The head stared back at him with lust-filled eyes and he slowly brought the face to his, kissing the mouth deeply, the woman's tongue slithering between her lips and into his mouth.

He was breathing shallowly, nearly panting, sexual tension tightened like an organic mainspring inside of him. He carried the head back to the car and leaned over the still closed door, to place the head back on the shoulders. The body immediately started moaning softly, the dead woman holding her arms out to him amid the carnage of the front seat.

The door opened easily, Denny falling atop the symbol of sexual frustration and liberation of his childhood. Her glazed eyes winked lewdly at him as quick hands reached between them to unzip his pants and pull his throbbing erection out into the moonlight.

He pushed her gown up over her hips, totally lost in the experience, and she squirmed around sideways, her head on the dead man's lap to facilitate his entry.

He slid into her with a loud groan, his mouth going to her breasts to take the small, pointy nipples between his teeth. The woman growled like an animal down deep in her throat and put her hands on his buttocks to pull him tighter against her, the little dogs jumping into the car and running around all over them.

And Denny was out of control, pounding against the woman so frantically her head fell off again and rolled onto the floorboards. But he continued fucking her, the pleasure turning to pain, then fear as the tension of climax built to a shattering peak . . .

* * *

He sat up straight, quaking, his orgasm not yet subsided, and jerked his head around, realizing after several seconds that he was on the living-room couch and it was still the middle of the night. He brought wildly shaking hands up in front of his face, the sight of his lack of self-control making him cry as his whole body shook with the horror and the shame.

He felt dirty and far worse than dirty. He was a junkie of the worst sort. This time he hadn't fought her entry to his mind. This time he had helped. The dream, so real, was Amy's free passage to the twisted back alleys of his unconscious where all the dark and slithering monsters lived. His mind had invited her into his dreams and his body had gladly responded to her soft ministrations of his libido.

It had been so real.

"What are you?" he croaked to the old masters who surrounded him on the large walls, then buried his face in his hands, sobbing loudly. As the shrink had said, Amy was fusing with him in her godlike way, and his ability to survive it had long been in question.

CUT TO:
CLOSE-UP—STACKS OF MONEY. Our vision is completely filled with bundled stacks of fifty-dollar bills, a hand moving in and out of the frame, dropping more stacks.

<u>MAN'S VOICE</u> (os)

Three hundred fifty thousand . . . three hundred sixty thousand.

ANGLE—A KITCHEN. We see the kitchen in a middle-class house. Dawn is just beginning to filter through a window over the sink. Two people sit at a small breakfast table, the table filled with stacks of money. There is a man, hair disheveled, wearing shorts without a shirt. A woman sits across from him in a long black raincoat. She wears dark glasses and has long blond hair. She is watching the man pulling stacks of bills out of a cardboard box beside him. On close inspection we realize that the woman is MOLLY HARTWELL in disguise. A small portable TV sits on a kitchen counter, tuned to WCN.

MAN

Three hundred seventy thousand . . . three
hundred . . . I'm really glad to get this out of
here . . . eighty thousand. You don't know what it's
like having to sit on this much cash.

MOLLY

You don't need to count it all.

MAN

Yeah I do.

MOLLY

I trust you.

MAN

I'm counting. Three hundred ninety thousand. Don't
be so casual about a million bucks. Four hundred
thousand.

As the man continues to count in a low voice, we drift over to
the television and the news that is coming through it.
ANGLE—TV. We are looking at a helicopter picture of the
WCN building. SMOKE is rising from within. The fences
have been torn down. Police cars and emergency vehicles are
parked everywhere around the remnants of the building.

ANNOUNCER (os)

. . . overran the station barely an hour after the air-
ing of newsman Dennis Stiller's on-air refutation of
fraud charges in connection with his participation in
the promotion of self-styled faith healer Tawny Kyle
and her daughter, Amy. It is unclear whether sup-
porters or detractors of the controversial Kyle were
responsible for the riot that left weatherman Red Bolton dead and thirty-seven other WCN employees
wounded, since both sides were represented in equal
measure. The station has been estimated to be a total
loss, World Cable News being forced to broadcast
from a secret location in order to continue operation
in the face of growing concerns for the welfare of the
entire city of Dallas.

ANGLE—TROOPS CLIMBING OUT OF COVERED TRUCKS.

> ANNOUNCER (cont, os)
>
> In related news, Governor Clements has declared martial law in Dallas in an attempt to restore order in what has taken on all the earmarks of a wartime city under siege. Hundreds of demonstrators and loiterers have already been arrested, many downtown buildings being seized by the National Guard as temporary jails for what is expected to be thousands of further arrests.

ANGLE—ANNOUNCER. He stares vacantly at the viewer, his background a straight black curtain. He seems unsure, shell-shocked.

> ANNOUNCER
>
> Also locally, Dallas psychiatrist, Abel Moreland who participated in the Dennis Stiller broadcast of last night was kidnapped from his home barely an hour after airing his views about Amy Kyle. Moreland's abductors, wearing ski masks, told the doctor's wife that he would be held for ransom. The price . . . one miracle to be named later. Moreland is just the latest victim in a rash of violence surrounding the televising of the so-called miracles. Yesterday, prominent Dallas attorney, Charles Kornfeld was killed and mutilated by a crowd seeking his intercession with Stiller. Kornfeld's funeral will be held tomorrow. His widow asks that no one but immediate family attend the funeral and stresses that Dennis Stiller will *not* be in attendance. For national and worldwide reaction to what is being termed the "dizzyness in Dallas" we switch to correspondent Margaret Chase in Los Angeles.

ANGLE—WOMAN REPORTER. She's standing outside holding a microphone, the Sunset Hyatt in the background.

CHASE

The series of stories initiated by Dennis Stiller into
the apparently miraculous powers of Tawny and Amy
Kyle has caused ripples all over the world. Here in
L.A., special effects expert Shorty Greenberg was
thrust into the international spotlight several days ago
when he challenged Dennis Stiller to conduct an experiment that would prove to him that Tawny Kyle's
miracles weren't special effects tricks. After reviewing
and analyzing Stiller's broadcast from last night,
Greenberg held an informal news conference here in
the Sunset Hyatt.

ANGLE—HYATT MEETING ROOM. Greenberg, looking
tired, sits at a long table, a television set behind him.
Reporters jam the room, flashbulbs popping as Greenberg
speaks into a large number of microphones all taped together.

CHASE (os)

Mr. Greenberg's message was simple and direct.

GREENBERG

Ladies and gentlemen . . . after spending the night
reviewing the Dennis Stiller tape, I and five of my
collegues have come to the inescapable conclusion
that it is absolutely genuine.

Noises fill the room as reporters come to their feet, all yelling
questions at the same time.

GREENBERG

Please . . . one at a time!

REPORTER

Would you, then, stake your professional reputation
on the truth of your statement?

GREENBERG
(smiling)

Somehow, I knew you'd ask me that. (everyone
laughs) I'll roll some tape and show you how we arrived at our conclusions.

A tape of Denny's broadcast comes up on the TV, just at the
section where he makes the food appear.

GREENBERG (cont)

This, to me, is the key section of the tape. There is
only one way to fake the materialization of an object,
and that is to stop the camera and place the object in
the frame, then turn on the camera. Right
here . . . this split second of materialization. To begin with, this show was broadcast live with no possibility of stopping the tape. Second, we studied the
tape over and over using still pictures and even running it through the computer and could find absolutely no edits that would show the camera had been
stopped. Finally, the clock on the wall runs
continuously . . . and we timed the seconds
exactly . . . finding no inconsistency with reality.
Three indisputable points were made, leaving us no
choice but to accept the reality of the materialization.
Six of us have signed affidavits to this effect and, yes,
I would stake my professional reputation on it. Couple this with the reports I heard this morning about
the Italian man whose fettuccine disappeared right off
his table in Milan in front of ten witnesses, and I
think we're into some serious weirdness at this point.

REPORTER

Do you think that Amy Kyle is God?

GREENBERG

Let's just say that if she started a religion right now,
I'd be the first to join.

ANGLE—CHASE.

CHASE

You may argue with Greenberg's findings, but you
cannot refute his qualifications—he's been nominated
for five academy awards and has won three. In Washington this morning, even the president got into the
act in his weekly news conference.

ANGLE—WHITE HOUSE PRESSROOM. The president stands at the podium with the executive seal on the front. The president is pointing into the audience.

REPORTER (os)

Mr. President, do you think that the Texas faith healer is God? (everyone laughs)

PRESIDENT

I'll leave the speculation and the fiction writing to you boys . . . you're better at it than I am.

REPORTER

What of the report from the United Nations this morning that a coalition of Communist Bloc countries and Third World powers are demanding access to Amy Kyle in order to test her abilities to see if she's a threat to the balance of power?

PRESIDENT

I'd say to them what I'll say to you . . . no way! No private citizen of the United States would ever be turned over to a foreign power in violation of his rights as a citizen. And that's enough on this topic.

ANGLE—DALLAS ANNOUNCER.

ANNOUNCER

And what of the effect of Amy Kyle, if any, on organized religion? We go to Martin Michaels in Chicago.

ANGLE—A CATHOLIC CHURCH. File-footage Mass is just ending, worshippers moving out of the Gothic splendor of the church and down the long, marble steps to the street.

MICHAELS (os)

The seat of Catholocism in Illinois is here, in the archdiocese of Chicago. We spoke this morning with his Eminence, Cardinal Bartello, about the phenomenon known as Amy Kyle.

ANGLE—CARDINAL BARTELLO. The man is in his seventies, dressed in red robes.

BARTELLO

We have received thousands of calls from parishoners and the news media about this child in Texas and her supposed "powers" and all that I can say is that many false prophets and messiahs have arisen since our Lord Jesus Christ was crucified and all of them have disappeared in the dust of ages. Such blasphemy can not exist for very long before it collapses under its own weight.

MICHAELS (os)

Are you, then, denying the existence of miracles?

BARTELLO
(stern)

Miracles certainly exist . . . the miracle of life, the miracle of birth, the miracle of Lourdes and its continuing healing powers. To become a saint in the Church one must have performed miracles and our records contain thousands of instances—

MICHAELS (os)

Then what makes this so different?

BARTELLO

Miracles are not performed in bars for money. They can only come about with the grace of Almightly God through his Son, Jesus Christ.

MICHAELS

Can anyone beside Catholics perform miracles?

BARTELLO

Only through the true faith will God's miraculous powers be felt on Earth. As is said in John, 3:16, the way to the Father is through Me. Anyone who claims otherwise is a heretic and lives in a state of mortal sin to suffer the fires of hell upon death.

CUT TO:

MEDIUM CLOSE—DENNY'S DOG. The animal is in the huge backyard standing on a patch of Bermuda grass between the tennis court and the swimming pool. It is staring vacantly down at the ground, as if intensely studying this one spot of earth. It stands for a moment, then walks around in a circle and studies the ground from another angle. A squirrel runs across the yard, passing close to the dog, but the animal takes no notice and instead sits and continues to stare at the ground. We ZOOM OUT slowly until the dog seems lost and insignificant in the vastness of the yard and sky.

Denny took one last look at the spaniel through the viewfinder of the video camera, then shut it down, pulling it away from his face. He moved from the kitchen window, removing the tape from the camera and putting it on the counter next to an ever growing stack of tapes dealing with Amy Kyle. The kitchen was a mess, trash strewn everywhere, some of it beginning to smell. He needed to take care of it; someone did, anyway, but he just couldn't seem to get himself around to it. There was so much clouding his mind, like layers of gauze, slowing his thinking processes. He felt as if his brain were the bug inside the jumping bean, trying to push its way out through an impenetrable shell, shaking the package but never breaking free.

It was late morning, but the house seemed dark to him. He had turned on all the lights downstairs but it hadn't helped. Neither did it help that when he stared too long at the paintings on the walls, which seemed to move and change positions.

His coffee sat on the breakfast table getting cold. He walked to it, tripping over the piles of money on the floor and nearly falling. Molly had gotten it earlier, their first payment for broadcast. It was scattered all over the floor now, just so much paper, so much waste. He'd always thought that a million dollars would be a wonderful thing to have, but now that he had it, it was just more trash clogging up the kitchen. His life was beyond money, beyond the small measure of security it could bring.

He kicked several more stacks of bills out of the way and sat down at the Early American table set beside the sliding patio door. The door was boarded up now, ever since last night when the dog had jumped through it, desperate, apparently, to get out to that spot of ground where he'd stayed ever since. They'd tried several times to bring the animal back inside and treat its cuts, but it always broke free and returned to its spot. Finally Frank dressed its superficial wounds out there in the yard and left it alone. It wouldn't eat; neither would it drink. It just stared unblinking at the ground.

The coffee tasted odd, uncoffeelike. He set it down and pushed it away from him. Nothing fit anymore. Nothing made any sense. As Amy tried to fuse with him, perhaps he was fusing also with her, taking in her world—whatever that may be. He could materialize solid matter and raise the dead, but he couldn't control his own bodily functions or his growing interdependence on this strange child. Even as he grimaced at the thought of the control she exercised over him, he wanted to go into the den and awaken her to photograph the plans he had made for today. Perhaps the story, the Truth of the story, was his addiction. And the more he gave himself over to her, the more he wanted. There were answers here; answers, perhaps, to questions he'd never even thought of—and turning back, oh God turning back, was something he was absolutely incapable of.

Molly could never understand that in him. The news was a job to her, just a job. She wasn't driven by it like he was. She didn't eat and breathe and exist just for the story—few of his collegues did. They were able to take some measure of self-worth from their lives, or their families, or their positions in the community and service to it. Not Denny. That was all meaningless to him, just time-filling stopovers on the way to the graveyard. But the story, the Truth of the story—that was something fine and beautiful and somehow important. It made him feel alive. It made him feel . . . real. He knew he was getting too close to the fire, that it could ultimately consume him like a meteorite exploding into the Earth's embrace. But what a beautiful fire it was. What a lovely, bright, pure flame the Truth of Amy Kyle could be.

And in that, he discovered something about himself and the girl. She was pure and so was he. She was unashamed Truth and he was its conduit, both of them unfettered by the lies that the rest of humanity tells itself to keep from committing suicide with the stupidity and pain of it all. Perhaps her purity was the root and measure of her power. Perhaps his surrender to it was the measure of his. She was the hammer, he the forge, and it was thunderbolts they were casting.

"Mama?" he heard her call from the den. "Mama?"

"I'm your mama today," Denny called from the table, his hand shaking on the coffee cup. "Come on in and get some meedle."

The girl came charging into the kitchen from her makeshift bedroom in the den. It was Denny's intention to live down here with her, the upstairs reserved for Tawny and the others. She ran past him, white nightgown flowing behind her, and charged into the bathroom that was set off the kitchen.

Amy hadn't seemed to miss her mother all that much, perhaps because she had a workable substitute in Denny. He doubted that she could really take more than one person into her universe anyway. Amy's head was a small and intense world, not much room for outside intrusion. As he listened to the sound of the toilet flushing, he thought about her powerful world and his role in it. He was the channel now, the hand on the tiller. It was he who had brought Teddy, the dog, back to life. She was the power, like an electric socket. He was the instrument that gave the power form. If there was a God to be found here, perhaps it was Denny Stiller.

He laughed out loud. In thousands of years of philosophical thought, from Plato to Maimonides to Aquinas to Luther to Martin Buber, no one had ever conceived of Denny Stiller as God. In fact, they had never even gotten close to the concept. What wasted minds and wasted words and wasted hearts.

He chastized himself. Even joking he shouldn't let his ego get control of the situation. He was a newsman; this was a story, plain and simple. He had covered in his time revolutions in Central America, riots in South Africa, terrorism in Greece, presidential primaries and conventions, hostage situations, and stray cats caught in trees. And he had survived them all because he had always kept his head in the story and his mind off himself. He couldn't back away from that now. Objectivity was the key, objectivity and taking care not to read between the lines.

Amy came out of the bathroom. Her hair was tangled and matted. They'd have to comb it before shooting. Her face was dirty and he wondered how long it had been since she'd bathed. He couldn't trust Tawny to give her a bath, and he doubted if Molly would do it. He'd have to figure out a way to get her cleaned up.

He got up from the table and moved to the kitchen area, taking a large jar of peanut butter out of the pantry and opening it. "Got some meedle here for you," he said, holding up the jar while getting out a spoon.

She squealed loudly, then began running around the breakfast table. He walked back, putting the jar on the table. She ran around him several times before he put out an arm and grabbed her, the shock of contact clearing the fuzz out of his brain immediately.

She wrapped herself around him, clinging desperately. The closeness frightened him and exhilarated him. He thought about last night and her nocturnal visit to his brain, suddenly frightened that dreams could become just as real as wants when connected to the power pack of her mind. He felt a surge of sexual excitement and forced her away from him, setting her firmly in the chair beside him.

The girl shook crazily, her eyes fluttering, and he put a hand on her shoulder to calm her, Amy turning suddenly and grabbing his arm and clinging to it.

"No," he whispered harshly. "Amy, let go. This is . . . this is too weird. I'm not . . . not . . . I can't." He pushed her off again and she jumped at him again.

"No!" he yelled and grabbed her shoulders, shaking. She screamed loudly, then turned her eyes to him.

He felt blinding pain in his head, then numbness. He'd later remember a sensation of movement for a second, but that wasn't until later. As it was, he simply found himself on the floor fifteen feet from her, his wooden captain's chair shattered, his hands covering his head, his mind searching desperately for some reality to hang onto, anything to stop the freewheeling carousel that his consciousness had become as images of his past twirled in a giddy dance with present memories, some real, others manufactured.

It subsided by degrees. After several minutes, he was able to roll over and sit up, a good bit of his body still numb; and what wasn't numb was sore. He'd taken quite a fall. He looked up at the table where Amy sat, quite happily, eating peanut butter with a spoon right out of the jar.

He stood on shaky legs and smiled, rubbing a sore shoulder where he must have taken the brunt of the fall. During the oil embargo of 1974, he'd stood in the midst of feuding gas station owners and people wanting to illegally top off their tanks and tried to get a story about need and greed. He'd ended up in the hospital with a broken arm and a fractured jaw. But it was the story that had made him do it. If conscience makes cowards of us all, then a story makes us brave—or foolish, by taking us out of ourselves.

"You stay here and eat," he said, working some circulation back into the shoulder. "I'm going for Frank."

He moved quickly out of the room, wondering if they'd had their first lovers' quarrel. He was anxious to get started with Amy today. As the range of her abilities increased more and more, the thought of finding a top limit, or at least a definition within boundaries became a consuming obsession. There had to be an end to this, although, obviously in Teddy's case, death was no limit. There was another thought intruding also. The safety factor. Charlie was dead, and the shrink, Dr. Moreland, had apparently been kidnapped. Of the people injured at the station itself, he'd heard that Dick Horton had been among them. For the first time he began to think in terms of finding parameters in order to bring this to some sort of conclusion. That was accepting the perhaps fanciful idea that there could be a conclusion.

He moved through the formal dining room and over to the stairway next to the living room, barely noticing how dirty and broken down the house was becoming. As he climbed the stairs, he dug the key to Frank's makeshift door out of his pocket.

The top of the stairs now had an old doorway blocking it off, the doorway was too small for the space, Frank filling out the rest of the space with scrap lumber nailed right to the wall. A heavy but weathered oak door was hinged into the frame. Denny put his key in the brass lock and opened the thing, stepping through.

He turned left down the dark hallway and moved to Frank's door. Knocking lightly, he opened it up and walked in. Frank wasn't there. Electronic and editing gear was scattered around the room, everything that WCN and his friends had let him scavenge, but Hargrave wasn't amid his transistorized flotsam and jetsam.

Puzzled, Denny left and walked down the hall, stopping in front of Tawny's room to the sound of Frank's voice. He knocked.

"Frank?" he called.

"Come on in, pard!" the man returned.

Denny opened the door, surprised yet not surprised to find

Frank wriggling into jeans as he sat on the bed, Tawny beside him smoking a cigarette. She was covered at the waist and was naked from there up, a situation she didn't try to hide and one that Denny gave no thought to one way or the other.

When she saw Denny, her eyes flashed hard. "What the hell are you doin' to mah little girl down theah?" she asked.

"Don't play grieving mother," Denny said. "It doesn't suit you."

"You son of a—"

"Stop!" Frank said, standing and zipping up his jeans. "I swear, you two are worse than bluejays at matin' season."

"But Frank," the woman said. "You heard 'em yellin' down theah afore, ah—"

"Just take it easy," Frank said, leaning over the bed to smooth her overbleached, dead hair. "This here's a bad deal all the way around, but old Denny ain't doin' nothing to harm Amy. I promise you that. I'm goin' to be here to keep an eye out, okay?"

"Ah want mah baby back," the woman said, pulling off the covers and pulling her naked legs over the side of the bed and pouring herself a drink from the bottle on the nighttable. She took a drink, her voice whiny. "Ah jes can't git along without mah baby, Frank." She turned to him, pleading with her eyes. "You know Ah need her."

Frank moved around the bed and took the glass out of her hand, setting it back on the table. "Why don't you go in and git cleaned up a bit, honey," he said. "I got to talk some business with Denny."

"Sure, Frank," she said, standing, trying to look dignified as she slipped a T-shirt on. "Ah know Ah kin trust you to look after mah interests."

She walked past Denny without a word and moved into the bathroom, closing the door, the shower pounding almost immediately.

"Denny, we got to git them two together soon," he said.

"And how do we do that?" Denny asked.

Frank pulled a shirt off the back of an easy chair and slipped it on, fighting with the buttons. "I don't know," he said, "but there's something weird about that relationship."

"What do you mean?" Denny asked.

Frank got the shirt buttoned and sat on the edge of the bed to try and get his boots on. "Don't laugh, okay?" he asked.

"Go ahead."

The man grimaced into his right boot. "There's somethin' . . . I don't know, physical, about it. I mean . . . it's almost like she's goin' through withdrawal or somethin' . . ."

"Like an addiction?" Denny asked.

"I give her all the booze she wants cause that's the only thing that keeps her from the d.t.'s." He struggled into the other boot and stood up. "I don't know what any of it means. I'm just afraid that somethin' terrible will happen if you don't let those two git together."

"I hope you're not getting too caught up with Tawny's side of this, Frank," Denny said. "You work for me, remember?"

"Don't put it like that, pard," the man warned. "You know you can't control me that way, you'll just make me mad. My personal life hasn't interfered with business yet, so don't git your head all rearranged."

"Sorry," Denny said, though he didn't really mean it. Didn't Frank understand how impossible it would be to put Tawny and Amy together at this point? He decided to change the subject. "You about ready to roll some tape?"

"Always," the man returned, smiling. "After last night, I'm ready for anythin'. You goin' to show them pictures of the dog on the air?"

"I don't know," Denny replied. "It's hot footage, but I don't know if the world's ready for it or not."

"It's the damn truth, isn't it?" Frank said loudly. "And ain't it the Truth you been lookin' for?"

"It's not that simple," Denny said.

"That's not the way you looked at it when you got into this thin', Denny. Don't forgit where you started or you'll lose sight before the end and all of it'll go out the window."

"It's not that," Denny said. "It's just that everybody keeps putting religious connotations on this and raising the dead is certainly something looked upon as a religious experience. I just don't want to confuse the issue even more."

"It ain't just the raisin' of the dead that messes this thing up, Denny," Frank said. "Molly tried to warn you of this before you even got started. It's that most religion is like white magic to people."

"White magic?" Denny returned.

Frank nodded. "Yep. The opposite of the nasty kind that everybody's scared of. Folks pray so that they won't die. They pray so they'll git stuff. They pray for solice and they pray for

revenge . . . and most of all they believe there's a God who
can perform magic for them and make everythin' all right
when it ain't. Cannibals got them a cannibal God and money
grubbers got them a God that gives out money like Green
Stamps. Well, I don't have no idea what God is, but what
you're doin' sure as hell looks a whole lot like what people
think God should be, and there ain't no way you're goin' to
convince them otherwise, cause they've all *made* their God the
way they want him to be and they're goin' to throw a shit fit if
they think you're tryin' to tell them somethin' else. People
tend to git real mad when you step on their God, you know."

"Then what do I do?" Denny asked.

"You already know the answer to that."

"Look for the Truth," Denny said, "and let the consequences be damned."

"There's only one thing harder then bringin' in a hard
story," Frank smiled, "and that's bringin' in a hard story good.
Let me ask you a question: what are you goin' to do with all
that money Molly brought in this mornin'?"

Denny shrugged. "Haven't given it any thought," he said.
"You got an idea?"

The shower went off in the bathroom and Frank lowered
his voice. "I'd like to spend a little of it to git some more
equipment to help with the recordin'."

"Reasonable," Denny said. "Take as much as you want.
Have Molly get the stuff for you."

The man nodded and stuck a large thumb in the direction
of the bathroom door. "We really do need to git them
together," he said. "I really worry about Tawny otherwise."

"We'll talk about it, okay?" Denny returned, trying to hold
down his annoyance. All he needed right then was for Frank to
get romantically involved with the Kyle woman and turn on
him. "Get everything ready. I want to shoot in a few minutes."

"On my way," Frank said, but continued to hang around
the room. Denny realized that the man wanted to speak with
Tawny before going down, so he simply left him to it and
moved down the hallway to Molly's room.

The woman's door was ajar, so he pushed it open. "Knock,
knock," he said sweetly as he poked his head inside. He was
determined to make things right between them, if only to
prove to himself that he still had some sort of control over
himself and his emotions.

She was standing at the window, looking out into the

backyard. She was still wearing the black raincoat and blond wig. Her open suitcase was sitting on the bed. She turned to him, sunglasses covering her beautiful brown eyes. "You look awful," she said.

"Really?" he said and walked to the mirror over her dresser. He barely recognized the man staring back at him. A light growth of beard soiled his face, the dark lines under his eyes were etched deep, like permanent scars. He ran a hand through wild, unkempt hair, realizing that he hadn't thought about his appearance in several days. "Guess I've been preoccupied."

"Yeah, I guess you could call it that," she said, and turned back to the window. "Teddy just sits there . . . staring."

"It's weird," Denny said. "I don't know what to—"

She flared around to him. "Is that all you can say, 'it's weird?' Damnit, that animal was dead and in peace until you decided to bring it back. It's suffering out there, Denny. Can't you see that?"

"It's fine," he reassured. "We checked him out last night."

"This isn't a game anymore," she said angrily. "You can't just bring the dead back to life and expect it to be like putting a Band Aid on a cut finger. You don't know what was lost while that animal was dead . . . what force was loosed never to return."

"Don't make it so damn metaphysical," he returned, still studying himself in the mirror. He'd have to clean up soon or risk looking like a maniac on television. "People return from clinical death all the time on the operating table and no one worries about what was lost."

"This isn't the same thing and you know it."

"I'm meddling in God's domain, right?" he replied, turning from the mirror to stare at her back.

She turned around slowly, as if in answer to his probing eyes. "It's nothing to make light of," she said.

He moved to her, taking her gently by the shoulders. "Oh Molly," he said. "I'm not trying to make light of anything." He reached out and pulled her sunglasses off, tossing them on the bed. Her eyes reflected deep sorrow. "I'm just trying to tell the story. Maybe I haven't done everything perfectly right, but we're having to make it up as we go along." He looked at the suitcase again. "You going somewhere?"

"Thinking about it," she said.

"Why?"

"Because I'm scared," she said. "I'm scared of losing you.
I'm scared for me and the baby. This thing has changed you.
You've pulled inward so far I don't think I can reach you
anymore. There're things going on in your head that I can't
even begin to understand, much less accept."

"You're wrong," he said, all the while realizing how right
she was. "It's still me. I've just been . . . preoccupied, that's
all."

"Tell me about it?" she said in exasperation. "The city is
under martial law, they're thinking about closing off all the
roads into the state. The goddamn station was attacked last
night . . . some of our friends were killed, Denny. And all
you can talk about is how many things you've got on your
mind!"

"I can't control the actions of others," he said. "Can't you
understand that? The story just won't go away. We're caught
up in a phenomenon."

"And it's tearing us to pieces," she said, the words choking
off in a sob as she turned her head from him. "I'm so damn
frightened."

"You're wrong," he heard himself say and knew he was just
searching for words. "This won't affect us."

"Why don't we sleep together anymore?" she asked.

He took her in his arms, panicking inside. "Well . . . I
have to stay downstairs with Amy. You wouldn't want her
running off during the night, would you? She's a big responsibility."

"I can come down to you," she said, burying her face in his
shoulder. "Oh, Denny. I just still need to know that you love
me and care about me. Fuck the other stuff. That's why I'm
packing."

"Of course I care about you," he said, stroking her hair
before realizing it was a wig and stopping. "Things have just
been . . . complicated, that's all."

"Well," she whispered. "Why don't I sneak down tonight
when everyone's asleep and see if I can uncomplicate your life
a little."

"That would be great," he said, his insides screaming.
What would Amy think about the intrusion of another into
their nightly rendezvous? The girl's power frightened him, but
not nearly as much as the nonexistent ethical system that drove
it. But he needed Molly, needed her to be his liaison to the

outside world. And besides, she'd stand no more chance on the outside right now than Charlie or Dr. Moreland.

She backed away from him. "Good," she said smiling. "It'll be great, you'll see. There's nothing we can't overcome if we love one another."

"Right," Denny lied, trying hard to match her smile. "Come on, why don't you get out of those traveling clothes and put the suitcase away?"

She nodded, smiling wanly. "And now, what are you going to do about Teddy?" she asked.

"Do?" he asked. "I don't guess I'll *do* anything."

She pointed out the window. "He doesn't eat. He doesn't sleep. He just stares at the ground. Have you seen his eyes?"

"All dogs eyes look like that," he said.

"His don't," she said. "His are dead."

"I get it," he returned, shaking his head and pointing at her as if he were holding a gun. "You don't think I have the right to bring Teddy back from the dead, but I do have the right to kill him."

"You have the obligation to correct your error and leave that poor animal in peace."

"Which is still a fancy way of saying you want me to kill Teddy."

She stared hard at him. "We're not communicating on the same level," she said, summing up the situation quite simply and correctly.

"It's because we don't share the same . . . I don't know . . . metaphysical reality," he replied. "Look. I don't believe the things that you believe. And ultimately, I'll have to follow my own instincts on this thing."

"Then what was all that talk about my input being so important?"

"It *is*," he said. "But the decisions are still mine, and I won't kill the dog. I couldn't even if I wanted to."

She pulled off the wig and threw it to him. "Some things are more important than being alive."

He put on the wig. "Not in my book, lady," he said, then made a face, hoping to divert her thinking. "Religion, patriotism and idealism are three pretty stupid reasons for killing or dying. I'm sorry, but self-preservation gets real high marks with me."

"Don't twist my words," she said, moving toward the door and taking off the coat to throw on a chair.

"I'm not," he said softly, then leaned over and closed up her suitcase, sliding it under the bed. When he turned around she had already moved out of the room and down the hallway.

He followed, stopping to lock the door at the top of the stairs, finding Frank engaged in a tug of war with Amy over one of the paintings in the living room. It was an early impressionist work by Seurat, apparently pulled off the wall by the girl. And as he watched, the seemingly random pattern of dots that merged together on the picture to make a pointillistic river picnic scene was being duplicated on Amy's arms, almost as if she were a painting.

No, he said, voice quaking. "Amy, stop!"

At the sound of his voice she dropped the picture and began crying. Denny moved to her and put an arm on her shoulder. She stopped crying immediately and fell to her hands and knees, crawling a circle around Denny, round and round.

"She's a strong little bugger," Frank said. "I could hardly git a grip on that picture."

"Crank it up. I want to shoot in here," Denny told him, then looked at Molly, who was standing across the room, physically removed from Amy. He called to her. "Get a wet washrag. I need to clean her up."

As Frank retrieved the camera from the studio, Denny bent to the girl, holding up her arm to study. The dots were fading, pastel blues and yellows, but they were definitely there. At least he thought they were there. He was afraid to ask the others, afraid of what they'd say. He turned and looked at the picture, still laying on the floor. In the background, a young girl leaned against a tree and stared straight back at the viewer. She looked remarkably like Amy. He stood and picked up the picture, leaning it against the wall, facing away from them.

"You need a comb, too," Molly said, tossing the rag to Denny from a distance.

"I don't guess you'd . . ." he began, hoping for help.

"You're right," she replied. "I wouldn't. But I will lend you my comb."

As Denny brought the washrag to Amy's face, Molly pulled her comb out of her bag and tossed it to him. Amy twisted frantically as he tried to wash her, and he finally had to catch her in a bear hug to hold her still while he worked.

By this time, Frank had moved back in with the camera. "Where you want it?" he asked.

"Just roll tape," Denny said. "And take it off the tripod, we may be moving around a bit."

"When I picked up the money this morning," Molly said, "Rankin reminded me that you absolutely must call the station today and give them an answer about going on the air under their terms."

Denny sighed as he rubbed color into Amy's cheeks with the washrag. "I'd hoped they'd get off that kick after last night," he said.

"They're insistent that they'll give you no more airtime until you go on with them. They've suffered big on account of you, and they intend to collect big."

"Where are they broadcasting from?" he asked.

"They've taken over one of the studios at KTVR, Gayler's local affiliate, and disguised it."

He put down the rag and began combing out the girl's hair, jerking through the tangles as Amy cried and twisted. This business with Gayler would be a pain in the ass, but probably wouldn't hurt him any. With Amy as his ace in the hole, he doubted if there were any situation he couldn't handle. In fact, the opportunity excited him a little.

"Get Horton on the phone," he said, "then bring it to me."

"You goin' to do it?" Frank asked, his camera focusing on Amy's pouting face as the comb dragged through her tangles.

"Sure," Denny said.

"It may be a trick," Frank said, moving in a little closer, the camera on his shoulder, "to get Amy."

"What makes you think so?" Molly asked.

"She's power," the man replied. "Nothin' people like the old man like better than power."

"We'll be ready," Denny said, and released Amy, straightening to look at his handiwork.

"I'm going for the phone," Molly said, leaving the room.

Denny looked up at Frank, the man pulling away from the viewfinder to stare at him. There was an electricity, an unspoken bond that existed between the two of them on this project, a shared excitement in the process of discovery. For Denny it was all internal and intellectual; for Frank it was all physical, video as truth—but to both of them it came together here in the merging of sight and sound. In the lunatic miasma of history and the swirling panoply of ideologies and shifting truths, the camera never lied. Its record was fresh and pristine, its memory never faulty. It was objectivity in a subjective world. Frank smiled slightly and nodded. Denny spoke.

"I worry a great deal about the consequences of our actions," he said, speaking loudly enough for the pole mike on the camera to pick him up easily. "Nothing in life is static. Every pebble thrown into life's waters causes ripples that extend out to touch the entire body. With this thought in mind, it becomes increasingly difficult to detail experiments that don't have ramifications elsewhere. To circumvent this, I try to choose situations that affect me, alone, and not ones that would have a negative effect on the rest of humanity. Perhaps this sounds oversensationalized, but that's precisely how I see it. And it certainly appears better in this case to be safe, rather than sorry."

He looked down at Amy as she stood beside him, her head at his chest level, her eyes wandering dangerously near the pictures on the wall. He put an arm around her and pulled her to him, getting her mind off the pictures.

"I want to try a couple of things today," he continued, "the main purpose of which is to see if physical contact is necessary to properly channel the power." He reached out, stroking Amy's hair, feeling the symbiotic electricity flow between them as he settled his mind and tried to pick up her wavelength. And he felt the power, felt the emotional boost that accompanied it, and fought hard to remember that it wasn't his power to do with as he chose.

"I want to fly," he said. "I want the power of controlled levitation."

He closed his eyes and pictured himself flying. Not in an airplane did he picture himself, but alone, without any device save his own directional sense. All at once, he felt a weighted push toward the floor, as if a car had been put on top of him. His legs bent, buckling, and he went, gasping for breath, to the carpet. He was being crushed, pinned to the floor by heavy gravity. And just when he felt he could stand it no longer, the feeling passed and he became light, like a balloon, and felt himself floating up off the floor.

Denny opened his eyes.,

"Mother fucker," Frank said, Denny laughing down at him from ceiling level.

"Watch the language," Denny said happily. "Amy might be

God, but we still have to bow to the *real* God, the almighty
FCC."

Both men laughed, Denny realizing that he was alone in
the air. Amy still stood beneath him, her attention distracted
by a ray of sunshine falling through the gap in the closed
curtains.

"It's unbelievable," he said, unable to keep the thrill of
absolute power out of his psyche, "as if my whole body, my
bones, my organs had simply lost all their weight. I feel
bouyant, like floating on an air mattress in a swimming pool.
I've never experienced zero gravity weightlessness, but it
must be something like this—but with a decided difference."

With that, he turned his thoughts to the other side of the
room, his body immediately moving in that direction. The wall
came up, too fast, on him, but with the quickness of a thought,
he stopped before hitting it, completely negating Newton's
laws of motion.

"I can control it!" he yelled for the camera, as Frank tried
to hurry over to keep him in focus. "I move with the power of
thought." He pictured himself turning somersaults and, tightening to the fetal position, he began spinning wildly through
the air.

He stopped the spinning just as easily and turned onto his
side, simply hanging suspended up near the Monets on the
high ceiling. "As you can see," he said, "I'm not in any physical
contact with Amy at the moment. In fact, it looks as if she's not
even showing any interest in what I'm doing. It makes one
wonder, then, just how far her power can extend."

Laughing, he dove for the floor, pulling out mere inches
from the carpet and zooming quickly over Frank's head to the
other side of the room. He let himself drift then, floating past
the old masters who had altered reality in their own earth-
bound ways when they'd thrown away the conventions of
photographic realism to use paint to express their inner
feelings. How appropriate that he should find his own inner
powers here among the French impressionists, expressing
physically what they could only dream about.

He began to swim, doing the breaststroke, then back-
strokes through the bouyant air, realizing that, perhaps, the
conventions of reality were merely symbols of the tethered
mind.

"Denny!" Molly shrieked, Denny going into a steep dive
that took him, laughing, in a tight circle around her head. She

turned with him, holding eye contact. "What the hell are you doing?"

"My love," he grinned, "that is one of the stupidest questions I've ever heard."

She laughed despite herself. "Well, maybe you'd better come down to earth long enough to talk to Dick."

She held the cordless phone out to him, Denny scooping it out of her hand to 'zoom back to the ceiling, Frank dutifully following with the camera as Amy lay on the floor, trying to enclose the sunbeam with a corral of trash that she built around it.

"Yo, Dick," Denny said into the receiver, unable to be serious, as if his own physical lightness was reflected in his mind. "How's it hanging?"

"Don't start with me, Stiller," the voice returned gravely. "I've got a broken arm, thirteen stitches in my head, a sick leave roster that reads like a wartime casualty list and a line-of-duty funeral to go to tomorrow. And it's all because of you and your fucking ego."

"Other than that," Denny said in mock seriousness, "how are things?"

"If it was up to me, Stiller," he returned, "I'd cut you off the air and never let you within a hundred miles of a television station again."

"But . . ." Denny helped.

"But it's not up to me. Mr. Gayler wants you tonight. Any problems result in cancelation immediately."

"Why, sure, old buddy," Denny said. "You just name it."

Horton let out a long sigh and Denny realized the man had been hoping that it could all end here. "You know where Gayler's house is?" he asked.

"The old man's digs?" Denny returned with a whistle. "Yeah. I had an audience there once when I was promoted to the Washington beat."

"We'll send a car out to—"

"No," Denny said. "We'll get ourselves there. Just give me a time."

"Tonight . . . eight o'clock."

"I bring my people," Denny said. "They're entitled to a good time, too."

"The invitation covers them," Horton said. "You'll be expected to appear on live feed and there will be questioners of Mr. Gayler's choosing."

Denny laughed inwardly. Mr. Gayler and all his myriad ways couldn't control him on this. He held all the cards, everything stacked in his favor. With Amy by his side, nothing was impossible. "You got it," he said. "Black tie?"

"Just be there," Horton said, hanging up.

"Or be square," Denny finished, stretching out his arm and tossing the phone to the sofa twenty feet below. He felt bad about all the trouble that had come about because of his story, but damnit, it wasn't his fault. He could only report. The actions of the rest of the world weren't his responsibility.

"Y'all get gussied up," he called. "We're going to a shindig tonight at the Gayler mansion."

"No!" Molly yelled, putting her hands on her head. "My hair's a mess and I don't have anything to wear."

Denny began gyrating, boogying in the air. "Baby!" he sang. "You'd look great in sackcloth!"

He turned, diving toward her. "Gimme a kiss," he called, his lips twisting wildly as Molly laughed from ground level.

And just like that, it was gone. The lightness, the control, everything. He was a bullet hurtling toward Molly.

"Nooo!" he screamed, as he put his arms out in front of him, trying to break the fall, Molly diving sideways toward the floor.

He caught her on the thigh, knocking her painfully aside as he slammed into an end table, a lamp smashing against the wall, the table crumpling beneath him as he met the floor, jarring hard, pain flashing through him, nearly blinding.

"Gawd!" Frank yelled, running toward them, still rolling tape as Denny tried to roll over through waves of pain, his mind set on Molly and the baby.

"Molly," he said through clenched teeth, "Are you . . . are you . . . "

She lay on her side on the carpet, crying softly and holding her leg, and as Denny crawled toward her, he turned his eyes to the girl.

Amy sat, twitching her fingers before her eyes, a frown etched deeply into her unlined face, and he could almost feel the waves of undiluted jealousy pulsing across the room to envelope him in a taut, confining web of guilt.

He slumped to the floor, afraid of his own murderous urges, afraid more of his servitude.

Scene 2

(that evening)

TWILIGHT—EXT—EST—A TV STATION. We are looking at KTVR in Dallas, Gayler's interim headquarters for WCN. The crowds have not yet discovered the new studio, so all is quiet, though in the bg we see a helicopter landing in the parking lot, several WCN people emerging and hurrying to the building.

CUT TO:

INT—KTVR. The quiet outside the building belies the turmoil within as we subjectively wander down a long hallway jammed with people, everyone from the KTVR staff to the huge WCN contingent to a large number of armed security personnel. We float unmolested down the hallway, a constant drone of voices our close companion until we stop before a door marked STUDIO 2. We ignore the flashing red ON AIR sign and push into the studio to see what's what. The area we stand in is swallowed in shadows, the floor littered with thick coaxial cables, but just ahead, we can see the male and female newscast team sitting in a bright egg of light on a news set that is draped all in black to disguise it. Three cameramen fluidly guide their electronic eyes around the area in front of the set. Behind and to the side of the newscasters is a blue screen upon which will be shown newsreel film for the people at home. The female's voice can be heard coming through a speaker set near us at ceiling level.

NEWSCASTER

. . . is the closest thing to disaster proportions we've ever seen without a catastrophe. Worldwide the story is similar. All international airlines are reporting flights totally booked to the United States, even though all domestic airlines are being routed around Dallas–Fort Worth and are not allowed to land.

While foreign governments are playing down the importance of the Dennis Stiller reports to their citizens, there is growing evidence of large cult followings gathering steam in many countries just as here in the States, reports are flooding in of large groups of citizens gathering in town meeting halls to discuss the broadcasts and pray. . . .

We turn to the right and see the broadcast booth set in a blockhouse just up a short flight of steps. We walk up and into the darkened booth where all the real action takes place. The director sits in front of the board wearing headphones, his head bandaged, two of his fingers fixed up in a splint. Beside him sits his assistant, a woman with her arm wrapped in gauze through which a small amount of blood has seeped. The sound man sits on the other side of the director as the assistant-director feeds TelePromTer scroll into the tractor. On the fifteen screens set in the board, we see various shots of the newspeople, plus insert feeds waiting to go on and test patterns. As the director coos in a monotone, we continue to hear the newscaster through a series of small speakers.

DIRECTOR

Okay . . . tighter camera one . . . tighter. Cut to one . . . bang! Loreen, get the hair out of your face . . . good. Give us a two-shot camera three . . . tighter. . . .

NEWSCASTER (os)

. . . while in the United Nations Security Council today, the United States was forced to veto a demand by the USSR that Amy Kyle be turned over to an international panel of judges and scientists who could, in the words of the Russian delegate, "test, verify, and determine the future" of the thirteen-year-old autistic girl. The Soviet Union claims that the Kyle girl's power, while not divine, seems to be generated by mental control and that her existence upsets the balance of power between the superpowers and could seriously affect the course of present and future summits and arms limitations talks if not dealt with quickly.

We continue to look around the booth, past the flashing board
to the tractor at the side of the room. As we watch the long
strip of paper feed into the machine, we hear the very same
words that we are reading.

NEWSCASTER (cont, os)
As Texas tries vainly to deal with the ever-increasing
transient population coming into the state, the National Guard has closed down all roads leading into
the greater Dallas area.

Our gaze travels upward until we can look through the window
of the booth at the newscasters without. Just beneath the
window we see a monitor showing the newscaster with a scene
on Interstate 35 leading to Dallas superimposed on the blue
backing beside her. Troops are all over the roadway, cars lined
up for miles leading up to the roadblock.

NEWSCASTER (cont)
But a great many people are ignoring the roadblocks
and are trying to get through by going overland.

On the screen we see a four-wheel drive Toyota leave the road
and crash off into the flat plain beside, engine gunning as it
spins off past the Guardsmen. The soldiers, shouting, raise
their M–16s and FIRE, first in the air, then directly at the
vehicle. It distances them by perhaps fifty yards before finally
coming to a stop, SMOKE pouring out from under the hood.

NEWSCASTER (cont)
The driver of that vehicle and one passenger were
killed in the exchange, bringing the total to twenty
dead and over a hundred wounded in connection
with the Amy Kyle phenomenon. Please heed the
warnings. Stay away from Dallas.

We wander out of the booth and back down the stairs, making
our way through the cables and past the cameras to move onto
the newscasters set. The man is talking now, keeping a
bandaged hand below the camera level.

NEWSCASTER
. . . to be no middle ground in the controversy,
with opposition large, vocal, and some
say . . . violent.

We move around the newscasters' desk and peek over their shoulders at the minimonitors inset into their desk. On the screen, we are seeing a large, nighttime demonstration before a huge bonfire in which effigies marked AMY, TAWNY and DENNIS are being consumed in the flames.

NEWSCASTER (cont)

This from Dearborn, Michigan, last night where an estimated twenty thousand people turned out at a rally condemning the faith healers and the broadcast-ing of their message.

We move in closer to the screen as the scene switches to a shot of Dr. Connover, speaking from in front of his church.

NEWSCASTER (cont, os)

The acknowledged leader of the opposition is evange-list James Connover, founder of the church of the Savior and chief executive officer of World Ministries.

CONNOVER

I didn't ask for it, but it seems to have fallen to me to expose these charlatans and their scam before the people of this world. We've received literally millions of pieces of mail worldwide condemning this ugly charade and we're using our Bumpercrop studios in Europe, Asia, and South and Central America as a rallying point for true Christians everywhere to make the Truth heard.

CUT TO;

EXT—DAY—THE CENTRAL AMERICAN JUNGLES. We are looking at a TV studio that is a miniversion of Connover's church. A large crowd has gathered. They are carrying signs written in Spanish and are chanting loudly, led on by an American with a bullhorn, "JESUS YES, STILLER NO." There is a billboard by the side of the parking lot that reads BUMPERCROP FOR JESUS.

CONNOVER (os)

Demonstrations are occurring at our worldwide stu-dios nearly twenty-four hours a day. We encourage this, the joining of the voices of True Christians ev-erywhere, for as our numbers swell and our voice grows louder, we will be able to drown out the blas-phemy that threatens to devour our land and its peo-

ple. I am here to assure those who are frightened by
the force and lunacy of the followers of this barroom
god, that truth and sanity shall win out, so help me
Jesus.

CUT TO:
ANGLE—NEWSCASTER.

NEWSCASTER

At this moment, the state of Texas can only hope that
Dr. Connover's predicted dose of sanity will take
place soon . . . before we have to bury any more of
our friends. And finally this . . .

CUT TO:
ANGLE—DR. MORELAND. We are looking at a crudely
made videotape of the psychiatrist who examined Amy. The
man is tied to a chair, a blindfold covering his eyes, a thin
trickle of blood running out of the corner of his mouth. We
MOVE IN TIGHT until our vision is totally filled with the
picture of the pathetic man.

NEWSCASTER

This was received this morning, delivered by a
spokesman for a group calling itself the United Moslem Front. Their demand, according to their spokesman, is that Amy Kyle miraculously free every
Moslem from every jail worldwide. As soon as that is
accomplished, the doctor will be set free. The FBI
has been called into the Moreland case, but any investigative procedures are sorely hampered by the
emergency situation that exists in Dallas today. And,
frankly, the Dallas police department feels that the
Moreland kidnapping is a very low priority right now.
A spokesman we talked to expressed the feeling that
the area psychiatrist had brought on his own problems.

ANGLE—SMALL MONITOR. We are watching the newscast
on a different television, the picture fluttering in black and
white. In the bg we hear a persistent BUZZING SOUND.
ANGLE—WCN MOBILE UNIT—INT. Denny sits before

the control board watching the monitor as he shaves with an electric razor, its sound drowning out the newscaster. Amy sits on the floor beside him, rocking back and forth, humming softly. It is dark in the van, except for the light coming through the monitor. Toward cab level, a curtain separating the ministudio from the cab has been pulled open. Frank is driving the van, Molly in the passenger seat. She's twisted around in her seat so she can watch the monitor. Denny turns off the razor and leans toward the cab.

DENNY

How much farther?

FRANK

(over his shoulder)

The houses around here are as big as airplane hangars. When they get as big as Rhode Island, we'll be there.

MOLLY

I feel so bad about Dr. Moreland.

"Yeah," Denny replied, putting down the razor and instinctively feeling the smoothness of his face. "I feel bad about everything that's happened. Why can't people be more reasonable?"

"Because they're fucked up," Frank stated flatly, as good an estimation as any. "And because they take their lives too seriously."

Molly rolled her eyes and turned to the man. "I guess they should just accept the fact that they're useless animals living useless, pointless lives, right?"

The man turned and smiled wide at her. "You got a great way of takin' everthin' to the extreme, darlin'."

"Perhaps you'll admit that we have at least a partial responsibility in all this," she said.

"No," Denny said loudly. "I don't accept that at all. We're not trying to influence public opinion. We're conducting a scientific survey. We haven't done so much as one thing to bias our report. It would be like saying that Bill Maudlin or Edward R. Murrow caused World War II because they reported it."

"TV coverage of the Vietnam War had a very direct

influence over people in this country," Molly returned. "Many
people attribute the antiwar effort and loss of the war to TV
coverage."

"Right," Frank said, "by showin' the Truth. The folks got to
see war close up for the first time right in their livin' rooms and
saw that it was nasty, not noble. It started makin' people think
about the reasons we was fightin' to begin with."

"Enough," Denny said. "Let's just worry about keeping
ourselves together tonight for now. We'll debate the morality
later."

"You've been saying that for a week," Molly said.

"We're comin' up on it! Frank said. "Jesus . . . there's
cops everwhere."

Denny leaned up and looked through the windshield. The
entire street leading up to Gayler's dark, gothic mansion was
barricaded, the house itself sitting halfway along the block atop
a small hill. A number of police cruisers were scattered around
the street on both sides of the barricades, their display lights
stabbing ineffectually into the curtain of night while shadowy
foot patrolmen armed with riot guns were scattered across the
lawns forming a loose cordon all around the property.

"Remember," Denny said, "stick as close as possible while
we're in there. Don't let them separate us."

"You act as if Gayler's the enemy," Molly said.

"Everybody's our enemy right now," Denny replied.

A blue-suited cop moved up to the driver's door, Frank
rolling down the window. "We're here to— " he began, the cop
cutting him off.

"We know who the hell you are and why you're here," the
man said, his voice dripping venom. He waved to the men on
the barricade and they hurried to side it.

"Well," Frank said, "hi-dee-doo to you too."

"Fuck you," the cop said. "If it was up to me, I'd shoot the
lot of you right here. Go on in."

He stepped away from the window and angrily waved
Frank on, and Denny realized for the first time exactly how
hard the job of the police had been for the last week. The
whole force probably hated him for what he'd done to their
town.

Frank rolled up the window and stepped on the gas,
Denny watching the men on the barricade glare at them as
they passed. This wasn't friendly territory. He was going to
watch himself every moment.

"My God, Denny," Molly said softly as they slid down the car lined street thick with elm trees. "This is insane."

"Not now," Denny said.

"Where should I park it?" Frank said.

"Out here on the street," Denny replied. "Somewhere we can't get blocked in."

"Gotcha."

Frank pulled up behind a blue, covered jeep with an air force tag and cut the engine. The night enfolded them, a hazy moon casting gray light over the silent, brooding landscape.

"Thin's movin' off in the dark," Frank said quietly.

"We're committed now," Denny said. "Stick with me and let's go."

As Frank and Molly climbed out of the cab, Denny picked up Amy and carried her out the back door, setting her on the ground, the others already waiting as he climbed down.

"Stay within touching distance," Denny said. "If anything happens, I'll try to wish us out of here or something. We move as a unit toward the front door."

They left the van with its cardboarded WCN logo and bedspread-wrapped transmitter on top and walked across the unlined asphalt of Gayler's drive, skittering along a line of cars and up the long driveway. Molly limped slightly, her leg still in pain from the collision with Denny that afternoon. Fortunately, neither of them had been seriously hurt in the fall, and Denny had blown past the incident, pretending that he had simply broken concentration at the wrong time and letting it go at that. The real reason for the accident he pulled gently by the hand as she pulled her hair out to arm's length and let it flutter across her face.

As they walked, Denny heard the screech of walkie-talkies in the distance, their sound silencing even the crickets. Gayler's house was set off all by itself on its hilltop, head and shoulders above the other mansions in the neighborhood that Ted's daddy had founded in the 1920s.

The house towered above its huge, meticulous lawn, which was left undeveloped in the usual fashion of the plains states. There the house's nod to its Midwestern roots ended, however. The place was Old World splendor in rough stone and stained glass, with buttressed walls and three-story round turrets that gave it the look of a castle. Ivy climbed the walls in large splotches, light escaping to the outside from well-trimmed holes fronting casement windows.

Amy began whining softly, throwing her arms around Denny's waist and squeezing, wanting to hang back. He could feel her trembling and emotionally sense her fear of this place and its inhabitants, a fear he was beginning to share. Maybe he'd been rash for accepting the deal, though as he felt her power flow through him, he knew that even Gayler was capable of underestimating his opposition.

"There's someone behind that car," Molly said, pointing behind them.

"I know," Denny said, gesturing out over the lawn. "And behind the trees."

"What's going on?"

"I think they's as afraid of us as we are of them," Frank replied, another walkie-talkie squawking nearby.

Dark shadowy figures were converging on them from all around— men with guns. Denny tightened his grip on Amy's hand and turned a circle, seeing them all around, twenty feet distant.

"Just keep walking," Denny said. "Security's just tight. We *are* an international incident, you know."

The circle tightened, their cordon moving to within ten feet of them, walking with them. The men all wore plain clothes and were in a semicrouch, like apes, ready to spring into some sort of action. Their pistols were drawn, but pointed upward. A small consolation. He thought of the Air Force jeep and wondered if he was meeting the Secret Service. The thought really bothered him. He didn't like the idea of the government involved in this one bit, especially given the nature of his relationship with the president.

When he couldn't stand it any more, he threw an arm wide, the plainclothesmen going to the ground, ducking beneath the arc of his harmless gesture.

"Gentlemen," he said. "Can't we be civilized about this? We're all adults here, right?"

They just stared at him, faces frozen hard in fear and hatred. Denny sighed. "Well, I wish you would at least put those guns away."

He closed his eyes, concentrating briefly and opened them to the sight of his "security team" holstering their weapons. "That's better," he said, winking quickly at Frank.

They walked on, still surrounded, passing the big WCN roving studio semitrailer by the front door, its motor running, thick black cables running from its underside and through a cathedral window in the house.

"Looks like we're fixin' to broadcast from here," Frank said, staring at the truck. "Sure would like to have all this stuff back at our studio."

They reached the front door and knocked, a man in a tuxedo opening it to smile at them. "Welcome folks," he said, pulling the door wide. "My name is Larry Gates."

The man stepped aside as they walked in, the plainclothes-men staying outside. Though it didn't seem to matter. Three other men packed in close around them on the threshold.

Gates spoke up. "I'm in charge of your security here tonight," he smiled. "We'll try our best to be unobtrusive. Just think of us as part of the furniture. And if you need anything—"

"I'll ask a couch," Denny said.

Gates laughed. "Very good," he said. "Now, if you'll step this way I'll take you to your host."

Denny and the others followed Gates into the guts of the magnificent house. The heavily wood-paneled entry hall led through an archway into a huge, open living room jammed with people in after-five attire. They drank martinis carried on silver trays by servants in starched white jackets and made small talk above the background music of a jazz pianist. When Denny, still dragging Amy along, walked into the room, everything stopped, the assembled crowd applauding politely.

If they didn't feel odd enough already, the difference in dress underscored their alienness. Denny wore a casual suit, nothing like the black tuxes here, and Frank just wore his jeans and a checked shirt. Denny waved self-consciously and walked into their midst, many people nodding and saying hello—some he recognized by sight, others by reputation. There were WCN personnel and local political leaders. Representatives from the nets were there, production and out-front people. He recognized media and entertainment celebrities, newspaper-men, and influential spokesmen from the professional sports fields, the clergy, and the uniformed military. Gayler was solidifying his position. If Denny was going to put it over the top, the old man wanted enough believable and trusted eyewitnesses present to spread the word through unbiased channels, The old man couldn't lose this way. If Denny fell flat on his face, Gayler could say that he uncovered the scam by forcing it out into the open.

The house itself was even more interesting than the assembled guests. It was a deliberate study in absolute contrast. A tribute to a lifestyle and elegance no longer existing, the house boasted polished wood floors and plaster walls trimmed in thick oak, and glittering crystal chandeliers. Its incredible vaulted ceilings were covered in frescoes done in the style of the Renaissance masters. Its draperies were thick, burnished velvet hung floor to ceiling. But like a crack in plaster, the whole atmosphere was cut by liberal splashes of ultramodern—stainless steel and glass tables and sculptures, a bar outlined with pale blue neon, minimalist furniture groupings and large Jackson Pollock paintings on the walls. The two motifs would never have worked together had they not been done so boldly or consistently— almost as if the mixture were a statement and not merely decoration. It impressed Denny in a way he couldn't understand.

"Wait here for a moment," Gates said, stopping their forward movement. "I'll see if Mr. Gayler is ready for you."

The man walked off, leaving them standing in the middle of a room full of people, their bodyguards drifting back to an acceptable distance. Beyond the living area, Denny could see the dining room through another archway. It was partially cleared out and set with klieg lights and cameras—their studio for the night.

While Denny searched the crowd around them for friendly faces, Frank reached out and grabbed a couple of drinks off a tray that was moving past. He handed one to Denny. "Might as well drink," he shrugged and downed his martini with one swallow.

Denny sipped his and smiled at the people nearby. They had all managed to clear a five foot area around him and stared with a kind of nervous bravado, as if he were a trained tiger sitting in their midst and they were trying to show their courage.

"I feel like I've got leprosy," Molly whispered.

Denny turned to her. Although she had fixed herself up and looked good in a double knit dress, there was still a wistfulness about her, a deep and troubled yearning that made her look small and nearly terrified. He held his drink up. "Maybe you could use a sip of this."

She shook her head rapidly. "No," she said. "I can barely maintain as it is."

"There you are!" called a familiar voice from the crowd,

Dick Horton's wife, Lynn, pushing her way through to reach them. The woman looked out of place in her off-the-shoulder evening gown and black-framed glasses. Mother of five and confirmed homebody, she always seemed more appropriately dressed in her official uniform of jeans and sweaters. She hugged Denny fiercely, jumping back, startled when she caught a dose of static electricity as her arm brushed against Amy. "My, my," she said, rubbing the place. "You sure put out the volts, sweetheart."

"Good to see you, Lynn," Denny smiled. "Sorry about—"

"Don't say it," she said, cutting him off. "You've just been doing your job. And don't pay any attention to what my old grouch of a husband says about it either. He's just a stuffed shirt." She turned to Molly. "My dear, you get prettier every day."

Molly blushed, a hand going reflexively to her hair. "I feel so underdressed here," she whispered.

"Oh pooh," Lynn said, her expansive face grimacing. "You put the other women here to shame." She looked at Denny. "I just can't figure out why some smart man hasn't scooped you up yet, that's all."

"Enough!" came a voice from outside the circle, Dick Horton, his arm in a sling that was trussed up at a right angle to his body, walking up to join them. "I could feel waves of embarrassment pulsating all the way across the room." The man had a martini resting atop his cast as if it were a small table. He picked it up with his good hand and took a sip.

"I'm just informing these good people of the obvious," Lynn said, walking up to sip from her husband's glass, a practice that was always guaranteed to drive him insane. She fit easily against him, his arm going around her waist, and Denny envied them their free and giving relationship.

Once Dick and Lynn had broken the ice, other people edged closer to their circle, listening with interest.

"Tonight's going to make it or break it for you, Denny," Horton said. "And I'm not sure I know which one I'm pulling for."

Denny shook his head. "I know how things are going to go," he said, "and I'm not sure how I feel about it, either."

"Oh, don't make such a big deal out of it," Lynn said. "Things always have a way of working out."

"Really?" Denny said. "Maybe you and I live in different galaxies."

She smiled and shook her head. "You don't get it, do you? Life just goes on, that's all. This, too, shall pass. Just do me a favor and don't let my old man get hurt anymore."

Dick raised his eyebrows high. "Get this—she cares about me!"

"Damn right," she deadpanned. "If anything happened to you, I'd have to get a job." Lynn looked at the girl, unconsciously rubbing the spot where they had touched. "She seems sweet."

Denny smiled at the power he felt surging through him as he held Amy's hand. "She's a nice kid," he said, and noticed that Molly's eyebrows had narrowed.

"Does she ever communicate with you?" one of the onlookers a newsman with NBC, asked.

"It depends on your definition of communication," Denny answered. "We communicate nonverbally."

"You mean like brain to brain?" someone else asked.

"It's more complex, more . . . abstract than that," Denny said. "We communicate through shared feelings, through brain images and . . . dreams."

"She plants dreams in your head?" the newsman asked and the surrounding group laughed, loosening up.

Denny frowned. He was already in deeper than he'd intended to go. It wasn't easy being on the wrong side of the gun. He looked at Molly, but she seemed as anxious to hear his answer as the rest of them. "It's more like she . . . manipulates the dreams that I already have."

"That's impossible," someone said.

"Do you realize what you're saying?" Dick asked, as Frank grabbed another drink off a tray and took it down in one gulp. "You're saying she reacts with premeditated calculation. You've always said—"

"I don't mean it like that," Denny said. "I—"

"Mr. Stiller!" came Gates's voice from outside the circle.

Denny sighed. Saved. "Over here!" he called.

The man gently but firmly shoved his way through the now large, curious group. "Mr. Gayler will see you now."

Someone pretended he was a dog barking.

"His master's voice," the NBC man said automatically, the crowd, nervously excited, laughing too much in response.

Denny exaggerated a shrug and followed Gates, Frank and Molly right behind, Amy struggling against his pull. As they

walked, several people who reached out to touch Amy were
rewarded with painful shocks.

They moved through the living room to the pianist's strains
of "Blue Rondo ala Turk" and walked into the makeshift studio,
their entourage of tuxedoed bodyguards closing ranks and
once again Denny couldn't figure out whether the guards were
protecting them or the guests.

The dining room was large and filled with technicians who
hurried around to make the place ready, moving lights and
setting chairs up in the area behind the two cameras that
would broadcast the action.

"Too bright," Frank said and swirled another drink that he
had acquired from somewhere.

"We'll worry about it later," Denny said, and they moved
into a hallway that branched off in two directions, taking the
left fork.

The house quieted the farther they got from the party. The
hallway was dark down here, barely navigable. "Can't we turn
on some lights?" Molly asked.

"Almost there," Gates said, ignoring her question. They
branched off down another, shorter hallway and arrived at a
closed door watched over by two men sitting on folding chairs
and dressed in blue suits.

Gates reached out, touching the knob, and looked at
Denny. "I'm sorry," he said, "but your friends can't go in with
you."

Denny met the man's hard eyes and decided it wouldn't
hurt to play along this one time. "Go take care of the lights,"
he told Frank over his shoulder, "and tell whoever's in charge
that I want you directing."

"You sure this is all copacetic?" the man asked.

"I can handle it," Denny said, then looked at Molly. "Work
the crowd a little. Play down the more bizarre elements."

"Like dream manipulation?" she asked, cocking her head.

"Just do it," he said, then added sweetly, "Please?"

"This is a mistake," she said, then turned and walked off,
Frank right with her.

Denny looked at Gates. "It's your party," he said.

With one hand on the knob, the man knocked lightly with
the other. Gayler acknowledged weakly from behind the door
and Gates opened it, gesturing Denny inside.

Denny handed Gates his drink as he and Amy walked into
a large library that took up two stories, a mezzanine balcony

running around the second tier of shelves. Gates shut the door behind him, staying outside. Dark oxblood leather furniture was scattered around the room, the deep plush of a Persian carpet warming the polished gloss of the hardwood floors.

Two men sat, legs crossed, like bookends on either side of a couch facing the door. One of the men was Ted Gayler, the other the President of the United States. Denny picked up Amy and set her on one of the nearby chairs, feeling relatively safe, and walked over to shake each man's hand in turn.

"Mr. Gayler . . . Mr. President," he said. "Kind of surprised to see you out in our neck of the woods."

The president stood, towering over Denny. "You're the world's hot spot, Stiller," he said. "Where else would I be?"

Denny laughed. "Surely you exaggerate."

The man simply stared down at him. "No," he said after a moment. "In fact I'm here precisely to talk to you about a matter of national security, and I ask that our discussion never leave this room."

"If it is truly a matter of national security," Denny said, "then I will gladly comply."

Gayler chuckled. "That's what they call a disclaimer, Mr. President."

The man nodded, never taking his eyes off Denny. "Use them all the time myself," he said. "Why don't we sit and be comfortable?"

"Fine." Denny grabbed a hard-backed chair from a corner and pulled it up in front of the sofa, a coffee table separating the men. "Now what can I do for you?"

The president, dressed in gray pinstripes, leaned forward, fixing Denny with intense eyes. "I want to ask you a question and I want the absolute truth in return."

"Tell you what," Denny said. "I'll answer a question for you if you'll answer a question for me."

The president smiled. "Go right ahead, you first."

Denny sat back, staring first at Gayler, then the president. He couldn't have planned this any better. "Did you pull strings to have me demoted off the Washington beat after our interview last year?" he asked.

The president looked startled, then turned to stare at Gayler. "What's he talking about?" he asked.

The old man smiled paternally, speaking in his quiet, authoritative voice. "Denny thinks you didn't like his questions in an interview once and talked me into bumping him down to regionals."

The president showed Denny empty palms. "If I tried to get rid of every reporter who ever gave me a hard time," he said, "there wouldn't *be* any Washington beat. Sorry, Denny. You've been kicking the wrong horse."

Stiller turned to stare at Gayler, the man's face an unreadable mask, though a glow of triumph seemed to hover in his steel-hard eyes. He said nothing.

He looked back at the president, feeling off balance now. "What was *your* question?" he said.

The man stood and walked to a large walnut desk, pouring a cup from a Mr. Coffee on its top. "Before you answer this," he said, staring down at the steaming brew in his fist, "I want you to consider the gravity of the stituation. Your broadcasts have aroused the interest of the entire world, our friends and our enemies. Decisions made by and about you and"—he nodded in Amy's direction—" the girl, will have far-reaching impact, not just in the United States, but worldwide."

"Yes," Denny said, "I understand what you're saying."

The president moved over near Amy, looking down at the girl and shaking his head as she sat rock still, staring into space with unblinking, unfocused eyes. "Is this real?" he asked, wheeling around to Denny. "I mean, is this really happening? Can this . . . this child really do the things you say she can do, or is this just a hoax or an entertainment or whatever else you'd want to call it. Think before you answer; evaluate your response."

"I don't need to think about it," Denny said. "I'm a newsman, not a stage magician. I'm looking for news stories, not 'entertainments.' I've never reported anything untrue before and I'm certainly not doing it now."

The president frowned deeply and took a drink of his coffee. "I was afraid you'd say that," he said. "Everything I've seen so far tell me it's true. I guess I was hoping against hope."

"I don't understand," Denny said.

"I'll spell it out," the president said. "That little girl is the human equivalent of a doomsday bomb. Her very existence upsets the balance of power to such a degree that our enemies could never allow us to keep her within the jurisdiction of our boundaries, and frankly, I can't blame them."

"Are you saying that the Russians would go to war over her?" Denny asked.

"A miracle is nothing more than a reverse holocaust," Gayler said quietly. "The unbridled power is the issue here."

"You see," the president said, moving back to the couch to take his seat, "our options are very limited. The girl's existence is a danger to everyone. I don't know if the Russians would go directly to war over this, but they would yell and first stop any negotiations we've got going with them and second impose sanctions economically, urging everyone else in the world to join with them."

"But she's just a little girl," Denny said. "It doesn't make any sense that everyone would get so upset about her."

"I don't blame them a bit," the president said, drinking again and setting the cup on the table. "Suppose, God forbid, the Soviets came on international televison and announced that they had a boy under their control who could mentally destroy the laws of nature for his own ends. And suppose then the Russians go on to prove it by having the boy perform incredible feats of will power right on live TV. How could we live with that as a country? The very first thing I'd figure him to do would be to make our weapon stockpiles inoperative from nuke warheads right on down. I'd be tempted to attack immediately, before it would be too late. If you've got the power, Denny, the tendency at all times is to use it. The Russians think it's possible now that we have a weapon they can't counter, and I can tell you from experience that the politburo is shaking from stem to stern because of it."

Denny turned and looked at Amy. He saw a beautiful little girl with a terrible problem. But he just didn't see World War III. He looked at the president. "I'm not going to try anything military with her," he said. "This is just small . . . you know, experiments."

"The temptation to use the power exists, Denny," Gayler said. "You'd have a difficult time convincing anybody that you've got the willpower to resist it."

"What, exactly, are you asking me to do?" Denny said.

"Turn her over to us," the president replied. "We'll do as the Russians suggested and turn her over to an international panel. I believe that's the only way to assure that not only the various countries, but the girl herself, will be protected."

"And what would keep you from giving into the temptation when you get hold of her, Mr. President?" Denny said. "How will you convince me that you've got the willpower to resist using the power?"

"I'm asking you as an American citizen to turn her over to us," the president said.

"I think that you might just want to kill her," Denny said. "That's one way of solving the problem to everyone's satisfaction, except the child's, of course."

"Watch your language, son," the president said angrily. "You don't know what you're saying."

Denny stood, walking back protectively to Amy and picking her up. "Don't be self-righteous," he said. "In the interests of national security, people like you consign millions of innocents to the flames of war and attrition and call them expendable. Well, Amy Kyle is *not* expendable. She's mine and you're not going to get her."

"There's nowhere to take this thing, Stiller," the man said, his voice tense. "There can't be any good end to this. How many innocents will die if you have *your* way?"

"Nobody has to die," Denny said. "All the trouble, every bad thing that's happened in connection with my broadcasts has been the result of choices made by people I don't even know, much less influence. It's you and all the people around you who persist in making decisions that have nothing to do with me or Amy. If you can't convince the Russians that Amy and I are harmless, well, maybe that's a problem with your communication, *not* with me. I haven't done anything wrong and I don't have to feel like a criminal or a traitor because of my association with this sweet little girl."

"Power corrupts," the president said, his face gone pale.

"No," Denny replied. "People corrupt power, but not all people, not all power."

"You have a lot to learn," the president said, taking one last sip of coffee before standing, looking old, looking tired. "This is your last chance to get away from this clean. You let me walk out that door and I'll consider you as much of a threat as I consider her." He pointed to Amy. "I feel that it's my clear duty as leader of this country to make sure that national security isn't threatened from without *or* within."

He turned to Gayler, his failure to move Denny seeming to drain and hobble him. "I tried."

The old man smiled calmly. "Go back to Washington," he said. "We'll talk later."

The president nodded and moved without a word toward the door, Denny following him with his eyes and trying to remain cool despite the threats implicit in the president's words. He was shaking slightly. This had caught him off guard, had him all tied up in knots. All he needed was to have the U.S. government after him, too. Then he began to wonder about the whole setup at the mansion. Was it designed to let him in but not out?

"Oh, Denny," Gayler said softly. "So impetuous. You're really pretty remarkable, actually."

"What do you mean?" Denny asked, turning back to face Gayler.

"Sit," the old man said. "You make me nervous."

Denny moved to the couch, taking the president's vacated seat. He set Amy beside him, but she scooted off the couch and began tracing the Persian carpet's designs with her fingers, following them on hands and knees.

"What did you mean when you called me, remarkable?" Denny asked, as Gayler watched the girl with interest, his eyes alight.

The man just touched Denny with his eyes before returning to Amy. "Most men at your age have already been beaten down by life," he said. "Most men are happy to accept compromise in any form and authority in every form. You just keep punching and fuming and trying to do things your own way. I guess in my day they would have called you a rugged individualist."

"And I guess today they call me a traitor," Denny replied.

The old man smiled broadly and shook his head. "I was certainly right to have picked you to explore Amy's powers. No one could have stood up under it like you have."

"You *were* there at Billy Bob's that night, weren't you?" Denny said.

"Oh yes," Gayler replied, and began searching through his three-piece brown suit for his pills. "I'd been a regular for about a month. would you mind getting me a cup of coffee?"

Denny stood and walked to the desk. The room was comfortable and elegant, surrounding him with wisdom and the stability of natural wood. So, why did he feel out of place? As he poured himself and Gayler a cup of coffee, he said. "You had an inkling of her power, then. Which means that you simply used me to confirm or deny, ready at any given time to throw me to the wolves if things got out of hand."

"Absolutely," Gayler said. "The girl and her power are important, perhaps even dangerous. Your existence means nothing to me one way or the other—no disrespect intended.

All things being equal, your life is relatively meaningless in the scheme of things."

Denny walked back and set the steaming cups on the table as Gayler poured a little yellow pill out of its amber, plastic case into the palm of his hand. "How about *you* telling me why I got bumped from the Washington beat," he said.

Gayler waved it off and took his pill, washing it down with coffee. "Old news," he said. "You should be worrying at this point about how you're going to stay alive. You're right between the rock and the hard place, Denny, and you can't stay there forever. No, sir. Can't stay there long at all. Face it, boy. You were never meant for the rarified air at the top. You don't have the training or the breeding for it. Save your ass while you've still got a chance."

"You want me to give her up, too," Denny said, tasting his own coffee. It was bitter, almost metallic.

Gayler sat back, slowly, with great effort, his body no longer as nimble as his mind. "Oh, yes," he said, nearly a sigh. "I'd have already had her except that I underestimated how quickly you'd act. You've been clever, but that's all over now. It's imperative that you turn her over to me."

"You want to use her, don't you?" Denny asked.

The man put slender, pale fingers to his temples, massaging gently. "Miracles don't impress me," he said. "I'm old. When you get old, maintaining the status quo becomes a miracle in itself. I don't deny that I might consider trying to become young again before I kill the girl, but kill her I will."

Denny stared at the man who could talk of murder so casually. What in God's name had he wandered into here? First, Gayler orders the president around as if he's a butler, then freely admits to Denny that he wants to kill his charge. It could only mean one thing: the old man didn't intend for Denny to leave his house.

"Why?" he asked.

"Believe me," Gayler said, "you really don't want an answer to your question."

"I'm a smart boy," Denny replied, checking Amy's position, not wanting to be too far from her reach. "Try me."

Gayler clapped his hands together to a dull thud. "All right, let's try. The world you live in, the world of Dennis Stiller and WCN and all the people and the news you report, is not the real world. It's a world of ideologies and religions and elections and issues that are important and meaningful. It's a world of love and hate, absolutes of emotion, terrible murders and heroic rescues."

"I'm still listening," Denny said.

"That's not the real world, you see," Gayler said. "I sort of hate to disappoint you, but your world is merely what Shakespeare would call, the stage, all its population merely the players. Your wars have never decided anything, your elections meaningless exercises in ego gratifications."

"Then what docs run everything?"

"Greed," the man said simply, "and a few people who understand its workings. Human beings deny the animalistic side of themselves to their own detriment. It's up to those of us more farsighted to use mankind's deterioration for his benefit."

Denny looked at his watch. They were supposed to broadcast in less than twenty minutes. Amy was crawling near him. He reached out and picked her up, holding her close for reassurance. "I still don't know what you're talking about," he told Gayler.

"You can't see the forest for the trees, can you?" Gayler asked, not expecting or wanting an answer. "Let me explain. Look around you, Denny. Look at all the books here. There are sixty thousand volumes locked away here in this room, all of them books on world history. I also have every historical videotape and 16-mm film ever made, plus copies of every major historical document ever produced by the mind of man. I've devoted my whole life to the study of history and of its ramifications. And one constant stands out amid all the pagentry and savagery—greed. Man succeeded as all animals succeed, by being greedy. Greed—individual and collective—is the perfection and dissolution of society. It is our greatness and our shame, our bursting forth in fire and the ashes that grow cold. For you see, our collective life on plant Earth has been nothing but a long, downward spiral, through greed, toward death . . . of the people, of the planet and its resources."

"Not everyone—"

"Stop," Gayler said, putting up a milk white hand. "I already know what you're going to say. It's a knee-jerk reaction to say that everyone's not greedy and selfish, but, inevitably, they are. It's the hallmark of the species, our best point, the thing that has made us master of all we survey. We take without thought; we take without guilt; we take our share and every other share we can get. To deny our motivating force is to deny our humanity. Those of us who understand that fact move the world very quietly and effectively along the path to destruction, while trying to maintain relative comfort and happiness for our people along the way."

Amy was trembling in Denny's arms. "Who are you talking about, international leaders . . . the pope . . . who?"

"Business makes the world go round, Denny, not politics. Countries rise and fall economically. A seeming disaster might be a well-planned blessing. Take the bombing of Hiroshima and Nagasaki at the close of the last world war, unprecedented destruction in order to bring on unprecedented growth. Japanese industrial interests precipitated their entry into the war to bring on the demise of its outmoded systems, hence ushering a new, stronger Japan, born of the computer, to emerge in full bloom into the twentieth century. It was a way of refashioning industry while increasing industry's revenue— a particularly Japanese solution to an interesting problem. Industrial interests on this side of the Pacific made sure the atomic bombs were dropped in order to force Japanese surrender before industrial resources reached depletion stage and the whole operation became cost prohibitive."

"You're out of your fucking mind," Denny said.

The man shrugged slowly. "I said you wouldn't want to hear it," he replied. "Everything is run basically the same way, the world moving along well-planned, homogeneous routes while presenting the facade of cause and effect to human dealings."

"Why the facade at all?" Denny asked.

"The myths of freedom and self-determination and righteousness tend to control people better than a giving over to selfishness," Gayler said. "We certainly don't want to see anarchy, that would be counterproductive for everyone. But if people think they are responding to higher motivations, they tend to channel their greed along acceptable lines. That's why religion was invented—the first truly great motivational control. That's why nationalism was invented. It's only good business sense. You give the people what they want. In this case an unjustified sense of self-worth."

"What's your place in all this?"

"Just trying to do my part," Gayler said modestly. "You know, our demise really is inevitable, Hell, we destroy millions of trees a year just to supply the world in toilet paper.

Look at America. With six percent of the population, we manage to use ninety percent of the earth's resources. Where do you go from there? I work to try to keep our standard of living intact for as long as possible. It's the most we can hope for as our greed takes us full circle. I guess my job is to help hold off the savagery to come for as long as I can. I suppose I'm trying to make us all as comfortable as possible as we die. It is, I think, a noble calling."

"Even if I did believe you, which I don't," Denny said, "what could any of this possibly have to do with Amy?"

Gayler leaned up and took another sip of coffee, his old pale hand still rock solid on the cup. "As our natural resources deplete and our environment becomes more and more undependable because of pollution and poisons, the balance of industrial might becomes very fragile. We must be wary of anything that might upset that balance and plunge us right over the brink upon which we already teeter. The fear is always new inventions unplanned for, but . . . Amy Kyle, now here's something. She could change everything, the entire power base, by simply trying to do good."

The man threw his head back and laughed loudly, falling back to sink into the couch. "You see, my friend, what we must fear more than anything, is the intrusion of unselfish behavior into our selfish world, an intrusion that the world could not survive. The gods we worship are selfish gods, their aims selfish aims. We are, all of us, the devil and mercy me, your cute little Amy could exorcise us all. So, you see I must attend this lovely child's destruction in order to save the world. Now, aren't you glad you asked me?"

Denny stared hard at the man, waiting for the punch line that wasn't forthcoming. "You're serious," he said at last, his voice a whisper.

Gayler straightened again, putting down his coffee cup. Most old men looked like somebody's grandfather or doddering uncle, but not Gayler. There was an energy about him that age couldn't touch, an untouchable air of command that placed him beyond humanity. He turned his eyes full force to Denny. He bore into the newsman, trying to wrest his soul right through his eyes. "Give her to me, Stiller," he said. "Give her to me now."

"No!" Amy screamed, a banshee cry that made Gayler start, his coffee spilling across the table. "No! No! No!"

The girl began writhing powerfully in Denny's arms, her hair whipping around her head, her eyes fluttering wildly as she broke from Denny's grasp and fell across the table, the cups skittering onto the carpet.

"Amy!" Denny called, the girl rolling off the table to the floor and screaming across the room to the door as sixty thousand volumes threw themselves out of the shelves to bang on the floor like thunder, books from the second floor raining down on the first. Denny stood, openmouthed, as books fell loudly all around him, covering the carpet and smashing lamps and knickknacks. The Mr. Coffee exploded with a loud pop as books bounced off the desktop, hot coffee spewing everywhere. A large globe, knocked off its stand, rolled up to Denny's feet. He kicked it away.

He looked at Gayler, the man's face white with shock as he realized that Amy wasn't as docile or as stupid as he'd thought.

Denny turned toward Amy as the door flew open, Larry Gates charging in with a drawn gun. The man saw Amy in front of him and reached for her. The contact spark arced blinding white, like lightning, throwing Gates across the room to crash into a bookshelf with a loud groan and fall atop a pile of H. G. Wells's histories.

"There's your answer," Denny said as he stared down at the horrified man. "You want us, you're going to have to take us."

With that, he turned his back on Gayler and strode to the door, taking Amy by the hand, the contact strong. Two secret servicemen stood in the doorway with their guns drawn, pointing. With a thought, Denny sent the guns flying from their hands, he and Amy casually walking past them and back down the long, dark hallway, leaving the destruction behind.

They had a show to do.

And quite a show it would be, too, as Denny, pumped up with anger and adrenaline and the raw power that flowed through him, moved with determination into the dining room-studio, ready to face the crazy world and anything Gayler could throw at him. His reality had crashed around him, everything topsy-turvy and up for grabs. If this was a new world he had entered, he was prepared to make a grand entrance.

The place was a madhouse. Frank, drunk, was weaving around the room arguing loudly with Russ Mallory, a WCN program director, and Dick Horton while Molly cried in the corner of the room, Lynn Horton and Barbara Walters trying to comfort her. He began to walk toward Molly to see what the problem was when he caught sight of James Connover, the man also talking loudly with a group of people who seemed to be keeping him from moving in Molly's direction.

"What the hell did you do to her, Connover?" he yelled loudly from across the room, everything stopping, the room full of people turning to stare at him. He didn't care anymore. They came here to see weird shit and he was just the man to give it to them.

Connover slowly eased his way through the people who stood around him and pointed a finger at Denny. "I called her the Jezebel she is and the harlot blasphemer who thinks she can destroy the word of almighty God!"

"What's the matter, asshole," Denny replied. Afraid to pick on someone your own size?" he cocked a fist. "I'll give you all you can handle, you low-rent shit."

Connover took a step forward, his ranks closing around him again, holding him back as Horton stepped between them. "Gentlemen," he said. "This is highly unprofessional. We're on live feed in five minutes."

"They won't let me direct _or_ change the lights," Frank called, Denny staring fire at Horton.

"Boss's orders," the man explained. "His exact words were, 'this is our party, not Stiller's.'"

Denny looked around. It was his move. He smiled confidently at all those around him. "Make a deal with you, Dick," he said, pointing at Connover. "You keep that son of a bitch away from my people and I'll go along with anything you have in mind."

Connover glared at him, but said nothing.

"I can handle that," Horton said, "but once we're on the air—"

"He can say anything he wants when we're on the air," Denny replied, smiling. "I'm more than ready for him. All I ask is that my co-workers be near me, just out of camera range would be fine."

"It's done," Horton said, moving quickly to Connover and speaking to him in hushed whispers.

As Denny gazed indifferently around the room, Amy pulled herself close to him, hugging him tightly, her bright white dress glowing like a candle under the glare of the kliegs. The music had stopped in the other room as people crowded around the archway separating the living and dining rooms. There were several chairs lined up within camera range for Denny's inquisitors, and chairs behind the camera already filled with dignitaries. Gayler moved slowly into the room, his face a mask, and took his place with the dignitaries, ignoring Denny's wide smile of greeting.

Technicians hurried all around him, taking care of the last of the hookups. One of them wheeled a monitor complete with VCR on top into camera range. Good. Denny had need of it.

"You got that tape?" he called across to Frank, who was still giving Mallory an earful as the man tried to get his board hooked up on the far wall.

Frank waved and turned his back to Denny, pointing to a videotape he had stuck in the waist of his jeans.

"Bring it here," he said, waving the man over.

Frank, his eyes bright, walked the tape over to Denny. "You really goin' to use it?" he asked.

"Hell, why not?" Denny replied, and took the tape, placing it in the VCR.

"Two minutes everybody!" Mallory called. "Let's get our places! Most of you are professionals here . . . please . . . when I ask for quiet, give it to me!"

An A.D. ran up and fixed a lapel mike to Denny's suit coat, resolutely shoving him in the process toward the black Xs taped onto the wood floor. He moved to the place as the other participants slowly took their chairs at the edge of the set on what would be the upstage side. Lynn Horton, her arm around a still sobbing Molly, moved the woman up close to the downstage side. Winston Turley, WCN's voiceover announcer paced nervously back and forth across the set, a finger in his ear as he practiced the intro he'd be reading from the papers in his hand.

"One minute!" Mallory called, most of the techs moving off the set, making way for the camera operators who were busy moving around, blocking their angles in unfamiliar territory. A woman in blue jeans and headphones frantically crawled around the floor, snugging loose cables to the wood with duct tape.

Denny leaned down and kissed Amy quickly on the cheek, the girl's eyes opening wide. "It's going to be all right," he whispered to her.

"Thirty seconds . . . Winston . . . take your mark!"

"I'm getting glare off Winston's forehead," the number two camera operator called.

"Fuck it!" Mallory yelled. "Fifteen seconds! Try to look as

if it's not the end of the world. Happy faces! C'mon, happy faces! Quiet on the set!"

Denny stood calmly amid the maelstrom that raged around him. He and the others had been lured there to be set up, but as he looked at Gayler now, he knew the man wasn't at all certain about the outcome of the night's events. As for himself: he was strong; he believed. The power energized him as it pulsed through his veins and it was the absolute power of purity and right. After tonight, there would be no doubt.

He looked at the camera, realizing that it was already on, that Winston was already reading recklessly. God bless him

. . . tonight is to either confirm or dispel, once and for all, the rumors surrounding the power of Amy Kyle," Winston said, the man's eyes jumping up and down from paper to camera, his nervousness obvious on the monitor that sat facing them from behind the cameras. "We have chosen to have this series of experiments conducted in front of a large group to alleviate the charges of camera tricks, plus we've brought together a panel of questioners, each an expert in religion or science or the paranormal. Let me introduce our panel . . ."

Denny turned and looked at the row of men and women who faced him at an angle on the edge of the lit area. The first was a woman named Goldblum, who was a professional psychic-buster, making a living touring around the country debunking psychic phenomenon. Next came a Catholic theologian with a Tip O'Neill nose and prissy lips, named Moran. Next a scientist, a physicist named Haupmann, who wore thick glasses and always appeared to be sneering. Connover sat next to him and next to Connover, a woman named James who claimed to be an astrologer and psychic investigator. The ludicrous panel was rounded out by Dr. Joyce Cousins, a pop TV psychoanalyst.

Denny turned and stared past the cameras to Gayler, realizing that even this was a setup designed to dampen Denny's impact by forcing him into a guilt by association situation with people no one save the *National Enquirer* would call "experts." It didn't matter. He was fixing to take control of the free access that Gayler had dropped into his lap. He'd heard someone say that this broadcast was going out over the satellites and would be reaching nearly a billion people. Good. The old man was playing for high stakes, willingly taking a public beating over everything that had happened if he could take Denny and Amy down with him.

He watched camera one move around to get him in the frame as Winston read his less than sterling introduction. ". . . we have Dennis Stiller, former newsman, now manager and self-confessed channeler to self-proclaimed healer, Amy Kyle. Stiller claims that the Kyle girl, retarded since early childhood, is the possessor of an unexplained power that enables her to circumvent the laws of nature and perform miracles. That is for our panel of judges to find out for themselves, as tonight, right here, we tackle the problem of the godhood of Amy Kyle, and the motivations of her mentor, Dennis Stiller."

Denny stared in rage at the camera. They'd already shot him down and dug the grave. All that remained was for him to fall into the hole and allow them to throw the dirt on him. "I would like to address—" he began, but was shut up by Winston.

"With all due respect, Mr. Stiller," he said, "You have had a great deal of free rein to deal with this subject matter any way you choose. Now it is time to put your claims to the test. Please, we have questioners. You may respond to them. We'll begin with Mrs. Goldblum."

He turned to the panel, let his eyes wander to Molly in the background, her eyes bloodshot, her face fearful. Frank stood with her, another drink in his hand, his face fixed in a hard frown.

"We're glad, at least, that you've come out into the open," the debunker said. "You realize, of course, that everything you've done behind closed doors and in preset conditions is useless for our purposes."

"And just what *are* your purposes?" Denny replied.

"We'll ask the questions, please," the woman said, her eyes hard. "First of all, I'd like to ask if you and the girl will submit to a full body search for optical devices, wires or any other contraband material."

"I will not," Denny said.

"I didn't think so," Goldblum beamed. "Second, I'd like to address the fact that in your earlier years you were a trained magician."

"I was not!" Denny said.

The woman snorted, producing a piece of paper which she waved in front of the camera like a battle flag. "Then perhaps you'd explain this program that lists you as, and I quote, 'Mysterio the Magnificent.'"

Denny laughed, shaking his head. "Where in God's name did you get that?" he asked.

"Just answer the question, Mr. Stiller."

"Look," Denny replied. "In junior high I entered a magic act in a talent contest. I was awful. My long scarf fell out of my sleeve in a lump and the rabbit in my hat died of suffocation. I never again—"

"So, you do admit that you had training as a stage magician," the woman said, writing furiously on a piece of paper as if she were a big-time attorney who'd just uncovered damaging evidence.

"I'd like to address these so-called miracles," the theologian said comtemptuously. "I'd like to ask Mr. Stiller about the Scriptural basis for making his claims of godhood, since the blessings of God's love and grace seem to be absent from his lifestyle and the lifestyles of the poor little girl and her larcenous mother."

"I've never claimed godhood," Denny said.

"Are you denying then, at this late date, that you perform miracles?"

Denny felt himself growing angrier. "Miracle is your word, not mine. I prefer not to think of Amy's abilities in religious terms."

"Are you denying, then," the man said loudly, "that miracles are signs from God as detailed in the Old Testament and the Gospels?"

"I'm not here to discuss religion," Denny said.

"Do you believe in Almighty God?" Connover interrupted. "Do you believe in the healing power of Jesus Christ here on Earth?"

"My beliefs are none of your business," Denny said.

"Listen to him!" Connover shouted. "He denies the very godhead that he pretends to emulate. Speak to us, prophet! Tell us of your blasphemous attempts to surplant God in the lives of the humans you hope to control!"

"This has nothing to do with—"

"And what of that poor little girl?" the psychoanalyst said. "Has it ever occurred to you, Mr. Stiller, that you could be dangerously affecting this autistic child's chances for recovery. When you reinforce the all-powerful nature of the autistic's world, you push them farther into darkness."

"But, I—"

"You're not being fair," the psychic investigator said.

"When I did Mr. Stiller's chart, I found that he had aspects of great power. It's barely believable. His Sun conjuncts Mercury, and the south node of the Moon *and* Pluto are sitting directly on his midheaven. He can control the masses for good or evil. I see clairvoyance and healing ability, with strong, perhaps dangerous sexual overtones, all of it in the public eye. It's amazing that—"

"This is all nonsense!" the physicist said, sneering at the astrologer. "Quite simply, this world is run by a series of natural laws, including the laws of thermodynamics and gravity and motion. These laws have run our planet since the beginning of time, my religious colleagues' quaint biblical interpretations notwithstanding. To calmly toss away the rules that govern us is laughable, like arbitrarily saying that red is really black. To even begin to attribute any credence to these unscientific sputterings is to deny the empirical research and theory of thousands of years by the most brilliant minds on this planet. When you brought all that food to your studio, Mr. Stiller, where did it come from? Was it created from nothing? Was it dematerialized, then rematerialized after being transported from someplace else? How far are you willing to take this idiocy?"

"Why don't you just test me with something?" Denny said. "Then I can show—"

"Your magician's tricks!" Goldblum said. "We've already established your professional credentials in that area, followed by your refusal to allow us to search for the devices you use in your act. I, for one, have no desire to see you conjure up cheap stage magic to help fool the trusting people of this world."

"Well, I have something else to show you anyway," Denny said, turning to the monitor containing the videotape of the dog's resurrection and juicing the set.

Amy was sitting, frightened, on the floor, her fingers blurring before her eyes. He reached down and pulled her to her feet, holding her hand tightly. He'd had enough. He'd been polite enough to let these fools have their say, but now it was his turn.

"I'm sorry," Winston said, "but this broadcast must be conducted according to our rules, and there is nothing in the schedule that would allow—"

"Shut up!" Denny said, and thought up a sore throat for Winston.

"Mr. Stiller, I—" the man's hand went to his throat and he

coughed, forcing himself to swallow. He tried to speak, but a dry rasp came out instead.

Denny looked back to the audience and saw Gayler giving the cut throat gesture to Mallory to make him end the broadcast.

"Don't touch that board, Russ!" Denny called, pointing a finger.

The man reached for the hardwire cutoff, an electrical shock driving him completely away from the board.

Denny turned on the VCR containing the resurrection footage and looked at the wide-eyed camera operators. "Get close on this," he said with authority, camera one hurrying to obey. Frank moved to camera two, shoving the operator out of the way and manning it himself, moving in tight on Amy. "Nobody moves . . . nobody leaves. You wanted power. I'll show it to you!"

He turned on the tape, watching himself, covered with blood, laying the dog on the floor of the fire-gutted, still-smoking studio. He wheeled around to Connover. "Can *you* do it, Jim? Can you raise the dead?"

The man was on his feet. "I can raise my voice in righteous indignation against you, sinner," he said loudly. "I can call on Jesus Christ to bring the scourges of Egypt down on you."

"Yeah?" Denny said. "Then do it. Do it right now."

The audience was staring in horrified fascination at the monitors as the dog's viscera slid back into its body, the wound sealing itself up. People gasped, several women crying.

"You wanted it!" Denny said loudly. "You wanted miracles."

"There are no miracles with you!" Connover yelled, trying to command the floor with the sheer force of his voice. "You are the whore of Babylon, twisting our words, using logic against the good Christians of this world. Only Jesus' power can work miracles. Only through Jesus—"

"Then call your fucking Jesus and do me a number!" Denny said. "Strike me down with your television satellites and with all the money you've taken from the pockets of old people who freeze in the winter because they've nothing left to pay for their electric bills."

Connover had turned red and was shaking all over. "God's will shall be worked upon you, disbeliever! The wrath of the Almighty is a great and terrible thing."

Denny looked at the other members of the panel. "And you

critic, how about a trick with wires? And my scientist friend . . . how about if we defy gravity together?"

He closed his eyes hard, feeling that same pull toward ground. He heard the screams, smiling, then opening his eyes. The entire panel was floating around the dining room shrieking. The psychoanalyst had somehow gotten upside down and was desperately trying to keep her dress from falling down over her head.

"You don't have the answers for everything," he told them as he walked around the set pointing to each in turn. "Don't you see that? Don't you understand that everything can't be cubbyholed and explained away. I've raised the dead, ladies and gentlemen, and I still don't know what the power is that drives me!"

"Let me down!" Connover yelled. "God damn you, Stiller. Let me down!"

Denny shrugged and thought away the field, the panel members falling all over the set, smashing into chairs and lights.

"More," Denny said. "How about some more?"

Frank was wheeling around the set, taking shots of collapsed chairs and sputtering lights at floor level.

Denny searched the group gathered by the archway, their faces slack, eyes frightened, picking out a small group of uniformed military. He pointed to a National Guard Colonel.

"You, sir," he said. "Ask me something. What would you want me to do for you? Get a camera on that man."

The Colonel shrugged, his heavily medalled jacket rising with the action. His face was dark, wary. "Can't think of— "

"Oh come now," Denny said. "There must be something important in your life, something—"

"The only thing I want right now is to catch that son of a bitch Cardera down in Colombia," the Colonel said uncertainly. "We got three divisions down there with their thumbs up their butts looking for him."

Denny smiled. "Cardera," he said. "Jesus Cardera." He walked around the people crumpled on the floor, the Catholic theologian whimpering like a baby, and stopped at the monitor. Cardera the drug king, What a marvelous thought. He shut down the VCR and hoisted Amy up into his arms, holding her close. The set was in turmoil around him as the panelists helped each other to their feet and technicians hurried to get the light poles set back up and the broken chairs out of the way. Connover staggered around near him, a hand to a cut and bleeding forehead.

Ignoring everything, Denny closed his eyes, thinking about Cardera's whereabouts, piecing together newsreel footage he had seen of the man with whatever facts he could remember. It hit him like a ball of white, electric light, making him stumble backward as a profusion of images crowded out everything else in his brain and he felt he *was* Cardera. City smells assailed his nostrils, sweet juices and frying peanut oil. He felt hot and began to sweat profusely.

Blindly backing up, Denny let himself bump into the monitor with the small part of his mind that was still his. The images fled instantly, draining him for several seconds as his own brain gradually seeped back in.

He shook his head, opening his eyes, and saw a street scene in Bogotá, Colombia, on the screen.

"I hope somebody's recording this," he said.

The scene moved subjectively into an ultramodern building sticking out of the urban rubble of the abject, forgotten poor like a rose growing up through a sidewalk, and Denny recognized all of it from the portion of the brain that he still retained. The roving eyes moved through a plush lobby, security guards waving and smiling and standing a little straighter, then into an elevator and up fifteen floors. The elevator doors opened to a suite of offices. On the wall was written in block, gold lettering RODRIGUEZ, INT.

"This place is a legitimate front," Denny said. "Its address is 1126 Bolivar Drive in Bogotá. The viewpoint eyes you're looking at are, I believe, Cardera's."

The crowd was buzzing, the colonel taking notes as the eyes moved into a large office marked CEO, an extremely dark secretary looking up and saying, "*Buenos Dias, Señor Rodriguez.*"

A hand reached out and picked up a stack of mail on the secretary's desk, then moved into a private office, the skyline of Bogotá stretching out dazzling and depressing into the distance, afternoon sunshine glinting off the rusted tin roofs of thousands of hovels like diamonds. The eyes moved to a desk and opened a drawer, a large bag of white powder and a small submachine gun laying side by side.

"That's it!" Denny said, pointing to the screen. "That's your man. He must live under an alias." He could see large pieces of a life, pieces that could probably fit together like a jigsaw puzzle. He saw something else, too, something strange and familiar that he wasn't prepared to talk about.

Denny turned to the audience as the picture faded. He saw fear in their eyes as they looked at him, and found he didn't mind the look. He took a step forward, everyone backing up a step, and set Amy on the ground.

"I suggest to the powers that be in Bogotá," he said, "that someone arrest that man before he slips away into another identity."

"You think you're so clever," Connover said from near him. Denny turned. Blood flowed in rivulets down the man's face, wetting his suit, covering his hands. "You use the Devil's power to turn these people from the Truth."

"What is truth, Jim?" Denny asked, walking up to the man and raising his hand. "Let me touch you. I'll fix up that cut."

"Behind me, Satan!" the man hissed, stepping away from Denny. "You'll never lay your Demon claws on me!"

"Just trying to help," Denny said.

"The Truth is the truth of this world and the next," Connover said, his voice gravel, his words choppy and disassociated. "The word of Jesus Christ as set down in the Gospels of Matthew, Mark, Luke, and John. Your works are blasphemy and sweet lies drip like honey from your tongue."

"You condemn quickly enough," Denny said. "but you refuse to test me."

"Oh, I have a test," the man said, raising up to his full height and staring hard at Denny. There was no fear in his eyes, however. "You play with TV sets and food and dead animals. If you really have the power, put it to worthwhile use, put it to godlike use."

"Name it," Denny said.

"Feed the starving," the man said. "Fill the bellies of the poor and the infirm and the weak. Multiply the loaves and fishes as Jesus did, and as I do with the money the Lord allows me to raise for his good works."

Denny looked at him, faltering. He'd never really reached beyond himself with predictable results. His fear of the consequences, of doing the wrong thing, held him back. "Pick something else," he said.

"No!" the man shouted in triumph. "That is the test of the godhead of Amy Kyle. Do good works. Perform this miracle if you truly have the power of God on Earth!"

"That's too dangerous," Denny said. "I don't want—"

"Dangerous!" Connover sneered. "Since when is feeding people dangerous? You can't do it, can you? I knew it. I knew that the wisdom of God would surplant the folly of this prideful man. Praise the Lord, my friends. A viper has been plucked from our midst . . . a very puny viper." The man started laughing then, several of the members of the audience laughing nervously with him. Denny felt his hands tightening into fists as the words forced themselves from his mouth.

"I'll do it," he said. "But it will be on your head."

"Denny, no!" Molly called, as Frank focused tight on Denny's face. "Don't give over!"

"On my head?" Connover said expansively. "I'll gladly take the credit for the feeding of hundreds of millions!"

Denny turned and looked at Gayler, smiling slightly. The man shook his head, mouthing a silent no.

"Ladies and gentlemen," Denny said, turning his eyes to the camera. "For this I'll need the help of every one of you in the viewing audience. Move up close to your televisions. Reach out. Touch the screen . . . lay your hands on the screen."

"Stiller, no!" Gayler shouted. He was standing, quaking. "For God's sake, somebody stop him!"

"Close your eyes," he said, taking Amy by the hand and walking closer to the camera that Frank was operating. "Relax. Think about the hunger of the poor, think about the burning hunger of the starving. Are you doing it? Are you thinking it?"

He moved up within a foot of the camera, then reached out and touched it, letting himself flow into it. "Let yourselves go . . . drift with it."

He let the thoughts come, remembering hunger, remembering the grotesque, bloated bellies of the children of the Ethiopian famine. He let himself float free on a monstrous wave of hunger and satiation, dealing with the entire situation in the abstract in his head.

The first blow was like a fist in his gut, knocking him to his knees, a terrible, burning need comsuming him. It was frightening, like imminent, inevitable death seeping through his weakened limbs. He wanted food, but knew there'd be no satisfaction in the eating, knowing that . . . that . . .

He opened his eyes to a nightmare. Everyone around him, the panel, the audience, the camera operators were all bent over, gagging, moaning with the same pain that he felt. People were stumbling to the kitchen, hands on their stomachs, but

Denny knew, he *knew* that the eating wouldn't help, knew that the mechanism of his brain had dealt with the hunger problem the only way it knew how.

Only feeding the hungry would make the pain of starvation go away for all of them. They were all locked into shared, empathetic pain until they did something to make it go away. CUT TO:

THE LIVING ROOM—TRACKING. We glide through Gayler's house like wraiths, in SLOMO, watching the pale, sickened faces of the guests as they double over, hugging their stomachs, their eyes distant and petrified. The old house throws deep shadows across the room as people crawl across the floor like animals toward the front door, driven by a vision of death experienced firsthand, committed through that vision to heal the body of mankind. We move with delicious slowness, savoring the images of the concrete gargoyles that leer down from the gothic rafters and the wailing, hollow faces of the religious frescoes until we come to a stop at the strained, pale face of LARRY GATES. The man has taken out a GUN, an automatic, and SNAPS a round into the chamber. We follow him as he staggers to the archway, holding the gun under his tux jacket as his arm hugs his stomach. He stares into the audiences, stares directly at . . .

ANGLE—GAYLER. Frowning and in pain, Gayler stares directly at us and NODS.

ANGLE—GATES—FROM BEHIND. He pulls out the gun and holds it stiff armed out in front of him, pointing at Denny Stiller, then slowly lowering the barrel until he has Amy in his sights. He pulls back the hammer.

ANGLE—DICK HORTON. He sees the gun, sees its intended victim, and runs between the two.

HORTON

No! Don't!

ANGLE—GATES—FROM BEHIND—SLOMO. The gun fires, the sound long and rumbling in slow motion, like thunder. Horton takes the bullet, twisting gracefully, almost a dance, as people dive for the floor. Stiller turns and stares. ZOOM IN on Stiller, eyes wide, almost maniacal, as he stares hard at Gates.

ANGLE—GATES. His hand is shaking on the gun, mouth

open, trembling, as his hand brings the gun up slowly, so slowly. He lays the barrel on the gun against his temple and, hand still shaking madly, pulls the trigger.
ANGLE—THE DINING ROOM. People are screaming, out of control, in their pain and in their fear. LYNN HORTON kneels before her husband's body, wailing loudly, gratingly. Denny looks at Horton's body and moves toward it, hand outstretched.

DENNY

Let me touch him. Let me help him.

ANGLE—LYNN HORTON. She looks up at us in anguish as she cradles her dead husband's head in her lap.

LYNN
(out of control)
Don't touch him! Leave him alone, you freak!

ANGLE—DENNY. He staggers back a pace, as if hit, then stretches out his hand to Frank and Molly.

DENNY

To me! Let's go!

The others come to him, touching, taking his hand. They walk from the room, people all around rushing from them, screaming, cowering.
ANGLE—THE STREET—NITE. It is quiet and dark on the street as we look up the long hill at Gayler's house. All at once, the front door bursts open and people come charging out, screaming into the night, followed after a brief pause by Denny and his entourage. As they walk silently back down the driveway, cops and secret servicemen, bent over in pain, attack but are thrown back great distances by an unseen force. Soon our ears our filled with the sounds of cursing and moaning that come distant and tinkling, like breeze through wind chimes. Far in the bg we hear the persistent rumbling of thunder. Another storm is moving in, a big one. A boomer.
FADE TO BLACK.

ACT FIVE

Scene 1

(later that same night)

NITE—INT. We are staring into complete darkness, the RUMBLING of thunder an ominous drumroll in the bg. This continues for several beats until, with a loud CRASH lightning flares our area bright white, flickering in and out for several seconds, allowing us to see the interior of James Connover's study. We are voyeurs waiting in the dark, casing the room like invisible burglars in order to steal the privacy and feelings and truths of the inhabitants of this place, perhaps a far more heinous crime than any real burglar ever performed. They only take things. We want hearts. The lightning FLARES again and we soak up more of the room. And as the thunder fades to a dull rumble, we detect another sound, MUFFLED VOICES, outside of the room, coming closer. We wait patiently in the dark until the door opens, hallway light spilling brightly into our cocoon. On the threshold we see DR. JAMES CONNOVER and his wife, MAMIE. Connover's head is BANDAGED and he is walking with a LIMP, his wife holding his arm, supporting him. Both of them are pale and drawn, obviously in pain.

MAMIE

Are you sure you don't want to go to the hospital?

CONNOVER
(shaken, voice weak)
The hospitals are jamming up already. But they can't
do anything. Nothing . . . helps. I feel so—

MAMIE
Empty?

CONNOVER
Maybe some coffee . . . something.

Mamie reaches into the room and SWITCHES ON THE
LIGHT, giving us a perfect look at a meticulously tidy room,
everything just so, all in its place—total order.

MAMIE
Sit down and rest, Jim. I'll get the coffee.

She leaves, Connover entering the room, standing barely
inside the doorway. For a large man, he now seems small,
shrunken. He puts a hand to his stomach, grimacing with the
pains of hunger and defeat. His suit is rumpled, the shirt torn
and dirty. His knees are dirty, the pants ripped there. He looks
up at the light, then reaches out and switches it off again,
plunging us back into darkness. There is the sound of furniture
moving, and in the next flash of lightning, we see that
Connover has pushed an easy chair up, facing the window, and
is sitting in it. Then all is dark again. We hear WHIMPER-
ING, then CRYING, lightning flashing again to a broken
James Connover, doubled over, sobbing into his large hands.

CONNOVER
(sobbing)
Dear God . . . what have you done to me? I've devoted my life to you, my every waking minute has
been lived in your service. Why have you chosen to
give the power of your healing hand to this godless
unbeliever? What kind of unholy comedy is this? I've
done everything, risked . . . everything to bring
your word to the world. Why do you mock me this
way? Why must you crush your champion?

Lightning FLASHES again, Connover's words dissolving into

inarticulate cries as he again doubles over with the pain. Light spills in again, as Mamie enters with the coffee. She turns on the overhead, brightening the room once more.

MAMIE

Honestly, Jim. Sitting here in the dark crying like a child.

She moves up near him, setting two cups of coffee on the edge of his big desk and pulling up a chair beside him. We TRACK slowly around the room until we are in front of them, the window behind us, lightning flashes occasionally brightening their faces somewhat. They both grab up the coffee and gulp it, although steam is rising from the cups. After drinking nearly the entire cup, Connover pulls it away from his mouth and frowns, flinging it away from him. She moves to put a hand on his shoulder, but a flash of pain also doubles her over, her cup falling to the floor.

CONNOVER
(concerned)

I-I've been so caught up in myself . . . how are you holding up? Is the pain . . .

MAMIE

You know how it feels . . . deep, gnawing hunger and longing. I . . . thought I was dying at first . . . I guess everybody . . . everybody . . . Oh, God, Jim. No one . . . no one should ever have to feel this way. I'd do anything . . .

Connover reaches over to the other chair and hugs his wife briefly.

CONNOVER

I know. I've turned the whole mechanism of the ministry over to this problem. We can get the message out. We can use our overseas studios as distribution points. The horror of the needy keeps crowding everything out of my mind. . . .

MAMIE

I've written a check . . . a big check. I hope . . .

CONNOVER
(shaking his head)

Do what you must. Life . . . happiness can't go on
until this is settled. I can't believe that Stiller is feeding the world. What kind of madness is this? What
mockery of God's word. *Is* he a prophet, Mamie? Am
I playing Salieri to Stiller's Mozart?

MAMIE
(taking his arm)

No! You're a great man, James Connover. These
things that Stiller does, they're not of God. Forced
giving is like forced anything—it's evil and dark.
You've brought love to the world every day of your
life.

CONNOVER
(in anguish)

Then why? Why has God let this terrible thing happen?

MAMIE
(in a small voice)

Perhaps he's testing us.

CONNOVER
(staring hard, grimacing)

Testing?

MAMIE

Don't the epistles of John warn us about false
teachers . . . false prophets?

Connover stares right at us, almost as if he can see us. Pain
shows on his face, but his mind is turning, his lips moving
silently as he forces the thought processes.

CONNOVER

Yes . . . he calls the false teacher the anti-Christ.
Perhaps you're right. Perhaps God is testing
our . . . no *my* reserve. This has all come from me.

MAMIE

Through your connection with Ted Gayler, Jim.
Maybe you should never have . . .

CONNOVER

Don't say it. Mr. Gayler's a fine man. Without him
there'd be no overseas missions. He's got everyone's
best interests at heart.

MAMIE

I know that. It's just that I'm so frightened. Will you
lose a lot of money halting the ministry's normal
course?

CONNOVER

We could lose everything . . . but . . . I can't live
with this . . . pain.

He doubles over again, lightning flashing, the sound of
BREAKING GLASS heard in the bg.

MAMIE

What was that?

CONNOVER

Here . . . on the floor!

ANGLE— FLOOR. A small bird lays amid broken glass on
the immaculate carpet, fluttering out its dying breaths, its
neck broken from its contact with the window. We PULL
BACK as the Connovers stoop to the small creature, Jim
picking it up, cradling it in his large hands.

MAMIE

Oh, how sad. It's a turtledove. The storm must have
driven it from its roost.

> CONNOVER

Turtledove? Are they common to these parts?

> MAMIE

Not common, but not unheard of either. Oh, it's dying.

> CONNOVER

Aren't these called something else?

CLOSE-UP—THE BIRD. It's wings flap spasmotically several times and then it lies still, its head bent at a nasty angle.

> MAMIE (os)

Some call them mourning doves.

> CONNOVER (os)
> (a hiss)

Yesss.

Connover stands, handling the dead bird gently, like Steuben glass. He carries it to his desk and lays it atop his blotter, then hurries to turn on the television-monitor at the other side of the room. Moving quickly, he wheels a tripod from near the monitor, a videotape camera attached to it. He wheels the camera over to the desk and turns it on, tipping the lens to photograph the bird. Then he grabs his gilt edged copy of the New Testament and opens it. His eyes scan quickly, with familiarity. Mamie moves up curiously beside him, peeking at the passages he is running through.

> MAMIE

What are you doing?

> CONNOVER
> (excitedly)

The dove, Mamie, the dove . . . it's a symbol of the Holy Spirit. Listen to me: "And behold, the heavens were opened to him, and he saw the Spirit of God descending as a dove and coming upon him." This is Matthew describing the baptism of Jesus, but all four Gospels describe it the same way, as God descending in the form of a dove as a sign.

MAMIE

But . . . the dove is dead . . .

CLOSE-UP—CONNOVER. His face is intent, his mind totally locked onto the miracle he feels he's witnessed. When he speaks, it is barely a whisper of dark fire.

CONNOVER

Exactly. We're being warned. About the death of Christianity and the rise of Dennis Stiller. Don't you see? It's Stiller . . . he's the anti-Christ.

We GLIDE AWAY from Connover, our eyes roving slowly around his meticulous room, the sounds of the storm drowning out any further conversation. We glide slowly, coming to a stop on the monitor, its screen showing a CLOSE-UP picture of the dead bird. We hold there for several beats, then drift to the window, lightning flashes illuminating the storm's fury outside. Then, slowly, almost imperceptibly, we ZOOM IN on the broken window pane until its access to the raging storm fills our vision completely.

MATCHING CUT TO:
A HUGE PAIR OF BROWN EYES. Our vision is completely filled with a glassy stare, as dark and empty as the raging storm that occasionally and unhappily flashes those eyes to light. For to look at them is to see naked pain without redemption, hurt so deep and all consuming that it tears our heart to see it. In the bg we hear a screeching sound that seems to occur over and over at regular intervals. What is it? A bird? Something mechanical? We hold on the eyes—far too long, longer than is proper, long enough to begin squirming in our complacency. And then, when we can bear it no longer, we slowly PULL BACK, finding ourselves staring into the bottomless pit of Teddy's eyes. He stands his vigil in the pouring rain, standing staring at the ground just as he was doing the last time we saw him. No longer a groomed, beautiful cocker spaniel, he is small and soaked to the skin, his demeanor more like a starved, disease-wasted creature from a famine area—walking death. We can barely stand to look at him, yet we can't turn away. All we can do is continue to slowly PULL BACK. As we do, more and more of the lawn and house comes into view, Teddy

becoming smaller and smaller, less important to our understanding. Finally the house is completely in view and we
detect the origin of the screeching. TAWNY KYLE leans out
an open second story window, rain slicking her face and
stringing her hair. The screeching comes from her open
mouth, the sound nonhuman and truly chilling as we see its
origin. LIGHT suddenly brightens the edge of our vision,
followed seconds later by a pair of headlights entering the
frame, the camouflaged WCN van stopping as near as possible
to the back door. The doors open, Denny jumping out of the
passenger side cradling Amy Kyle, followed by Molly, Frank
jumping out of the driver's door, cutting the headlights. As the
others rush to the back door, Frank moves into the yard,
staring up at Tawny.

FRANK

(pleading)

For God's sake, Tawny. Please stop . . . please go
on back in.

He watches her for a moment, his words swallowed in the
storm, having no effect. Finally he, too, runs for the back door.

Denny moved through the broken patio door and into the
darkened kitchen area, Molly, groaning softly, right behind
him. His arms ached from carrying the girl, but he hated to
break the contact at this point. While he held her he felt
confident, powerful . . . right. He feared the reality of letting her go. He feared facing up to what he had done.

Molly turned on the light, bathing them in harsh glare. She
threw herself on a kitchen chair, doubling over in pain, as
Frank, dripping wet, came through the door.

"I'm going' up and bringin' her down to see her baby." he
said.

"No," Denny said, holding Amy tighter, his clothes wet
and uncomfortable. "We can't risk it."

"I ain't riskin' nothin'," the man replied. "I'll keep an eye
on her."

"Frank—," Denny began.

"It's goin' to happen," Hargrave said with finality. Then he
turned and walked out of the room.

Molly sat up straighter, her arms wrapped around her
stomach, face strained pale white. "God, did you see the
people on the streets?" she said. "It was h-horrible. . . ." She

doubled over again as Amy began squirming in Denny's arms, trying to get down.

"I can take your pain away," Denny said, looking down at her.

She snapped her head up, staring hard at him. "What did you say?"

"The pain," he said. "When we were driving back, I wished my pain away. I only wanted to try it on myself to make sure the result wasn't dangerous."

"And . . . and it went?" she said hopefully.

He nodded. "Just like that."

She leaned back in the chair, limp as a doll. "Thank God," she sighed. "You can end this nightmare. It's not too late to bring this thing to a close. Just take that pain away and turn her over to somebody who can handle this insanity."

Hargrave spoke from the doorway. "Insanity's a word people use to describe lifestyles different from theirs. Ain't no such thing as sanity."

The man had his arm around the Kyle woman, supporting her, for it was obvious she could never stand on her own. She was limp drunk, her eyes merely twin video cameras recording blindly for future playback. "Mah baby," she slurred instinctively. "Where's mah, . . . baby?"

"There she is, honey," Hargrave said, using his free hand to tilt Tawny's face in Amy's direction. "See, she's fine."

Denny stared at the pathetic countenance of Tawny Kyle, immediately realizing his own growing dependence on the girl's touch.

"C'mere darlin'," Tawny said, trying to lift her arms out to Amy, who still squirmed in Denny's grasp.

He was beginning to get arm cramps, knowing he'd have to let her down soon.

The woman tried to walk toward Amy, but the second she was out of Frank's protective reach, she crumpled into a heap on the kitchen floor.

"Let's take care of this now, Denny," Molly said. "We can't let this hang over our heads any longer."

"It's not that easy," Denny said. "Extending beyond ourselves is unpredictable."

Molly threw her hands up and yelled. "Then why did you do it to begin with?"

"Because I had no choice," he replied. "They pushed me . . . forced it on me."

Molly, grimacing with pain, shook her head. "No, Denny. You did it because you wanted to, because you lost control of yourself and wanted to teach everyone a lesson. It was your mind that made everybody sick, *your* mind that invented this whole thing!"

He stared down at her in godlike calm, realizing there was no way she could ever understand what it felt like to see things as clearly as he did and be able to affect them. She didn't understand the power, and she couldn't even imagine the force for change he represented.

Frank had bent to Tawny and was helping her, lovingly, to her feet. "You can get rid of the pain?" he asked.

"I did it for myself," Denny said, moving up close, but turning so that Amy wasn't within touching distance of her mother. "I can probably do it for you."

Frank held out a large hand. "Try it now on us while Tawny's senseless," he said.

Denny nodded and took Frank's hand, immediately feeling a feedback of the gnawing, overpowering emptiness of starvation. It was so deep, so much more than a physical thing. It was like a bludgeon, constantly battering mortality into the brain, a constant reminder of the uselessness of struggle and the utter inanity of all human institutions in comparison. Worse, it was a totally defeating pain that made it impossible to forget how close to the dreamless sleep of death we all are at each moment. That was the worst part—the remembered frailty. It made everything else in life pale when set up against it. That's why it was so effective. Normal life could not continue as long as the feeling persisted.

Denny closed his eyes and wished it away. They say that man is the only creature who can comprehend his own end. What a curse. Humans don't design their feelings for endings. He felt a horrible stab in his gut that nearly drove him to his knees, but within seconds all of it faded away and the pain was gone. His mortality once again became nothing more than a bad dream.

Color immediately began returning to Frank's face, his posture straighter, a glow back in his eyes. Tawny was still as drunk though, beyond physical pain of any kind.

"Thanks," Frank said. "It'd be hard for us to work like that."

Denny turned to Molly. "You ready?" he asked.

The woman nodded fearfully. "Please don't hurt the baby," she said in a small voice.

"The baby's fine," Denny said, reaching out a hand to her. "Really. Nobody's going to hurt either one of you."

She nodded, but the fear never left her. She put out a tentative hand, locking fingers with him. He felt the pain again, surprised by its sheer intensity, but as he tried to wish it away it merely inflamed his brain like a fireball with a molten core that tore from his head and shot down his right arm before he knew what was happening.

"Aaaahh!"

The jolt shot through his hand and broke their grasp, sending Molly halfway across the room to bounce against the wall, lightning flaring the room in and out.

Amy screamed, jumping from Denny's grasp to disappear in the den, the withdrawal forcing Stiller into the cold night of his own soul. He ran to Molly, who sat on the floor, holding her stomach and sobbing.

He knelt before her. "Are you all right?"

She looked at him, her wet eyes icing over. "W-what the hell did you do to me?"

He put a hand on her arm. "Molly, I . . ."

"No!" she yelled, pulling away from him. "Every time I get near you now, I get hurt. What is going on?"

"It's not me," he said. "It's Amy. I think she's—"

"She's what?!"

"Nothing," he replied, as if ignoring Amy's jealousy would make it disappear. "Is the baby . . ."

"I think I'm okay," she said, then cocked her head, thinking. "The other pain is gone, too." She struggled to her feet, waving off any attempt at help from Denny.

He watched her rise, using the wall for support instead of him. Without Amy to lean on, the doubts and fears and vulnerability began creeping in again. It had been a hell of a night. From Gayler's illuminati nonsense to Dick Horton's murder to the broadcast itself, it seemed as if the entire world had gone insane and that he was to blame. He couldn't get past the vision of Lynn Horton's hate-filled face as she looked up from the body of her husband. She blamed him, everybody blamed him, and yet as near as he could figure he hadn't really *done* anything.

"Before this gets any crazier," Molly said, running hands through her wet hair, trying to physically, and by extension— mentally, put herself back together, "we've got to set things right."

"How so?" Frank asked, as he scooped Tawny Kyle up off the floor, the woman's head lolling around, her eyes flirting with unconsciousness.

"How so!" Molly yelled. "We've just put God knows how many people in an advanced stage of starvation, and you ask me, 'How so?'"

"I think that before Denny tries anything else fancy," Frank said, "we ought to watch the TV first and see how widespread this thin' is and how it's workin' out."

"Good idea," Denny said, turning toward the den. "Let's get in there."

"What's to check?" Molly said. "What's wrong with you people? We've caused a lot of pain. We need to alleviate that before we do *anything* else."

Stiller moved into the den, turning on the overhead and bending to the remote on the coffee table. Amy lay on the couch, her face slack with tiredness as she wiggled fingers in front of her eyes. Molly was still talking in the other room, but he didn't want to listen to what she said. Her constant moralizing in the face of an entirely new ethic was beginning to get old. Her unwillingness to try and understand *his* viewpoint was no longer a welcome dissent. Things had gone too far now. She would either have to stay in the boat or drown in the turbulent waters outside it. He wasn't going to baby her along any more.

He touched the power button on the remote, a picture jumping onto the screen seconds later. He fell back on the sofa, watching the sickly face of Neil Brenner, WCN's midnight to four A.M. man.

". . . that nothing short of the black plague has infected so much of the world's population. Ladies and gentlemen, please. Try and stay calm. All information is sketchy right now, but listen to what we've discovered so far and try to apply it to your own situation. First, do not, I repeat, do *not* go to the hospital. The hospitals are jammed to overflow already, and we have reports of hospital riots in major cities, but the simple truth of the matter is: there's nothing that can be done for your pain at the hospital. Nothing touches it, not antibiotics or narcotic central nervous system depressants or psychotropics. The pain continues. This is still early, but the initial reports coming in from doctors say that the pain is all created in the mind. There is no physical reason for it or any physical damage occurring, despite how it feels. There have been suggestions from psychiatrists that what we are experiencing is a form of mass hysteria brought on by Dennis Stiller's broadcast."

"Why are you just sitting there?" Molly asked from the doorway. "Can't you *do* something?"

Frank had come in with Tawny in tow and placed her gently on the rocker, her head falling against her left shoulder. The man walked over close to the big-screen TV, squatting down Asian-style in front of it as if he were worshipping an electronic god.

"Gawd . . . old Neil looks awful," he said.

Brenner had doubled over at his desk, a wave of pain clenching his fists to white knuckles, a whimper escaping Molly's lips as she stood watching, a hand to her mouth.

Brenner sat up again, his eyes frightened, like the eyes of victims. "E-excuse me," he said, wiping sweat from his forehead. "We have m-more information for you. Please listen. Please. Don't stuff yourself with food. It won't help either. All you'll do is make yourself sick for real. What you are suffering is not starvation, but a symptom of starvation. Many, many people are suffering just as we are. The phenomenon is worldwide. We're not sure yet h-how many people are involved with this, but . . . it seems that anyone who was watching the broadcast, or was near the television while the broadcast was on has become infected. We're talking about, perhaps, as many as two billion people . . . all as hungry as you are.

"On another front, calls have been pouring in from people asking how to give money or time in order to halt the spread of hunger in the world. At the bottom end of everything, is this common realization that the hunger can only go away when no human being is suffering from it. High-level meetings and phone conferences are taking place in Washington at this very moment, the leaders of the world working harmoniously for the first time in history to initiate a hunger program even as they condemn Dennis Stiller and call for his arrest and that of Amy Kyle."

"Arrest!" Denny said, sitting up straight.

"There," Molly said in triumph. "*Now* are you going to do something?"

Thunder crashed loudly outside, the den lights and TV flickering in and out for several seconds before finally dying, plunging them in total darkness.

"There goes the electric," Frank said. "I wonder if they got any candles round here."

"There're candlesticks on the dining room table," Denny said. "Let's try the drawers in the breakfront."

Denny stood and felt his way toward the dining room, Molly stumbling after him. "Why are you wasting time?" she demanded. "You have no right to prolong this suffering for even another minute."

"You heard the man," Denny said over his shoulder as he felt his way into the dark dining room, lightning flashing long enough for him to find the breakfront. "The pain is mental . . . not physical."

He could smell her perfume, sense her near him. "How do you tell that to small children and babies?" she pleaded, Denny opening the cabinet drawers, searching them by braille. "How do you tell that to pregnant mothers and deaf or retarded people? You caused this Denny. You must undo what you've done."

"Why?" came Frank's voice from the entryway. "Maybe if there ain't no other way to make people appreciate their fellow man's sufferin', this might just be the best thing that ever happened."

"God, you're both crazy!" Molly said.

"Here," Denny said, pulling several long tapers out of the bottom drawer. The owner of the house must have been a nonsmoker. Book matches were stuffed in the drawer near the candles.

He tucked a candle under his chin and used his free hands to strike a match. As the candle flared to life, both Molly and Frank took on a ghostly, flickering appearance. Denny set the candle in a holder on the large, polished table, then proceeded to light several more.

"Don't leave Tawny alone in there with Amy," he said to Frank, the man moving quietly out of the room.

Denny kept lighting candles and putting them in the multilayered candelbra, exposing a room filled with electronic equipment, stuff that Frank had talked Molly into procuring for him earlier in the day. The table itself was jammed with monitors. Denny shoved them all to one side so they could sit at the other. Seconds later, Frank came back, pulling Tawny along with him, the woman still sitting in the rocker.

The three of them sat then, Denny at the head of the table, Frank on his right and Molly his left. The storm raged and kicked outside, wind whipping rain frantically against the windows, all of them feeling small and alien there in the flickering darkness that overpowered everything.

Denny looked at each of them in turn, his feelings that the discussion they were about to have must be something like the meetings held by Harry Truman before his decision to drop the bomb on Japan. The issue was major, the decision earthshaking. With Amy in hand he felt supremely confident in his ability to handle anything. Without her, he was in way over his head. What he wanted to do now was try and reconcile those opposite poles.

As he looked at Molly, she returned his gaze in puzzlement, unable to understand why he had a problem at all. But Frank, here was something different. There was a light behind the man's eyes that he had never seen before, as if Hargrave were waking up from a decade's long dream.

"You've got something on your mind," he told Hargrave. "What is it?"

"This is it, Denny," he said, his voice bursting with excitement. "We've crossed over."

"What do you mean . . . crossed over?" Molly asked suspiciously.

"Television . . . it's like magic," Frank said, his large hands out in front of him, selling the point. "We been usin' it, all this time we been usin' it, tryin' to break out of the bounds of reality and we finally done it."

"Great," Molly said. "So, we've broken free of reality and used it to hurt millions, maybe billions, of people. You'll excuse me if I don't bake a pie and raise the American flag."

"Wait," Denny said, putting a hand on her arm that she shrugged off. "Frank is getting at something."

"You damn bet I am!" the man said loudly, happily. "We crossed over into a metaphysical reality. We're dealin' with insights into the human condition now, with the power to back it all up. Amy *is* God, the power of God to do good anyway."

"I don't like using the word, God," Denny said. "You know how I feel about that. God implies direction and motivation. Amy's actions are random at best."

"Don't you get it?" Hargrave said. "*We* provide the motivation and the direction. Who's to say what the definition of God is? I like this one as good as any."

"God is God," Molly said. "If we read the Bible, we know

what He's like. For my money, this is not only stupid, but sacreligious."

Frank looked at her in exasperation. "Expand your horizons a bit," he said. "Think about it. There are a bunch of different religions in this world. Are you saying that the religion that wrote the Bible that you read is the only one, the only definition of God, the only possibility of insight?"

"Well . . ." Molly said. "Not exactly."

Frank brought a heavy hand down on the table. "That's all I needed," he said. "Just listen to me. Hear me out, then tell me I'm crazy. All thin's being equal, we're all of us, even a heathen like Denny, looking for God . . . for some reason to make our lives worth a shit. Every culture looks and defines in its own way, from Amish to Zen and everythin' between, and people with an open mind to study, find that all religions contain the selfsame seeds of discovery and personal responsibility. Way back . . . before I went to Nam and lost it all, I used to live with a hippie chick who was real hot on Eastern religions, especially Hinduism and its offshoot, Buddhism."

"I don't see . . ." Molly began, but Frank cut her off.

"I asked you to let me finish," he said. "Please. Listen. Her name was Debbie, and anytime she ever hurt herself . . . you know, a sprain from joggin', a finger burned on a fryin' pan, she always called it a dakini sign."

"What the hell does that mean?" Denny asked.

"I'm gettin' to that. A dakini is somethin' the Buddhists believe in. It's a demigod, a wrathful lookin' deity who is kind of the human being's personal emotional harpy. The point of the dakini, is that sometimes, as we take different realities onto ourselves, we forgit what we're doin' and stray from our real life path. The dakini will hurt us through injury, forcing us to examine the directions we've taken and hopefully make us think about it and perhaps change our realities. A psychiatrist might say that the dakini is our subconscious tryin' to tell us to move in another direction, which to me is just another way of agreein' with the original premise."

"You're trying to tell us that what happened tonight is a dakini sign?" Molly asked.

"Bingo," Frank said. "The biggest old dakini sign there ever was. Think of it. All these people are hurtin', knowin' firsthand the pain that a lot of people on this planet get for real. It ain't hurtin' them none, it's just makin' them think, makin' leaders who won't give each other the time of day, sit down for the first time and work on somethin' major."

"You don't *want* me to take the pain away," Denny said. "You want me to leave it alone."

"I dropped out of life because I couldn't handle the misery of others," Frank said, "or the callousness of my fellow man. Maybe I *am* crazy, but I don't see nothin' but good comin' out of what Denny done tonight if even one person gets a meal and knows what it's like to feel human again."

"What gives you the right to blithely bequeath pain on others?" Molly asked loudly. "Who made *you* God?"

"Ted Gayler and his satellite system!" Hargrave responded, coming out of his seat to pound the table. "Open your fuckin' eyes, lady. We live in a world where a hundred thousand people *die* of starvation every day, and I don't mean no mental pain either. I'm talkin' about swelled up bellies and rickets and dead eyes. I'm talkin' about slowly wastin' away, fallin' down and dyin' in the dirt when you can't walk no more. I'm talkin' about real starvation in a world of plenty. Hell, in America today, folks throw away enough food out of their refrigerators a year to feed a *bunch* of countries. And *we* are in a position to do somethin' about it! What we're really doin' is makin' folks feel guilty enough to take care of their fellow man."

"You know as well as I do that feeding the world is an impossibility," Molly said. "Well-funded organizations have been trying for years to no effect."

"That's cause of human greed, honey," Frank said. "People put it in their pockets instead of where it belongs."

"Gayler says that the human animal isn't perfectable," Denny said. "He says that greed is our inevitability, our climb to the top of the heap and our downfall."

Frank leaned against the tabletop on stiff arms. "And I say that everbody just brought the dakini sign on themselves and are goin' to do the right thin' if it kills them. You see, Molly, Denny didn't do this to folks, they did it to themselves because of their greed. We're defining God right here, right now. If it ain't superstitious enough or religious enough for you, Molly, I'm sorry. But we've got to move with our own definitions now."

"Frank Hargrave, philosopher," Molly said with contempt. "I have to believe that Adolf Hitler used the same sort of logic when he was putting into effect his final solution to the Jewish problem, too."

"We ain't killin' nobody, Molly," Hargrave said, sitting down. "We might be savin' people's lives."

Molly turned and looked at Denny with a real mask of frail desperation on her face, and he couldn't help but wonder if she was really worried about the pain in the world or just trying to keep her own notions of religion intact.

"You're not going to listen to him, are you?" she asked. "This is the biggest pile of horse manure ever unloaded on a cabbage patch. Good cannot come out of bad."

"Define good," Hargrave persisted. "Define bad. From where I stand, we live right now in the worst of all possible worlds. It was you guys who brought me back to this awful place; you guys who asked me to get involved again. Well, here it is, on the damned table. We can remake a world, right here, tonight. I'm in now, and I'm excited. I can't believe you're not!"

Denny took a long breath, watching their faces lit brightly by the jumping candles, sweating like baked apples as the lightning flared outside and the wind stirred the rain to thunderous tumult, and he had to feel as if this was *the* moment of creation, that all before, man's greed and folly and wonder, were simply rehearsals for this moment. He was making no one do anything. As Frank had said, they were, indeed, doing it themselves. There was no premeditation here. He knew a little Buddhism, too. This is what a good Tibetan would call auspicious coincidence and the pope would call divine intervention. Both the same thing, be he the instrument or the musician. How could he stop this song once in progress? All the technical complications aside, this *was* the moment of the world—mankind giving to save those less fortunate. Besides, to believe otherwise was to accept Gayler's definition of life.

He looked at Molly. "I'm not seeing your side of the argument," he said.

"Then you're as much a hypocrite as Frank," she said, voice hard, eyes flashing in the candlelight. "How easy for you to take the pain away from yourself, then condemn the rest of the world to suffer for their own good. Don't you really see what you're doing? No good can come of this. People aren't going to do the right thing. They're simply going to want you dead and out of their lives."

"I could believe that if I hadn't experienced it myself," Denny said. "You know what I'm talking about. When I had the pain, I absolutely knew—*knew*—that feeding the hungry was the only way to stop it. This will work. It must."

"You don't have the right to make decisions like this," she said.

"Then who has the right?" Hargrave asked. "Tell me."

"No one!"

"I'll remember that when I fill out my income tax," Denny said, shaking his head. "I just don't see your viewpoint, Molly. I can't help feeling that you're speaking from fear and not concern for the Truth."

She stood, walking to the window, lightning flashes defining her. "Of course I'm afraid," she said. "I'm not the one getting to play God." She flared around, imploring, her hands held out in front of her. "Think, Denny. You've taken on a responsibility that you neither earned nor deserve. Up until the last week, the only concern you ever had for your fellow man's welfare was whether or not it was a good story. I don't *want* you to be my God. I'd rather choose that for myself. You'll have to excuse me if I find you underqualified for the job."

Denny sat back, watching her stare at him. Not a bad point, really. He'd been playing God long enough by this time that he had begun to think of himself as a natural for the job. But that still didn't alter the situation as it stood. The starvation pains existed as a separate entity from him. He never planned it; he never willed it. It had just happened through some combination of Amy's power, Denny's analytical mind, and the fears of the affected audience. Frank was right. The world could turn right here.

"I think we'll leave things as they are," he said. "We'll see what happens."

"Then you just signed your own death warrant," Molly spat, "because those people out there are going to hunt you down and they're going to kill you . . . and Frank . . . and that devious little bitch *and* her mother! And you'll have to excuse me once more, but I, for one, don't intend to be here so they can kill me, too. You've looped out, Denny. You're completely around the bend. I love you, but I'm not going to stay around here and watch this anymore."

She moved back to the table, pulling one of the candles out of its holder. "Please change your mind," she said low.

Denny just stared at her. There were no more words,

nothing left to say. Molly searched his eyes frantically, then turned and hurried from the room.

"You goin' to let her go?" Frank asked.

Denny slumped. "I just can't bring myself to stop her.

"What if she gets caught? It means the end of all of us."

Denny nodded, his eyes drifting toward Tawny. The woman was restless, her head shaking from side to side, a single word sputtering over and over from her lips—Amy. Was he looking in a mirror when he looked at her? Was this him a littler farther removed down the line? "I'll work on the thing with Molly," he said. "We haven't come across anything we couldn't lick yet."

"This is goin' to work out just fine," Frank said excitedly. "Tomorrow I'm goin' to git all this shit hooked up so I can watch Amy better . . . closer. We're on the right trail now, I tell you. You'll see, Denny. Gayler ain't right. This don't have to be the end."

With that, the man stood, moving to the rocking chair and gently, lovingly taking Tawny Kyle up in his arms and hugging her close, more like a child than a bride. "C'mon sweet thin'," he said, "let's git up to bed. We got a big day tomorrow."

Like Molly, Frank took a candle and left the room, Denny suddenly alone with the storm and the little girl who had just set the entire world on its ear. He had been angry with Molly earlier, but somehow that had all melted away. He knew the source and reasons for her viewpoint; it was the same liberal-pragmatic rap he had shared before Amy had come into his life. But things were different now. Inevitable change had taken place, and it was his duty to move with the changes. But that meant the end of the life he had known, and Molly's leaving was the symbol of that ending. And this, he realized, was the reason he had been so insistent upon her staying to begin with. It wasn't for love, or sex, or dissension. It was simply because she represented the stability of his former life. He had, indeed, crossed the pale, for he had become an active voice in Amy's power, a force of change and not of definition. Quite subtly and through small, unnoticable progressions, he had given over. He no longer reported the news; he *was* the news.

And he was big news.

He stood slowly and moved toward the den, feeling his way without a candle. Amy lay, asleep, on the couch, her fingers twitching even as she slept. An afghan was draped across the couch back. He used it to cover her.

"What have we done?" he quietly asked her sleeping form, realizing that for the first time in his life he had made a real commitment to something. The thought frightened and liberated him. He had changed somehow in a fundamental way. Unfortunately, in all the pain and confusion, he wasn't sure if that was a good thing or not.

Leaning over, he kissed the girl lightly on the cheek, feeling the electricity, then straightened. Now that he was a part of it, he was anxious to continue his explorations with Amy. Only it was different. The exploration was as much his own as hers. He was ready to turn the journey inward. Tomorrow. Tomorrow was soon enough.

He moved out of the den and took a candle from the dining room table before making his way to the living room and sleep. Despite what Molly had said, he didn't feel like God. Gayler, who *did* pretend to godhood, was as much a reason as any for his decision, almost as if this were a personal battle between the two of them.

The living room was a mess, as the trash that was beginning to fill the rest of the house spilled over. Chairs and tables were knocked over, equipment and food wrappers thrown carelessly about. In the barely lit darkness, it was as if he were making his way through an obstacle course.

"I came back down," came a small voice from behind. Molly.

Denny turned to her, the woman moving up close, coming into his halo of candlelight. He stared at her, surprised at how distant he felt, as if she had already left and become a part of the outside, a part of the problem. "Why?" he asked.

"Maybe a last chance," she said, voice husky. "I-I just can't believe that it could all end this way."

She moved up close, sneaking around his hand carrying the candle to wrap her arms around him.

"What are you doing?" he whispered low, as she ran gentle hands up and down his chest. "You don't want this, not really. . . ."

"Denny," she whispered in his ear. "It's me, Molly . . . remember? You're not so far away that you don't remember." She leaned up and brushed her lips lightly against his, her body hot where it rested against his at chest and pelvis.

"Molly . . ." he said, knowing that she was trying to bring him back to her reality through the physical connection. He didn't want her like this. She meant more to him than a prize for good behavior. He wanted to push her away, but his senses were keen as a knife edge, his wants immediate and impossible to ignore. That in itself scared him, but he was already caught in the feeling.

He wrapped his arms around her, returning the kiss, hoping her concern wouldn't backfire on her. For her to come on like this meant she thought he was confused and out of control. He may have been out of control, but he knew *exactly* what he was doing.

"Shhh," she said. "Things have been rough, Denny. God, I understand that." She reached between them, her hand dancing lightly to his crotch. "It's been so much to deal with. I don't know if anyone could have handled it as well as you have."

She knew what to do, knew what emotional center of gravity to kick out from under him. He felt himself growing hard beneath her touch and frightened of the feeling. "I'm not going to change my mind," he said. "Do you understand?"

"Just give me a chance for a few minutes," she said, taking his free hand and moving it to her breasts. "Just listen to me . . . let me reach you."

She was moving against him, her body undulating, incredibly liquid as she moaned down deep in her throat.

And the passion rose in him, strong like a wave, a blinding rush of sensation that slapped him, an overpowering shock to the system. He tried to tell himself that Amy was fast asleep in the other room, but thick, drippy colors throbbed in his eyes as all the paintings on the walls began moving, throbbing with life. Even the walls pulsed slowly, rhythmically, as if breathing. He had entered Amy's territory, but the sensations were not too overpowering to turn back.

He dropped the candle to the floor, his arm going around Molly to pull her tight against him. His erection ground insistently against her, his penis tight, painfully tight, as he beat his hips against hers. He was going fast, too fast, but his feelings were out of his control right now.

"Easy . . . easy," she said, pulling away long enough to look in confusion into his eyes. Then she reached down to the hem of her double knit dress and lifted it slowly over her head.

She was naked beneath, her body throbbing, bright pink to his enflamed mind.

He wanted her with a need beyond will, a fire blazing in the pit of his stomach as he watched her hard pointed breasts swaying gently from the action of removing the dress. She wasn't Molly anymore, but all women, his own desire the unconsumated scream of the ages. Somewhere down inside a warning voice was calling to him, but it was buried deep, deep beneath layers of animal desire, no more than the tinkling of a distant bell.

He reached out and took her breasts, the nipples hot coals searing his palms, and her own hands worked his pants, sliding them down his legs then cupping his throbbing, painful erection.

A small cry tore from her lips. "Denny, it looks . . . bigger!"

Beyond words, he went slowly to the floor, pulling her down with him. In the darkness she was pillow soft and smooth as velvet as he tore his shirt off and fell upon her, his jutting penis pushing insistently against her still closed thighs.

"Come back to me," she said, her hands sliding up and down his back and buttocks, her legs still closed, denying him entry. "Walk away from this thing. It's taking control of you. Back off. You can't handle it . . . nobody can."

He heard her words, heard them individually and in groups, all words that he had heard before in a variety of contexts—but he understood nothing. He was a beast, a hawk descended upon helpless prey in the desert.

He grabbed her wrists, pinning them to the floor as he slid down her torso to take her breast in his mouth, sucking greedily, biting.

"Denny . . . please . . . not so r-rough."

He couldn't deny the pain in his belly any longer. With a loud wail, he used a knee to force her legs apart, then thrust against her, the head of his throbbing penis jamming against her furrow.

"Put it in," he growled. "Hurry."

She reached for him, her legs going wide, but the second she touched him, she recoiled in horror. "It's so b-big . . . Denny . . . what's wrong with . . ."

He looked down, uncomprehending. His organ was huge, massive, its purple head beating like a heart as it stood straight out from his loins, quivering like a high tension wire in a hurricane. And it appeared to be growing!

Denny rose on his knees and threw his head back, his wail high pitched and screeching, the walls wheezing in and out all around him, the trash moving under its own power around the room, piling itself up in abstract shapes as the pictures jumped in their frames, trying to get off the walls.

Molly screamed, Denny looking down to see his hands covered with hair, his penis growing larger, the pain nearly unbearable as the woman scooted away from him, shaking her head in openmouthed terror.

He grabbed his penis with both hands, squeezing against the unbearable pain, his mind racing through burning corridors, desperately searching for some kind of rationale before he lost himself completely.

Molly kept screaming, screaming, the sound echoing, rebounding in his head, confusing him. He toppled to his side, his organ an obscene, bloated sausage vibrating against the floor as weakness overtook him, fear that all the blood in his body was pulsing through his member.

He fought for control, watching Molly reacting to the moving walls. She saw them too! He closed his eyes to the woman, afraid of his desire, afraid that he'd still try and take her. It was Amy . . . Amy doing this. "Stop it!" he yelled, pain in his gut knotting him up on the floor. "Stop!"

"Oh God, Denny!" Molly called, and he opened his eyes again. The floor was pitching wildly, like the deck of a ship rolling through a storm, as lightning flashed bright red, yellow, and green outside, throwing the wildly undulating room in and out of brilliant, colored light. And at the end of the room, a horse stood, blood pumping from bullet wounds on its side, the sickly smell of death permeating the room, the odor thick and overpowering. The horse had a rider. He was short and wearing jogging clothes. The top of his head had been cut away, blood streaming in thick rivulets down his face and onto the horse—Charlie Kornfeld.

"Hi guys!" Kornfeld called, urging the horse forward, Molly's screams turning to hysterical shrieks. "Haven't you missed me?"

"Damn you, Amy!" Denny called through teeth clenched in agony. "Damn you . . . stop it!"

He forced himself back to his knees, the weight of his penis, thick and long as a femur, nearly toppling him forward.

He looked at Molly, the woman's eyes filled with unreachable terror, her hands holding her face as she convulsed without control. He turned to the apparition, Charlie riding right up to them before dismounting.

"How's it hanging, Denny?" Charlie said, winking a bloody eye. From close up, the man was battered horribly, the way he must have looked when he died. He limped forward.

"You're not real," Denny said loudly. "Go away!"

"I'm not here to see you," the man said, turning to Molly. "I've come for this good looking woman."

Molly fell backward, writhing wildly, inhuman cries tearing from her sputtering lips.

"Yes, sir," Charlie said, bending to her. "If you don't know what to do with this fine looking woman, I sure do."

Charlie reached out bloody, gnarled hands, running them all over her naked body as Molly shook with hysteria. Denny fought down his own hysteria, forcing himself through layers of fog and ripping pain to try and concentrate. "It's not real, Molly!" he yelled. "Amy's doing this to our heads."

Kornfeld threw himself on Molly, laughing down deep in his throat as Denny tried to move across the rocking floor. He reached the man, pulling at him, trying to knock him away, Kornfeld turning to blow fetid, rotten breath in his face, the aura of death rolling from the man in waves.

Denny fell back. Molly's head was as responsible for this as his. He *had* to get her cooperation. "It's not real!" he yelled in her barely recognizable face. "Stop believing it! You must stop! It's a vision . . . a vision!"

Kornfeld had pulled his jogging shorts down, his profusely bleeding mouth clamped on Molly's throat as he softly cooed words of endearment to her while forcing himself upon her.

"Look!" Denny yelled. "Please look!"

He grabbed Kornfeld by the hair on the back of his head and snapped the head back. Then ignoring the fear and revulsion that coursed through him, jammed his hand into the man's mouth, fingers held stiff. "He can't bite! He can't hurt! He's not real. It's a nightmare . . . a nightmare."

She met his eyes, her lips moving silently.

"It can't be real!" he yelled. "It's not real. Look!"

He jammed his fingers farther into Charlie's mouth, not feeling anything, his hand disappearing to the wrist in Kornfeld's mouth, then to the elbow. "Nothing!" Denny yelled. "Nothing!"

And it was gone. Just like that.

INT—NITE—POV. We are at floor level at the front end of the long living room. A small fire is burning paper trash beside where Denny dropped the candle, throwing jumping shadows all over the walls and ceiling. At the other end of the room, Denny sits on the floor, his head buried in his hands while Molly lays on the floor, crying softly. Both are naked. The storm still RAGES outside, lightning FLARING from time to time.

DENNY

I'm sorry. I'm so . . . sorry.

MOLLY
(crying)

W-what's happening? What—you called Amy's name. You called—

She suddenly SITS UP STRAIGHT and stares at Denny. Her face is strained and pale. She looks years older.

MOLLY (cont)

What does she have to do with this? Why did . . . did—

DENNY

She gets in m-my head . . . controls things.

MOLLY

Tell me this isn't what I think it is!

DENNY

Molly, I . . .

MOLLY

Oh God, what a fool I am. Why didn't I see? It's sexual, isn't it? This thing between you and her. Christ, Denny . . . not that. What kind of . . . madness is this?

Suddenly Molly LOOKS UP, staring straight at us, her face twisting into a posture of hatred.

REVERSE ANGLE. From Molly's POV, we are staring at the
end of the room. Amy Kyle sits there, turned from them,
watching them peripherally. Her face is set hard, no compassion evident in her angelic features occasionally lit by lightning
flashes. We are staring at amorality, and it chills.
ANGLE— MOLLY AND DENNY. Denny reaches out a hand
to her, the woman shrinking from him.

DENNY

It's not like you think.

MOLLY

No.

DENNY

Please. I know things are a little bit weird right now
and. . . .

MOLLY

No!

DENNY

I can't keep her out of my head, can't you see? I
can't control. . . .

MOLLY
(screaming)

NO! NO! NO!

She scrambles to her feet as Denny reaches for her again,
backing away from him with her hands out in front of her.

MOLLY (cont)
(out of control)

This is insane! Everything's gone crazy, I. . . .

She suddenly STOPS TALKING, then turns slowly, looking
toward the back of the house. Then she turns back to Denny,
keeping watchful eyes on him as she backs toward the
swinging door to the kitchen.

DENNY
(suspicious)
What are you doing Molly . . . Molly!

Molly turns and CHARGES FROM THE ROOM, Denny jumping up to give chase.
EXT—NITE. As the storm rages around us, we stand in the backyard, watching the house. In the fg, TEDDY, THE DOG, stands absolutely still, watching the same spot of ground he's been watching since Denny resurrected him. We hear noise from the direction of the house, immediately followed by MOLLY, who runs out of the back door, still naked and crying. She charges into the yard, falling down once, then picking herself up. She's found a SHOVEL on the ground and carries it as she charges toward us, Denny, also naked, rushing out of the house, CALLING HER NAME.
ANGLE—MOLLY. Streaked with mud, she runs up to the dog, who is just below our line of vision. She STARES at it, then turns once to watch Denny coming for her. She turns back, raises the shovel and brings it down with all her might on the dog. She does it again, then again, then again, Denny in the bg, HESITATING at her act of violence, then moving forward at a slower pace. In the bg we see FRANK, dressed only in jeans, come out of the back door and move toward them carrying a bundle. She comes around to Denny, SWINGING out in his direction with the shovel, then swinging back.

MOLLY
(screaming)
Leave him alone! Don't you come near him! So help me God, I'll kill you!

Denny BACKS UP, his hands out in front of him as he tries to calm her.

DENNY
I won't touch him, Molly. I promise.
Please . . . come in now. It's all over . . . come in.

ANGLE—MOLLY AND THE DOG. Drained, she sags to the ground, petting the dead animal, crying softly.

MOLLY
(sobbing)
No. He needs . . . he needs peace. I'll take care of
him. I'll give him . . . rest.

She stands again, obviously in a state of total exhaustion and
paranoia, and begins DIGGING in the mud beside the carcass, crying as she digs.
ANGLE—MOLLY AND DENNY. Frank has walked up
beside Denny. He has a video camera wrapped in a slicker and
is photographing Molly as she digs. All at once, the shovel slips
from her hands and she totally dissolves in tears.

MOLLY
What am I doing? Oh God, look at what I've come
to. I can't . . . can't . . .

She runs away, her arms wrapped around her breasts in
modest embarrassment. Frank turns and follows her, the
camera cranking the whole time, as Denny looks down. He
leans over and PICKS UP THE SHOVEL. His face is a mask
as he looks down at the dead animal. Then he turns, stares
once at the house and turns back. After several beats he begins
digging, rain pouring down his face and body, his hair slicked
tight against his head.

ANGLE—THE GROUND. We are watching the shovel
gouge into the muddy ground, the dog's head just visible at
the left of our vision. Denny is digging at the exact spot the dog
has been staring at. He is digging the dog's grave.
FADE TO BLACK.
FADE OUT.

Scene 2

(the next day)

INT—DAY—TAWNY'S BEDROOM. We are standing at the threshold to Tawny's room, the barest morning light seeping through cracks in the curtains. The room is a shambles of electronic equipment and empty whiskey bottles and full ashtrays. Clothes and trash are strewn everywhere. On the bed, amid a clutter of bedclothes, we can see Frank asleep on his stomach, snoring lightly. Beside him, Tawny is sitting up in bed. She's wearing a Dallas Cowboys nightshirt. She sits stock-still, statuelike, a cigarette dangling from the corner of her mouth. She is frowning, her eyes staring off at some distant place that we don't want to know about. Her hair is a tornado around her face and her skin is milk pale. She looks sick.

ANGLE—TAWNY. We look closer, close enough to see her red, swollen eyes, almost close enough to smell the booze and the depression that rolls from her. We don't want to ever get any closer, but she seems to have us wrapped in some sort of spell, or perhaps it's just the human fascination with the perverse, like the gawkers at an accident, for Tawny Kyle is surely a human accident in the purest sense of the word. With no change of expression, she reaches up and REMOVES HER CIGARETTE, dropping it into an empty bourbon bottle that's already filled with butts. She slowly pulls the covers aside, and we realize that she is trying not to move her head at all, the hangover is so bad. She carefully slides her legs over the edge of the bed and tries to stand, falling immediately to the floor.

ANGLE—FLOOR. We get down there with her, watching her trying to crawl. She makes her way slowly across the floor to the bedroom door, where she reaches a hand up to the knob, only to find it locked.

ANGLE—BATHROOM. We are watching through the bathroom door as Tawny, using the wall for support, stands and moves toward us. Laboriously, she reaches the doorway, leaning against the frame and breathing heavily. Then she makes the sink, leaning against the porcelain bowl on stiff arms. She looks up, into the mirror, and sees herself as we've already seen her, realizes herself what we already know. She begins to cry, softly, so as not to wake Frank. We are watching her reflection, the tears running slowly down her cheeks, etching a hopeless path down her weathered face. Without Amy she's nothing and realizes it. She looks down at the sink, eyes roving, finally coming to a stop on . . .

ANGLE—TOILET TANK. Frank's shaving kit is open on the top of the toilet next to an open bottle of booze.

ANGLE—TAWNY. She reaches into the kit and pulls out Frank's razor, an old Gillette double edged. With easy familiarity, she unscrews the bottom of the razor, the top hatching open to reveal the double-edged blade within. She removes it, almost reverently, holding it up to her face for several beats. She closes her eyes, squeezing out more tears, then lowers the blade to her left wrist. Her right hand hovers above the wrist for several seconds, then begins to quake, her hand shaking wildly as she finds herself unable to complete the action of ending the pain. The blade FALLS FROM HER GRASP and she once again grabs the sink, her whole body quaking the way her hand had done, her placid face now contorted to an ugly mask. Her eyes go to the bottle on the toilet, and she GRABS IT UP, tilting it full to her lips as she gulps loudly.

MATCHING CUT TO:

A COKE BOTTLE—CLOSE-UP. Someone is drinking the coke. We PULL BACK to find it in the hands of a National Guardsman in uniform, an M–16 loaded with a full magazine strapped to his shoulder. Behind him is a tank barricade blocking the road, armed soldiers all over the tanks. In the bg we hear loud voices, moaning and shouting. Sometimes the sounds are unbelievably loud. We take to the air, pulling way back and up . . . up . . . above the people and the noise. Below us, we can see the Red River, the dividing line between Texas and Oklahoma. The tanks sit squarely in the center of the bridge just on their side of the dividing line, as per the dispute that decided who owned the river many years before. We can barely believe what we're seeing. On the Oklahoma side of the river, millions of people are jammed up to the barricade. The highway is filled with cars as far into the background as we can see, even from our vantage point. The land around the highway is also filled with people, people on blankets, people wandering aimlessly. Most of them seem to be suffering the pangs of starvation, symptoms we've already seen too much of. Helicopters flit around the area, loudspeakers telling people to disburse without avail. They've come to see the healer, the punisher. They won't leave until that happens. Large groups pray together, prayers they've made up for their new God. Others take up collections for the poor of the world, everyone giving everything they've got. The hundred-yard-wide river itself is patrolled by large fanback boats, armed soldiers firing warning shots at those who are trying to cross. Abruptly, we TURN AWAY and look the other way, down the deserted ribbon of highway that is the Texas side of the border. We fly above that empty road, searching. Then we spot it, a lone car speeding north on I–35, a sports car that seems remarkably like the one parked in the garage at Denny's hideout. We once again turn north, following the car's progress as we dip down for a closer look only to find that the CAR HAS NO DRIVER.

ANGLE—BARRICADES. The soldiers who'd been drinking the coke spots the speeding car and unslings his rifle.

GUARDSMAN

Cap'n Jenks! Somebody's comin' up double time.

JENKS

(from a tank, loudly)

Give them a warning shot, then use your own discretion!

GUARDSMAN

Yes, sir!

REVERSE ANGLE. We are looking down the bridge from behind the guardsman as he gets in his sights, then deliberately FIRES A SHOT too high. Brakes screech as the car comes across the bridge, stopping dead about thirty feet from the barricades. The guardsman, weapon at the ready, charges toward the car.

ANGLE—CAR. The guardsman RUSHES UP to find an empty vehicle. He looks all around, then moves to the edge of the bridge to look down.

ANGLE—OKLAHOMA SIDE OF BARRICADE. We are amid a
crush of faces, desperate people seeking desperate solutions as
they shove up to the barricade and look up into the down-pointed
barrels of the M–16s and listen as the guardsmen SCREAM AT
THEM to leave. The hunger is getting to everyone. The crowd is
a crystallization of all the people who go to Lourdes, or rush to see
the pictures of crying virgins, or sit on the top of Superstition
Mountain waiting for the aliens to come and rescue them. There
is no reasoning with them or trying to turn them back—there is
simply toleration. And in the crush of people and egos everyone
fails to notice that a miracle is happening right before their eyes.
Slowly MATERIALIZING within the crowd is a woman in a black
slicker with long blond hair and sunglasses. We recognize MOL-
LY'S DISGUISE, though no one else does, so unable are they to
see beyond their own fears and desires. Curious, we follow her as
she moves slowly through the crowd and watches the suffering and
hopes of those around her. Chants of, HELP US, AMY, ring in
our ears from all quarters, along with groans of pain and
discontent . . . so much discontent. She moves off the road to
the impromptu campgrounds on the hillside and forests surrounding the river, ending up beneath a huge billboard at the top of a
hill that states WELCOME TO OKLAHOMA. A woman sits,
leaning against one of the posts that holds up the sign. A baby lies
in her arms, crying hoarsely, its little face red from exertion. The
woman is trying to console the child.

> WOMAN
>
> You don't need no more, honey. You'll just make
> yourself sick. Please don't cry. Please . . . don't.
> It'll go away soon.

Molly kneels in front of the woman, watching her intently.

> MOLLY
>
> I'm so sorry.

> WOMAN
> (tearfully)
> Be sorry for everyone, ma'am. What kinda world do
> we live in anyway?

MOLLY
(reaching out)
May I hold him?

She takes the child in her arms, lovingly, her face straining
back the tears as she thinks of her own child, and then all the
children everywhere. Suddenly, the baby STOPS CRYING,
Molly and the woman sharing a long, intimate look as the
woman takes her child back and stares at Molly.

WOMAN
I guess the Lord works in mysterious ways.

CUT TO:
CLOSE-UP—DENNY STILLER. We are looking at a trancelike face, Denny staring in deep concentration, apparently at
nothing for he seems more inside of himself than outside. We
watch him for several seconds of immobility, then PULL
AWAY to see that Denny is standing in the living room staring
at a picture on the wall. He is HOLDING AMY'S HAND.
Scattered around the mess of the room we see a number of
cameras and monitors, all running, as pictures of Amy fill TV
screens all over the living room, taking the measure of Frank's
growing obsession with physical realities. We slowly circle the
room, drinking in its schism with the order of the everyday
world, finally ending with Denny's picture, the one that draws
him with its power. We look over his shoulder at the French
impressionist work of Manet, *The Bar at the Folies-Bergère,*
somehow acquired from the Courtauld Institute Galleries in
London. SLOWLY, SLOWLY we PULL TIGHT, the picture
filling more and more of our reality as we stare at the beautiful,
but sad looking face of the barmaid who is staring at us, her
unseen customer. She is surrounded by her counter holding
bottles, a compote of fruit and a glass vase holding two roses.
Behind her, angled slightly and filling the entire painting is a
full-length mirror, showing us the customers behind us, but
angled enough that we don't show in its reflection, except,
perhaps, as a ghostly reflection in the upper right hand corner
of the mirror. It is a large, gay crowd dressed in their finery
and carrying opera glasses, and we despair for the barmaid
who is unable to share in their happiness. Her sadness
pervades everything, a lingering look of deep pain.

There was no demonstrable point of debarkation for

Denny. It was as if he had simply "osmosed" into the world of Manet. He had watched the barmaid, feeling her sadness, and in so sharing, perhaps became one with her. He heard the music then, smelled the perfumes that barely covered the pungent odor of sweat.

"And what for you, *Monsieur*?" the barmaid asked.

Denny started, as if waking from a dream, but the reality of the picture did not go away. He turned, the music loud—the cancan. The room was bursting with light and life, an idealized kind of sensation direct from the artist's pallet. Thick smoke wafted in blue-gray clouds through the large room, a combination of tobacco and coal oil residue. The colors were bright, truer than life, and Manet's special talent for pulling the impressions of life among the common man existed intact in this place. A real world, but real only to itself. This *was* the Folies-Bergère, at least Manet's Folies—a never-ending party, a celebration of life amid the barmaid's pain. He was standing smack in the middle of the decadence of the Montmartre, the Mountain of the Martyrs, where St. Denis, beheaded in 272, picked up his severed head, washed it off in a nearby fountain and walked four miles before collapsing. This was the world of trivial pleasure and gruesome realities, blended together like a societal smorgasborg.

"*Monsieur* Stiller," the woman persisted. "May I help you?"

Denny turned back to the woman, her features real, but unreal. She was the physical embodiment of the artist's impression of the world and as such was somehow indistinct, like everything else in the club. He caught sight of himself in the mirror, smiling at a great artist's rendition of Denny Stiller. "You know my name," he said.

"Of course I know your name—visits work both ways," she said casually. "How about a nice cognac?"

"Certainly," Denny said, leaning against the bar, realizing for the first time that Amy wasn't there with him. "Will I be able to leave this place?"

The woman nearly smiled as she set the snifter of cognac on the polished wood of the bar and slid it in front of him. "Hardly the words of an explorer," she said.

"Is all this real?" he asked loudly, above crashing cymbals.

"What is real, Mr. Stiller—"

"Denny," he said, taking a sip.

"You can call me Adele," she replied. "As I was saying

Denny, reality is a difficult thing to define. There are many shades and hues to reality."

"What am I supposed to do here?"

"I don't know if anyone is ever *supposed* to do anything," she replied. "Though you do have a meeting scheduled, do you not?"

"I do?"

"Your party is waiting for you . . . through that door beside the stage."

"I don't suppose there's any hurry."

This time Adele did smile, if only briefly. "There is only now," was all she would say.

"I've got to ask you," he said, draining the glass, feeling a pleasing warm glow at the end of his nose, "why do you seem so unhappy?"

"I am the unhappiness of my creator amid the simple realities expressed by the ignorant simple minded."

"How can you say that about such a great painter as Édouard Manet?" Denny asked, remembering back to his college art history class. "He elevated the lower classes."

"Just as a way of attacking the establishment that rejected him," she returned casually, removing his glass and wiping at it with a wet towel. "I was his last major statement. He died, bitter and undiscovered, soon afterward, condemning me to an eternity of unhappiness. No, *Monsieur,* I have no great love for my creator. His bitterness died with him. Mine goes on forever. I think you should carefully consider what I've just said as you go about creating your own realities."

"I'll keep that in mind," Denny said, unable to accept any of this as more than a strange hallucination. Everything looked and felt real, the cognac even gave him a faint buzz, but that was far removed from reality. "You say I have a meeting?"

But Adele did not answer. She had already resumed her posture of haunting sadness at the bar, her baleful stare designed to tear out the viewer's heart.

He turned from the woman and walked into the guts of the boisterous music hall. All around him bright, giddy, impossible colors throbbed with a beating, dancing life, as the crowd cheered and the cancan proceeded onward toward a conclusion that never seemed to come. The entire place was caught in stasis, knowing a moment frozen in time, with nothing to compare it to. He watched the faces of the men and women at the tables, drinking from unending bottles, laughing with drunken giddiness and sexual fire—but now he was tainted by Adele's words. He saw those people as runners, desperately charging away from Truth and real beauty, on a headlong rush toward incomprehensibility and escape from thought and hence, from catharsis and betterment. It filled him, also, with sadness. But it was Manet's sadness, and he knew it.

He moved through layers of smoke, past the madly playing orchestra in the pit, past the smoking, sodium footlights that turned the sweating faces of the perpetually dancing ladies bright pasty white, and he thought that utopia was only positive if there was something far darker to compare it to.

There was a door opposite the stage with the word *privé* written upon it in flowing gold script. He reached out and took the glass knob in his hand and turned. There was no fear, no apprehension within him—it was all too bizarre for that. It had to be a vivid hallucinatory dream, a head trip, and he was determined to make the most of it.

The door opened easily and he walked into total darkness, standing hesitantly on the threshold.

"Close the door," a gentle voice said.

He pushed the door, letting it close behind its own weight, the music outside muting out nearly completely. A match flickered immediately, a coal oil lamp brightening the room to a dull haze. Denny wasn't prepared for what he saw.

A mythological creature stood before him, a woman with six arms wearing a necklace of human skulls and a girdle of snakes. Her hands held swords and a skull full of blood. And, incredibly, she had Amy's face and wore a Grateful Dead T-shirt with six armholes and Chic jeans with tennis shoes.

"A-Amy?" he said fearfully. "Amy Kyle?"

"We get to speak together at last," she said, smiling angelically.

"You look like . . . like . . . "

"Say it Denny," Amy urged.

Denny searched his brain. This was familiar, this was "Kali," he said. "Hindu Goddess, wife of Siva. Wrathful deity."

"Wrathful only in appearance," she replied, her arms waving in rhythm, hypnotic, the body swaying gently from the movements of the arms. As terrible as the image was, Denny didn't fear it. In fact, he was attracted, incredibly attracted.

"What, exactly, is happening here?" he asked.

"Come closer," she said, and reached out a hand to pat the bed that materialized beside her. "Sit."

He moved to the bed, the odor of sandalwood incense spinning his head back to the explorations of his college days. And somehow, he realized there were answers there for him.

"You willed us here," she said, sitting cross-legged at the head of the bed, her arms still undulating harmoniously. "So here we are."

"But this isn't real," he returned. "I mean . . . I'm still standing in the living room looking at a painting, right?" He found himself getting aroused just talking with this apparition, the feelings taking him back to when sex was young for him, and mysterious.

She just smiled sweetly at him. "Does it feel real?" she asked.

"Yes, but—"

"Then you've answered your own question."

"You're telling me that I'm literally creating realities," he said, watching her face, excited by the concept of actually communicating with her.

"It's no big thing," she replied. "Everybody does it constantly. We all live in mind-generated realities all the time. Yours simply has gone in a different direction."

"This is crazy," he said. "Am I talking to Amy Kyle, then, or my mentally created version of Amy Kyle?"

"You can ask your question another way," she said, smiling. "Is God within or without. That *is* the question, isn't it— within or without?"

"I-I suppose so," he replied.

She just smiled at him, then flicked out a tongue to wet her lips. Her movements, all her movements, were sensual and rhythmic, his mind whirling to his teenaged reading of the *Kama Sutra* and the wild sexual explorations that followed.

"You're not going to answer," he said.

"The question, dear sir, was rhetorical. Though I must say that you and I are probably here for different reasons."

"Why have you appeared in this form?" he asked.

The instruments of destruction had disappeared from her hands, as had the skull necklace and the snakes. She lay back on the bed, her arms waving sensually in front of her, beckoning him. "You've asked another rhetorical question," she said. "You tell me the answer."

He looked at her, feeling the overpowering sexual pull and knew why she had said they were there for different reasons. His mind raced backward. Why Kali? How did he even know the name? Ever since Frank's pronouncement last night about the dakini sign, something had been sticking in his mind, something from his own past. In college he had taken a course in comparative religions. He knew nothing of the dakini, but there had been something else . . .

"Shakti," he said at last, the pieces slotting into place. "You're a shakti, am I right?"

"Nothing's that easy. You tell me."

He looked at her, his mind opening in areas he hadn't thought about in years. "Siva is the main Hindu God. He's male, but passive. Kali is his wife, and one of a number of shaktis, the realities of power, searching only for Siva's direction. Kali is the physical form of Siva's omnipotence, the catalyst of power. My God, almost like the power you give to my mind."

"Interesting," she said.

"But that's bullshit," he returned angrily. "Just made-up stories to explain the unexplainable."

Kali-Amy laughed loudly. "You call yourself a searcher for Truth, but you are only willing to search in certain directions. Within or without—what's the answer?"

"There is no God," he said. "Either within or without."

"You're victimizing yourself, Denny Stiller. Perhaps you are not the one to search."

"What's that suppose to mean?" he asked

She answered with another question. "Does life exist only on a physical level?"

"Yes," he said "No! I don't know. What could there be beside what we see?"

She shook her head, and wagged six index fingers in his face. "No, no," she said, teasingly. "I will not help you there. Perhaps we should dispense with this discussion and get to what we really came for."

"I didn't come for anything," he said.

"So stubborn," she said. "This is no way to treat your lover who has been pining away for you. Besides, didn't you get rid of the other woman for me?"

"What do you mean—my lover?"

She sat up and moved closer to him, her six hands reaching for him, stroking his arms, his chest, his face. "You judge others so easily, with such a stern yardstick," she said. "Will you not be honest wtih yourself? You cannot hide behind the camera here, Denny. There is no place left to hide."

"You've intruded into my mind," he said. "Without my consent, I—"

"*Without* your consent!" She laughed again. "What a poor, weak-willed little boy you are that helpless, retarded teenagers can masturbate your mind without your consent. Is there no truth at all for you, Denny?"

He looked at her and saw, really saw, what it was she (or was it he?) was trying to say—that his entire existence was a lie. He lived with an image of himself, not a reality. He thought of himself as sophisticated and intelligent and honest, but he was probably the most dishonest person he'd ever met. He ran from relationships, ran from the inner pull of his own being, hiding behind the safety of the television screen, behind another created reality. No wonder people in television seemed so shallow. They picked apart the bones of others, like the vultures who devour the carcasses of good Buddhists without ever turning that all-seeing eye upon themselves. God, it was so groundless! He wasn't a real person at all. His search for the truth of Amy Kyle was nothing but a cheap show to help his career. He didn't want Truth. He wanted fanfare.

He looked hard at the shakti with Amy's face. "I'm totally empty," he said.

She shook her head. "Now you're substituting self-pity for reality," she said. "Don't be so hard on yourself. The fact that you've gotten this far puts you ahead of most everybody else on the planet. Truth is not a great motivator, my love. Honesty is basically a word used to describe an unattainable ideal. People throw the word around like manure on strawberries. We rationalize animal instincts and call them truths. You're smart enough to know that's not what Truth is."

"But dumb enough that I can't do anything about it."

"Can't or won't," she said. "Everything is choices. And right now, you'd better give in to the urges of your own biology without kidding yourself, because my dear, the two of us have a pressing engagement."

Suddenly, both of them were naked on the bed, Kali's hands spider dancing across his body, exciting in a million different ways. "B-but it's not right," he said as she scooted ever closer. "You're just a child, and a . . . special child at that."

"We're talking dueling libidos here," she said, stroking his already erect penis gently, lovingly, "not indecent liberties. Sex is a mind game anyway, is it not? I am your fantasy,

Denny, and I can give you *everything* you've ever
wanted . . . ever dreamed about."

She drew his mouth hungrily to hers, her tongue hot and
demanding within his mouth. His hands went to her involuntarily, fondling, stroking, the fire between her legs hot and
wet. She moved against him, moaning gently, urging him on
with tiny screams and he was a man with no soul, his desires
totally ruling his world. He took her breasts in his hands, large
and heavy, her nipples erect, straining upward. He hated
himself even as the passion overwhelmed him.

"I can't s-stand it," he choked, pulling her fiercely to him,
trying to merge their bodies together. "I've got to have you
now."

She laughed, wrapping all her arms around him and
mounting him with a loud groan face to face on the bed, both
of them sitting. A wave of sensation tore through him as he
pushed in and out of her, his body straining for immediate
release, so intense was the feeling. But, she held him even
more tightly, taking control of the movements herself, drawing
the agony out slowly, slowly. She screamed, red lips drawn
across white, clenched teeth as she pumped slowly up and
down on him, the pain of postponed release spinning his brain
beyond any type of rationality. She looked at him with eyes
that reflected eternity, deep pools that knew only Truth. "You
could have walked out of here a-any . . . time."

As he pulled her close again and hungrily took her red, red
lips, he knew she was right. He'd been more than happy to
place the blame for his sexual yearnings all on her, a child
barely able to feed herself. She smelled of jasmine and cocoa
butter and he closed his eyes, letting her six hands work magic
on his body. He was always able to slip away from the blame,
in everything he did, but here, as he drove himself into her, he
had to face the fact that her passion couldn't exist alone,
without his.

She pushed him backward until he was flat on his back and
she could rise higher upon him, her angelic face twisted in
perverse pleasure as she slammed down hard this time, nearly
driving him over the edge, knowing exactly when to pull back
and when to stoke the fires. Her arms moved in clockwork
symmetry, undulating like rolling waves.

Be it in mind or body, he was fucking Amy Kyle, both of
them equal partners in statuatory rape. As with everyone else,
he needed something from her and she was giving him what he

wanted. He was using her. Even with her enthusiastic consent and exotic complicity, it was his relationship to control, not hers. She was a child, incapable of giving consent in something like this. God, how many other lies did he tell himself on a daily basis?

His body was tightening, winding like a mainspring as she continued to ride him, and he couldn't have stopped had he wanted to—but he didn't want to. He rolled her over and pushed in from the superior position, her hands everywhere, exciting, exploring. His head went to a heavy brown breast and he took the hard, sweet, dark copper nipple into the cavern of his mouth and bit down gently.

He felt shame, but it was lost in the overwhelming passion that controlled him. She was a matrix of passion, as always the essence of the experience—and it was all so real. And even as the wild winds tore through him, he wondered if the sex equated with domination, domination of her power. What a hypocrite he was, condemning everyone else for wanting a piece of Amy Kyle while *he* wanted all of her.

Her head twisted wildly from side to side, sleek black hair fanning around her as she choked out a strangled release, his own climax building painfully down in his stomach. Her hands went around his back, pulling him in, urging him faster and faster now, letting him take the control, and he came—screaming—the release like an explosion as he collapsed upon her.

"My love," she cooed as he lay panting atop her, feeling himself drain into the perfect vagina created by his own mind. "You are mine forever, our love a binding pledge."

What was she saying? Surely his mind wouldn't turn him toward responsibility. She *was* in there, somewhere, her own emotions twisted by childlike notions of emotional reality. God, what was he doing? What was he thinking? Who was *really* in control here?

"Denny!" came Frank's voice, distant, urgent. "Denny, come here!"

He rolled from Amy, the girl using all her arms to pull him back. "It's Frank," he said. "He needs me for something."

"Forget it," Amy-Kali said. "We're just getting started." Her hands went to him again, stroking, arousing.

"Denny!" Frank's voice was closer now, just outside the door.

"I've got to see what he wants," Denny said, pulling away from her and sliding off the edge of the bed.

"Come back here!" she hissed, eyes flashing. Her wrathful posture had returned. Swords flashed in her hands, working intricate patterns in the perfumed air, the skulls clattering around her neck as she opened her mouth to razor sharp fangs for teeth, the lights dimming to sharp, angular shadows. "I'm not finished with you yet."

"No!" he said, backing toward the door. "Not this time."

He turned to the glass knob and pulled the door open, staring into Frank's face, the man's eyes wide with fear. "We made a terrible mistake," he said.

"What?" Denny replied, and he was standing back in the living room, turned away from the picture. Amy jerked free of his hand and ran from the room.

"It's all hit the damned fan," Frank said.

"Everybody's gone nuts. We gotta do somethin' to git ourselves out of this."

Denny grabbed the man's arms. "Slow down and tell me what's going on," he said.

Frank looked at the ground, shaking his head. "What the hell was I thinkin' about last night?" he said. "I was all pumped up after the damn show—"

"Frank!"

Frank stared at him, Denny coming face-to-face with a truly frightened man and for the first time realizing just how fragile Frank's psyche really was. A day of revelations.

"They's talkin' about bombin' Dallas on the television," Frank said. "They's talkin' about war!"

"No," Denny said. "That's ridiculous."

"Come look," Frank said, turning and walking toward the den. "Look for yourself."

Denny moved through the house, the place now filled with monitors and cameras mounted on the walls. Frank had been working furiously all morning, making the entire house one huge eye. He moved into the den, the big TV screen filled with a United Nations in turmoil. Delegates moved around the great hall, shouting angrily, most of them sick, pale, weakened from hunger. There was no order, or sense of civilization evident in this place. The atmosphere was close to riot proportions.

An off-screen announcer was talking. "These pictures are coming to you live, from the United Nations, at 11:33 Eastern

Time. Everyone has been waiting for a hastily announced visit from the President of the United States who, it is said, will address the world hunger issue and the Amy Kyle problem."

"Amy Kyle *problem*?" Denny said.

"Thing's have gone nuts, man," Frank said. Denny had never seen him so agitated, the man walking around nervously. He was even smoking, the cigarette bobbing between his lips as he spoke. "We should never have done that last night."

"What did you think?" Denny asked. "That everyone would just go along quietly?"

The man flared around him. "I don't know what I thought, okay? I just wasn't thinkin' straight."

On the screen, the Secretary General was banging a huge gavel on his raised dais to no effect. The announcer continued. "It has been reported that the president is now in the building and is approaching the great hall. At this time we'd like to show you the scene as it was here about an hour ago."

The scene switched immediately, a shot of the Russian ambassador standing at his desk, his hand cutting wildly through the air as he screamed, the voice of the translator providing a dull monotone for the inflammatory diatribe. " . . . as long as this . . . menace is allowed to roam free, the peoples of the world are in . . . precarious . . . danger. With every minute people get sicker . . . and what is next? That is the question we must all ask ourselves. It has been demonstrated that this child and her accomplice are capable of any kind of behavior. It is imperative that . . . steps be taken to insure all our . . . survival. We should stop at nothing to protect ourselves . . . even the razing of this city should not be beyond our limitations. Just as my ancestors burned Moscow to protect all of Russia from the evil of Napoléon . . . so too we must do whatever is necessary to stop Amy Kyle and Dennis Stiller!"

The hall went wild with applause, the fear cutting through any political allegiances, as Denny felt the anger grow within himself. Didn't they realize they *couldn't* stop him? Wasn't the starvation enough to make them realize the possibilities?

The announcer spoke again. "We're back live. The president has just entered the hall and is approaching the dais." On the screen an old, pale-looking man, stooped over with hunger pains and responsibilities climbed the steps of the Secretary General's dais. He didn't look like the president now; he was simply a worried, bothered man. He took his place at the podium, gripping its sides for support, and surveyed the angry crowd that had abandoned their seats, crowding around the aisles and the foot of the dais.

"This is a time of international crisis," he said weakly, the audience responding with boos and catcalls. He waited for the noise to quiet before continuing, a hand going to his stomach. "Amy Kyle was not my doing, but she's become my problem! I have heard the world's voice on this matter since late last night, and though I cannot compromise the security of my country, I want you to know that your voice has been heard. The threat of Amy Kyle is a threat to all of us. The people of the United States are suffering as much as everyone else. We are not to blame for this great sickness, but are, in fact, as much victims as the rest of the world, and in so saying, I would like to make an historic announcement that will, I hope, make the people of the world realize that this danger is not political or motivated by any political ends.

"The city of Dallas, and in smaller part, the entire state of Texas, has been sealed off. Martial law is in place and house-to-house searches in the greater Dallas area conducted by the military are beginning as of this morning. I have asked the Secretary General to ask this body for approval of a United Nations peacekeeping force to be sent to Dallas to help in that search. I do not make this offer lightly—foreign troops have not occupied this country since the War of 1812. Further, I charge Amy Kyle and her legal guardian, Dennis Stiller with crimes against humanity under the rights of international law. These people and their accomplices are to be considered extremely dangerous fugitives, their live capture effected only if safe to do so. We sincerely hope that these steps will lead not only to greater international understanding of a complex problem, but also to the end of our present stage of emergency.

"On the second front, the battle against hunger, I approach you humbly and with excellent news. Within the last twelve hours, we have heard from the ruling bodies of every nation on earth, all agreeing to open their borders without exception to the efforts of those in the spearhead of Project: Hunger. There will be international cooperation in feeding the needy!"

Applause rang out, the delegates talking excitedly, the president continuing above the din.

"Already, work has begun at the highest levels, pinpointing

the major trouble spots in the world. We've already had good news from smaller pockets of need. In places where the hungry are not part of a national famine area, their neighbors have hurried to their defense with gifts of food and money, a natural outpouring of affection and generosity. On the larger scale, major food distributors along with transportation companies have already pledged their financial and physical support to our efforts to feed everyone—food pipelines already being set up to take care of the trouble areas as they're discovered. Construction companies the world over are also pitching in, building roads and rail lines and airport landing strips in inaccessible areas, trying to solve the problem of delivery. All in all, we are all doing a splendid job and should be proud and excited about the most humanitarian undertaking the world has ever known."

"Those sons of bitches!" Denny shouted. "They've separated us from the hunger project and are taking credit for it as if we had no connection!"

"I'm telling you, Denny," Frank said, pulling out his cigarette to flick ashes on the floor, "we need to get out from under."

"But look at the good we're doing," Denny said. "If we stopped right now, the hunger thing would collapse under its own weight. This was bound to happen."

"Denny," the man said, his hands shaking. "I'm not put together for this sort of thing. It's what whipped me to begin with. I-I'm too open to the pain now."

"Just get yourself together," Denny said, blowing past the man, angry. "I can protect us from anything they can throw at us."

"Didn't you hear them?" Frank yelled. "They're bringin' in the damn Army! They're goin' to shoot us on sight."

"I can stop them!" Denny said.

Frank pulled another cigarette out of his breast pocket and lit it on the butt of the one still in his mouth. "This is too damned weird," he said, dropping the butt on the carpet.

"Go out and crank up the transmitter," Denny said. "We're going to broadcast."

"What makes you think they'll *let* us broadcast after what's happened?"

"Two reasons," Denny said. "One, they're going to try and trace us and they'll have to let us transmit to do that; and two, they just won't be able to help it. I'm still the best show, the best ratings, around. Gayler knows we'll get an audience. It'd be like choosing to not air the Super Bowl."

"What do you want the air for?" Frank asked.

"You just crank it up," Denny replied. "I'll take care of the rest."

Frank stared at him for a minute as if he were going to say something. Instead, he turned and walked from the room, going out the back way, through the busted patio door.

The cordless phone lay atop the coffee table. Denny picked it up and got the information for the Gayler affiliate that was broadcasting CNN's stuff. He rang it up, reaching the highest level of organization there at the time, Chuck Primrose, a long time producer who was temporarily filling in until a successor could be chosen for Dick Horton. The man wasn't happy to hear from him.

"God, Denny. Don't hit me with any shit my first day," he said. "Things are going to hell enough already!"

"I want on the air, Chuck," Denny said without emotion. "I want on in five minutes."

"Impossible! I'm not authorized to simply drop programming and run anything that comes—"

"How would you like me to turn you into a frog, Chuck," Denny said. "How important would your authorization be then?"

There was silence for half a minute. "You're . . . serious aren't you?" Primrose finally said, his voice distant.

"I'm glad that I've impressed that upon you," Denny said, menacing. He didn't want to be so hard on the man, but he didn't want to spend the day fucking with petty bureaucrats either. "Will you give me the time?"

"Yes," Primrose said. "We're making arrangements now."

"I'll be ready in just a couple of minutes," Denny said, smiling.

"We'll be waiting," the man returned, then said hesitantly, "Is that all?"

"For now," Denny said, hanging up immediately. Maybe if they thought he was a hard ass, they'd find less to argue about.

He moved out of the den and walked the hall to the studio. He felt energized, the power pumping him up a bit. Amy had exposed that nerve in him, that urge to power, to where he could no longer deny its attractiveness. He was still the best person to use it, though. Look at how well he had helped get Molly out of the city, making her invisible until after crossing the state line. He could handle it, could use it properly. He knew he could.

The studio was a mess, still filled with the carbonized remains of the dinner he had conjured two days ago. What hadn't burned was rotting and he made a mental note to get rid of it as soon as possible.

A camera was set on the tripod. He moved to it, turning it on and checking the lens to make sure it was clean. He had to keep his wits about him. Theoretically the house-to-house search could take a great deal of time to accomplish, but he had a feeling they'd concentrate on the wealthier neighborhoods. Someone would recognize the studio as a steam room, and that, by its very nature, limited the range they had to search. He'd need to lay plans quickly.

He blamed Gayler for the way events had turned. After watching the way the old man had handled the president, there wasn't a doubt in his mind that Gayler was pulling all the strings on this. But why? How?

There was something else, too, something that had stuck him last night when he'd been the persona of the Colombia drug dealer. It wasn't anything that showed up on the screen, nothing concrete, just the barest hint of a word, a name perhaps—bumper. Bumper. The name had been drifting through Cardera's mind like the ubiquitous theme phrase from a popular song. The same name for the bank account that provided James Connover with the bulk of his overseas donations. Coincidence? Probably. But such a strange parallel strain, enough so that it piqued his reporter's interest. Maybe it was because Gayler had invited Connover to the show last night, but he was not going to be quick to dismiss any thoughts of conspiracy between the principle players. *Something* was going on. That, if nothing else, he was positive about.

So, now it was time to take a lick back at his chief adversary. He picked up the headset and put it on, turning on the small transmitter to Frank.

"You got it?" he said into the small mike.

"Makin' contact now," came the man's static filled voice. "We're go in . . . thirty seconds."

"Gotcha."

Denny pulled off the headphones and ran around in front of the camera. He had instant access to the world. What a unique position. The funny thing was, if all this were, indeed, an act of God, Denny Stiller would be the perfect one to carry the message to the world. He was literate, well-spoken and camera wise—and he had access—and a certain amount of public trust went along with the job like extra baggage.

He turned and watched the last few seconds run down on the big clock, it's face slightly blackened by soot. When the thirty seconds were up, he turned back to the camera. "Ladies and Gentlemen," he said, putting on his most sincere face. "I awoke today to find myself the most hated man on the planet. Why? Because I was the cause of a great deal of discomfort to you while helping you to perform a noble and human act. For your discomfort, I am truly sorry. For our nobler purpose, I applaud every one of you. Many of the needy are already being served, while I'm sure that human ingenuity and creativity will solve the rest of the problem very soon. It seems to me that feeding the hungry has simply never been a human priority before. Now it is the number one priority. I see nothing wrong or threatening in that. I see only good. Those who hate or blame me for this, I accept it gladly in the cause of world hunger.

"I also want to assure all of you that I mean you no harm. My power will only be used for good, but along with that must go a warning. Stop looking for us. Leave us alone. You can't harm us at any rate. All you'll accomplish is hurting yourselves and innocent people. We can't be touched. The same power that has given you the pains of starvation can protect us now. Think about it. Turn your attention to the priorities. Leave anger and barbarism in your other suit. I'll be back in touch."

With that, Denny moved out of camera range and flipped the thing off. He picked up the headphones and held the earpiece to his head, talking into the mike. "That's it, Frank," he said, feeling good. "Wrap it up and get back in here."

"What the hell did you just do?" Hargrave said, his voice all but hysterical.

"What do you mean?" Denny said.

"You practically announced yourself as God Almighty! I thought you was gittin' us out of it!"

"We're already committed," Denny said. "Don't worry about it."

He turned off the transmitter. Maybe he had gone a little heavy on the omnipotence, but it seemed that the hunger issue now had to be settled in order for him and Amy to be able to walk away from all of this sometime. If thinking he was God helped bring people around, then God he would be.

Hallelujah!

NITE—EXT—EST. We are looking down a long deserted roadway, thick jungle lining the road on both sides. We listen quietly for a moment to the sounds of the night, predators calling complicated mating rituals, night birds flapping quietly across our vantage point, crickets, and something else, something more distant and mechanical, like a swarm of angry mosquitoes. As we listen, the sound gets closer, more distinct —a POLICE SIREN. Within seconds, a black Lincoln, lights blazing on bright, SCREECHES past our position, followed quickly by several police cars, horns, lights, and sirens blaring. After they pass, the jungle is dead silent for several seconds, then resumes its eternal course.

ANGLE—ROADBLOCK. We are farther down the jungle road, a patrol of AMERICAN NATIONAL GUARDSMEN, has blocked the road with jeeps and a tank, all painted olive drab. A guardsman with a walkie-talkie stands in the fg, as the rest of the patrol stands behind the roadblock, smoking and talking amiably.

GUARDSMAN

It is 1323 hours, sir . . . we are in place. Over.

He brings the phonelike apparatus to his ear, his eyes widening.

GUARDSMAN

Yes, sir! We are ready, sir, and more than willing. Over and out!

He turns back toward the barricade, captain's bars gleaming on his shoulders in the moonlight.

GUARDSMAN
(loudly)
The son of a bitch is five minutes from here and comin' on quick! Take him alive if you can!

CUT TO:
JESUS CARDERA—MEDIUM CLOSE. We are looking at Cardera through the windshield of the Lincoln. He is staring,

intense. Behind him we can see the police cars in pursuit not fifty yards behind.

REVERSE ANGLE. We are looking through the windshield. We are Cardera's eyes speeding down the unlit road, just barely keeping up with our headlights. All at once, the barricades are right there, on top of us!

ANGLE—FLORBOARDS. Cardera JAMS both feet on the brake!

ANGLE—BARRICADE. The Lincoln skids wildly, smashing sideways into the tank on the passenger side. There is silence for several beats, then Cardera opens the driver's door and FALLS OUT ONTO THE ROADWAY just as the police cars skid to a stop inches from him. Fifteen men with drawn guns charge Cardera's position.

ANGLE—CARDERA. Battered and stunned, he looks up from the ground and smiles sheepishly.

CARDERA

> ¿Cómo estás, amigos?

CUT TO:
DAY—EXT—EST. We are looking at the outside of a small Catholic church in Dayton, Ohio. The service schedule on the lawn informs us that it is SACRED HEART CHURCH. Many cars are pulled around the church, people going in and out with boxes.

INT—CHURCH. We are standing in the back, looking toward the pulpit. Food is piled high all around the church, canned goods and commodities such as flour and sugar. People, hungry people with hollow eyes and pained expressions, pass through our vantage point, but it is the young priest on the pulpit who draws our attention. His name is FATHER RYAN and he is trying desperately to answer the questions his parishioners are voicing from around the sanctuary.

FATHER RYAN

> How can I know the answers to your question? I
> can't pretend to understand the ways in which God
> makes himself heard among Man.

We begin to PULL IN TIGHTER. Slowly, barely noticeably, we move toward the priest as he talks.

FATHER RYAN (cont)

How can we deny the possibility that this is, in fact,
a message from God, working through that little girl?
We have been entreated with taking care of our
brethren. We *are* our brothers' keepers, but have we
discharged that duty with honor? No. Millions starve
every year while we wallow in a land of plenty, in-
dulging ourselves, giving over to the selfish sides of
our natures!

The priest fills our vision now, and still we PULL TIGHTER,
focusing on his face, so obviously torn by doubts.

FATHER RYAN (cont)

We suffer now, as others suffer daily. It makes me
feel so . . . cheap, so . . . dirty to know how I've
turned my back on my fellow man's suffering for so
long. I welcome this pain, for it is the pain that Jesus
must have felt when taking the sins of all the world
on his shoulders. And if my superiors continue to
condemn the person who has done more toward
bringing understanding and humanity to the world in
one week than my religion has in two thousand
years . . .

We are very close now; his face fills our vision; his fractured
humanity and painful honesty tears at our souls. Tears fill his
eyes.

FATHER RYAN (cont)

. . . I don't know what to say, my friends. I l-love
my religion. I love God and have dedicated myself to
his service and the service of my fellow man. Perhaps
the best way to do that is by preaching the Gospel of
Amy Kyle.

PARISHIONER
(loudly)

Amen!

Scene 3

(the next day)

EXT—DAY—CLOSE-UP—SLUDGE. We're looking at decaying compost, old leaves and filth deteriorated together and jammed in an out-of the way spot. We PULL BACK enough to realize that we are exploring the guttering system on the roof of a large building, metallic channels crisscrossing with mathematical precision, in their own way, quite beautiful, albeit unseen. We jump into one of the gutters and slide along its length. The roof is steep and we pick up speed as we ZOOM down its length, the wind WHOOSHING in our ears. Suddenly, the guttering STOPS and we are flung into the air, FALLING rapidly, landscape blurring past us until we abruptly HIT THE GROUND to find ourselves looking at a side entrance to James Connover's CHURCH OF THE SAVIOR. We move through the door, finding ourselves in the beehive activity of the office complex that runs the ministry. The halls are barely lit, and from somewhere distant, we can hear an organist practicing Wagner, a funeral dirge. We pass open doorways, the offices bustling with people, all of them sick looking, all of them working feverishly despite their sickness. The phones are ringing all around us as Connover's organization takes a lead in helping to feed the hungry of the world. But this isn't what we're looking for. We travel onward, finally stopping before a door with the word CONFERENCE written upon it. The door DISSOLVES before us and we move through as if it weren't there. James Connover, his vigor obviously dissipated by worry and pain, stands at the head of a table. His eyes are dark and sunken, his face pale. A hand stays at his stomach. A group of men are sitting around the conference table, some wearing suits, but most dressed in jeans and T-shirts. They are a ruddy-looking lot, teeth clenched against the hunger as they stare at Connover in deadly concentration. On the table before Connover sits a pair of rubber boots, beside them, elbow-length rubber electrician's gloves.

CONNOVER

There is no way that the government can understand this danger, no way that the secular humanist and left wing socialist conspiracy that runs this country would even want to believe the religious implications of the events of the last week. But friends, I believe it. I believe it because God himself told me about it last night. And you believe it because you're here, because you've heeded God's call to prepare His way for the Second Coming.

There are mumbled affirmations around the table, Connover nodding gravely as he listens to the amens.

CONNOVER (cont)

Quite simply, Dennis Stiller is the anti-Christ, using all his wiles to steal our souls and our minds away from Jesus' saving grace. And he could succeed—unless *we* stop him. As Christians, we've always made our own way. Not by governments do we survive, not by laws or by shifting attitudes. It is by the Holy Book that Christians take their lives, and breath and sustenance, and the Book must sustain us in this time of trial.

A man in a Ranger's ball cap and gray T-shirt sporting a Confederate flag, clears his throat.

MAN

Dr. Connover, can't you jest go on the TV like Stiller is doin' and tell the people what's goin' on here?

CONNOVER

I shall, but my voice is a small one. Denny Stiller has the ears of the world. All I've got is fourteenth place in thirty-eight markets worldwide. *Leave it to Beaver* reruns poll higher than us. By the time my voice is heard, it will be too late. Stiller and the girl must be stopped now!

Connover SLAMS HIS HAND on the table for effect. When we look at him, a little of the fire has returned to his eyes.

CONNOVER (cont)

We are fighting for the souls of the entire planet. Ignorance of our mission and salacious defeatism conspires against us. We must do this thing! We must save the planet for the return of Jesus Christ. If you join with me, you will be performing one of the greatest services a human being could ever hope to perform. And if you perform it well, there will be rewards in both this world and the next.

ANOTHER MAN

Let's talk about the rewards in this world.

CONNOVER

I am prepared to offer a bounty of a half million dollars for the whereabouts of Dennis Stiller, and another half million for his, and the girl's, heads. They must be killed. They are serpents and their power is great. This is not an undertaking for the faint of heart. (he holds up the boots) Her power is electrical in origin—ground yourselves when dealing with her. Rubber shoes, rubber gloves. Kill them on sight. Don't give them the chance to kill you first. Shoot for the head; Jesus will guide your aim.

FIRST MAN

Where do we go about lookin'?

CONNOVER

My reward for knowledge of whereabouts goes on the air later today. Believe me, at that kind of money, we'll have plenty of reports to check out. We'll establish a command post right here. Try and work in the daytime to avoid the curfew. You were all called in because you are hunters, marksmen, and former combat veterans. Your prey this time will be the Hellhound. Steel yourselves—this is holy work.

As Connover finishes talking, we move around the table, watching the faces of the hunters. They are all lower-middle class, blue-collar types. Two of them have hunting rifles laying before them on the table. They return Connover's fire with pride and determination. A wounded tiger has arisen among them, a man-eater, and it is their task to stalk and kill the beast with the triple numbers on its head.
CUT TO:
CLOSE-UP—AMY AND DENNY. They are sitting at the kitchen table, a large breakfast set in front of the girl. There is no sound as Denny puts scrambled egg on a fork and tries to feed her, Amy knocking the utensil away, her face set in a hard frown. We PULL BACK to find Frank, in Tawny's bedroom, watching the breakfast from a terminal board containing a large number of small monitors, all of them, at this moment, showing Amy eating breakfast.

FRANK
(mumbling)

Just a sign little girl . . . something that folks can't deny. If they just see it . . . the Truth . . . what else we got? Ain't no lyin' goin' on, people. What's so bad about the real shit? Things are real or not, that's all. Real or not. Maybe more cameras. . . .

ANGLE—TAWNY. She stands near Frank, staring in an oval mirror hung crookedly on the robin's egg blue walls. Her eyes hold horror as a hand gingerly explores the lines and creases of her weathered face. She staggers, drunk already. Neither she nor Frank look at one another as they speak.

TAWNY

Gawd, Frank. Why do Ah look this way? Ah ain't never looked like this bafore. Ah'm . . . Ah'm ugly, Frank, and Ah hurt, baby. Ah hurt so bad. . . .

FRANK (os)

It could be so damn simple . . . you show folks your stuff and, if it's true stuff, they believe it. What could be so simple? How could people want to kill the truth?

TAWNY

What's happening to me? Why has ever-thin' gotten
so nasty and painful? Ah'm jes rung-out guts, Frank.
How kin you stand to even make love to
this . . . this . . .

FRANK (os)

If I just run enough tape, you know Tawny? If I just
run enough tape, then they'll see. They're so
angry . . . worse than Nam somehow. Why should
true things make people angry?

ANGLE—BEDROOM. We are watching Frank and Tawny
from the distance of the other side of the room, the two of
them not five feet apart—the distance to another galaxy.

TAWNY

Ah never felt like this when mah baby was around.
Ah felt good . . . Ah looked good. Ever'thin' hurts
now, and gawd, some of it hurts so damn deep.

She turns and looks at Frank, unable to bridge the distance
between them.

FRANK
(oblivious)

Somebody told me once, Man appoints and God dis-
appoints. But that's the God in their heads. This
one's for real. I got tape, tons of tape. I could prove
it in court. Yes, sir, any court of law would accept my
evidence, any court in the world would say, yes, sir,
Frank Hargrave, that's proof positive all right. But
instead they want to bomb us. Bomb us! Do we love
killin' so much?

TAWNY
(in desperation)

Ah'm really sceared, Frank. There's a pain deep inside and it hates me . . . it wants me to hate mahself. And the drinkin' don't touch it no more. The
drinkin' don't even touch it. Only mah baby kin take

it away. Ah cain't git along without mah baby no
more, Frank. Ah feel like Ah'm gonna die. Ah think
Ah'm dead already. . . .

FRANK
(agitated)

What's the word?—preponderance. A preponderance
of evidence. That's what I need. A lot more tape and
a lot more cameras. I'll choke them with evidence,
then they'll understand. I just need more tape, that's
all.

CUT TO:

Amy picked up the plate full of eggs and bacon and slung
it across the room like a Frisbee to smash against the breakfast
room wall, runny egg sticking, sliding slowly down and ruining
Denny's chance at assuaging his guilty conscience. Forced to
look at his own selfishness while visiting the Manet painting,
he had to realize for starters that as a substitute father he was
a complete bust. Since Amy had been in his charge, he hadn't
provided her with as much as one good meal. She was a child,
a growing child and needed proper nourishment.

TV cameras and monitors sat everywhere, all of them
running, all but one showing pictures of Denny trying to feed
Amy. The other one was now hooked up to outside reception
and was now running WCN news. If he'd had any doubts about
the importance of what had happened at Gayler's party, the
news put it all to rest. There was nothing going on in the
world—nothing—that wasn't directly tied to Denny's action.

The world had, in just thirty-six hours, totally realigned its
priorities with devastating effect. Most all work had come to a
halt that wasn't directly connected with feeding the hungry as
people everywhere volunteered in staggering numbers to
donate their time to establish pipelines of food. Business had
turned its vast resources to the problem, ignoring all other
types of production. Several more days of the same would
bankrupt the entire world. Governments protested in vain,
while suspending all the ideals and priorities that had seemed
so important in order to cooperate with the rest of the world,
all differences put on hold without reservation.

It was incredible. Kicking and screaming, the people of the

planet were working together for a common goal, though economic ruin seemed quickly inevitable. There were other minuses— hospital riots in every major city on Earth, babies going comatose from continual crying, severe religious condemnation from all major religions save Buddhism and Hinduism, which found the priority change totally compatible with their outlooks. Even with the condemnation, large numbers of people from all over the world were breaking with their religion and gravitating toward something that was being called Divine Miracle. And for all of those people, there were greater numbers of people calling for the death of Amy Kyle and Dennis Stiller.

It was high drama on a grand scale, the future of the entire world tied up in its ability to carry off the dream quest, but to Denny, it was all simply pictures on the television. His problems were a lot more immediate, and the way he worked them out would affect everything else. And the crazy thing was, the problems were personal ones. He wasn't sure of anything else that was going on, but one fact had slapped him so hard he couldn't deny it any longer: he wasn't who he thought he was. He was merely an image, a television creation. He used Truth as a bludgeon that hurt people, never turning that damned all-seeing eye on himself. But no more. He was a part of it now, part of the muck, the craziness. He had treated Amy like a bug under a microscope, just like he had always treated everything, never caring about her welfare on any level—physical or emotional. What did that make him?

He had to gain some sort of control over this thing. He doubted at this point whether taking away the pain would be able to change the downward economic spiral. It meant that he was going to have to take the blinders off his own mind and look at himself the way he had always looked at everybody else. What a fool he was! He'd always thought he was so pure, so honest and above everyone else. Why?

Because the camera *was* God. Because it showed Truth and invented truth. Because whatever it showed *became* Truth for the audience, the very size of the audience in an age when worldwide communications were instantaneous, feeding back approval and rightness to the endeavor. McLuhan's famous maxim— the medium *is* the message—was never more true. If half a billion people saw the same thing on television, the very act of sharing information with that many people made the information correct and important. The cathode-ray oracle at Delphi.

And because he stood at the right hand of the vacuum-tube god, he then became the voice of the oracle and, consequently, pure himself.

But it wasn't true! It was all invention, and he was no God. The truth of the matter was that he was an emotionally retarded product of a shattered childhood who hid behind an image rather than deal with his own demons. He was a created person, unreal on every level, unable to communicate emotionally with the rest of his species. To make matters worse, he had finally come to realize that he enjoyed the power. It threatened at all times to reach out and consume him rather than let him find himself. So easy to retreat behind the power, just as he had done with the camera.

Denny Stiller was scared to death.

He and Amy were linked inextricably and the power had already been extended. For him to somehow put this in proper perspective, he'd have to learn more about himself and who he really was. And he'd have to communicate, really communicate with Amy Kyle. And he'd have to do it quick.

He looked at the girl. She sat rocking back and forth on the dinette chair and pulling her beautiful hair out in long strands that fanned before her face. She was at once the most fragile and most hardened person he had ever seen, although amid all of that, what he saw most was loneliness and a desperate desire to merge with what was human. Shakti, dakini—whatever she was, she embodied energy in unbelievable measure. He had tried to explore her power by using it. But that wasn't the answer. It went far deeper and far more human. Denny had been wrong about everything.

The television switched to a picture of a 747 converted to military use landing at the Dallas–Fort Worth Airport and disgorging troops in green uniforms, the U.N. peacekeeping force insignia on their shoulders. He reached out and turned up the sound, listening to the announcer.

". . . where thousands of citizens turned out to demonstrate against what they feel is an unlawful invasion of foreign troops on American soil. The mood was dark here, the protestors carrying signs condemning the peacekeeping force and shouting slogans threatening violence. A message from the president asking for help and understanding was read to the crowd, but was shouted down with anti-intervention chants and finally a rock-throwing melee."

The TV showed pictures of the troops being pelted by rocks and debris, and finally dispersing the crowd with tear gas, rubber bullets, and nightsticks. It had to send shudders through every American who saw it—a foreign invasion of the United States, including Russians, with the support of the government. The plan called for fifteen thousand U.N. troops, plus a like number of National Guard. At that rate, they could cover the rich part of the city pretty quickly.

Denny reached over and smoothed Amy's baby-fine hair then stood. It was time to go to the place of communication with her, another crack at Edouard Manet. He reached out to shut down the television, when another story caught his attention. It was a film of Jesus Cardera being taken aboard an Air Force helicopter for parts unknown, the government not wanting to let the graft of the civil authorities steal their prize away. The man was smiling at the camera and waving with manacled hands.

"With information supplied by Dennis Stiller, Cardera was captured at a roadblock outside of Bogotá by U.S. troops last night," the announcer said. "Access to his office building has provided the beginnings of a strange tale of foreign intrigue and big business. Much is still unknown, but the preliminary investigation into the computers at Rodriguez International seems to show that Cardera had led a double life, using his legitimate enterprises as a cover for his drug empire, apparently trading high-tech hardware for cocaine, which in his ledgers was always referred to as 'bumper.'

"Further, and even more startling, there are continual references to a CIA contact known only as Trent, who bartered everything from computer chips to video cameras in exchange for large quantities of the controlled drug. Who this Trent is, or what he is, still remains to be seen as the investigations continue. Cardera will be tried in federal court on international drug smuggling charges and thirteen counts of murder. He can be sentenced for up to two hundred and thirty years if found guilty on all counts."

The scene changed again, more on the hospital riots, and Denny turned off the set. There was that word again— bumper, and on top of that, a CIA connection. This got stranger all the time. The story attracted him strongly, instinctively. If only everything else wasn't so weird, he could think about pursuing it. But not now. There was so much on his mind. Everything was so unreal.

"Amy," he said softly to no reaction. "I know you can hear me so please listen. I want to go into the painting again. I want to talk some more. Please, no sex this time. We've got to talk together, to make some sense of all this. Nothing makes any sense to me anymore and I feel like I'm losing my grip. Do you understand?"

She cocked her head, then jumped out of her seat and ran to the smashed up plate and the remnants of breakfast on the floor. She squatted before it and began playing with the eggs.

He stood up and moved to her, trying to hold down his own growing sense of frustration. No wonder it was so easy to use the power. Trying to establish a link with the child was so nearly impossible; she clung so desperately to her godhead, so fearfully. He half-smiled when he realized it. Amy Kyle was God because she was afraid of the pain of being human. Adele, the barmaid in the painting, had said that we all created realities every day. Perhaps that drive to control the world was an extension of the same fears that drove Amy, and perhaps the same fear that had tied Denny so inextricably to the TV camera.

He moved to her, hating himself for the growing excitement with which he anticipated their mental joining. Even as he tried to rationalize the power, it seduced him.

He leaned down and picked up the girl, who clung to him immediately, nuzzling familiarly against him—bonding. As he held her, it was as if the blood heated in his veins, energizing him, pushing away the fears that only a moment ago had seemed so totally overpowering. What an addiction the power was, not because of its potential for gain, but because it was a protection against the fear of being human.

As always, when he took her into his arms, he felt his mind extend outward like an open electrical connection. Colors became vibrate and alive, pulsing, inanimate objects seeming to breathe with a life of their own. It was as if the house around him was a huge, living organism.

He moved with her into the living room, the paintings that covered the high-ceilinged wall like so many movie screens, the work of the French impressionists bursting forth as subconscious reality: Pissarro's marvelous Parisian street scenes with his indistinct market figures calling and moving in harmony; Monet's dotty landscapes with falling leaves and choppy waters moving sailboats whose bold white sails caught unreal winds in billowy excitement; Degas's twirling ballerinas bursting forth in pastel beauty and grace. Denny could see, actually see, what the artists had seen in their imaginations. The impressionists had somehow understood the created nature of reality and had extended their minds to physical form.

With ever growing excitement, he moved to Adele behind the bar at the Folies-Bergère, smiling as he saw the reflected customers at their appointed seats, drinking and chatting happily as the cancan pounded its driving rhythm in the background, loud enough that he could hear it in the living room.

He set Amy on the floor and took her hand. Straightening, he stared Adele straight in the eye, accepting her eternal sadness as an unhappy reality.

"You've returned," she said. "Didn't get enough last time?"

"Is my appointment waiting for me?" he asked.

"I do not know of any appointments, *Monsieur*," she said, and it seemed to him that something was troubling her.

"What's wrong?" he asked.

"Your visit here is more dangerous than last time," she answered, and he could barely hear her voice above the din of the music.

He turned and leaned against the bar, staring out at the boisterous crowd. They seemed to be having *so* much fun. "How can it be dangerous?" he replied. "It's only my own mind."

"Have you decided that now?" she asked.

"You always respond with questions," he said, turning back to her, "and you always try and depress me. Give me an answer this time: why is it dangerous here if it is only my own mind?"

She stared directly at him, her eyes emotional spikes driving into his heart. "Your own mind is the most dangerous place in the universe," she replied. "Please go now."

"Gladly," he said, angry at her. Adele reminded him of a roommate he'd had at college who never saw the good in anything. No matter what happened, he'd find its depressing aspect. When he saw a man set foot on the Moon, he saw nothing but pollution being taken into outer space. They had taken his roommate away in a straitjacket after a semester and a half. Of course, to Denny, the only thing interesting about the Moon landing was the fact that a cloud of dust had risen around the astronaut's foot when he stepped off the ladder. It was a nice visual.

He moved away from the bar, working his way through the crowd until he reached the stage and the never-tiring dancers who still frolicked through their paces, the feet pounding and shaking the flimsy stage. The private room sat across from the stage in its accustomed place. He moved to it and entered.

He found himself standing in an office. A man wearing a porcelain collar with slicked back hair and a pencil-thin moustache looked up at him in surprise. "Yes," he said in English with a heavy French accent. "What do you want?"

Denny looked around the room. It was decorated warmly, obviously a manager's office with ledger books and a filing cabinet. A small couch covered with purple velvet sat in the corner. "I . . . uh, had an appointment with . . . Amy," he said.

The man frowned, shaking his head. "There is no one here by that name," he said. "If I cannot help you with anything else. . . ."

"Yes!" Denny said. "I mean, no. I met her here yesterday. I must speak with her. This is my mind. *I* control it."

"Then you will please control yourself and leave this office immediately," the man said, half-standing and closing a ledger book. "The person you are looking for is not here. Wait." The man bent once more to the desk, rapidly writing something on a pad with a fountain pen. He tore off the paper and held it out to Denny.

Denny took the paper. It was full of French writing. "Give this to one of the waiters. You will have a free drink on us. Please. Go, take a table. Enjoy yourself."

Denny wandered out of the office, idly watching the never-ending dance. What to do? He looked at the paper in his hand. It didn't really look like French. It was more like a combination of Spanish and gibberish. Perhaps, though, the thing to do was take the advice of the manager.

He moved into the audience and found an empty table near the orchestra pit, the maestro's baton waving a heavily punctuated rhythm, the musicians, faces intent, letting the baton issue their life force in pianoforte and 4/4 time, cymbals clashing loudly on the upbeat.

The beat was elemental, intoxicatingly sexual when coupled with the chorus line's pounding, leggy gyrations, the young women's faces puffed red with exertion, their little cries like strangled, ecstatic moans. He found himself getting aroused, and fought back the feeling. That wasn't why he had come here.

"What can I get for you?" asked a waiter in English, a young man, womanish-looking, in a starched white apron and pastel pink cheeks highlighting Manet's sickly pale skin tones.

Denny handed him the note, the young man nodding pleasantly, then setting a glass of burgundy on the wood table. The wine had somehow materialized on a tray he carried above his head.

"Enjoy the show," he said, then walked off before Denny could ask him anything else.

The wine was dry, the way he liked it, so he decided to drink this one glass and enjoy the show before returning to the house. Obviously, nothing was going to happen this trip. Perhaps it wasn't that easily controllable. All around him men in top hats and women with boas and hair piled high atop their heads, laughed and drank. At a table near him, a man and woman kissed, her hand furiously rubbing the front of his trousers, Denny unsuccessfully attempting to divert his eyes because of the feelings it aroused, his own sense of voyeurism so strong he could only sit, mesmerized.

"Hello, Dennis," came a soft voice beside him.

He turned and stared into the eyes of his dead past. "M-Mrs. Parsons?" he said.

"Call me, Jane," she said. "You're all grown up now. You can call me that."

He couldn't believe it. He had lived with the Parsonses through most of his twelfth year. It had been his fifth foster home since the death of his parents, and the one he'd most loved, until—

"You look . . . just the same," he said, staring into her hazel eyes, feeling a tinge of excitement at the low cut sweater she wore, just the barest hint of cleavage pecking out of the V-neck, her freckled breasts heaving as she laughed.

"You're far too kind, Dennis," she said, smiling with red lips. "I hope you've forgiven me for what I did."

"It wasn't completely your fault," he said, and her hand slipped into his, fondling. "I've carried the image of . . ."

She stopped him with a hand to his lips. "I was jealous of you, you know. Barry and I couldn't have any children. When he became so fond of you I guess I just got a little crazy."

He looked at the tabletop, at her hand upon his, so fine, like alabaster, the nails trim and perfect as always. "I've carried your image around all this time."

"I know," she said, bringing his hand up to his lips, then crushing it against her chest. "I think it's sweet." Denny was shaking with excitement. He had fantasized making love to this woman for well over twenty years. To have her here like this before him, so beautiful, so pristine, was almost more than he could stand.

He forced self-control by reminding himself why he had come here. This wasn't real—was it?

"Did Amy send you here?" he asked, mouth dry.

She smiled and brought his hand back to her mouth, sucking gently on his index finger. "Why blame everything on that poor little girl?" she asked. "Isn't this *your* party?"

"I've hated you," he said.

"Hate and love are just words," she said. "Guilt. Now there's something. Guilt is a good reason for hatred." Her eyes twinkled. "And in your case— lust."

"I remember Mr. Parsons shoving me out the door that day," he said, "and that tiny little smile on your face."

"This smile?" she asked, pulling her lips tightly across her teeth.

He nodded. "I wanted to fuck that smile off your face."

"Like I said, Dennis: it's your party."

He reached across the distance between them and grabbed her by the back of her curly black hair, pulling her roughly to him and jamming his lips against her, his tongue and teeth angry, biting and invading her lips and mouth. And her lips were soft like butter, her mouth yielding.

She pulled away from him, eyes like blue flame. "Not yet," she said. "Things aren't perfect yet."

"Why am I here?" he asked.

"I live here," she said. "You're the one who came for a visit."

"I wanted to talk to Amy."

The woman looked coy. "Well, maybe we can go find her," she said, and stood, smoothing her sweater over a pleated skirt that revealed incredible legs, the sweater pulling tight across her breasts, large excited nipples pushing out the material.

"Where are we going?" he asked, an erection throbbing within his pants as he tried to ignore it.

"You'll see," she said, and moved up beside him, their arms

slipping easily around one another as they picked their way through the crowd toward the front entrance.

The year had been 1962 and Dennis Stiller, a sullen and unhappy child going through the metabolic change to manhood, had suddenly found himself living in a nice neighborhood with people who had taken him into their lives for reasons other than the monthly stipend that the state paid for foster kids.

The woman had been in her thirties then, and cool toward him. But with the husband, Barry, an immediate chemistry had taken place. The man had been desperate for children, and Denny had been desperate for a man's guidance, both of them throwing everything they had into the relationship, trying to build something out of the ruins of both of their lives. But Jane Parsons wasn't happy. Unable to have her own children, she adamantly refused to consider adoption, not wanting "someone else's mistakes." Barry had been able to talk her into trying a foster child situation, but for her, it never took. It may have simply been a reminder to her of her own inadequacies. Whatever the reason, she searched for, and finally found, a reason for her husband to remove Denny Stiller from their lives.

"This way," the woman said, opening the double front doors. "It's not far."

They walked out into a beautiful warm evening in 1882, gaslights glowing the cobbled beauty of *Rue Richer* to a warm, bunlike yellow as music and laughter tumbled up and down the streets like paper trash on a stiff wind. They turned left, toward the *Rue du Faubourg Poissonnière*, the uppermost spire of St. Vincent de Paul Cathedral just evident above the tops of the uneven, balconied garrets that lined the streetstairs going up the great hill of the Montmartre.

The air smelled of perfume and baking bread as he pulled the woman closer to his hip, delighting in having such physical control over someone who had done so much to ruin his life.

He heard a shout, then a muffled groan, his attention drawn to a lamppost on the intersection. A man in a wool suit and wooly top hat had been run up against the lamppost by a shadowy man in black, his hat falling to blow away down the street. The man slid slowly to a sitting position, as the dark man pulled a long stiletto out of his stomach, blood dripping from the blade that sparkled in the light. Denny's first thought, his very first thought, was that he wished he'd had a camera with him. The dark man knelt before his victim, going through his pockets and extracting his purse before fleeing into the alleyway behind the bakery on the corner.

"Exciting, isn't it?" the woman said as they hurried to the man on the ground. He looked up at them, eyes fluttering, his mouth moving to bubbling blood that was a shade of red that only Édouard Manet could have come up with.

Denny stared down in horrified fascination dismissing the scene as unreal before understanding that everything he ever showed on television was unreal to the people who viewed it.

"Looks like a goner," came a familiar voice from the shadows, Frank Hargrave dressed in Hawaiian shirt, jeans, and cowboy boots stomping up to stand beside them. He had something black and plastic draped over his shoulder.

"Frank?"

"My work ain't never done," Frank said, kicking the man, who groaned loudly in return and fell prone in the street. "Oh well, might as well git to it."

He bent to the man, laying the length of plastic beside him. A body bag, that's what it was. Frank unzipped the bag and tried to roll the man into it.

"I'm not d-dead," the man protested weakly.

"Fuck you," Frank said, pulling harder, finally succeeding in getting the man atop the bag. Then he began bending the guys legs, trying to fit them in the bottom as the man continued to protest.

"C'mon honey," Jane Parsons said. "This isn't what we came to see." She took Denny by the hand and led him away, Frank and the dying man arguing over the disposition of the body.

"Mrs. Parsons!" a little girl called from across the street, waving.

"Penelope, hello!" the woman called. "I have some sweets for you!"

The girl giggled and charged across the street, just as a horse-drawn carriage thundered around a corner at breakneck speed. Screaming, the girl was knocked under the horse's hooves, then the wheels of the great carriage, her cries mangling with her body, Denny hearing the snap of her breaking bones as the carriage rumbled on down the street.

"Stop!" Denny called running toward the fleeing coach.

The coachman turned then, laughing, and tipped his top hat—it was Charlie Kornfeld, blood oozing from the open wound on his head. The horse was Oater, Molly's dead stallion.

"Remember!" Charlie called to him above the thunder of the wheels on the street. "It's all bullshit!"

"What's happening?" Denny said, walking back to join Jane Parsons on the sidewalk.

"Isn't this wonderful?" the woman said. "Paris is such an exciting city!"

They started up the stairs, the street rocking with an explosion from the bakery. Denny turned back to the store, a man running out onto the street, his body ablaze, lighting up the night.

Denny stopped, transfixed, as the human torch stumbled toward him, arms outstretched. With a mixture of fear, revulsion, and inquisitiveness, Denny watched the man get closer and closer, the smell of his roasting flesh strong in the air. Just as he was about to reach them, he fell face down on the stairs, his body twisted up like a twig. The woman moved up to the now-unrecognizable hulk and bent to it, a cigarette in her mouth. Leaning far forward, she lit the cigarette on the body, inhaling deeply, then letting out a streamer of gray-white smoke.

"Ahh," she sighed. "I needed that."

She straightened, taking another long drag on the cigarette.

"Where are we going?" Denny asked. "What has all of this got to do with Amy?"

She blew a lungful of smoke into his face. "What's the problem?" she asked. "Isn't this what you like? Come, follow me."

She turned and continued up the stairs that were the *Rue du Faubourg Poissonnière*. Her hips swayed gently as she walked, the sight of her almost unbearably exciting. He was moving in an almost dreamlike way, totally caught up in the reality around him. And, if nothing else, it *was* real. Perhaps for lack of a better term, a real dream. He saw, smelled, tasted—felt—the atmosphere, and not as something separate and apart, but as a totally involving reality.

His entire professional life he had spent in the pursuit of the story, the filmable event. Everything happening around him aroused feelings of excitement that he was responding on a very elemental level, well beyond rationalization. Gutty emotion was pulling him up those stairs, was arousing him at the sight of Jane Parsons. Though he knew it was important for him to exercise his reason now, he couldn't bring himself to do it. This was his mind, putting on some kind of show for him, and he had nothing to do but sit back and enjoy. Could anyone resist such a safe and fulfilling dream trip?

They continued up the stairs, climbing higher, *Rue Richer* small and indistinct far below them, all of Paris stretching out, twinkling like grounded stars around him. He felt above everything, breathing cool, clean air from the mountaintop.

The woman stopped at a crooked doorway high above the city. She reached for the handle, then turned to smile wickedly at him. "Here we are," she said. "You'll see. The trip will be worth it."

"Will I find Amy in there?" he asked.

The Parsons woman frowned deeply. "When in the *hell* are you going to figure out that *you* can't ask the questions here?"

"Denny," came a soft voice behind him. "Don't go in."

He turned to see Molly standing behind him on the stairs. Her stomach was huge with pregnancy and she carried Teddy, the dog, in her arms, the poor animal's intestines hanging out, running down the length of her swollen belly.

"Molly," he said, embarrassed. "What are you doing here?"

"That's a stupid question," she returned, then held the dog out to him.

"No," he said, pushing the animal away. "That dog isn't mine. I'm sorry for what happened, but it had nothing to do with me."

"You have responsibilities. Everything the human being does touches everyone else."

"It doesn't have to," he said adamantly. "I've lived apart . . . for no one but myself."

"As I raise our son I'll tell him that," she said, pulling the dog back against her and hugging it close, the animal responding by licking her face. "Oh God, Denny. Why have you been so afraid of me? All I've wanted was to make you happy."

"No!" he said loudly. "You've wanted plenty. You've had expectations, desires, plans, hopes . . . all of them revolving around me, all of them designed to keep me from being free."

She jumped back, startled. "You think you're free?" she asked, incredulous.

"That's enough, bitch," Jane Parsons said, walking between Denny and Molly. "Go peddle your guilt somewhere else. He's *mine* tonight, and he's a free man, far too smart to let

some hard-times chick tie a weight around him and sink him in
the river of life."

"*You're* the one who wants his freedom," Molly said.
"You're just giving him enough rope to hang himself."

"That's it!" Parsons said, exasperated. She turned to
Denny. "Quite the little fruitcake you've gotten yourself all
mixed up with. Well, that's okay too. . . ."

She turned back to Molly and shoved her hard, Molly
losing her balance and falling backward. She went down the
steps hard, screaming, the back of her head cracking open as
she hit the steps to a rush of blood.

"Molly, no!" he called, reaching out for her, watching in
horror as his hands grabbed empty air, Molly Hartwell tumbling down the long stairs, still hugging the dog to her,
protecting it as her body slammed, cracking and breaking.

And she fell to oblivion, tumbling all the way to the streets
far below, her cries choked off in dream death long before she
hit bottom. He stood, staring down, trying to simply look at it
as another story, another facade to hide behind.

"Come on, let's go in," Parsons said breathlessly. She
moved up to him, pulling in close, her body lush and smelling
of a perfume he hadn't been around in years—her perfume
from before. She pushed up against him, her breasts mashed
against his arm.

"But, Molly. . . ." he said, not resisting as she turned him
from the view down the stairs and drew him through the door.

"She made her own choices," the woman said, "and you've
made yours."

They were standing in a simple room of blue walls and
wood floor. A plain table with a gaslight stood in one corner, a
walnut four-poster bed in another. An iron stove for cooking
and heating rested near the center of the place. On the far
wall, a doorway covered by a beaded curtain, sat directly
opposite the front door.

The woman fit herself into Denny's arms, molding to him
from lips to feet. She kissed him deeply, his insides jangling
with the excitement. The kind of sexual excitement he hadn't
known since childhood.

She reached between them, patting his erection. Then she
pulled away, red tongue darting out to lick her lips. "I can see
you're ready," she said, moving toward the doorway with the
beaded curtains. "Stay out here until I call you."

He stood alone, shaking, wanting more of the woman. He

tried to concentrate on why he had come, but these images were more than he could handle. They drew on his soul, on the base instincts that motivated him. Greed, Gayler had called it, summing up thousands of years of human history with a word. But Denny began to realize there was a concept that drove humanity even more than greed—fear.

"I'm ready," the woman called seductively.

Without hesitation, Denny moved to the beaded curtains and pulled them aside. He was greeted by a billow of steam that within seconds gave way to the look of a modern bathroom.

"My God," he whispered, stepping in.

It was 1962. Denny was a kid again, walking into the Parsons's bathroom just as he had done that day. He moved to the tub, the woman sitting smiling in the water that slicked her skin, making her shiny; making his stomach dissolve in butterflies. Her large breasts floated, bright red nipples jutting upward. He had never seen a naked woman before.

"Don't be shy," the woman said, just as she had done that day. "I know you've wanted to see me like this. Come closer."

He moved to the tub, his knees threatening to buckle and knock him to the white tile floor.

"Scrub my back," she said, handing him the washcloth. "Soap it up good first."

He soaped the washcloth with trembling hands, his penis throbbing. He reached out tentatively and rubbed her back in a slow, circular motion.

"Hmmm," she said, closing her eyes. "That's nice. Why don't you do my front, too?"

He looked at her fearfully. "It's all right," she said. "Barry won't be home for hours. It's time for me to take a hand in your education."

He moved around before her, soaping her chest, then her breasts. His mouth had gone dry, his breathing erratic as he fondled her, the woman throwing her head back and moaning.

Then she reached for him, unzipping his pants, his erection plopping out into her hands. And he leaned against the tub, all strength gone as she stroked him with soapy hands.

Then it happened—the noise at the front door. Barry Parsons had come home. "Honey! Where are you?"

She looked up at Denny then, smiled once, then screamed, high and shrill, frightening. He froze to the spot, reliving the moment, his penis stiff and jutting as Mr. Parsons walked into the bathroom, his wife covering her breasts with her arms.

"My God!" she screamed "He . . . he forced himself in here. He was trying . . . was trying . . ."

"What?" the man shouted, grabbing Denny's arms and shaking him wildly. "You did what!"

"No, sir," Denny said, frightened. "She . . . called me. She t-told me to, I—"

"Liar!" the woman screamed. "You lousy little fiend."

He looked at her then, understanding of the trick he had walked into flooding over him. And he hated her then. He wanted to kill her with sex, to hurt her.

"Mr. Parsons!" he yelled. "I didn't! I swear I didn't!"

"I know you didn't, son," the man said, breaking from the reality of the situation. "She's just a dumb, stupid bitch. Go ahead . . . take her! She deserves it!"

Denny turned to stare at him. The man was smiling. "Go ahead, son," he said, fatherly. "She's yours. Fuck some sense into her."

And Denny realized the purpose of the dream. He moved to the tub, frustrated, angry, and excited, climbing right into the water with the woman. She didn't resist as he threw her legs over his shoulders and pounded into her, twenty-six years of pent-up emotion draining out of him as Barry Parsons cheered him on. And as his breath came ragged and the tensions convulsed his body, he heard someone crying from very far away and realized that it was him.

CUT TO:

NIGHT—EST—PARKLAND HOSPITAL, DALLAS. Crowds surround the hospital entries. They are screaming and charging police barricades. From our vantage point beyond the activity, we see the occasional streamer of a tear gas canister as it is lobbed into the crowd. We PULL TIGHTER, moving through wafting tear gas smoke, then the crowd. They magically part for us and we reach the wooden barricades with shoulder-to-shoulder riot cops blocking the way. We pass the cops, who don't notice us, then move through the hospital entrance. We are searching for something. People JAM the inside of the hospital as we move through the emergency room crowds, people with bad stomachs and people with accidents or with gun shots from run-ins with the police. It is obvious that there is no way the numbers of people here can possibly be treated by the hospital staff, who move around trancelike, doing what they can, trying to tell the difference between the truly sick ones and the weak ones who refused to live with their mental pain. But this isn't what we're looking for. We PUSH ON farther, moving past the packed waiting room, TV blaring within, Dr. Connover talking about Denny Stiller, to take the darkened hallway branching out from the emergency room. People fill the hall, sitting on the floor or walking back and forth. We anxiously SCAN THEIR FACES to no avail. That for which we search isn't here. We move on, stopping finally in front of a pair of double doors that have the words WARD 2 printed on a transom above. We hurry THROUGH THE DOORS, walking into the darkened ward, passing a night-duty nurse who doesn't see us. We are moving more quickly, sensing an answer to our questions. Beds rush past us in a blur as we TRACK toward the end of the line. We pick out a certain bed, hurrying up to it.

ANGLE—A SLEEPING MAN. We recognize him, PULL-ING IN TIGHT. He JUMPS, startled, at our approach and BOLTS UPRIGHT in bed, staring straight at us, but not seeing us. It is ROY GEIST, the insurance investigator from Act III.

ANGLE—WARD ENTRANCE. We watch, from a safe distance now, as the man jumps out of bed and walks toward us, toward the door. He passes us and moves. . . .

ANGLE—THE HALLWAY. We watch the man walk down the hall toward us, but as he passes the waiting room, he looks in. We look with him, at the television screen showing Denny's picture.

ANGLE—TV SCREEN. We are watching Denny and listening to James Connover in vo.

CONNOVER

Remember, the reward will be paid confidentially. No one need ever know who you are if you prefer. Our number is flashing at the bottom of your screens. If you have seen this man or any of his accomplices, please contact me at the number shown. If your information is valid, the half million dollars will be paid immediately, no questions asked.

CLOSE-UP—ROY GEIST. He is staring dumbly at the television, eyes narrowed as he tries to think.

CUT TO:
ANGLE—NURSES STATION TELEPHONE. Geist picks up
the phone while no one is watching and dials the number that
he is mumbling over and over to himself.

GEIST

Y-yes . . . is this the number on the
television?. . . . Yes. I-I think I was at that man's
h-house four days ago. . . . No . . . no, I don't
remember. . . .

CLOSE UP—GEIST. Tears are running down his cheeks.

GEIST (cont)

Please help me . . . I don't
remember. . . . No . . . no! Please! I don't remember m-my name. . . .

FADE TO BLACK.

Scene 4

(early evening, the following day)

MONTAGE. We are the eyes of the world, folding through
mists of cascading Truth, a vortex of events swirling round us
like the hair of the opium eater in Coleridge's *Kubla Khan*—
beware, beware. We are looking at a huge map of the globe, a
map thirty feet by twenty feet that fills one wall of a large, open
room. People rush around the map, climbing ladders to stick
pins and draw concentric circles over specific areas as tables
full of telephones and Styrofoam coffee cups jangle noisily
amid a jumble of voices. We PULL TIGHT slowly on the map,
seeing the circled areas are areas of need, centered over
Africa, the Middle East, China, Russia, Central and South
America, Mexico, along with a few sections of the United
States. As certain areas are dealt with, flags are stuck

into the circles, sending up cheers from the myriad of workers in this one room. The cheers DISSOLVE into the sound of TRUCK ENGINES revving up, as crates of food are being loaded into a convoy that blocks up a large highway for miles in both directions. We PULL TIGHT on a crate with the word MEXICO stenciled on it, the crate DISSOLVES into another crate, the words BUENOS AIRES written across this one, as it is loaded into the cargo hold of a 747 jet, a commercial jet donated into service, the entire airport turned into a distribution point. We DISSOLVE again, this time to a bird's-eye view of Beijing, China, hundreds of thousands of people gathered at the Forbidden City to stack food on their bicycles and on trucks for distribution to famine areas. We DISSOLVE again, to a scene of an empty diamond mine in South Africa, as we PULL BACK to see an incredible scene. Stretching from our vantage point all the way to the horizon, millions of people, black and white, are toiling together, building a massive road for food transportation right through the heart of the African jungle. DISSOLVE to airplanes, flying low overhead, dropping crates from their holds, thousands of parachutes popping open like summer flowers as food drifts down to the waiting arms of Ethiopian villagers, who run, laughing to the downed parcels, even as engineers from Europe stand to one side, going over plans for irrigation systems to bring water to this region on a regular basis. DISSOLVE to food trucks crossing the Mexican borders. DISSOLVE to an Israeli agricultural expert giving farming advice to a roomful of Syrian farmers, experts in all aspects of agricultural needs giving their time and talents a free rein as the world works together on the problem. DISSOLVE to a series of rapid-fire scenes of people working—loading, harvesting, teaching, transporting, building roads and irrigation systems, a dizzying series of flashes making us realize how much of the world is involved in this thing, to be quickly replaced by another series of rapid-fire scenes of people eating—and smiling. White people, brown people, black people, red people all eating, all feeling the simplest, most basic pleasure of the human animal, many of them for the first time in their lives.
CUT TO:
A WCN CONTROL ROOM. It is dark in the booth, the control panel lights and small monitors providing the only light. On the hardwire monitor, we see a very weary-looking Dr. Abel Moreland being interviewed from a hospital bed.

Through the booth window, we can see two newscasters on the
set. Someone is in the booth whispering urgently to the
director as we listen to Moreland's voice through the booth
speaker.

MORELAND

I-I'm not sure what happened. They were waiting for
me in my garage and b-beat me, trying to make me
tell them where Stiller was. I told them I didn't
know, so they kidnapped me and tied me
up . . . but after Stiller's broadcast that made everybody sick, they thought it was some kind of trick designed to make them give up some sort of
information they thought they had. I know it doesn't
make much sense. They just . . . took themselves
very seriously. . . .

The director nods to the man whispering, then leans up in the
booth and speaks through the speaker on his headphones.

DIRECTOR

Harv . . . we've got live feed coming in from Stiller
and we're supposed to run with it. Get this off. We'll
cut to you on three, camera one. Ready . . .

MORELAND

. . . They just . . . committed suicide. I just don't
know how else to say it. They shot themselves in the
head while praying from the Koran. It took me two
days to get myself loose, I . . .

ANGLE—ANNOUNCER. He's looking concerned.

ANNOUNCER

We interrupt at this time to bring you a live broadcast from Dennis Stiller, in hiding. We switch live to
that address.

ANGLE—MONITOR. We are looking at a very strange
Denny Stiller. He stares, half-angry, half-asleep at the camera.
His face is slack and pale, with a three-day growth of beard.
His hair hasn't been combed and he's wearing a dirty T-shirt.
We lock onto his eyes, trying to ferret out the truth of this

man, and we see fear—not the chilling terror of Nature or
inhuman Man, but a more deeply abiding and debilitating
fear: the fear of oneself, the lack of self-control. We PULL
TIGHTER and listen to his words.

<u>DENNY</u>

. . . You just don't understand. Your life is lived up
here, up in your head. The stuff that goes on around
you is just window dressing, you know? Am I making
any sense? You decide up in your head what your life
is going to be and then you simply do that. If you're
oppressed or controlled, it's because you *choose* to be
so. *You* decide what is right. *You* decide what is
wrong. And all of it is selfish—selfish greed, selfish
fear. These are the motivating forces of the universe.
Ted Gayler tells me that Man is not a perfectable
creature, that our greed will simply end our existence
when we've depleted everything. I believe he's right.
I believe we are all victims of ourselves.

We PULL TIGHTER, Denny's face filling the screen, drawing
us into his private hell, the hell world of his own creation, the
wrathful shakti of his own invention. And because we *are*
Truth, we can feel the forces that are tearing Denny Stiller
apart.

They needed to know, to understand how useless it all was,
and Denny was telling them. Perhaps someone would listen.
He stared hard at the camera, trying to overpower it with his
sincerity, but felt he was falling short for some reason so he
kept talking.

"Don't you see?" he said, fighting his brain back to the
topic before it was too late. "There is no Fate, no Justice, no
Fellowship. There is only abuse, of our resources, of ourselves. We use ourselves and our world up and then we die.
Our heads rule our hearts and our heads are full of slavish
devotion to our overpowering needs!"

He had been up for almost a day and a half, living in his
head, letting himself float through one selfish experience after
another. When Amy would fall asleep from exhaustion, he
pulled her close and used her as she slept. He had taken
himself through every major experience of his life, reliving
them to his own ends. He'd had sex with every woman he'd

ever dreamed of having sex with, those he liked and those he hated. He domineered the dominating ones and let the others bask in his glory. He'd beaten up and killed most of the men who'd ever gone against him. He'd mixed stories together and had large casts where he got to live out his will on any number of other people he'd known all his life, all the experiences real, all of them coming out just the way he wanted them to. He was able to indulge himself without measure, each experience fresh and dependable. And every time he did, he gave away another little piece of himself. Every time he did, another part of the civilized Man who must live together with the rest of the society disappeared, leaving behind bitterness and resentment. Leaving behind something far worse—humanity. After enough indulgence he was able to see the Truth as he understood it, and the Truth was that Ted Gayler was right in everything he had said. Mankind was addicted to its vices, and that addiction would always keep us as jungle animals. Gayler had told Denny that his negative reactions to that postulate were simple knee-jerk. After living in the excesses of his own head for over a day, Denny understood *exactly* what the man had meant.

"Sickness, health, love, hate—all conditions of the spirit," he said. "Religion, patriotism, unionism, political activism—all meaningless words that we use to justify our continual search for ego gratification. Freedom and dignity—control words from a society that uses our gratifications against us. Don't you see? It's all nonsense. Nothing means anything. We're animals that live and die and are controlled because we don't understand the nature of control. Amy Kyle is God all right, the God of gratification. She's loved and hated, not because of what she is, but because of what she can give. That is God to us, unlimited gratification with no responsibility attached, thank you very much. We're all a festering sickness, killing ourselves and our world. There's not a drop of humanity among us. Isn't it interesting that everyone has come and said, 'What can you do for me?' Not one person has said, 'What must we do?' Responsibility is a word of fourteen letters, nothing more. And without responsibility, there is no civilization. So, all of you are feeding the poor because your bellies hurt. And after you've gratified the pain in your bellies, you'll come after me for daring to force you to assume responsibility for your starving brethern.

"I hate all of you. I hate you all to death. I hate you almost as much as I hate myself. Take away your troops and your threats, because the way I feel right now, I might just do something . . . drastic. This is Dennis Stiller reporting, live from nowhere."

Denny moved away from the camera after staring silently at it for several moments and shut it off, picking up the headset to contact Frank, but the man had already broken communication. Denny could hear him coming in the back door.

"Frank!" he called, moving out of the festering garbage of the studio and into the hallway to the kitchen, meeting the man as he walked through. "How was it?"

Frank, frowning deeply, just shook his head. "I can't handle this anymore, Denny," he said, and there was a wildness to his face. "You may be able to handle this crazy shit, but I'm not strong enough."

"What are you talking about?" Denny asked, moving to the sink for a glass of water. "Crazy . . . what's crazy?"

"You are, man. This whole damn thing is." Frank was looking at the running monitors, looking for Amy. He found her in the living room, sitting on the floor before one of the paintings, and just stared at her image. "You and her have gone on past this world, partner. You're livin' in another world . . . the place where people go nuts."

The counter was covered with dirty glasses, Denny unable to find a clean one and giving up. "You're not making sense," he told Frank as he opened and closed every cabinet door, then began opening them again. "Nothing's changed."

"You've changed," Frank said, pulling a chair up in front of the monitor as he stared at Amy. "You're livin' in the hell world, the place where people see so clear they go nuts if they ain't strong enough. This is a trip I can't make with you. No, sir. Been there before. I can't handle it."

Denny moved to him, looking hard at the man. He was nervous, almost disoriented. "I'm just looking for answers," he said.

Frank looked up, then reached out for Denny's hands, taking them in his own. "I love you like a brother, Denny. Hell, I knew it was you who kept me workin' at WCN when all them other fellas wanted to let me go. You ain't never judged me." A tear formed in his eye, slowly working its way out and down his weathered face. "I'll die if I go where you are. Tawny's already dyin'. I come out of my shell for you and took up that poor lady's welfare. Then I just let her go and drink herself to death, cause I got all caught up in the girl and cause I didn't know what to do for her. I'm not strong. I think we got God in our hands and we're goin' to be punished for it. Believe me, if I don't pull out soon, it's all over for me and the woman. We can't breathe the air that's filled up your lungs and head. I'm on the edge already."

Denny just stared at him, afraid of losing him, afraid of losing all perspective. "But I *need* you," he said softly. "Everybody's deserted me."

The man released Denny and lowered his head, burying his face in his hands, the light from the monitor bathing him in a pale glow. "You don't git it," he said, voice shaking. "I been gone before. I don't mean nervous breakdown . . . we're talking all the way out in the back woodshed, Denny. I don't handle that place. I'll die without stability around me. Not many are cut out for the journey you're takin'." He suddenly looked up at Denny with understanding. "You don't even know what you've done, do you?"

"What I've . . . done?" Denny returned, knowing full well what the man was talking about. He had retreated to his mind and had begun questioning the value of everything.

"Reality, ethics, values, motivations," Frank said. "You've gone to the place where that stuff ain't real, where everythin's groundless. It's the place of madness."

"Then I've always been mad," Denny replied, "because none of those words ever had any meaning for me."

"Then God help your immortal soul," Frank said, standing, his eyes still glued to the television. "I'm goin' to have to save myself and Tawny. The energy's too weird around here. We need space, me and that woman, before she drinks herself to death and I have to take the blame for it. And if you got any sense left at all, listen to me. People got to believe in things, even if they ain't big, important things. If we don't believe . . . trust in something beyond us, we're all done for. Find some way to save yourself or you're goin' to end up in a padded room with electrodes strapped to your head. Either that or you'll be dead. Believe me, I know what I'm talkin' about."

He turned and walked from the room, quickly, without looking back. As Denny heard his footsteps charging up the stairs he began to feel the largeness of the house all around him. The house was like his mind, a fine structure that had become jumbled and chaotic. It was full of rooms with many doors, all of them open and filtering light from all the others. He feared it, not xenophobically, but for the answers it might give him. He had never believed in anything but his job, and now he found that his job created as many realities as it explored. What was left for him? What good all the power in the world if it didn't give peace of mind?

He wandered into the living room, the evening glow lighting up the curtains as sunset pulled the reds and yellows from the visible light spectrum and splashed them across the sky in ways that people who believed in things would think were a gift from God. And above it all, the low roll of thunder and a darkened crown of sky, another storm moving in.

Amy sat nearby on the floor, holding a painting of Claude Monet's titled *Woman in Garden, Springtime*. As Denny entered, she sat stiffly, half-turning to him. He could feel a pull from her, a sexual stirring that made him feel cheap and dirty, his mind filling with the image of the RCA dog sitting in front of the Victrola listening to his master's voice, just like the joke they'd made at Gayler's party. It wasn't a joke anymore.

The surroundings faded to the background as he walked toward her. All that existed was the glow that radiated from within her. She had successfully merged with Denny, successfully made him a part of *her* world just as she had done with Tawny. He thought about how much they'd taught her. She'd learned about grasping from Tawny, jealousy from Molly, and selfish lust from him: the three major motivators of human existence—greed, fear, and sex.

He had been such a good teacher and such an easy conquest. It had never really occurred to him to help the girl. Consequently, his own demise was no worse than what he deserved. He'd wanted God just every bit as much as those poor, frightened souls who had journeyed to Dallas looking for a miracle to make their lives better. If they looked hard enough they'd find what he'd found. Contentment is the only happiness, and contentment comes from within. Unfortunately, he'd had to lose himself to find that answer.

What is God? It's the thing people want that will make them content.

He moved to her and sat on the floor, taking her hands in his just the way Frank had done. The confidence surged immediately back into him, pumping him up—the ninety-seven-pound weakling ready to kick sand back into the bullies' faces. With her near him, he could do anything, have anything, want anything—except that one thing peace of mind could bring—happiness. But how to find peace of mind? He'd been working on that one for nearly forty years without success.

Amy jerked her head toward the front of the house, Denny hearing the rattle of Frank and Tawny coming down the stairs a second later.

"Where ish she Frankie?" the woman called loudly, her voice slurring badly, the nasal twang like an ambulance siren on a foggy night. "Where'sh mah baby?"

Then Frank's voice, low, reassuring, unintelligible. Then they came around the corner and into the living room. Frank had a suitcase in one hand and Tawny in the other.

Denny started when he saw the woman. She was an ambling shell with nothing inside. Frank had to support her, for walking was beyond her ken. Years ago, when he had tried to join a college fraternity, Denny had been forced to guzzle a quart of vodka as part of the hazing ritual. He had lost total control of his mind and bodily functions, and had had to be hospitalized for two days to keep from choking on his own vomit. In looking at the woman, his own mind was forced back to the event, if only to realize how sober he had been then by comparison. She was in desperate trouble.

"Where are you going to go?" he asked Frank.

"Don't know," Frank said, his face dark, brooding. "Away from here."

"How are you going to go? I need the truck here."

Frank glared at him and walked closer, dragging the woman. "I'll hot wire somethin' on the street," he said. "I don't know."

He moved closer, bringing Tawny up near her daughter, Denny feeling uncomfortable signals from Amy and standing to move between them. "What are you doing?" he asked.

"Her body's poisoned, Denny," the man said. "Only the girl can help her now."

"Amy grabbed Denny's pants leg, a frightened surge charging his brain. "No," he said. "Amy doesn't want to."

"What the hell you know about what Amy wants?" Frank replied venomously. "She's Tawny's daughter. Her mama needs her bad, and I'm goin' to see that she gits what she needs."

Thunder rumbled outside as Frank tried to move past

Denny, who stood firm, blocking access in response to the frightened signals of his soul mate.

The two men stared at one another for several seconds, a look in Frank's eyes that he had never seen before. Then, in a flash, Frank dropped Tawny and grabbed Denny with large hands, jerking him out of the way and throwing him halfway across the room to bang heavily, Sheetrock cracking, against the opposite wall, several pictures falling like rain around him as he slid to the floor.

Pain charged hot through Denny's head, temporarily blocking out any contact with Amy. Hands to his temples, he looked up in time to see Frank dragging the nearly comatose woman right up to the girl, flopping the woman's head in her lap.

"No! No!" Amy screamed shrilly, convulsing with the touch of her mother, a bolt of lightning strobing the darkening room blinding white.

"Make her do something!" Frank yelled to Denny. "God damn you . . . make her help!"

"Don't you see she's scared half to death?" Denny yelled back, pain in his head nearly blinding him as he got to his knees, still too shaky to stand.

Amy, still screaming, wiggled out from under Tawny and charged to Denny, throwing herself in his arms and crying wildly. Frank turned to her, moving again.

"You stay away from her," Denny warned low. "Tawny's too far gone . . . the energy's too incomprehensible."

"Her mama needs her," Frank returned, his hands coming out in front of him.

Denny stood, using the wall for support. He held Amy fiercely to him, both of them strong in the contact. "I'm warning you, Frank. Get back! I don't want to hurt you."

All at once the front doorbell rang several impatient times. Everyone stopped, turning to the door. The bell rang again, then there were fists pounding on it.

"You will open the door!" came a voice with a thick Russian accent. "By the terms of the United Nations charter and international law we demand ingress to this dwelling!"

Thunder crashed again, the two men looking hard at one another. "The fuckin' troops!" Frank said. "Oh Jesus, it's all over now."

"No!" Denny snapped. "Not yet."

There was more pounding, this time with rifle butts.

Denny's mind worked frantically. He had intended to prepare for this eventuality, but had gotten so wrapped up in his own head that he'd let it go.

The pounding continued, the door cracking, finally breaking inward to slam open, two men charging in immediately with Kalishnikov rifles and throwing themselves prone in the entry hall, guns at the ready as others huddled around the door frame on the outside.

"Aw shit," Frank said, putting up his hands and walking toward the men. "Don't shoot. We ain't goin' to hurt you none."

"They can't hear you," Denny said, Frank turning quickly to him, his hands still in the air.

"What do you mean?"

"You can put your hands down," Denny said.

The men at the door had climbed cautiously to their feet, strained faces relaxing by degrees as another flash of lightning illuminated them from behind. They walked into the living room, slinging their rifles back over their shoulders. Their faces had the gaunt pale look that Denny had come to recognize as the starvation pain. Their demeanors were stoic as they gutted up and did their job in the fashion of military men everywhere.

"Come ahead," one of the men called back toward the door, three more soldiers, one with communications equipment strapped onto his back, entered casually. This man had a Swedish accent, Denny realizing that, being a multinational force in an English-speaking country that they'd share that language in common.

"What the hell is goin' on?" Frank asked loudly, his hands still in the air.

"I've convinced them that this is an abandoned house," Denny replied. "Please put your hands down."

Frank dropped his hands and got out of the way of the man with the Swedish accent. The men wore green fatigues with long blouses and white ball caps bearing the U.N. insignia.

The Swede turned to the man who'd come in with him. "What a place," he said, taking a flashlight-nightstick out of his belt and turning it on, playing the light all around the room. "Watch your step, the floor looks rotten."

"It doesn't look as if anyone has lived here for a long time," the other man, the Russian accent said.

"Damnit, Denny," Frank said. "This is too weird. Why don't we just end it here . . . give ourselves up, and—"

"No," Denny said. "It's not finished yet."

"The place didn't look this bad from the outside," the Russian said. "Why would they let it go like this?"

The radio man laughed without humor, then spoke with a German accent. "You know how the damn Americans are," he said, "they waste everything. I think we're about finished with this neighborhood."

"Set me up with Central," the Swede said. "We'll see what they want next." He looked at the other two men who'd come in with the radio operator. "Check out the rest of the house just in case."

The men left, Frank going up to the Swede. "Please," he said. "End this for us. We can't do it ourselves."

"Would you just stop it," Denny said, the room a throbbing kaleidoscope of color and moving pictures, the lightning outside throwing rainbow hues all over the walls and men. He held tight and rode with it.

"Fuck you," Frank growled, then grabbed the Swede by the arm, spinning him around. "Will you listen to me now?" he screamed in the man's face.

The soldier, a first lieutenant, shrugged Frank off as if he hadn't felt anything. "So many cobwebs," he said. "They got *big* spiders in America."

The Russian had walked over near the wall and unzipped his pants. "Maybe they feed them to their poor, huh?" he said grimly, and began to urinate on a Degas pastel drawing titled, *Woman Scratching*.

"That's not funny," said the radioman from the floor where he had set up his unit. "You wouldn't want to be fed spiders when you're starving."

The Russian nodded gravely and zipped his pants back up. "The night of the telly show, I ate fifteen cans of C-rations before I knew it wouldn't help me. I maybe would've eaten spider that night."

"I can't stand this Denny!" Frank called, agitated. "I just can't stand it!"

"Got them, Lieutenant," the German said from the floor, holding a telephone receiver out to the man.

The Swede took off his ball cap, and wiped sweat from his forehead, blond hair falling around his face as he took the receiver, switching the phone to the outside speaker. "This is Green–5 leader to Cabbage Stew. Over."

An American New England accent answered the call. "Go ahead Green–5. Over."

The man had pulled a map out from his breast pocket and was looking at it in the light of his flash. Denny moved to the wall switch and turned it on, brightening the room. The troops never noticed.

"We are just completing our swing through section C–13 with negative results . . . over."

"C–13," the staticked voice replied. "Check Any trouble? Over."

"Several verbal confrontations," the Swede replied. "Animosity, but nothing physical. Is there a problem? Over."

"You will go to full combat gear, Lieutenant Turgen," came the cold voice. "Steel helmets, live ammo. Our forces are meeting with heavy resistance in several neighborhoods. There have been a number of deaths. The most serious firefights are taking place in the Oak Cliffs area, E–24 on your map. Do you see it? Over."

"You've got to stop this," Frank said. "The whole damn world's falling apart."

"Precisely why I can't stop it," Denny said. "I keep looking for a way to work it out."

"There ain't none!" Frank shouted.

"I've found section E–24," the lieutenant said. "Over."

"You will proceed there immediately and report to Captain Jergennson, rendering any assistance the captain deems necessary. Do you read me? Over."

The other troops returned from their tour of the rest of the house and sat on the floor, lighting up cigarettes.

"Do it now, Denny," Frank said. "For God's sake, do it now!"

A hard rain began to fall outside, the troops groaning and sorting through their packs for ponchos.

"I read you loud and clear," said the Swede. "Am I to understand that we are returning civilian fire?"

There was a long silence of static, everyone turning to stare at the radio. "Affirmative, Green–5," came the quiet reply. "Out."

The Swede stood slowly. "You heard it," he said. "Crush the butts and get back to the truck. We're breaking out the combat gear."

"You know," the Russian said. "There's a lot more of them than there are of us."

"A lot more what?" the Swede said.

"Americans," the man answered, slipping a plastic poncho in camouflage over his head and pulling up the hood. "Fucking Americans. And they've all got guns."

The Russian picked up his rifle and slung it over his shoulder, trooping back toward the front door and into the rain.

"Stop!" Frank called, running up to grab the Swede again. The man pulled away, acting as if nothing were holding him.

"Dear God, please," Frank whined, walking next to the man as he headed for the doorway. "Please hear me. Please take us out of this place."

The troops left, not even bothering to try and close the busted door, rain pouring in, puddling in the entry hall.

Denny looked at Frank, watching him carefully and holding tightly to Amy's hand. The man looked wild, his eyes crazed, not connecting up consciously with his brain. Denny couldn't risk letting him come near again. He had no idea of what Frank could do if he were able to separate the two of them.

Frank paced for several seconds, wild walking, then he stopped dead, flaring around to Denny, lightning flashing his face demonically. "It's all comin' down," he said, talking rapidly. "The whole fuckin' world's comin' apart. I've got to git out of here . . . got to find a place to hide. Somewhere away from people . . . that's it. Yeah . . . the mountains . . . birds . . . streams. I can hide away. I can . . . forgit, and . . ."

He stopped talking and looked at Tawny. The woman lay on the floor where he had dragged her. She wasn't moving, her glazed eyes staring at the ceiling.

"C'mon, honey," he said, moving toward her. "Me and you. We'll hide out, git off the booze. We can do it, baby. We can save ourselves."

He bent to her, scooping her up in his arms. "You're so cold, baby. Why are you so . . ." He stopped talking, his face a mask as he turned to Denny. "Oh God," he whispered.

"What?" Denny said, starting across the floor toward them, then pulling back.

Frank carried Tawny to the couch and lay her down,

feeling her face, her arms, rubbing them vigorously. "I'll warm you up."

Denny's mouth went dry as he understood what was happening. "Take her pulse, Frank," he said slowly, trying to stay calm. "Please take her pulse."

Frank dropped her arm and just stared at her. Then he leaned up and kissed her on her parted lips.

"Frank!" Denny said.

"Don't need to take her pulse," he replied. "I stuffed enough body bags to know meat when I see it."

He bent to her then, picking up her thin, frail body and holding it close, rocking her, moaning down deep in his throat as the storm raged inside and out.

Denny's mind raced. A body. They had a body on their hands. And it wasn't just a dog they could bury in the backyard, but a real, dead, body.

Amy was agitated beside him. She vibrated, squeezing his hand with all her strength as he tried to think. They needed to record it all, somehow get it down so everyone would know he wasn't responsible. There was only one way to do that.

"Frank, get your camera," he said, "the one in the studio."

The man looked at Denny, his eyes draining tears, even as he held the woman to his breast, rocking her like a baby. "She understood," he said. "Tawny knew my weakness and never questioned . . . and I let her down."

"It's not your fault," Denny said mechanically. "Please, get the camera."

"What are you goin' to do?"

"Just get the fucking camera!" Denny screamed.

"Git it yourself!" the man said through clenched teeth.

Denny closed his eyes and willed the studio camera to him. By the time he opened them again, the thing was sitting, tripod and all, right in front of him.

He moved to the viewfinder and turned on the machine. It had already plugged itself in. He lined up Frank and Tawny, PULLING BACK just a touch to take in more of the scene. He was moving without thinking, taking care of business no matter how grisly.

"Come back here, Frank," he said low. "Come back here and roll tape."

The man looked up at him, eyes wild, crazy. "What are you goin' to do?" he asked shrilly.

"Get your ass back here," Denny said calmly. "Do it now."

Frank, moving mechanically, lay Tawny back on the couch and walked to Denny, his eyes narrowed, suspicious. "It's the end of the fuckin' world," he said. "And *we* did it, Denny. Me and you, we screwed everything."

"We've just searched for Truth, Frank," Denny replied, reaching down to pick up Amy, who immediately began writhing in his arms, trying to break free.

The man wiped his calloused hands across his red, wet eyes. "Don't you see . . . that's just the problem. This world don't work on no Truth. It's bullshit keeps us goin'. Just bullshit." He began to whimper softly, a large man now small and indistinct. He shook weakly, broken. Denny had brought him out of his shell only to destroy him.

"I want you to roll some tape now," Denny said softly, like a doctor with an Alzheimer's patient. "Just give me a little of the old magic."

"Roll . . . tape?" Frank said from far away, and the thunder crashed again.

Denny, holding Amy tightly, walked over to the couch, trying not to stare at the body. The girl in his arms shook and cried with horror, Denny grasping her tighter to hold her for just a while, just a little while. He addressed the camera.

"Behind me, on the couch, lies the body of Tawny Kyle, mother of Amy Kyle. She died just a little while ago, I believe, of alcohol poisoning. Her death was her own fault and her own making, tragic though it may be. Since I am currently not in a position to call in medical people or law enforcement officers, I want to convince you of me and my crew's blamelessness in this unfortunate woman's death. Since I don't expect you to believe me without proof. We will ask the Kyle woman herself what happened."

"Denny, no!" Frank screamed. "God, no!"

Denny leaned down and grabbed the dead woman's arm and squeezed, wishing life back into her. Immediately he felt the chilling pull toward the void, Amy's horror mixing with the death feelings as he slumped to the couch, darkness closing all around him only to flee seconds later to the sound of Frank screaming, hoarse and gutteral.

Amy broke from him, running to the far end of the room as he turned, staring straight into the dead, unblinking eyes of Tawny Kyle. The woman was sitting bolt upright, her face barely a foot from his.

"Tawny," he said, but Frank's screaming drowned him out "Tawny!"

Bright colors swirled all around him, the room tilting wildly. The Manet *Folies* hung nearby, Adele sticking her head out of the painting to see what was the matter.

"Amy! Aammmy!" Tawny yelled, her nasal voice grating, even in death. "Ah want mah baby! Amy!"

Frank had fallen to the floor, his hands covering his ears, his mouth open, screaming now without sound. The woman reached a clawlike hand toward Denny, grabbing his arm like a vise, her strength unbelievable.

She pulled him toward her, bringing their faces together, her breath carrying the rot of decay. "You fffucker . . . hellllp me. Ah need mah baby . . . it hurts!"

Denny jerked, pulling free of her, a large chunk of the skin of his forearm ripping off in her grasp as blood flowed freely down his wrist and hand, dripping to the carpet.

"I'll send you back," he said, moving away as the woman stood, her limbs already stiffening with rigor mortis. "Just tell us what happened. Please. I'll send you back."

Frank had regained his feet as he stared, uncomprehending, at the woman who walked stiffly past him, movements jerky. He was gone, lips sputtering, brain spinning wildly as he walked to the camera, his hands running lovingly over its contours.

Denny kept backing up, slowly, the room elongating and rocking all around him as the babble of voices from the paintings filled his ears. The dead woman kept advancing, jerking comically to the side, smashing through furniture that got in her way.

"How did you die?" Denny asked, hearing the shakiness in his own voice. "Tell us how you died."

"Died?" she said. "Died? Yessss. Send me to dead. Send me now! Amy . . . come . . . too!"

Frank had picked up the camera and moved it toward the window, tilting it skyward. "Damn good twister weather," he said, face glued to the viewfinder. "Whoo-ee! Look at that squall line. Might git us a boomer tonight. Yes, sir!"

Denny backed into a trembling Amy, her arms going around his leg, her power flowing into him as the colors brightened, lightning flashing her mother's wide eyes like car headlights.

"Did you drink too much?" he prompted. "Drink?"

The woman's lips moved with great difficulty, word commands traveling slowly along dying brain passages, stiffening muscles tightening. "Drrrinnkk," she said, her mouth twisted nearly sideways. "Giivvve meee mahhh baaaby. Yesss . . . drruuunkkk. S-send toooo dddeaddd. Hhheellp meeee."

She reached Denny, her arms enfolding him, steaming bile bubbling from her lips to drip in long stringers down his front as her putrid breath flamed hot on his face. He tried to push off, but her grip was death, crushing the air right out of his lungs.

"Tonight may be the night," Frank said, still looking through the window. "Got pretty close to one in Euless last year . . . but tonight I'm gonna catch me a twister. I can feel it sure."

"Dddeadd," Tawny rasped, fetid gas rising with her words.

He fought frantically against her, the revulsion nearly overpowering as her dead weight drew him to the floor beneath her, her mucus encrusted eyes staring deeply into his, tearing at his soul as he writhed and twisted in her grasp.

Frank ran to him, looking down excitedly. "I can feel it this time, Denny. There's goin' to be a humdinger tonight, and I'm goin' to catch it!"

"Dddeaadd," the woman pleaded, Denny himself fighting for breath, his free hand scrabbling for a hold on Amy, who had scooted out of his grasp and was sobbing on the floor, rolled up in the fetal position.

He couldn't breathe, his vision filling with fuzzy brown dots as he inched along the floor beneath Tawny, fingers stretching, reaching . . .

His finger touched cloth as he began to lose consciousness, and his mind filled with thoughts of death. Death. Death.

"Yesss," Tawny said, her voice only a croak now. She raised herself from him and rolled onto her back, arms outstretched, welcoming her unseen lover, her lips turning with difficulty into a crooked smile, her eyes upraised and happy. "Commme . . ."

And the face froze once more, smiling this time, embracing peace for the first time in her life. Denny, shivering with disgust, scooted away from her, then turned and stared hard at the body, his breath coming in ragged gasps. He heard Frank behind him, and realized the man had gotten between him and Amy.

"You'll help me," Frank told the girl. "I know you, and I know you'll help me with that twister."

Denny was still gasping, still trying to get past the extreme dizziness. "Frank . . . wha . . . what. . . ."

"Don't you worry none," Frank said, and bent down, grabbing up the girl.

Bright light arced from the contact, scorching Frank's face and arms, the smell of his burning flesh filling the room, Denny rolling onto his stomach and retching. But still the man held the girl, a strangled gasp, like a dying animal's, straining through clenched teeth.

"Frank, no!" Denny said, forcing himself to one knee, his own blood all over everything as the open wound continued to pump.

Frank looked at Denny, eyes alight, his face inhuman, totally lost as smoke rose from his skin and clothing, tiny electric sparks flaring everywhere he was in physical contact with Amy.

"C'mon sweetheart!" he yelled. "Let's git us one!"

He turned toward the back of the house and ran, Amy crying in fright and confusion as her body unsuccessfully fought the forced contact.

Denny rose on weak legs, staggering after them. He moved through the doorway to the kitchen and saw Frank and Amy, lit by flashing lightning, in the backyard near the pool, the man screaming at the sky.

The plywood that had been covering the broken sliding patio door had been knocked out, rain pouring unhampered into the breakfast room. Denny moved through the broken place, ferocious winds whipping rain, stinging him, as the sky swirled crazily above.

Flinching against the rain, Denny moved into the yard. "Let her go, Frank!" he called. "Please!"

Frank turned, a crazed smile plastered onto his face. "She's bringin' in the boomer for me!" he yelled. "Three hundred mile an hour they turn, Denny. That's somethin'!"

An arm up to his face, Denny moved out across the lawn, yelling Frank's name into the teeth of the squall. Then suddenly, there was dead calm, the sky quiet as a grave.

"That's it!" Frank called, and the sky had a yellowish tinge, the silence profound and horrifying.

The man was laughing. He set Amy on the ground, the girl

charging back for Denny, crying, and throwing herself in his arms.

"Listen to that hiss!" Frank yelled, then pointed upward. "There . . . there she is!"

Denny looked, and saw. Out of a black cloud overhead a dark finger was emerging, stretching for the ground, pointing to Frank, and as the hissing got louder it was replaced with a whooshing sound that drowned out everything in a stentorian hum.

Denny wrapped the girl to him and backed toward the house as Frank opened his arms wide to embrace the inevitable. And it was huge, a turning roiling mass totally consuming the backyard, the power of nature venting anger on the Earth as the sound came deafening, roaring insanely in Denny's ears, a monstrous beast descending over him.

It came to ground, a hole in heaven, sucking everything up as debris from the lawn and the water from the pool rose, alive, and danced crazily around Frank, the man's hair standing straight up as he laughed in the face of the thing, Denny finally realizing that the tornado was for Frank the dark, storming mass of a humanity he couldn't understand or live with, a humanity that was finally taking him to its bosom.

Denny made the door, fighting against the raging, screaming winds to get inside. He took one last look at Frank. The man had risen with the winds, swirling an exotic, alien dance, his laughter rumbling with the thunder.

Denny folded Amy tightly to him and inched through the kitchen, all the trash and paper flying around the room, dirty glasses smashing themselves against the walls as if all of their blasphemy was being repaid in one cacophonous orgy of destruction.

He folded himself in a corner, under the overhang of the breakfast bar, his only real thought to protect Amy. The wind rose, breakfast table coming off the floor and smashing against the far wall, electricity kicking on and off. Then, with a loud roar, the storm literally cried in rage, something large smashing through what was left of the glass in the sliding doors.

Then silence.

He sat there, breathing heavily, the only sound the pounding of his heart . . . then the gentle crying of the small girl in his arms. The lights flickered several times, then caught and came on for good.

Slowly Denny unfolded himself and climbed out from

under, Amy clinging to him. He stood, feeling weak from loss of blood and emotion. On the floor near the sliding door lay the remains of Frank Hargrave that the twister had given back to Denny.

In death, the man looked calm. He seemed almost to be asleep. There were no marks on him, nothing except . . . except the leg. His left leg was gone, cut off perhaps on the trip through the glass door. It was the new leg that Amy had given him.

And in Denny's arms, a small, frightened little girl was crying. Not God. Not the Devil. Just a small child who needed to be cared for and made well.

"I'm so sorry," Denny said, tears flowing from his own eyes as he held the girl tightly and stroked her hair. He whispered to her, "I'll take care of you. I promise."

DISSOLVE TO:

ROY GEIST—MEDIUM CLOSE. The man looks confused and frightened. He is sitting in a semidark room on what appears to be a dentist's chair.

> GEIST
> (agitated)
> You must understand how c-confusing it all was. I was face-to-face with this man. . . .

> VOICE (os)
> Dennis Stiller?

> GEIST
> Whatever. And suddenly his face was the only thing I knew. It was as if I had just come into existence that moment. My mind was a clean slate.

> VOICE (os)
> Did you drive away from the residence?

> GEIST
> I-I think I . . . had a car, but you've got to understand . . . I didn't know if the car was mine. I didn't even know if I, if I could d-drive.

VOICE (os)

Then what?

GEIST

Again? I just wandered away until the police picked
me up because of the curfew. A-at first they took me
to jail . . . but after a while, they decided to t-take
me to a hospital.

VOICE (os)

What about identification?

GEIST

I may have had a . . . what do you call
it . . . briefcase with me at that man's . . . Denny
Stiller's . . . house. I must have l-lost it
somewhere.

ANGLE—A ROOM. TED GAYLER and JAMES CON-
NOVER are standing in a darkened room, watching Geist and
his interrogator through thick glass, their voices coming
through a speaker in the room. We PULL BACK a little and
realize this is the control room of the recording studio from Act
III, the chair sitting where musical instruments had once
been.

CONNOVER

What do you think

GAYLER

I think it's too weird for him to be making it up. This
guy doesn't want anything except to remember his
past. If we work it backward, from Stiller's position,
it would seem logical, when faced with discovery, to
do something to make that person forget.

CONNOVER

So, now what?

GAYLER

Now we get serious.

Gayler moves to a telephone and picks it up.

> GAYLER (cont)

Let's start him on the pentathol. Okay.

He hangs up and looks at Connover.

> GAYLER (cont)

I'm in touch with a hypnotist. If the drugs don't
work, we'll try that.

> CONNOVER

What about the other stuff, though, the stuff we can't
control?

> GAYLER

You worry too much.

> CONNOVER

They've got Cardera and they're onto Trent and you
tell me not to worry.

Through the booth window, we see two men enter the room
and walk right up to Geist. They begin strapping him to the
chair, the man protesting, his voice loud and frightened in the
booth. Gayler reaches out and FLICKS A TOGGLE, the
man's voice gone immediately.

> GAYLER

There's *nothing* in this world that can't be taken care
of, Jim. You just worry about using the information
we're going to get from that gentleman in there. *I'll*
take care of everything else.

Through the booth window we see the interrogator moving
toward a silently screaming Geist, a long syringe in his hand.
CUT TO:
NITE—EST—THE TROPICS. We are looking at palm trees
and a white beach that glows in the moonlight. Waves are
lapping gently against the shore. At the bottom of our vision is
SUPERED: VIRGIN ISLANDS.
ANGLE—A BUNGALOW—EXT. All is quiet as the wind
gently blows the trees. No lights are on in the house.

ANGLE—A BUNGALOW—INT. We are inside the quiet house, a shadowy figure moving around, occasionally backlit by the moonlight sifting through the curtains. We don't know who he is or why we're here, but we can almost smell the fear that permeates the room.

ANGLE—THE CURTAINS. We watch as a pair of headlights move across the material from the outside. Our figure RUNS to the curtains and PEEKS AROUND THEM. We follow the figure back across the room to the front door, hearing the sound of a car door closing outside.

ANGLE—THE FRONT DOOR—POV. We become the shadowy figure's eyes as we turn on the outside light and pull open the door. A friendly looking man in his twenties wearing jeans and a T-shirt and a windbreaker stands smiling under the light.

> MAN

Hi ya, Trent.

We are Trent, and we feel happy to see this man.

> TRENT
> (relieved)

Thanks for coming. Everything's falling apart here.

> MAN
> (laughing)

So I've heard. I think everybody in the company's running around looking for you.

> TRENT

I hope you don't get too messed up with this. I need passports and help out of here. You're the only person I could trust.

The man SHAKES HIS HEAD, clucking his tongue in an irritating manner.

> MAN

The only one, huh?

The man reaches into his windbreaker and pulls out a small .22 made long by the silencer attached to its barrel. He points the weapon at us!

MAN (cont)

That was always the trouble with you, Trent. You never knew who your friends were.

ANGLE—GUN. The man pulls the trigger, again and again, emptying the entire gun as gray-white smoke oozes sensually out of the barrel.
FADE TO BLACK.

ACT SIX

Scene 1

(the next day)

INT—DAY—A HOTEL ROOM. We are staring at louvered French doors, closed and shuttered tight, small lines of bright sunshine slitting through the cracks. The room is nearly completely dark. Outside, os, we hear NOISES—car horns, people talking loudly. The sounds increase. We slowly PAN the room, admiring the barely seen French provincial furniture, finally stopping at the bed. A lone figure, wrapped in covers, is stirring because of the noise outside. We see the shadowy figure reach out and SWITCH ON A BEDSIDE LIGHT. It is MOLLY HARTWELL, her blond wig askew on her head, turned sideways covering half her face. She frowns and pulls the wig off, then leans toward the bedside clock.
ANGLE—CLOCK. It is 7:33 A.M. In the bg we hear Molly GROAN.
ANGLE— MOLLY. She pulls the covers aside and slides out of bed, fully dressed. She's obviously very tired as she stumbles toward the French doors. A portable television, out of place in this Old World splendor, stands near the foot of the bed. Molly TURNS IT ON, then continues to the French doors, throwing them open.
ANGLE—THE STREET—MOLLY'S POV. We are looking down at streets jammed with people. We are in New Orleans, the French Quarter, and farther down the end of the street lies the harbor. All the people, on foot and in cars and trucks, are

all heading toward the harbor, where we see ships are being loaded with food and medical supplies—for starvation entails a great deal more than just eating. Everyone's carrying food on the streets, thousands of people all magnetically drawn to the ship loading.

ANGLE—MOLLY. She stares down, her face unreadable, then slowly closes the doors. She moves back to the bed and retrieves her wig, putting it on. Then she picks up her sunglasses from the nightstand and puts them on, too. She walks to the foot of the bed and sits, staring at the television.

ANGLE—TV. An announcer, pale and hollow eyed, is reading the morning news.

ANNOUNCER

. . . on this, the fourth day of what many are calling P.S., Poststarvation, reports from around the
globe continue to astound. Despite a death toll from
worldwide hospital riots that continues to rise, today
passing the eight hundred mark, the prognosis for the
drive to eliminate hunger continues to be good. Gov-
ernmental cooperation on this issue has had a number of unexpected benefits, as this excerpt from a
press conference with Secretary of Commerce, J.
Emmett Feldman shows.

CUT TO:
A HOTEL BALLROOM. A man stands before a huge bank of microphones. He is the Secretary of Commerce.

FELDMAN
(tired)

It is my pleasure to announce this morning the signing of a number of trade agreements with other countries, most notably: Japan, The Soviet Union, China,
the Common Market of Europe, Sweden, Yugoslavia,
Poland, Spain and the independent nations of Africa.
The agreements are free and open ended for all parties concerned and have been brought about, in large
measure, because of food negotiations in connection
with the starvation issue. We've found that the ease
of bargaining to mutual fruition has made a great
many of our other concerns obsolete and outmoded.
Free trade is now the key administration phrase

these days, and why not? We've just taken steps that
should zero out our balance of trade deficit within the
next two years.

QUESTION (os)

Are these agreements a direct result of mental or
physical pressure attributal to the mass hysteria?

FELDMAN

That's the amazing thing. The trade bargaining was
simply a natural outgrowth of negotiations over food
shipments in good faith. We've all simply got the ma-
chinery in place and our attitudes are healthy. It's the
most positive thing I've seen in my twenty years in
government, unselfish bargaining.

ANGLE— ANNOUNCER.

ANNOUNCER

And if you think that hostile government cooperation
is a miracle, just look at the tape we received this
morning from our crew in Damascus, Syria . . .

CUT TO:
A STREET IN DAMASCUS. Unbelievably, we are watching
Israeli Army trucks rolling through the streets of their most
hated enemy, the huge convoy carrying food, not soldiers. The
streets are lined with Syrian military, standing in straight rows
and saluting the passing motorcade, and behind them, the
civilians. They are crying and applauding and cheering the
Israeli troops, who wave happily back, their errand of mercy a
bond of love and respect between human beings.

ANNOUNCER (os)

Syrian police officials at first worried that people who
didn't see the Stiller broadcast would cause trouble in
this war-torn region. They solved the dilemma in a
most unique fashion.

CUT TO:
INT— SYRIAN POLICE STATION. We are watching a
number of young Moslem men being brought, handcuffed,
into a room that is empty except for a television. They are lined
up before the screen and the TV turned on.

ANNOUNCER (os)
It was discovered that a replay of the broadcast had
just as much impact as the original.

We watch as the young men begin to double over in agony, the
very real pain of hunger driving the arrogance out of them as
they watch a replay of Denny Stiller's broadcast. The language
barrier means nothing as the concentrated energy affects them
anyway.

ANNOUNCER (os)
After these films were made, the young men in question returned to the streets where they joined in the
labors of their community in the battle against
hunger. . . . Unfortunately, in Dallas, Texas, today,
the story is somewhat different. . . .

CUT TO:
BIRD'S-EYE VIEW OF DALLAS. We are looking at a city
under siege, thousands of people roaming the streets along
with Army tanks and armored personnel carriers.

ANNOUNCER (os)
Despite harsh measures, people continue to flood to
Dallas, all of them trying to find Dennis Stiller and
Amy Kyle, all of them taxing a system already
brought to its knees by huge, unruly crowds.

CUT TO:
THE STREETS. We are watching a line of National Guardsmen with fire hoses keeping back a large crowd of cripples as
people charge them, only to be knocked down by the pressur-
ized spray. People are screaming, angry, German shepherds
snarling on taut chains at those who get through the spray.

ANNOUNCER (os)
This was the scene this morning as demonstrators
clashed with police and National Guard in the sixth
straight day of rioting. And in the melting pot Oak
Cliff section of the city, United Nations troops searching for Dennis Stiller met even heavier resistance
from local citizens.

CUT TO:
A BOWLING ALLEY—EXT—DAY. We are watching the outside front of the Don Carter Bowl. A line of pickup trucks rings the entire building, hundreds of men dressed in quilted vests and cowboy hats, wielding shotguns, use the trucks for cover and look toward the building.

> ANNOUNCER (os)
> Several thousand members of the U.N. peacekeeping force have been trapped here since last night by Dallas residents angry over foreign intrusion into their homes.

ANGLE—A PICKUP TRUCK. A burly, red-faced man looks over the bed of the truck at the front of the building and a huge white flag that is being flown from the doorway. A line of Red Cross workers is walking up to the door pushing supermarket carts loaded down with bags full of McDonald's hamburgers to distribute to those under siege.

> NEWSMAN (os)
> Why are you keeping these troops prisoner here?

> MAN
> (turning to camera)
> Listen . . . as long as I got strength enough in my finger to pull a trigger, ain't no Ruskie gettin' into my house. We're just gonna keep 'em here until somebody sends an airplane down to ship 'em back where they come from.

> NEWSMAN (os)
> But the president sent the troops in to help search for Amy Kyle.

> MAN
> This is my home, Mister. Ain't nobody comin' in less I invite 'em. If the president let these (bleep) in here, then he's just as bad as they are.

The man turns back to the building and fires a shot high and wide to the right, driving everyone in front of the bowling alley to the ground. He turns back around, smiling wide.

NEWSMAN (os)

What would you say to people who would tell you these troops are serving an important function here right now.

MAN
(suddenly serious)

Nuts! I'd tell 'em, nuts!

CUT TO:
BOGOTÁ AIRPORT, COLOMBIA—EXT—DAY. We are looking, from a distance, at a MAC 727 on a secluded runway south of the airport. A man is being led across the tarmac in chains, surrounded by American Marines.

ANNOUNCER (os)

In related events, Jesus Cadera was put aboard a military jet today and flown to the United States, the State Department ignoring extradition laws by spiriting him away without ever turning him over to the local authorities.

ANGLE—ANNOUNCER.

ANNOUNCER (cont)

What is believed to be the body of the mysterious CIA link to Cardera, a man known only as Trent, has been found today in the U.S. Virgin Islands. So far, no one from the government is claiming the body, but informed sources told WCN earlier today that CIA files impounded by the Justice Department will show that Trent is listed as TDY to Colombia on the same dates that Cadera's files show major cocaine purchases. The president has already initiated a blue ribbon panel from the House and Senate to look into the allegations of CIA involvement in illegal drug smuggling, while CIA Director E. Melvin Porter is saying no comment to reports that he and Deputy Director Russell Buchner personally authorized Trent's expense vouchers and, in fact, signed off on the temporary duty orders themselves. More on this story as it developes.

CUT TO:
CLOSE UP—FRANK HARGRAVE. We are staring at the
dead man's face, eyes closed. We are amazed at how relaxed
the face looks, how, in death, it knows the peace it never could
know in life. We feel strangely glad for Frank, incomprehend-
ingly happy that he has escaped, finally, the mortal chains that
always bound him. He was a man never meant for Ted Gayler's
universe. We slowly PULL BACK to see that we are in the
basement of the mansion, Denny struggling with the body of
Hargrave as he tries to hoist it into a freestanding freezer, the
top hinged open.
ANGLE—THE FREEZER—FROM ABOVE. We are looking
down as Denny, grunting, gets the body partway into the
freezer, the body of Tawny Kyle already in there. Amy stands
beside him, her fingers wiggling crazily before her eyes.
Denny GROANS loudly, then hefts the body up, letting it fall
into the white box atop the women.
ANGLE—DENNY AND AMY. He SAGS against the freezer,
wiping his forehead. Then he straightens, staring sadly down
at the bodies. He looks at Amy.

DENNY

What do you think—maybe I should say a few words?

AMY
(loudly)

Meedle? Meedle, Den-ney?

DENNY

Not right now, sweetheart. I need to do this first.

Denny walked closer to the freezer, better to see the
bodies. He didn't want to look at them. What he wanted to do
was slam the freezer door and turn and run away. But he
wouldn't, not this time. For once in his life he was going to
take the responsibility for his actions.
He stared down at Frank's body, piled like cordwood atop
Tawny Kyle, both of them dead because they couldn't breathe
the rarified air on the mountaintop where Amy lived, a
mountaintop that *he* had forced them blindly to climb. There
were things that made sense now, things he'd been unable to
see before. Molly had understood best of all. She'd told him
that the path he had chosen would lead only to disillusionment

and death. But he had, of course, ignored her. He'd ignored her for one simple reason: he'd mistaken his job for his life. As a newsman, he'd only had the responsibility to report, not stand good for the things he'd reported. As a human being undertaking an entire new course of experience, he should have considered the ramifications and his part in them. So good he was at running away that he'd thought he could ultimately run away from himself too.

He'd been wrong.

"I'm so sorry," he said to Frank. "Your life was sad and tortured, but it was still your life. I had no reason to force you to this point and take it away from you. If there is forgiveness, I beg yours."

He felt the pain of loss, surprised at his depth of feeling for someone besides himself. "Oh Frank, what a tragic clown you were—so boisterous and crude on the surface, so deeply sensitive and frail underneath. You may be the best man I've ever known. I'm only sorry I didn't get to tell you when you were alive." He smiled. "But maybe if you were alive, you wouldn't have let me tell you. Good-bye, old friend. Good-bye, Tawny. You used your daughter, but with love. You deserved better than me, too."

He reached out and gently closed the lid, smiling sadly when he realized that he'd just uttered his first prayer. Denny Stiller, loner, had just realized how very much he needed people.

Reaching out, he pulled Amy to his side, ignoring the sexual feelings that rifled immediately through him. "It's just you and me now," he said, looking down at her as she twisted her head all around and hugged his waist tightly. "You're my responsibility now, and I swear on the bodies of Frank and your mother that I'll do right by you. Let's get you something to eat. We've got to journey inward just once more."

"Meedle?" the girl said sadly.

"Yes," Denny replied. "You'll have meedle, but this time we're going to try some vegetables with the mix."

He led Amy upstairs to the kitchen, cleaning it up a bit before finding some canned vegetables in the pantry and a steak in the freezer. As he cooked, he found his thoughts returning over and over to Molly. Everyone else close to him was dead now, just like his parents. Only Molly remained. Molly, the woman who'd stuck by him through everything no matter how he'd treated her. He'd let her get away so easily, like sand slipping through his fingers, all his thoughts, his feelings, his life— dust. He wondered where she was, if she—and the son she carried—were all right. Melancholy threatened to engulf him, but he fought it off. There was still much to do. If Molly had, indeed, gotten away, she was far better off without him than with him.

He watched Amy pick at her food with a grim determination. The girl had brought him into her universe, but he intended to get out of it again. It would take a strength that he'd never known before, but an idea was beginning to take shape in his mind that might answer many of the problems. So interested he'd been in exploiting the girl that the concept of helping her had never seriously motivated him. Perhaps, knowing something of the nature of Amy's mind and power, it wouldn't be impossible to do her some good. If he could confront her when she was open, mentally, to him, perhaps he could force her out of her godhead. It was just a chance, and a dangerous chance at that in worlds that Amy's egocentricity controlled—but he didn't know what else to try. Unfortunately it would take another inward journey, for he would ultimately have to face up to his own weakness in order to attack her strength.

It was with great trepidation that he took her hand and led her into the living room, the hall of realities, as he'd begun to think of it, for it contained the essence of the artists' minds and hearts, a forever living legacy of their ruminations on the nature of life. It was here that he'd face his own demons, here among the bold statements of a previous age. It gave him heart.

With the power of Amy Kyle in hand, the living room throbbed with boisterous life. He could hear the pictures' inhabitants talking animatedly from within their frames; he could feel the warmth of summer and the sweet smells of flowering still lives; he could sense the joy of living and the pain of loss; and he marveled that oil on canvas could be so much more alive than the flesh on his own bones and the blood in his veins. So much he had cut himself off from.

He moved directly to Manet's *Folies*, his unofficial entry into the world he and Amy could share. As he stood before Adele, she seemed almost to smile . . .

"You seem never to tire of punishing yourself, *Monsieur*," she said, shaking her head. "You wish to see your past again . . . through the girl?"

Denny moved up and leaned against the bar, turning to stare at the revelers still enjoying the cancan. He was beginning to feel quite comfortable here. "Give me a champagne, Adele," he said. "I need a bracer."

"You *are* searching for something," she replied, filling a glass and sliding it across the polished walnut. "That will be four francs."

He reached into his pocket, pulling out a roll of American money and laying it on the bar. "This is all I have," he said. "You've never charged me before."

"You've never looked seriously before," she replied, taking the money. "Everything serious in life has a price. Do you understand what I'm telling you?"

"Yes, I think so," he said.

She nodded. "This time you've only had to part with money. For whom do you search?"

"God," he said, his mouth going dry. He took a sip of the champagne. "I'm looking for God."

"I thought you did not believe in God."

"I will give God the chance to reveal Himself to me."

"This isn't a newscast, *Monsieur*. One cannot just take from God. One also has to give . . . to pay."

"What price?" Denny asked, and drank the rest of the champagne in one gulp.

The woman looked at the top of the bar. "Your heart . . . your mind, your . . . essence."

"I don't understand."

"You will," she said unhappily. "And now I must go. I have other responsibilities."

Adele turned and walked farther down the length of the bar and began washing long-stemmed wineglasses in a basin of murky water.

Denny stood alone for a moment, twirling the crystal champagne glass by its thin stem, watching the play of light oozing elongated patterns across its length. He felt nervous, Adele's dire warnings making things even worse. The music pounded loudly in his ears, the smoky room burning his eyes. He was here for answers. It was time to find them.

He moved back through the noise and the crowds, toward the office he had originally entered when he'd come here the first time. The door still sat in its accustomed place, but the word *privé* written on it had been replaced with large block letters proclaiming *DIEU*.

He turned the glass knob and entered the totally dark room. As soon as he had closed the door behind him, the barest orange light, like sunrise, began to illuminate the way before him. He walked toward the light and it became brighter.

He found himself on a straight road stretching to infinity, the sun climbing quickly now, brightening the world around him. The sky was bright blue overhead, but the landscape all around him was bland, all straight lines and sharp edges. In the distance, a plume of gray-black smoke drifted straight up as far as he could see.

There was something familiar about the road, as if he'd been on it before. He was almost entirely sure that the landscape he walked was the measure of his own mind, that the images created were being created by his subconscious. Perhaps not the best place to search for a deity, but the only place he knew.

He walked for an indeterminate length of time, time itself losing all meaning when subjected to the vacuum of the unchanging landscape. He used the plume of smoke as a reference point, but it never seemed to move, to get any closer.

And then he was upon it—just like that. The smoke came from a single car wreck, the hulk of the old Lincoln blocking the roadway, its metal twisted by fire and attrition, and he felt the chill run up his back, making his neck hairs stand out. It was the wreck of his parents' car, the photographic sight of the twisted thing that had etched itself indelibly into his mind at age six and haunted his dreams thereafter.

He felt it first in his stomach, a wave of nausea rifling through him. Then it hit his brain, unreasoning panic backing him away from the wreck and the two bodies, covered with sheets, that he could see shimmering through the orange fire on the other side of the car.

This was stupid, crazy. There was absolutely no reason for him to torture himself with this vision from the past. There could be nothing to gain here except . . . pain. He turned and walked away from the wreck, all the while knowing that it was precisely pain like this that he had avoided all his life. He turned back.

From a distance of twenty feet he surveyed the wreck. He felt his nose tingle, the prelude to tears, and he had to fight to keep from turning and running again. Adele had said there would be a price. He hadn't appreciated exactly how high that price would be. To face this blazing, crackling nightmare went against his entire outlook on life.

With his whole body screaming a warning, he took a step toward the burning car. Then another, and another until he stood right before the wreck. He could feel its heat, feel it trying to burn his flesh. How many times in his career had he blithely covered killings and accidents, totally detached, totally separate from the pain and metaphysical questions of death? It all came flooding back to him now in shame as he realized just how much he had exploited over the years in the name of Truth.

His truth wasn't Truth at all, it was his lashing out with the camera-weapon to strike at everyone who'd experienced emotional pain. It was *his* truth, his way of convincing himself that he was greater than the pain.

But he wasn't. He was as human and as fragile as anyone else. He stepped around the fire and stood staring down at the white-sheeted bodies with the covered heads. His insides told him to bolt again, but he fought against the feeling. He'd come this far. He'd have to go through with it.

This was a vision from his childhood, a nightmare he'd been unable to overcome. He had handled it by burial, a proper, Christian burial. But unfortunately, the dead don't stay that way.

He felt himself leaning toward one of the bodies, reaching for it with a shaking hand. With nausea choking his throat and a terrible tightness in the back of his neck, he jerked the sheet back. His father, unscathed, smiled up at him.

"Finally," he said. "You finally remembered we were here."

Denny looked at the ground, feeling guilty. "I-I always knew where you were," he said. "I've just been too scared to come and find you."

The man nodded, pulling a pipe out of his shirt pocket and sticking it in his mouth. "You haven't made things any easier on yourself this way," he said. "You've just built the walls higher."

"I know," Denny said. "It's good to see you, Dad."

His father stood, looking just the way he'd remembered him—tall, with a clean, honest face. "Come on," he said. "Let's get your mother and go home."

"Home?" Denny said, and felt tears stinging his eyes.

Home was the place he'd hated, the place where everyone but him got to know joy and happiness and closeness.

"I know what you're thinking," his father said, pulling the sheet from Mary Ann Stiller's form, the woman standing immediately. "You can only take life as it comes, Denny. Be happy with what you have and have had."

Denny Stiller turned to his mother. She was still young, her face alive with love, her red lips trembling. "Oh, Dennis," she said, holding out her arms. "How I've missed you."

"Mama," he said, embracing her. She was warm and soft and smelled of Chanel No. 5, and he closed his eyes and never wanted to let go of her. "It's been so . . . difficult, these years, so terrible . . ."

"Shhh," his mother said, cradling his head on her shoulder. "It's all right now. Pain isn't accumulable. It's not going to eat you alive."

"It has though," Denny said, pulling slightly away from her. "It has!"

Mary Ann looked sadly at Denny, then shared a look with her husband. "Can we take him home, Norman?"

Mr. Stiller removed his pipe and folded his arms across his chest. "Of course we can," he replied. "In fact, I think we've got to. Come on, it's just off the road here."

Mary Ann Stiller put her arm around Denny's waist and turned him away from the wreckage. The empty landscape had transformed itself into his old neighborhood in San Antonio, Texas, moss-covered trees lining a shady street of fancy adobe houses. He turned back to the wreck. It was gone—vanished like his pain at seeing it. And in that, he'd already learned a lesson about fears.

"I haven't thought about the old street in years," Denny said, looking around, smiling as he passed old lady Morrison's precious apple tree that she'd never let him climb and that he'd climbed anyway. "These were the happy times for me."

"Good memories are wonderful," his mother sighed. "You should work at making some more."

"I c-can't," Denny said, choking back tears. "It all ended with you guys."

Norman Stiller lit his pipe on a silver Zippo, the sickly sweet odor of burnt cherries curling happily through Denny's mind. "Sounds to me like you're blaming us for dying," he replied.

Denny laughed coldly. "I guess I am," he said.

"Here we are!" Mary Ann said happily, Denny looking up to see the white two-story Spanish-style adobe house that he'd spent his first six years of life in. The place looked like it had just been painted, all the wrought-iron trim shiny black. Spring flowers were blooming in the front garden.

"Can we go in?" Denny asked, looking at Norman. The man smiled and nodded, the three of them starting across a lush green lawn, slightly in need of mowing. Denny remembering that his mother had to always be on his father to get it taken care of.

As they neared the house, the front door burst open, a young boy charging out. "Mom!" he yelled. "Dad!"

Denny narrowed his gaze, recognition settling in. Of course *he'd* be there.

The boy raced up and threw himself in Norman's arms, the man laughing and swinging him around, setting him back on the ground in front of Denny.

His mother bent to the boy, tousling his hair. "Dennis," she told the boy. "I'd like you to meet somebody. And guess what? He has the same name as you do."

"Really?" the boy said, looking up.

Denny smiled at the inquisitive eyes. "Really and truly," he said. "Tell me something. You still like to climb old lady Morrison's apple tree?"

The boy looked around uneasily. "Are you here to make me stop?" he asked.

Denny laughed despite himself. "That's the last thing in the world I'd do, Denny," he said. "I used to climb that old tree myself."

"You lived in the neighborhood?" the boy asked, eyes alight.

"Better than that," Denny replied. "I used to live in this house." He pointed to a second-story window. "That used to be my room right there."

"That's my room!" the boy squealed. "Would you like to see it?"

"Would I," Denny said, then looked at Norman. "Is it all right?"

The man just smiled, relighting his pipe. "No reason to stand around out here," he said.

They walked the rest of the way across the lawn, young Denny's hand firmly trapped in his adult self's grasp. Denny hadn't had much use for kids over the years. But this

one . . . this was different. He thought about Molly's child—
his child.

They moved into the house, Denny slammed in the heart
by the look of the place. He had blotted out his earlier
memories almost completely. To walk into this time of his own
happiness, and to recognize that happiness, was almost more
than he could bear. Everywhere he looked—at the old Muntz
TV with its two dials; at the kitchen swinging door that he'd
painted with liquid shoe polish; at the low-slung mahogany
table where he used to play with his trucks— was like opening
a floodgate of memories. Warmth, love, laughter—all had
been his; all had been lost.

"Hurry," the boy said, calling from the stairs up. "I want
you to see."

Denny looked at his parents. "Go ahead, dear," Mary Ann
said. "We'll meet you back down here."

Denny turned and hurried to the stairs, surprised at how
far and fast his grown-up legs took him compared with what
he'd remembered from childhood. He took the stairs up, the
boy already way ahead. The sixth step creaked loudly, Denny
smiling as he remembered how hard his father had tried to fix
it, and how the noise had only gotten louder.

Everything was as he remembered it. Nothing had
changed. No matter where his eyes settled, memories resided,
memories of feelings, and he realized how empty his feelings
had become. A stupid smile was plastered to his face and
wouldn't leave. He would stay here forever if he could.

"Hurry!" came the unseen boy's voice.

He wound around the banister at the top of the stairs and
trod the familiar pathway to his old room. He walked in, young
Denny jumping up and down on the bed.

"Better take your shoes off when you do that," Denny
warned.

"That's what my mother says," the boy replied, out of
breath, and let himself fall to the bed. "How do you like it?"

Denny Stiller looked around at his work in progress, his
young life. The room was just as he'd fixed it up. His Davy
Crockett coonskin cap and toy flintlock rifle hung on the wall.
His miniature turtle, Freddie, sat contentedly on his rock in
the middle of his goldfish bowl. Clothes were strewn everywhere, and baseballs and baseball cards and pennies and
pocketknives and toy doctor kits with tiny candy balls in pill
bottles. An electric football game sat poised on the floor, all the

players, plus tiny toy soldiers, laying on their sides. The five-year-old version of interior decorating.

"It's a great room," Denny said.

"Yeah," the boy answered, lying on his stomach, cradling his face in his hands. "But I wish I had bunk beds."

"But you don't have a brother to sleep in a bunk bed," Denny said.

The boy jumped up and ran to the dresser. "Maybe I'd *get* a brother if I had bunk beds."

Denny nodded. There was logic to that.

All at once, the boy's face got serious. He put his hand on something covered with a pillow case on the dresser. "This is what I wanted to show you."

Denny walked to the dresser, not sure what he was going to find. When he walked up close, the boy pulled the pillow case away.

A bird sat in a cage. It wasn't a small domestic bird, but rather a full grown robin, nearly too big for the cage. It chirped loudly and seemed to make eye contact with Denny.

"I call him George," the boy said, "on account of that's what I'd like my little brother's name to be if I had a little brother."

The name tore through him like a knife, and Denny remembered what it was he'd come here for. He was shaking all over as he forced himself to speak. "What are you going to do with him, Denny?" he asked.

The boy looked sadly at the floor. "My daddy says that I should let him go," he said, nearly sobbing.

"Why does he say that?"

"'Cause he's mean," little Denny said, running to the bed and throwing himself on it. He buried his face in his folded arms, sobbing into his shirt sleeve. "Mean!"

Denny moved to the bed and sat with the boy, putting a hand on his shoulder. "Birds are meant to be free, Denny—"

"No!" the boy shouted, raising his head, his eyes red, cheeks wet. "No! I raised the bird when a cat killed its mama and its little brothers. It was a baby. I fed it and tooked care of it all by myself. It's my friend on account of neither one of us has no brother. I can't let him go. I can't!"

"I know how badly it will hurt to set George free," Denny said. "But sometimes . . . we have to face hurt. Just think about how much it will hurt George to stay in that cage with no other birds to play with or start families with."

"He's mine!" little Denny yelled.

"No," Denny said gently, stroking the boy's hair. "We can't own somebody else's life. We'll just hurt ourselves more by hurting them. We can't run away from pain." Denny wasn't sure at this point whether he was talking to the boy or to himself. "There's a great thing that my own daddy taught me when I was your age and didn't want to get rid of a bird."

The boy sat up, rubbing his eyes. "*You* had a bird, too?"

Denny nodded. "And his name was George, and I didn't want to let him go either."

"What did you do?" the boy asked, eyes open wide.

"I realized that I couldn't make myself happy by making George unhappy," Denny said. "I realized that he needed to be free and live among his own kind, and that to get happiness, you first have to give it."

"What did your daddy teach you?" the boy asked.

Denny took the boy to him, hugging him fiercely. "He taught me that glory lies just on the other side of pain. That they're both just the same thing."

The boy pulled away from him, cocking his head when he saw Denny's own tears. "I don't understand, Mister."

"No, I'm afraid you don't," Denny said. "You see, the only way to discover that truth is to sacrifice first. You must set the bird free. You must do the right thing and face your own pain. If you really love George, you'll let him go."

"I don't want to."

"I understand."

The boy looked at Denny for a long time, trying to figure it all out. Then slowly, he walked up to the cage and looked at the bird. "Do you want to go, George?" he asked.

Silence hung loudly in the room, Denny realizing the melancholy nature of all things and knowing how much he'd lost by blotting out these years in his anger at his parent's death.

After several minutes, little Denny picked up the cage and carried it to the window, leaning it against the sill as he opened the glass. Denny watched him proudly, knowing how hard his actions must be for him.

The boy opened the cage door. "Go on," he said, the bird refusing to budge. He shook the cage. "Go on, you stupid bird!"

George tentatively jumped from the cage to the sill and sat there, cocking his head just the way the boy had done earlier.

"Go on, I said!" the boy called loudly, and the bird spurted out the window and flew off. Little Denny angrily threw the cage to the floor, scattering feathers that would have to picked up. He looked up at Denny. "There! You happy?"

Denny Stiller shook his head. "No," he said. "I'm not. But I think we may soon be."

"What do you mean?" the boy demanded.

"I want to show you something downstairs. Come on, I'll race you!"

With that, Denny charged from the room, the boy running after, both of them tromping down the stairs in a manner his mother would lovingly call, "an elephant stampede."

They ran through the living room and into the dining room, its back window overlooking a heavily wooded lot that declined to a small creek fifty feet away. Norman and Mary Ann sat at the table drinking coffee. They both smiled when they saw Denny and Denny run in.

"Now I know why you brought me here," Denny told his father.

Norman smiled and puffed on his pipe. "You left a lot behind when you went away," he said. "A whole lot."

"What did you want to show me?" little Denny said, panting, out of breath from his race.

"Here," Denny said, pointing out the window. "Look up in the maple tree."

The tree grew near the kitchen window, its heavy branches slung low not ten feet from their vantage point. Evident in the lowest branch of the maple, a robin sat in a nest, feeding worms to a number of hungry, cheeping mouths straining upward.

"George!" little Denny cried. "You didn't leave after all!"

"Maybe Georgette is a better name," Denny said. "I told you that if you give, you get in return."

The boy looked around, his mouth falling open. "I'm a grandfather!" he yelled, running into Denny's arms and hugging him tight. "I love you, Mister."

This time the tears came hard, Denny not holding them. "I love you, too, sport," he said.

But life is motion—growth and decay—and soon the boy broke the hug and ran outside to get a better look at his new "family."

Then he sat down and drank some coffee with his folks, loving the moment, but feeling drawn away. They discussed old times until the boy called his father outside for something, leaving Denny and Mary Ann alone.

"You're going to go again, aren't you?" she said.

Denny shrugged. "I can't stay here."

"Where do you go next?" she asked, reaching across the table to pat his hand.

"I need to find Amy," he said. "I don't know. I need to find some way to help her, though I'm not sure what I can do."

"Maybe I can help," his mother said, reaching down to pick her purse up off the floor. "I want you to look at something."

She rummaged around in the handbag for a moment, the way women do, then pulled out a round compact, handing it to him.

"What's this?" he asked, taking the compact.

"Maybe the answer to your questions," Mary Ann said. "Go ahead, open it."

Denny opened the plastic device. It contained powder, a puff, and a mirror hinged on the top half of the case. "Nothing here, I . . ."

He caught sight in the mirror, seeing not his own face but Amy Kyle's. No matter how he turned it, all he saw was Amy. "I don't . . . I don't . . ."

"Tell me what you see, son," his mother said sweetly. "Go on, look closely."

He stared with wide eyes, Amy's opening wide. His saw his own sadness mirrored in her look, his own pain shining through on her face. "She's just like me, isn't she?" he asked.

"Exactly," his mother said. "She fears the pain, too."

He stood, laying the compact on the table. "I've got to go to her," he said.

Mary Ann stood with him. "Don't you want to say good-bye to your father and—"

"No," he interrupted, taking her in his arms and squeezing tight. "It's tough enough to say good-bye to you. It'd be impossible to leave all three of you. Do you know which way I must go?"

"It's dangerous," Mary Ann said. "There are a great many fears waiting there."

"I've got to, mama," he said, pulling reluctantly away from her. "I'll come back again."

"Often?" she said, eyes twinkling.

He nodded and kissed her on the cheek. "Now that I know the way, you'll have a hard time getting rid of me."

"Just a thought is all it takes," she said, leading him through the kitchen and down the hall to the cellar. They stopped at the cellar door. Mary Ann pointed. "She's down there."

Denny looked at Mary Ann, trying to memorize her

features the way he'd never been able to do previously. "I love you so much, mama."

She hugged him one more time. "I love you, too," she said, her own eyes wet.

Denny opened the cellar door. Darkness awaited him at the bottom of the long flight of wooden steps. "I guess this is good-bye for now," he said and started down.

"Wait," his mother said, taking his arm. He turned back to her. "A little advice. When you go looking for God . . . don't look any farther than relationships. You couldn't buy one for a million dollars."

He nodded. "The price is much higher than that. So long, mama."

"Good luck, my son."

He moved cautiously down the long stairs. At the bottom he searched blindly on the wall until he found a light switch. He flipped it on, finding himself staring down a hall at the living room of Tawny's trailer, trash and cigarette butts strewn everywhere. He turned back toward the stairs, finding himself looking at a closed door.

He opened the door and entered the bedroom of Tawny's trailer, the woman herself standing by the window. She was there, but not there, her body transparent, like a double exposure. Amy sat on the bed, staring up at him.

"I want to get inside of your mind," he said.

"You are in my mind," she answered. "We are one mind, sharing life. Come to bed."

"No," he said. "I want to see through your eyes, to live in your head."

She reached out to him, undulating slowly on the mattress. "I want you," she said. "We'll make all this go away . . . we'll live for pleasure. That's all we need."

He shook his head, feeling the sexual stirrings again, the sign of his bondage. He ignored it, and the growing discomfort. "Let me in your mind first," he said. "I want to share everything with you."

"And then you'll come to bed?" she asked.

"And then I'll decide," he replied.

He felt an electric jolt, the intensity a blinding white light before his eyes, forcing him to squeeze them tightly closed. When the pain subsided, he slowly opened his eyes.

He recognized the bedroom of the trailer, but only because he knew that's where they were. The eyes he saw through were not human. They reduced everything in the room to geometric shapes defined by bright areas of color, as if the intensity of light, all light, was increased a thousandfold. Everything gave off its own heat and reflected light. The intensity of light spilling through the window was blinding, so much so that he couldn't look at it. The television on the dresser played loudly, light pouring through the screen as concentrated as a spotlight at a new-car dealership. He was bombarded by light of various colors, all of it intense, overpowering. Light bludgeoned him from every direction.

He looked up and saw himself standing by the bed, his body pulsating between bright green to yellow to hot white. He couldn't stare at the pulses, having to look at himself peripherally. What was it the psychiatrist had said about overstimulation?

He could barely stand the bombardment of pulsing light and began waving his hands in front of his face to mitigate it. The craziest part of the whole thing was that he knew he could control that light, just by a touch, and that the light filled its own value scale. It was organic and abstract, but he began to realize the reason for and the extent of Amy's power. She existed to neutralize and harmonize the light. With a touch, she could give the harsh light what it wanted to cool it down. With a touch, she could make harmonic the cacophonous clash of erratic energy and hence stabilize her world.

He stood on shaky legs and walked up to the television and its unbelievably bright, directed, light. He touched it, just a touch, the light flaring brightly, then settling to a steady, soft blue haze. He had neutralized it.

It all made sense. Amy craved stability desperately, unable to deal with the overstimulated energy of those around her. She didn't want what he wanted, or even understand what any of it meant. She had grasped the beauty of sex as merely a physical release from the hormonal changes and tensions normal in a girl going through puberty. Anything else to do with it, *anything else*, was simply the product of Denny's own mind. The girl wasn't seducing him. She was simply giving him what she perceived he wanted from her without conscious understanding.

Waves of shame washed over him. It was him, all him. The hard, binding energy was hers, the selfish drive for release— but *he* had given it form. Be it the desire to be close to the source of such power or simple midlife yearnings for young girls, the fault was entirely his. Without his motivation, Amy could never have fused with him, physically or mentally. And in his own headlong rush to avoid personal responsibility for his feelings, he had simply refused to accept his own direction in this. If he had, indeed, lost control over himself, it was because he had never *had* control over himself. He was Gayler's archtypical selfish man made flesh. He had never been above the problems. He *was* the problems.

Amy Kyle was a frightened little girl, an alien little girl, who needed protection, not abuse. How could he have been so selfish? He could help her now, but it would mean breaking her hold on him, the hold he had allowed her to get through his own out-of-control ego.

He fled her mind, retreating to the safety of his own head, self-disgust threatening to eat him alive. He looked at the TV he had touched. The front was busted out, a thin trickle of smoke curling from the guts of the thing with a burnt toast smell.

"Now will you make love to me?" she said, reaching her arms out to him.

"No," he said, putting his hands to his eyes, feeling the overpowering attraction. "No, I can't. It-it's not right."

"Come to bed," she said huskily. "Please."

He took two faltering steps toward her, then tightened up inside. "No!" he screamed. "No!"

He turned and bolted from the bedroom, charging down the narrow trailer hallway, the floors tilting crazily beneath him, threatening to pitch him to the ground. His heart pounded as he hurried through the kitchen and reached the front door.

"Come back!" her voice called behind him.

Afraid to look back, he pulled at the door, the thing coming off in his hands. He jumped from the doorway to the ground, the trailer park suddenly filled with people, all angry.

"There he is!" somebody shouted, the crowd roaring.

"Let's get him!"

Denny ran, shoving his way past angry faces as they closed in on him. He pumped hard, running for all he was worth, breath coming in gasps, as the angry crowd closed in, their fingers like talons, threatening to tear him to shreds.

CUT TO:
CLOSE UP—A MAN'S FACE. He is looking directly at us, speaking softly, sonorously.

MAN

You're really getting to be a big boy now. You can
play in the backyard all by yourself and help your
mother hang up the wash. And it's time for a birth-
day party. Do you know how old you are?

CHILD'S VOICE (os)

I'm f-four years old.

MAN

Excellent. Four years old is really big. I'll bet you're
big enough to know your whole name.

CHILD'S VOICE (os)

Uh-huh.

ANGLE— SOUNDPROOF BOOTH. We are looking through
the window into Gayler's recording studio. Two men in suits
are standing in there with us, both of them pale and doubled
over from hunger. Through the window we see ROY GEIST,
smiling crookedly, eyes wide, sitting strapped into the chair
where the man we've been watching is talking to him. We can
HEAR THEIR VOICES through the speaker in the booth. On
the control panel before us, a large audiotape is running,
recording every word.

MAN

Now this is very important, Roy. I want you to tell
me your whole name.

GEIST
(in a child's voice)
My name is Roy Jerome Geist, Jr.

MAN
(looking toward booth)
Very good, Roy. I'm really proud of you.

REVERSE ANGLE. We are looking at the young, nondescript
men in the booth. One of them is furiously writing on a piece
of paper, the other has picked up a phone. We can't hear them

because of the booth glass, so we PULL TIGHT, moving right through the glass and getting into the booth with them.

MAN ON PHONE

Please, it's urgent. I was told I could interrupt anything. . . . Sure . . . I'll hold.

The man puts his hand over the receiver and turns to the other man in the booth.

MAN ON PHONE (cont)

They're getting him now.

He suddenly stiffens and pulls his hand from the mouthpiece.

MAN ON PHONE (cont)

Yes, sir! The regression seems to be working. . . . Yes, sir. We've got a name!

CUT TO:
A CONFERENCE ROOM. Ted Gayler is sitting at the head of a large walnut table, a telephone to his face. Five men in business suits fill the rest of the table. Briefcases and stacks of paper are sitting in front of them. Empty Styrofoam coffee cups litter the desk. We PULL TIGHT on Gayler, listening to his conversation.

GAYLER

Good . . . keep working the regression from your end. Meanwhile, use my people at the Dallas Police Department and run a computer check on all missing persons cases around the country. If he's not from Dallas, *somebody* is probably looking for him, and maybe they know where he went. The second you come up with something concrete, get back to me. We're close now . . . let's don't lose it.
Yeah . . . and Curtis, when we've got what we need from that man, Geist—take care of him. You know what I mean.

Gayler puts a finger to the switchhook, then let's it off again. He is staring thoughtfully into space, his mind working. He pushes the switchhook again.

GAYLER (cont)

Annie . . . get Connover on the line. Whatever he's
doing . . . I need to talk to him now.

Gayler hangs up again as we PULL BACK to take in the whole
room. Gayler looks to his left, at the two men who sit on that
side of the table. The tall one, dressed like an undertaker in a
black suit is, MEL JAKES, Gayler Enterprises' chief accoun-
tant. The other, smaller, with black, plastic-framed glasses is,
JEFF SLUTSKI, Gayler's financial adviser. We recognize
most of the others present as Gayler Enterprises' lawyers from
Act I.

GAYLER (cont)

You were just explaining to me, Mel, why we
shouldn't sell off our marginal operations at this
point.

MEL

They're liquidity right now, Mr. Gayler, and the less
successful ones, operating losses, tax breaks. You've
been selling everything off, tying it up in a declining
gold market. If you tie up too much, you'll have no
loose capital. Any setback could be devastating.

GAYLER

What you're saying, is that when I lose my ass on the
gold speculation, I should have something to fall back
on.

MEL

I wouldn't exactly say—

SLUTSKI

Well, I'd say it, Mr. Gayler. The gold market has
gone bust with this hunger thing. Nobody's tying
their money up there anymore. You're buying into
the *Titanic*.

GAYLER
(smiling)

You gentlemen are like geese . . . waking up in the morning to follow the first asshole you see. Don't you understand that the flow is a lot larger than what you're looking at now, today? If this hunger problem goes on much longer, the major corporations throughout the world will go bust, collapsing the world's monetary systems. Gold will be the *only* thing of any value.

SLUTSKI

I understand the theory, Mr. Gayler, but it's not lining out that way. I think we're beginning to look at a restructuring of the wealth.

GAYLER

What do you mean?

SLUTSKI

The corporations aren't going broke. Most people can't do anything about direct contributions of food and help, so they're doing the next best thing— investing money in the companies that can do something. The businesses that are doing the most for hunger right now are actually *making* money. Hell, the stocks you sold off to buy gold have gone up in value. Companies are beginning to hire all the free help they've been getting . . . actually making the feeding of the poor a physical part of their business. It's nearly evolutionary . . . the wealth and more importantly, the *motivation* of the world has shifted into a different direction.

GAYLER

I've built an empire on the predicting of human greed, Mr. Slutski. Believe me, this is all artificial, based on the pain in people's bellies. Hell, I've donated millions myself. We can't help it. Just as soon as that belly pain goes away, people will get back to some realistic greed.

MEL

I hope your businesses can hold together that long.

GAYLER

What are you saying?

MEL

We've gotten a call from our man at the Securities
and Exchange Commission. He says that the government is looking at all the gold you've been picking
up. You know . . . hoarding gold is against the law.

GAYLER

That's no problem, the president will protect me.

MEL

The president's on the run right now over this CIA
drug thing. Another problem with the hunger is that
it's making people look around them more closely.
Their stomachs hurt, but their brains are sharper
than ever. If SEC confiscates or makes us sell off at
the current price of gold, (he looks at a piece of paper and shakes his head) which is fifty-three cents an
ounce, you'll be ruined in one day. In fact you'll have
to sell off *everything* just to meet your promissory
notes. Whatever you do, you'd better do it fast.

SLUTSKI

I second that. I can't emphasize enough the concept
of reorganization of the world's wealth. If the corporations proceed in the direction they're moving right
now, which includes a whole shitload of new business
agreements in Third World countries to build facto-
ries in partnership with those countries'
governments, it could become *impossible* for them to
go back to the old ways. Mr. Gayler, feeding people
has *become* the new business trend. There's even talk
of putting the world on a currency standard built
around food and farmland. I'm watching it change
before my eyes. Even the companies that are being
hurt financially by this are finding ways to retool and
fill support areas in the food distribution chain.

You've climbed off the train, Mr. Gayler. You must
find a way to get back on.

GAYLER

No! It will *never* happen. Nothing ever changes. People don't change. Just wait and see. Just as soon as
the hunger goes away, we'll have it all again.

The phone beside Gayler rings, the trilling of a bird. He stares
at it for a moment, then picks it up, swiveling away from the
men at the table.
ANGLE—GAYLER. We watch him on the phone. Behind
him, all the men at the table are talking, arguing vehemently
just below our range of hearing.

GAYLER (cont)

Jim. . . . Good, good. Listen to me. We've got a
name on our mystery man . . . I think we'll have it
all within a matter of hours. Will you be able to
move on this when the time comes? . . . Yes. . . .
Yes. . . . I understand all that. You just need to understand that if it doesn't happen quickly, both of us
lose everything. Just answer my question,
Jim . . . can you control your people?

ANGLE—CONNOVER. He's dressed in his vestments,
standing in the wings of his cathedral, his full orchestra and
choir singing "Gather at the River" in the bg. People hurry
around him as he talks on the phone.

CONNOVER

My people understand the gravity of this situation,
Mr. Gayler. We are, all of us, prepared to fight, to
die if necessary, to remove this blight from our land.
Rhetoric . . . What are you talking about? This is
far larger than our business dealings. . . . Yes. . . .
Yes. We've been chosen to defend mankind in the
final battle for the Earth. . . . I'm *not* being irratio-
nal. I've seen a sign, Mr. Gayler, a wonderful sign.
We *will* win this battle . . . I promise you that.
God's word is stronger than any pagan hypnosis. I've
got to go, I'm on the air. . . . Yes. . . . Yes . . .
my people will do *anything* I tell them to do.

Connover hangs up the phone, staring directly at us for several beats. His face is transformed, angelic. He is a man at peace despite the pain in his stomach, a man secure in his place on Earth and in heaven. His secret knowledge is a certainty, an unshakable fact. As he sees it, Truth is his cloak, and who are we to disagree? He turns from us and strides out into his sanctuary.

ANGLE—CONNOVER —FROM THE AUDITORIUM. The man moves toward his podium, then stops, turning toward his audience instead. He walks down the stairs and into the congregation. People reach out to touch him, to shake his hand as he passes. They are pale and weak, seeking solace and understanding in the midst of confusion.

                              CONNOVER
                        (with great sincerity)
Friends. Today I must share my heart with you. I
must prepare all of you for the battle that is yet to
come, prepare you for the vision that has rent my
soul and torn my heart to pieces.

Connover's face slackens, tears filling his eyes.

                          CONNOVER (cont)
I held the Lord, God, in my hands the other night. I
held Him in my hands in the form of a dying dove, a
dove whose life ebbed away even as we cried over it.
And God spoke to me then, just as He's spoken to us
through the Gospels. My friends, it's frightening,
nearly beyond belief. We live our lives, day to day,
never thinking of the larger battles that rage between
God and the forces of Darkness. But now that battle
has come to us; the fight must be ours, for the anti-
Christ is among us in the form of Denny Stiller!

We look at the crowd, watch their faces as they try to match their feelings up with the gut core of their beliefs. We see angry faces, faces in pain, faces in confusion. We see belief as a subjective reality for most people, a measure of the lonely, seeking mind. People continue to reach for Connover, touching him, mumbling amens, trying to comprehend the immensity of the task their God has set out for them.

CONNOVER (cont)

I didn't want this fight . . . I *don't* want it now, but that doesn't matter. God has chosen me, has chosen us, to be his champions. Stiller has apparently made us do good, but what happens after? Think of the turmoil he has brought, the confusion that is even now plunging our world into chaos. Did you think that the Devil would come in a cloak with a pitchfork? He comes grinning and charming, trying to confuse us with the illusion of good works that hides his true purpose from our eyes. Ancient is our enemy, my friends. Elusive are his ways. The Lord speaks to us in Isaiah 5:20, saying: "Woe to you that call evil good, and good evil: that put darkness for light, and light for darkness: that put bitter for sweet, and sweet for bitter."

We PULL TIGHT on Connover, the light in his eyes like a smoldering fire, the energy that consumes him feeding directly from his soul.

CONNOVER

These are not idle speculations, friends. John the Apostle spoke eloquently about our response to the anti-Christ. "As for you, let that which you have heard from the beginning abide in you. If that abides in you which you have heard from the beginning, you also will abide in the Son and the Father. And this is the promise that he has given us, the life everlasting." Hear me friends. I have been your helper on the spiritual path for many years. This is the moment of our lives. This is the moment for which this restless Earth has waited for two thousand years. If we are ever to look upon the saving face of Jesus, our Lord, we must strike at this demon in our midst. We must strike him with words and with cold steel. Our religion, our ways, our *world* have been given to us by God. We must abide in the ways that God has made holy. Even now, the anti-Christ plunges God's

marvelous creation into turmoil as the secular world
crumbles beneath his boot. It is up to us, to God's
people, to take up arms and destroy this creature
from hell's depths. We can bring our message of salvation to everyone, but first . . ."

CLOSE UP— CONNOVER'S EYES. He locks eyes with us,
his intensity nearly overpowering.

<u>CONNOVER</u> (cont)
Dennis Stiller and Amy Kyle . . , must die.

CUT TO:

Denny walked slowly through a surrealistic combination of
Dallas, Texas, and Manet's Paris in which the *Folies* and Texas
Stadium were the same building, chorus girls dressed in
shoulder pads and helmets dancing before fifty thousand
screaming fans drinking champagne from tall glasses under the
joyful luminescence of thousands of gaslights and candles. As
he moved through the T-shirted, top-hatted crowd looking for
a vacant seat, he tried to work through his shame and his fear.

He had run from Amy, run from her when he should have
stood his ground and dealt with it. Then he'd run from the mob
she'd conjured to bring him back, finally escaping through a
maze of back alleys that resembled Manet's Paris by way of
good-ole-boy Dallas. And here he was, trying to lose himself in
crowds rather than face up to the inevitable. He had to break
her power over him, and the only way to do it was by meeting
her power head on, by shaking that egocentric universe and
reminding her of her humanness. It wouldn't be easy—
especially given his own weakness.

He found a seat near the fifty-yard line about thirty rows
up, reaching it just as the crowd jumped to its feet, cheering.
He stood with them, staring down at the field, which was
actually a hundred-yard-long wooden stage with footlights
running around the perimeter. The dancers had shed their
uniform pants and were dancing around in sparkling-sequined,
black net hose and G-strings. They bounced a huge, round
balloon among them, the crowd cheering every time the
balloon was tipped into the air again to keep the rhythmic
pantomime going.

He watched the wondrous around him without wonder, his mind no longer dazzled by created realities. He was searching desperately for the root of real Truth in his own life. The truth that paraded around him was simply window dressing.

The crowd sat, Denny with them. He looked to his right. A man sat beside him dressed in a long wool coat and a fuzzy top hat. He had huge mutton chops and a sprinkling of smallpox scars lining his cheeks. He continually shouted to the women below in French. To Denny's left, a woman in modern dress sat on the edge of her seat, caught up in the action on the field. There was something familiar about her, something he almost recognized.

Then it hit him, an excited tension choking him up almost immediately. "Leslie Toland . . . Les?"

The woman turned to him, more beautiful than he had remembered. She stared at him in disbelief for several seconds, her face slowly brightening into the most loving look he'd ever seen. "Oh my God, Denny," she whispered, her hand, the touch electric, taking his arm. "I've prayed for this moment for years."

"Come here," he said, opening his arms, the woman falling joyfully into them. Her touch filled him with love and with lust. She was firm, resilient, her body shuddering with excitement as he heard her crying gently into his shoulder.

It had been so many years, so many. Les had worked at the same television station that he had in Waco, an office romance blossoming slowly between the two. He had been in his early twenties, single, and lonely in a new town. She was five years older, the victim of a bad, early marriage. He'd been sympathetic; she'd needed a hand to hold, and after a while, one part of the anatomy becomes the same as the next.

She pulled away from him, cheeks wet, and stared deeply into his eyes, hers so clear, so deep with understanding. "So funny," she said, "like fate."

"What do you mean?" he asked, kissing the end of her nose, then, lingeringly, her deep warm mouth, her love alive in him.

"Our last time . . . together," she said, "was in the same place."

He looked around, the dual reality had solidified into the recent past. They were sitting in a brand new, just-built Texas Stadium, watching Don Meredith quarterback the Cowboys into another mediocre season. The view was even the same.

Waco was a small town, Les's husband a local, connected politician. Afraid of consummating their relationship in Waco itself, they had both arranged, separately, for a weekend in Dallas. It had been the most glorious sexual relationship of his life. Les had been desperate for gentle affection and was more than willing to give double in return. Their first, and last, weekend had been a Moslem heaven dream to Denny, all feasts of flesh and pleasure, perfumed hair and shared fantasies. After, her husband had found out, kicking her out of the house. Denny, characteristically, had refused to let her move in with him, afraid of the effects on his life and career. Les had moved away. He'd never seen her again.

Yet never, ever had she left his mind. All other relationships had to suffer in the light of his weekend with Les. All other fantasies had paled to transparency when stacked up against the epic nature of his WEEKEND. And now she sat beside him, real, as real as any reality, and her hand was rubbing his leg.

"Oh Denny," she sighed, the crowd cheering a pass completion, jumping up around the two of them, leaving them alone in their private universe. "Nobody's ever . . . affected me like you did. I don't think a week goes by that I don't think of you."

"Me either, Les," he said. "I-I'm so sorry about . . ."

She put a hand to his lips. "Past history," she said. "We've got now, that's all that matters. And brother, I want you so much it hurts."

He smiled at her, seeing in her face the same vulnerability that had attracted him so many years before, feeling the same chemical reaction that could attract him across a room full of people. "What a romantic I must be to think things could still be the same between us," he said.

"They are the same," she whispered. "Remember what happened the last time we were here?"

He grinned. "Sure. We got so horny that we snuck out to your Cadillac at halftime and got it on in the back seat."

Her eyes twinkled. "I've still got that same car," she said. "It's out in the parking lot right now."

She stood without another word, taking his hand, leading him down the stairs to the ramp out. He went without much thought, knowing somewhere in the back of his mind that this wasn't really happening, that it was just a product of his mind, perhaps even Amy's mind; but none of that mattered. For nearly twenty years he had carried Les Toland around in his mind like a personal love slave. To have the genuine article here, in his hands and as slavish as his imagination, was more than anyone could possibly walk away from. He *had* to have this woman. He'd handle breaking away from Amy later.

As they moved out of the bowl and down the ramp into the guts of the stadium, she moved up close to him, reaching a hand inside the overcoat he had somehow acquired, to rub and squeeze his ass—just as she had done that November day back in 1971. "Remember the time we made love in the shower?" she asked in a tiny voice.

"Hmmm."

She shook her head. "I've never been that free before . . . or since, I guess. For some reason I never felt ashamed or embarrassed with you."

"We were totally open with each other," he said. "We had nothing to hide or to fear."

"I'm shaking inside," she said. "I can't stand it. Walk faster."

They picked up their pace, Denny's breath coming fast in his excitement. They moved through the building and into the parking lot, Les stopping to throw herself into Denny's arms for a deep kiss. She molded her body to his, her pelvis thrusting sharply into his, his legs weakening. He slid his hands to her buttocks, pulling her up even tighter against his erection, the woman bucking against him and moaning orgasmically down deep in her throat.

Then she shuddered, breathing out a long, frost stream of air against the side of his face. She leaned away from him, eyes closed, cheeks rose red in the winter chill. She opened her eyes, smiling coyly, then taking a deep breath. "Let's get to the car," she said. "Quickly."

They began to jog, hurrying into the asphalt, past one of the movie screens used during the summer when the place was a drive-in. They passed a Dallas mounted policeman on horseback, Denny smiling obliquely in the direction of the black leather clad cop as they went by. Then he noticed the horse, blood streaming from its neck. He stopped dead, his neck hairs prickling.

"Denny, come on!" Les said, her long auburn hair swaying gently in the wind. She was now several paces ahead of him, turning quizzically.

His eyes moved up the horse's neck, then to the cop.

Beneath the leather clothes and gloves, and beneath the white helmet, Molly Hartwell sat staring down at him, and her eyes held infinite sorrow.

"Molly," he said, guilty. "I can't help it. You understand?"

"Denny!" Les called, not ten feet distant. "Come on! It's cold out here!"

"Honest to God," he said. "There's too many years, too many memories. I've got to go with her . . . just this once."

Molly just stared at him, occasionally reaching out a hand to pat Oater's blood-soaked mane.

"I'm going!" Les called. "If you want me, come on!"

She took off at a quick pace, Denny jerking between her retreating figure and Molly's accusing face.

"I'm sorry," he said. "I've got to go."

He turned from Molly and ran as hard as he could, catching up to Les just as she was reaching the old, bright red Caddie. She turned to him, smiling brightly, as he ran up.

"Will you be a gentleman?" she asked in a put-on Southern accent while holding out her car keys, "and unlock the door for a lady?"

He snatched the door key from her and plunged it into the lock. "That was no lady," he said, wiggling his eyebrows, "that was my sex object."

The door came open, Les falling into the car on her back, legs spread, her miniskirt pulling farther up her thighs. Just as she had done that day, Denny checked all around their island in the sea of cars for privacy before climbing in.

Les had already taken off her coat and unbuttoned her blouse, the silk material gaped open, revealing her naked breasts; and she was shinnying out of her pantyhose. "Now," she said. "Now you'll be mine."

Denny froze at the words he had heard the shakti say to him, the words that marked Amy's desperate desire to fuse totally with him. He couldn't do this, not again. He couldn't begin the cycle again. If it weren't Les, it would be somebody else he couldn't resist. His fantasy life had been rich and varied. And it was beginning to occur to him just how to get both of them out of it.

"We can't do this," he said, half in half out of the car. "It's not right."

She licked her lips, reaching out to stroke his still throbbing erection right through his pants. "*We* make right,

Denny," she said. "You know that. Now stop talking nonsense and get in here with me. I'm going nuts I need you so bad."

Here it was. He'd hit the wall, and now he was going to have to hurt her and himself. He'd avoided responsibility for his actions his entire life because he couldn't face pain. He had to drive her to pain, to responsibility for her own actions or she'd never come out of it. He took a hard breath and slapped her hand away. "Of course you need me, you retarded little shit. It's me who doesn't need you. You disgust me."

Les jerked as if she'd been hit. "W-what are you saying, Denny. You love me."

"How could I love an ugly, smelly little pile of garbage like you," he said, moving totally out of the car to lean against the one beside. "You're gross. You make me sick."

She slid out of the car, too, her blouse hanging open, her cylinderlike nipples bunched tight in the cold. "But, Denny," she pleaded. "All of your feelings . . . your desires . . . I can be anything you want me to be—any woman you've ever known or met or thought about. . . ."

"And it would still be greasy little, stupid Amy Kyle," he spat, grimacing. "I played up until now just to see how far you'd go with this thing, but I just can't stand it anymore. You're just too gross to even think of touching. I wouldn't dick you again for all the money in the world. So, you just climb in your little red car and get the fuck out of my sight before I throw up."

The sky suddenly became dark, angry clouds roiling, thunder like cannon fire roaring in the distance.

"You son of a bitch," she said. "You lousy asshole."

He reached into his pocket and pulled out a quarter, tossing it to the ground before her. "Here's two bits," he said. "Why don't you just go call somebody who gives a shit?"

Les's beautiful face had twisted dark and ugly, strained pale with furious anger, as a lightning flash lit it to a harsh white glow. "I'll fix you so you don't ever dick *anyone* ever again. You'll pay you son of a bitch. You'll pay."

He heard shouting as lightning flared again nearby, Les laughing as he turned to see an angry mob charging him.

"There he is!" a man yelled, and he was waving a rifle over his head. A good thirty people ran with him, all of them armed with guns, knives, and baseball bats. This was a hanging party if he'd ever seen one. And they were the same mob from before, all mobs the same mob. They were twenty feet and closing fast.

"You're meat," Les said low, menacing, then she began to shout. "Help! Rape! Rape!"

The fear nearly paralyzed him as he realized that if sex was real in his dream world, so too could pain . . . or death be. The keys were still in the back door lock. He shoved Amy-Les out of the way and grabbed them, running around to the driver's seat.

He jumped in, trying to start the engine. They were right up on him. He'd never get away. Then he heard shouting, Molly charging Oater in front of the mob to hold them back, buying Denny some time.

The car kicked over, Denny gunning the engine and squealing out of the parking slot just as the mob flowed around Molly to overtake him. He turned sharply, still in the lot, charging for the exit, realizing, finally, just exactly how little control he had over his own vision. The steering wheel went crazy in his hands, turning into a snake that dropped to the floorboards as the car swerved, smashing into a Cowboy-blue pickup truck.

Denny jerked forward, smashing into the windshield just as he had done at Molly's house. It gave way, his body following the glass through, Denny bouncing painfully off the hood and rolling onto the ground.

Blood was streaming down his face, the pain driving all other thoughts from his mind as he tried to stagger to his feet, the mob bearing down upon him once more. So little was his in this world; so much was Amy's. He had no control here at all, and worse, had no idea how to get out of it. Taken from the reality of his entry point at the *Folies*, he had been unable to wish the dream away.

And the pain: it was real, as real as the sex had been. He was dizzy, his head throbbing, blinding him. An arm, broken, hung limp at his side. Blood streamed from the area of his crotch where the glass had torn him coming through the window. The pain was intense there, Denny fearing that he had left his balls on the dashboard and afraid to look.

And they were right on top of him again, Denny nearly resolving himself to the inevitable when he thought of a last desperate shot. His physical body was standing before a wall, looking at a Manet portrait. If he could move that body, break the spell on that side somehow. . . .

"We've got him," came a hard, female voice, and Denny looked up through a curtain of pain to see Adele, the melancholy never leaving her face, staring out of the crowd at him. They surrounded him on all sides, their faces full of hate, faces that he had seen many times before—in war, in riots, in corporate boardrooms—the single, angry eye of the mob, an existence beyond humanity, Gayler's jungle pack animal. And the pack was hunting.

"He's the one," Les-Amy said, pointing from the fringes of the crowd. "He forced himself on me. I'm underage!"

They closed in a step, as he doubled over in agony. *Was* this Amy? Or, perhaps, maybe it was his own guilt come to take recompense. Were higher sensibilities punishing him, punishing him to death? He could still do right by Amy . . . he could!

With a loud groan, he forced himself to stumble toward the mob, using whatever powers of concentration he had to try and move his real body, too.

"Kill him!" Les-Amy shouted. "Kill him now!"

He stumbled toward Adele, the woman bringing a long knife out of her cloth coat and smiling as she thrust the blade at him. He saw its blur, felt its kiss, then. . . .

"Ouch!"

Denny bounced off the wall, the Manet falling at his feet as he staggered back, holding his nose where he'd bumped it, the contact enough to break the spell.

He turned immediately to Amy, the girl, hysterical, shaking uncontrollably in the middle of the room, tears sloughing out of her eyes as her head twisted wildly back and forth.

He reached for her, just holding back, his arms shaking. "I'm sorry!" he yelled. "Amy . . . it's all right. I'm here!"

He took her in his arms, the contact arcing bright light, throwing him back to hit the wall, pain shooting through his back and head.

The instinct to bolt rose in him and he fought it down. "No!" he said. "You won't retreat! I won't let you!"

He grabbed her again, the electric charge numbing, blinding, as he was thrown to the floor. He jumped up again. "I love you, Amy. I love you. I want to help you. Please let me."

He took her again, the contact burning him this time as he fell to the floor, just on the edge of consciousness, his clothes smoldering.

"Amy, please," he said, shaking his head slowly, bringing reality back as he got to his knees, then his feet. "I love you, but I won't fuse with you. You're *not* God. You're a young girl who needs love and attention. Please listen to me . . . please."

He took her by the shoulders, the electric charge shooting through him, numbing, hurting. He wouldn't let go, the pain increasing, shaking him. "Amy . . . you'll have to k-kill me. I l-love y-you."

And the wind rose in his ears, the power intensifying, driving all conscious thoughts away on quavering currents of white fire. And when his insides were boiling and his head was ready to explode—it stopped, the only sound a gentle rainfall in the distance.

Reality came slowly back to him, and he realized that the rainfall wasn't rainfall at all, but Amy's tears dropping onto his arm. He looked down at her, the girl's head slowly raising, her eyes searching out his. They looked at one another for the first time, her frightened eyes melting his heart. "Den-ney," she said, halting. "Mama . . . where mama?"

"Oh, sweet thing," he said, taking her into his arms lovingly, fatherly. "I'm so sorry about your Mama."

She cried then, like a little girl, Denny rocking her gently, soothingly, knowing the truly monumental joy of giving for the first time in his life. His mother had said that God was relationships. He finally understood what that meant.

CUT TO:

NITE— EXT—A NEW ORLEANS STREET CORNER. The streets are filled with people, even though it is very late at night. None of them are in the Bourbon Street bars, though. They are just walking, somnambulistically, their stomach pain not allowing sound sleep. We pick Molly out of the crowd. She is walking with the rest of them, in disguise, just watching. A middle-aged nondescript woman stands beneath a streetlight, its glow bathing her almost like a spotlight. She is blind, wearing dark glasses, a Seeing Eye dog sitting at attention next to her. We are drawn to the solitary woman and move in that direction, taking Molly with us until we have moved right up to her. Molly lays a gentle hand on the woman's arm.

MOLLY

Are you all right? Can I help you get anywhere?

WOMAN

Oh no, honey. Thank you. I was just standing here
watching all the activity.

MOLLY

Excuse me. I thought you . . . were. . . .

WOMAN

Blind? There's all different kinds of blindness. What's
your name?

MOLLY

Mo . . . Martha.

WOMAN

People call me Angie, and I mean to tell you that my
physical blindness has been the least of my problems.

MOLLY

I don't understand.

The woman reaches out, tentatively taking Molly by the arms.

WOMAN

Don't you see, Martha? We're all of us alike, all of us
seeing in a different light. I've been blind for twenty
years, twenty long years spent living in my own private hell, hating the world, feeling sorry for myself.
And then the hunger came and opened up a whole
other world for me. I felt the pain and the loneliness
of others, and I knew it wasn't just me, that we all
share the good and the bad of this world.

MOLLY

But so much pain. . . .

WOMAN
(laughing low)

Maybe God is viewpoint, Martha. If you can truly
feel the pain of others, doesn't that pain become your

own, that sorrow, that happiness? Maybe viewpoint is
what will take us out of the jungle and help us to live
together as civilized human beings. All I know is that
I've finally reached out of myself and into the hearts
of others. It's a wonderful, godlike feeling. We're not
alone . . . any of us. We've got each other.

The woman begins to cry through her laughter, tears streaming from beneath her dark glasses. She removes them to wipe
away the tears, her eyes merely white sockets reflecting the
street light.

> WOMAN (cont)
>
> And when we pray now . . . it's different, isn't it?
> We no longer pray selfishly for salvation or benefits.
> Now we pray in a single, united voice, not for our-
> selves, but for the pain of others.

Molly's face is torn as she reaches out a hand to smooth the
woman's hair out of her face.

> MOLLY
>
> But it's forced. Can that be right?

> WOMAN
>
> Who cares how or why it happened? That's like ques-
> tioning the rain because it brings tornadoes. All that
> matters is that we've been taken out of our selfish
> minds and forced to see life through the eyes of oth-
> ers. You're me, Martha, and I'm you. I know your
> pain and your desires, just as you know mine. We're
> all in this life . . . together, and this world can be
> our paradise. We all understand the way now. We
> must share it . . . together. How can I see so much
> better than you when I'm blind? Don't you be blind,
> too, honey. The human race is learning how to sing.
> Would you want it to croak again?

Molly begins to cry, too, as she hugs the woman fiercely to her,
both of them holding on tightly, sharing. Slowly Molly pulls
away, looking down at her hand. She reaches out and places
her palms on the woman's eyes, closing her own tightly. The

woman jumps slightly, a jolt, and when Molly removes her hands, the skim is gone from the blind eyes. They are a bright clear blue. She stares incredulously at Molly.

                            WOMAN
    What did you . . . how did . . .

Molly puts a finger to her lips, shaking her head slightly.

                            MOLLY
    I've shared your pain. We are one.

                            WOMAN
                    (shaking with excitement)
    But I can see!

                            MOLLY
    You've always seen a lot clearer than me. Please
    don't say anything about this.

The woman looks down at her dog, going immediately to one knee and hugging the animal, cooing to it.

                            WOMAN
    What a beautiful animal, I . . .

She looks up at Molly, reaching out a hand to her.

                       WOMAN (cont)
    How can I thank you? What can . . .

                            MOLLY
    It's me who needs to thank you.

Molly turns and disappears in the milling crowd. We pull TIGHT on the woman as she stands, trying to spot Molly, but it's too late. The woman stares right at us, her features bunched up, eyes narrowed as she searches the crowds. Gradually, her face relaxes, a small, knowing smile just curling the corners of her lips.

Scene 2

(the next morning)

DAY—EXT—BLUE SKIES. We are staring up into the morning sky, a large number of aircraft too distant for us to identify are grinding through the air above Dallas, too distant for their sound to reach us as anything more than a mosquito buzz. Crates are FALLING from inside the planes, PARA-CHUTES OPENING like distant umbrellas to float their payloads of food gently down to the Dallas crowds.
ANGLE—TED GAYLER—CLOSE-UP. Gayler, face stoic, is watching the sky from outside, a coffee cup poised at his lips. He is dressed in a black suit with black tie.
ANGLE—PARACHUTES. We watch again a sky full of open chutes, the gift of food raining as manna from heaven.
ANGLE—GAYLER. He lowers his gaze, sips his coffee, and reaches out.
ANGLE—TELEVISION. The TV is off. It is sitting outside, on a table facing Gayler's huge, open backyard. We see Gayler's hand come up and TURN ON THE TV. The screen flickers to life as we PULL TIGHT on the newsman who materializes magically for us.

NEWSMAN
(pale, hollow-eyed)
. . . Tokyo Exchanges have just closed, mirroring
what analysts are seeing everywhere. It's a new
morning here on Wall Street, the dawning, apparently, of a new financial age. With the price of gold
now down to thirteen cents an ounce, we must con-
clude that the worth of precious metal will no longer
determine the wealth of nations and that gold, as a
transferable commodity, is now worthless.

ANGLE—GAYLER. We watch his unchanging face as he listens to the market report.

NEWSMAN (cont, os)

Why has this happened? This is a fundamental concept having to do with the sovereignty of nations. I
certainly don't have anything besides my own speculations to offer on this topic, but it seems to me that
the texture of world finance has simply changed. Corporations worldwide have now moved into the realm
of mammoth multinationals, taking advantage of the
free and open policies between nations because of the
hunger issue to strike a large number of mutually
beneficial business deals in partnership with other
countries. These deals, more than any other single
source, are having the combined effect of moving us
toward one, economic world, a world in which political boundaries mean nothing. With free trade and
mutual profit the order of the day, the xenophobic
hoarding of precious metals becomes pointless. The
gold standard was based upon the mutual fear and
paranoia of the various countries in competition with
one another. Now that the entire world is buttering
the same economic slice of bread, that philosophy is
no longer operative. Everything has changed. Food
producers have moved to the economic top of the
heap on the big boards, support industries lining out
behind in accordance with their importance to the
new scheme of things. Many of the old giants, the
old money, are tumbling. But, as the poet Robert
Bruce once wrote, "Look abroad through nature's
range. Nature's mighty law is change." This is Martin
Beswich for *The Morning Board*.

We are still watching Gayler's face as he reaches out, the sound
of the TV dying immediately. He hasn't moved or uttered a
sound, but we can sense a heaviness to him, a deep-seated
anger, the kind of harsh sentiment that moved him to the top
of the heap to begin with. It frightens us.

VOICE (os)

Mr. Gayler . . . someone to see you.

ANGLE—PATIO DOOR. A black maid in starched white

uniform is standing at the door with Jeff Slutski, Gayler's
financial adviser from Act VI, scene 1. We PULL BACK to
take Gayler and the table into our vision, too.

GAYLER

Martha, get Mr. Sluski a cup of coffee.

SLUTSKI
(moving toward the table and sitting)
No, thanks. I won't be here that long.

The maid departs, leaving Slutski and Gayler alone at the
table.

GAYLER

Come to tell me I'm wrong?

SLUTSKI

No, sir. I've come to tell you I'm quitting. They're
setting up a new government board to oversee famine
areas and the integrity of the food chain, and I've
been asked to sit on the panel.

GAYLER

Kind of out of your line, isn't it?

SLUTSKI

Not really, Mr. Gayler. I came out of college in the
late sixties with a degree in psychology. I worked as a
social worker for several years before the urge to get
rich struck me and I began to use my psychology
training in more selfish ways.

GAYLER

Nothing wrong with a little healthy greed, son.

SLUTSKI

I don't believe that, not anymore. I frankly can't believe that you still do.

GAYLER

Look. Even if I allow that we will continue to feed

the world, the number of people who *don't* die of
starvation will soon get top-heavy and choke out
what's left for everyone.

SLUTSKI

Maybe. But as the food distributors build their facilities overseas, and the support industries spring up
around them and local help is hired, people will get
richer. Wealth brings education and a fuller life, you
know that. People start thinking birth control. History, Mr. Gayler, has shown us the cycle.

GAYLER
(smiling)
You just wait . . . it'll all come back.

Slutski stands and moves to the door, turning back one last
time to face his old employer.

SLUTSKI

It's over Mr. Gayler . . . all of it: your life, the old
ways, the old . . . urges. Change with it, sir.

Slutski leaves, Gayler, neck craned, staring at the still open
sliding door. A phone on the table RINGS loudly, Gayler
jumping, startled, before answering.

GAYLER
(aggravated)
Yes, what is it?

We watch a large smile slowly spread across the old man's
withered features, the most emotional we've ever seen him.

GAYLER (cont)
Wonderful. . . . Yes, let me write down that address.

He picks up a pen and writes on a small notebook.

GAYLER (cont)
Yes. . . . Got it. Turtle Creek. Fascinating. What

about Geist? Good. . . . Good. . . . But not in my
building. . . . Fine. I'll take care of everything from
here on.

Gayler hangs up, taking a deep breath, his mood now light as
he prepares to take back the empire he has just lost.
CUT TO:

Denny strained to hold the sheet out as far as he possibly
could before tacking it down with the staple gun. He hit it
once, then a couple more times for good measure before
standing down from the stepladder to examine his handiwork.

The sheet was in place, covering the busted-out glass of the
patio doors. His solution wouldn't do much but keep out the
bugs, but it was more important to Denny for its moral, rather
than physical ramifications. He had been all morning cleaning
house, trying to set the chaos back in some sort of order. He
would start with his own house, then see what he could do for
everyone else.

He moved to inspect the rest of the kitchen. The trash had
been picked up, dishes done, and he had even waxed the floor
after enjoying the first good night's sleep he'd had in almost
two weeks. Outside, through the kitchen window, he could
see a huge pile of garbage bags, the physical manifestation of
his internal changes.

The kitchen passing inspection, he moved to the living
room. It looked pretty good in here, too, except for the burned
spot on the carpet. The pictures still lived for him, but it was
passing, as if he were still working off residual bleedoff of
Amy's power. He could still hear the paintings talking and
laughing together, even see the occasional oil and canvas head
poke out of a frame to glance around, but all that was definitely
ebbing. The moment that Amy had come down from the
mountaintop to admit her humanity had been like the breaking of fever. The power had just left her, quite simply and
without fanfare. It was over. Before long, he'd be locked again
into his own realities, shut off from those without. But he'd
never forget what he'd learned about ethics and about giving,
and he'd never stop talking about it.

He would go on the air soon to announce that Amy had lost
her powers. He was, at first, surprised to find that people still
suffered from the hunger even though Amy's power no longer
existed, but then he realized that more of their own minds

went into the creation of that reality than Amy's. Just as with him, Amy had provided the power, but the people themselves gave that power form. People weren't as bad as they liked to pretend—they just need a little boot once in a while. And if he was oversimplifying, so was Gayler in saying that selfishness was all that existed. Even if the old man had been right, that the human being wasn't perfectable, did that alleviate the ethical man from trying? An artist friend had once told him that the most essential trait of the artist was that his reach exceed his grasp. Isn't all life like that?

So, he'd go on the air and bring people his message of hope. If they didn't listen, he'd keep bringing it until they did. Interestingly enough, he found for the first time that the idea of going on the air didn't excite him, not anymore. TV news had been an escape from reality for him, and to go back now would only wipe out all the personal gains he had made. No, service was in Denny's future somewhere. He had a lot to make up for and was anxious to get started. If only he hadn't run Molly off.

Amy was showering upstairs, an aspect of her personal hygiene that he had ignored since incarcerating her mother. He'd have to check on her. Had he hoped for a miracle with the girl, he'd have been disappointed. Her moving out of her shell, her protected world, was going slowly, with numerous setbacks. But she trusted him now, trusted him as someone ready to help, and had rejected the autistic turn of her personality completely. This was obviously the first step toward human autonomy for Amy, and if the price had been a destruction of part of Denny's ego structure, it was cheap at twice the price.

He moved up the stairs, making a mental note to remove the stairway door at the first opportunity. Bringing Amy out of the autistic dream proved another point also: her power diminished with the distance from her created reality. She wasn't God, wasn't even living in God's territory anymore. Her godhead had simply been another created fantasy. Though Denny, interestingly enough, had found a resurgence of what could only be called faith within himself with the working out of Amy's problems.

He moved down the hallway and into the room that had been occupied by Tawny and Frank, listening to the sound of the shower in the attached bathroom. The control board still sat on the floor, although Denny had cleaned the rest of the room. The machines multiple monitors were all juicing pictures of a now-clean house. He smiled down at the physical testimony to the hard work he'd been doing.

His new found positive attitude had, of course, a severe downside. He understood guilt now for all the things he'd done in his lifetime, coupled with a tremendous need for recompense. Whether it had been Amy punishing him in his dream state or his own mind, the results were the same—there were higher principles that ultimately triumphed over greed and selfishness. And, worse, were the feelings he had about Molly, feelings he could never do anything about now. She'd been the best thing that had ever happened to him, something he could never recognize without the benefit of distance. Unfortunately, that distance, both physical and emotional, would keep his newfound knowledge his own, sad secret.

Ultimately, he and Amy were a lot alike. Both had been living in a created reality that let emotion neither in nor out. Both had needed the jump-start of human compassion to bring them back—but how different were they from the rest of the world? Weren't they simply extreme examples of the very greed that Gayler had expounded upon, the basic nature of all men?

He heard the shower stop and walked quickly to the closed door. "Amy!" he called. "When you get through drying off, put on that robe I left you and come out here."

"Den-ney," her frightened little voice called from the other side. "You . . . love me?"

Denny smiled, choking back the tingling in his nose. "Yes, sweetheart. I love you very much."

He went back to sit on the bed, marveling at the resiliency of youth. Apparently her entire, autistic life was nothing but a rapidly fading nightmare to Amy. She seemed to remember nothing of what they'd been through over the last week and a half. The only baggage the kid seemed to be carrying around with her was a smattering of knowledge of those closest to her and a desperate need for reassurance and affection. It was as if she had just been born, except with the knowledge and understanding of a four or five-year-old. With the proper supervision, though, she could come along quickly.

He winced when he realized that the supervision he envisioned might not include him. In fact, with all that had happened, he might be lucky not to go to jail. He shook it off, unable to worry about it now. All he could do was the right thing. The consequences would have to take care of themselves.

The door opened, Amy, scrubbed bright white, walking out with a dissipating curtain of steam, looking small and swallowed up in the big, green, terry cloth robe that had belonged to Frank.

"There you are," Denny said, walking up to the girl who came midway up his chest. He hugged her quickly, Amy squealing with delight, then smiling up at him.

"Den-ney . . . my daddy," she said happily, as Denny held out her hands, checking the fingernails.

"It's too dark in here," he said, dropping her hands and moving to the window five feet distant. He pulled the string on the blinds, the metal strips clattering around the bright morning sun.

Amy screamed loudly, falling to the floor and covering her face with her hands, Denny hurrying to her, kneeling, taking her in his arms.

"It's all right," he whispered, pulling her hands gently away from her face. "You can face the light now."

She looked up in wonder, fingers coming up to gently touch her cheek were the sun had fallen upon it, a tiny smile creasing her lips.

"Let me show you," he said, helping her to her feet, leading her, shyly, to the window. "Look out there. Look at your new world. Isn't it beautiful?"

"Bu . . . ful," she repeated as she grabbed playfully at the dust particles dancing in the light. Denny took her hands again, studying the nails.

"You're not completely clean," he said in mock sternness, tilting her head to examine behind the ears. "No lunch for you, young lady until you've gone back in there and scrubbed good behind the ears."

She frowned. "Scrub . . . hurts!" she said.

"So does growing potatoes in your ears," Denny replied, stifling a smile. "Just go do it. You want to look pretty on television."

Amy pouted, just like every teenager Denny had ever seen, then stomped loudly back into the bathroom, slamming the door behind her.

He shook his head at the door, surprised at just how much he really loved her. If they were going to take Amy away from him, he'd give them the fight of their lives first.

He looked at his watch. It was nearly ten-thirty, time for him to be thinking about getting on the air with his last message to the world. He moved over to the monitor board, finding the one that Frank had hooked up for outside reception and turning it up, the sound coming from beneath the panel somewhere.

Molly's old nemesis, Gloria, was reading the news again, but it wasn't the Twinkie Gloria of old. There was a somberness to her face born of adversity and the gauze bandage on her left temple lent a certain trench warfare grittiness to her words.

"Tho hungor hot spots seemed to have reduced themselves to three or four areas of incredible, widespread famine," she said, "but operation organizers say that the end is in sight . . . a truly . . . unbelievable thought as we move into the fifth day of Poststarvation.

"Here in Dallas today we've gotten a large boost from an unexpected source. For unexplained reasons, the citizens of Dallas have been opening their doors for two days to those who made the pilgrimage quest to see Dennis Stiller. This hospitality, plus massive food drops by the Air Force have taken the burden off the National Guardsmen who have been deserting in large numbers over the course of the last week. Even the United Nations peacekeeping force has been released after a two-day siege in a metroplex bowling alley with the promise they'd be sent home immediately."

Gloria stopped and took a breath, closing her eyes against a wave of deep pain that coursed through her. No one apologized or explained these things anymore. It was simply an accepted part of the human condition.

She continued when the wave passed. "More on the strange case of Jesus Cardera and his association with the American intelligence community," she said, voice shaky at first, then gaining authority.

The picture switched to a scene at Miami International Airport, Cardera being led in chains to a black limo with tinted windows. A large crowd of men carrying automatic weapons in plain sight surrounded him. Gloria's voice continued off-screen.

"Cardera was taken into custody by U.S. marshals in Miami today. He will be kept in a maximum security facility, the identity of which is unknown, until being brought to trial on federal charges of murder and smuggling controlled substances. Cardera has openly boasted that his contacts will rise up and free him from American jails, and that he will serve no time. Meanwhile, the Justice Department is carefully going through confiscated CIA files pertinent to Cardera and agent John Trent, the mystery man's full identity released to the press this morning. According to Cardera's files, Trent, while employed by the CIA was engaged with Cardera on what has come to be known as Project Bumper, where large supplies of cocaine were exchanged for high-tech hardware, computer chips, and Japanese digital technology, which Cardera sold legally in his native country, building a second life as an honest businessman."

The scene switched to the Virgin Islands, films of Trent's body being taken away by American military personnel.

"Though as with the effects of the death of William Casey on the Iran–Contra scandal, Trent's death may serve to cover any Agency involvement with the illegal operations, the Justice Department already admitting that large gaps exist in the paper trail tying Trent to the organization that paid his salary. A spokesmen for the Justice Department said in a prepared statement this morning that, 'Without the ability to question the principle witness in the Bumper Project fiasco, the full details of the operation may forever elude us. . . .'"

Denny frowned at the screen. It was reading out like a whitewash, typical Washington behavior. He'd seen it in everything from economic predictions to income tax statements—admit the problem, call it something else, then deny any knowledge of it and take credit for calling it to attention.

It struck Denny that to work from the assumption that the government was, if not directing Trent's labors then certainly allowing them, they were then giving tacit agreement to the project. The question, then, becomes, why? Why would the government trade technology for dope? There could only be one reason—money. Illegal money was nonreportable money, nonreportable money was nonexistent money, nonexistent money could be spent any way one chose without telling anyone else. Without any other confirming evidence, Denny was then able to make the jump to Connover. The Bumper fund, Connover's Swiss account was full of nonexistent money, that's why he couldn't and wouldn't report its source. The motivation for such actions was beyond anything Denny could come up with at the moment. He held in his hands a male and female plug. He had no idea of what they connected to, but they fit together perfectly. Unfortunately, perfect speculations did not fit the criminal justice conception of "beyond reasonable doubt," otherwise, probably half the world would have been implicated in the assassination of John Kennedy.

He stared into space for a moment, trying to work all the elements together to come up with a reason, but it eluded him on any rational level. And besides, it wasn't his problem anymore.

Leaning forward, he reached out to turn off the monitor, a painful static charge jumping from his fingers to the toggle. He fell back, sitting, on the bed, putting his stinging fingers in his mouth. And then he looked at the control board.

All the monitors were working, fuzzy pictures coming through, fading pictures. It wasn't the house on the screens, either. Different scenes, like movies, were playing on the screen, many of them through subjective cameras.

"My God," Denny whispered, leaning forward. He must have intellectualized Amy's residual power, getting the Bumper story right through the screens. They were running everywhere, fading, very light. He had no time to find a VCR to record it. A pencil and paper lay on the nightstand beside him. He grabbed them up and excitedly took notes.

The first scene showed money burning, a huge furnace, flames licking out, being filled with money by a forklift that picked it up on pallets and slid it into the flames.

The second screen showed a viewpoint shot of a line of frightened, pleading men in a dark room. Then there were loud pops and flaring light, the men falling to the ground.

The third screen showed another pov shot, a car driving into a small town and parking before a place called First National Bank of Cordell. Through intervening static, Denny watched the pov walk into the bank and up to the information desk to look down at the young woman who worked there. "Yes?" she asked.

"My name's Trent," the pov said.

The woman nodded. "Mr. Gaetano is waiting for you in the president's office."

Denny moved to the fourth screen, showing men loading boxes from a Quonset hut into an unmarked truck. A sign hanging on the outside of the hut proclaimed DEPT OF COMMERCE, QUARANTINE #3, NO ADMITTANCE.

The fifth screen was fading totally. Through the haze that

threatened to blot everything out, Denny saw another pov shot walking across a quaint street in an obviously foreign— Scandinavian?—country. The viewpoint moved to a car and climbed behind the wheel, which was located on the opposite side of American cars.

"Connover!" Denny shouted, as the pov looked at the other occupant of the front seat. Connover in dark glasses and a suit nodded to pov, then looked down at an open briefcase full of money. Atop the money lay a piece of paper with numbers written across it. Denny strained his eyes on the dying image, trying to get the numbers written down before they were gone forever.

The screens were all dying, Denny's remaining charge not strong enough to hold the images. He desperately searched the screens, finding a faint image left on number three, but no others. On number three he was looking at a man with a hard face in a nice office. The man was speaking, but the words were lost in distortion. The man exchanges open briefcases with the pov, one filled with cocaine, the other—money. The image crackled, breaking up, for several seconds, then the whole board went blank, immediately rejuicing to the previous hidden camera scenes of the mansion.

Denny sat with a paperful of scribble. The aftertaste of power hadn't been very strong, but it might have been just strong enough to break a big story. He reached out and picked up the night table phone. He had a few calls to make.

CUT TO:

DAY—INT—CHURCH OF THE SAVIOR. We are MOVING with JAMES CONNOVER down the middle aisle of his media church toward the outside doors. His face is set in determination, eyes hard, as he leads a large crowd of loud, angry people. They are all walking quickly, all of them wearing black rubber gloves and rubber boots. They are armed with every kind of weapon imaginable. Above them, and to their left, we focus momentarily on Connover's empty CHARIOT PULPIT before BANGING THROUGH the doors to the outside. Outside we KEEP MOVING distancing Connover who stands just outside the door, pushing his people onward.

CONNOVER

We are God's people, the people of the Bible! We go to give glory to the Lord and His holy name! We are the saviors of the world . . . give glory to God!

People are streaming around Connover, their faces the same face, their eyes the same eyes—the crowd monster. They are charging into the parking lot, jumping into pickups with camper shells and wagons and beat-up Pontiacs, Connover now rushing into the black Cadillac that pulls up before him. He shouts as he climbs in.

CONNOVER (cont)

Follow me! Follow me! Victory is in our grasp! The
Lord had delivered the ungodly into our
hands . . . praise God! Praise Jesus! Tonight we
feast at the table of the Lord!

Connover climbs in the passenger side of the Cadillac, the car SCREECHING away immediately, cars passing in all directions in front of us. We DRIFT UPWARD, looking down at the confusion of the lot as the machines, looking now like small, burrowing animals, jockey for position and drain out of the huge lot like sand through an hourglass, the drivers screaming and hooting, celebrating the elevation of the animal instinct to supernatural status.
CUT TO:

Denny stood in the back of the mobile van, switching toggles, turning on everything there was to turn on. He was barely competent on the control board, but figured if he pushed enough buttons, the right things would happen. He watched the board as it slowly ground to life, electricity flowing like blood through its system, and he marveled at exactly how much like a living organism the concept of television was. It was just like an extended human being, its images showing truth, but interpreting that truth through juxaposition of the image for its own end. Truth may be God, but who is godlike enough to interpret it?

He sat heavily in the director's chair, the suit he had put on feeling tight and confining, a reminder of just how ill-fitting his profession had become to him. No, Denny Stiller was through with the news, but he was going to go out with a bang, with the biggest story of his life.

The modular phone sat, waiting for him, just beside the control board. He dialed up the WCN number and reached programming quickly enough. "I've got everything juicing dead air," he said, looking at his watch. "Give me . . . ten minutes, then hardwire me in national."

They were more than happy to do it, Denny knowing that the extreme broadcast time he was giving them would be enough time to trace the source of the broadcast. At this point it didn't matter. Amy's power had been neutralized, taken away by exposure to reality. He doubted whether it could ever be brought back. Autistics, once cured, didn't return to their private universes, wouldn't know how if they wanted to. So, better that the authorities should take him now, rather than the public at large. Bureaucracies he could handle. The mob was a mercurial, unpredictable emotional animal.

He climbed out of the van, its motor running as it sat in the driveway. He went back in the patio door, passing the devastation of the backyard, where tree limbs, trash, and roof tiles were strewn everywhere. Even the pool was empty.

The white sheet blocked his entrance to the house. He pushed it aside and went in, looking at his watch again. He was tired of deadlines, tired of being married to the clock. In his next career he'd find something that didn't require slavery to time.

Amy sat at the breakfast room table, paging through a magazine, her eyes lighting as she looked at the photographs that introduced her to a world she'd lived in for thirteen years but had never known. She was wearing a simple blue dress he'd found in her mother's closet, and her hair was combed. Amy was truly a beautiful child, though she still needed a little weight on her. Denny didn't know what she weighed, but he'd been able to carry her around with ease and, at her age, that didn't make sense unless she was severely underweight. He wished he'd have enough time with her to work on that. He shook his head. There he was, thinking like a parent again. The funny part about accepting responsibility was that once he'd stopped fighting it, it had really been quite easy and natural— the cycle of life.

"Hi, sweetheart," he said, sitting beside her at the table.

She smiled at him. "Den-ney," she said. "Where go?"

"I was outside starting up the van," he said. "We're going to be on TV, did you know that?"

Her eyes widened. "TV?" she said, hooked after only one day's viewing in her new reality.

He nodded. "We're going to go on TV and let everybody see how pretty you are. Now, come on. Let's get ready."

They went into the living room, Denny having moved the studio setup in there rather than take the time to clean out the steam room, which was still full of smelly, rotten food. This was better in here, brighter, airier. He wasn't trying to hide anything at this point, so the pictures formed a good background.

He moved her into position on a chair very close to Manet's *Folies*, Adele staring sadly at the proceedings. He checked his watch. They only had about a minute and a half before air time. After checking through the viewfinder one last time to make sure they were centered, he walked around and sat on the chair next to Amy, putting his arm around her shoulder, the girl cuddling up against him, smiling happily.

Denny pulled her close, wanting so desperately to protect her from what was to come, yet knowing he couldn't. If she only knew the troubles she'd caused.

He checked his watch again. Only thirty seconds. He felt an uncharacteristic nervousness overtake him, a feeling he'd never experienced to this degree, and he wondered if the problem was that he had been thinking too simplistically with this thing. The nervousness could quite possibly be fear. For once, he was facing the world without Amy's power to protect him.

He glanced at his watch again. Ten seconds. "We're getting ready to go on," he said, pointing her toward the monitor just out of camera range. "See?"

He counted the time down, then gave it about ten extra seconds in case they were doing an intro. Then he began.

"This is Dennis Stiller," he said, professionalism replacing the nervousness, "reporting from Dallas, Texas, where my ongoing experiments with Amy Kyle and her unbelievable power have finally come, thankfully, to an end. But before we talk about the closing down of this truly remarkable study, I'd like to indulge myself in a little amateur detective work."

Denny smiled and took a breath. He was excited about this part, anxious to get it all out. "Ever since the capture of Jesus Cardera, in which Amy and I played a small part, I have been fascinated by the discovery of his secret files and especially with Project Bumper; for six months ago, I was also involved with something known as Project Bumper that was, on surface, totally unconnected to Cardera's files. But I've been digging ever since and believe I've come up with an incredible theory to explain what has happened.

"I'll make it as brief and simple as I can, give you my evidence, and let the courts and the American people judge this for themselves. The first question is: did John Trent, an American CIA agent, trade cocaine for technology with Jesus Cardera? The answer is yes, already supported by corroborating evidence in company files. Next question: was this done with the knowledge and support of the United States government? The answer is also yes; I'll offer the proof in a moment. What I want to get at now is the why of it all. You see, when I did the original story about Project Bumper, I was investigating evangelist James Connover and his source of income, discovering he had a secret Swiss bank account called, Bumper, from which he had drawn *all* the money for his overseas operations. I was also doing a series of interviews with the President of the United States, which had been adversarial, to say it nicely. I was demoted with these broadcasts down to regional features. For months, I thought I'd been bumped down because of the presidential story. It was only this morning that I realized that it was the investigation of Connover that threatened my career, for the proceeds of those cocaine sales are what went into the account that Connover used to build his overseas televangelical empire. Here's how it worked, and we'll see the why of it immediately.

"John Trent was the key man, the autonomous agent in charge of this clandestine operation. At least twice a year, he'd go out to California with government authorization and go to the Commerce Department's quarantine buildings near the major harbors where shipments of illegal equipment or over-quota items, mostly from Japan, were stored. He'd take what he needed and go to Colombia, where he'd trade the commodities to Cardera for cocaine. He'd then fly the cocaine back to the U.S. on authorized, secret military flights to avoid customs. At this time, he'd transport the cocaine to Cordell, Oklahoma, where he'd trade it for 'hot' cash to one, Buddy 'Fingers' Gaetano, a convicted Mafia kingpin who's been living under witness protection for the last five years. The money would then be put into the vaults at the First National Bank of Cordell, where it would be traded for 'clean' bank money that was then deposited into the Swiss account of James Connover. Why the bank route? Because Gaetano would be willing to pay top money if he could unload his marked cash, cash he wouldn't normally be able to dispose of except at a severely reduced rate. The bank could then simply hold up the marked cash as old money, trading it to the Federal Reserve for burning, all of it, of course, replaced with new money.

"Now, why Connover? I believe that Connover and the CIA had struck a deal. If the CIA would supply Connover the cash to build his Bumpercrop studios around the world, Connover would, in turn, allow the CIA to use part of those studios as clandestine stations, perhaps for the planning of counterinsurgence. In other words, a source of worldwide policy and upheaval that didn't go through the regular channels for funding and overseeing. Further, I believe that the murder of the fourteen DEA agents in Colombia was not carried out by Cardera, but by Trent himself, acting out off Connover's studios in Bogotá to protect his source, Cardera, from arrest and keep this pipeline of funding open.

"My proof, I believe, will rest in the bank records of the First National Bank of Cordell, and I've already gotten the FBI to work on that aspect. I also feel that amounts and times will match up with deposits in the Swiss bank, the numbered account of which is 2Q2–1719. There is only one more point of major interest to me. You see, I've not only been an employee of WCN for many years, but I've also been a stockholder in Gayler Enterprises through profit-sharing programs, and in such capacity have been sent regular stockholder reports, all of which, in the list of holdings, tab Ted Gayler as the president and chief executive officer of the First National Bank of Cordell. Gayler, the owner of the station you are now watching, is the glue that holds this entire network together. Close friends with both James Connover *and* the president, it looks to me as if Gayler was the man who set up this whole operation at the behest of the president, who wanted a clandestine operation not answerable to the Congress of the United States to carry out covert operations.

"He got it, and so, ladies and gentlemen, apparently have we. According to my rough estimation, Project Bumper has brought approximately two hundred tons of cocaine illegally into the United States in the last three years, to an estimated profit of eight billion tax-free dollars to Gaetano and his pals on resale. Really reaffirms your faith in democracy, doesn't it?"
CUT TO:
EXT—DAY—A DEMOLISHED HOUSE. We are watching Connover and his people at the demolished house across the

street from Denny's mansion. They are all kneeling, cradling
their guns and baseball bats in their rubber-gloved hands,
their heads bent reverently. Connover stands at the head of
the group, eyes closed, rubber hands held high.

CONNOVER
(reverently)

. . . and guide our steps and our hands this day,
Lord. Help us with your saving grace to do what we
must. Our love for you is boundless, our separation
from Your Divine light painful and confusing. Though
we be but mortal sinners, pity us in our hour of
need. Steady our aim; harden our hearts to mercy,
for we are performing your holy work. In Jesus' name
we pray. . . . Amen.

CROWD
(heartfelt)

Amen!

Connover watches them rise, his face set in determination as
they move toward the road.

CONNOVER
Surround the entire house. Attack on my order or
upon discovery. No one must leave that house alive.

CUT TO:
DENNY'S MONITOR. We are back in the house, watching
Denny on his own screen. He is smiling, happy, a lightness to
him that has never existed before as he hugs Amy, occasionally
tousling her hair.

DENNY

. . . we're the ones who made her God, not Amy.
She had a power and now it's gone. While it was
here, all of us tried to take it and use it selfishly, trying to promote our own egocentric ideas of what God
is in order to satisfy that ego. I'll tell you the truth: I
think the search for God is highly overrated. We're
all simply looking to make ourselves feel special, better than others. I've not been immune from this. I've

simply called it something else, which brings me to the point of this broadcast. I have no special insight, no unique knowledge to impart, except this: When we search for God, we won't find Him in the mirror. Everyone talks so much about self-esteem. The term means nothing. We *all* have too much self-esteem. What we need to do is get out of our own selfish heads and look for the esteem in others. If you can walk a mile in somebody else's shoes, you will have discovered God, who is compassion. Dwell on this: in the Bible, God destroyed Sodom—not because of orgies or idolatry as Cecil B. de Mille would have us believe, but rather because of inhospitality to strangers. Compassion. Viewpoint. As you've been feeding the world this week, you've been discovering that capacity for hospitality, for compassion within yourself. Isn't it wonderful? Isn't it the greatest feeling you've ever known? We all seek happiness, contentment, and the peace that will make those things happen. I think we've all been taking a very large step toward that happiness.

CUT TO:
EXT—DAY—THE BACKYARD. Men and women with guns, many of them wearing ski masks, are charging into the backyard and flattening themselves against the side of the house. One man breaks from the others to peer cautiously into the kitchen window.
CUT TO:
DENNY. He is holding Amy very close, the girl smiling innocently at the camera, the man's love evident on his face.

DENNY

Amy Kyle isn't God, but she's shown me God by making me look at life through other eyes, purer eyes. We are capable of rationalizing away right and wrong if we stay in our own heads. We must balance life according to higher good—unselfishly, justly. Don't trap yourself in your own mind. Walk out of it, and if you must judge—judge only yourself. Shun those who speak with absolute Truth, for no man of flesh and blood is able to know the meaning of that absolute. Believe me, that is my own sin.

Denny suddenly jerks, seeing something.
ANGLE—WINDOW. We see a number of shadows flit past
the living-room windows.
ANGLE—DENNY. He reacts to noise at the front of the
house, a breaking window.

> DENNY
> (frightened)
>
> My God, someone's here!

ANGLE—TAWNY'S BEDROOM—THE CONTROL BOARD.
We are watching the board containing all the monitors in the
house, watching people coming through all the windows on the
monitors. A MAN in ski mask comes through the bedroom
window, passing in front of the board.
ANGLE—LIVING ROOM. Denny has run to the middle of
the room, windows breaking all around him as he twists
around in horror.

> AMY
>
> Den-ney! I scared!

> DENNY
> (frantic)
>
> No! It's all over! She doesn't have the power any-
> more! It's over! Please, God!

They are coming through the windows and doors, an angry
mob, led by Connover. Denny rushes toward a woman coming
in a window, a rifle butt smashing into his face and knocking
him down. The mob descends upon Amy, their angry voices
muting as they form a semicircle around her, Connover in the
forefront brandishing a large, silver cross. The little girl, terror
in her eyes, backs against the wall just beneath the Manet, her
chair clattering to the floor.

> AMY
> (frail)
>
> I . . . I Amy. Please . . . friends . . . friends?

The crowd stops its forward progress, the people looking at

one another. Several of the raised weapons are tentatively
lowered. Connover takes a step forward.

CONNOVER

It's the Devil himself you're facing! Don't back away!
She beguiles you! Take her!

AMY

Please . . . no hurt. I . . . love . . . you.

Connover screams loudly and runs to the girl, grabbing her
around the throat, choking, using the cross as a garrote.

CONNOVER
(screaming)

Die beast in human form! Dear God, take the viper
from our midst! Destroy the ungodly!
De . . . stroy . . .

Connover stumbles backward, clutching his chest, his face
drained of all color. He begins to turn in a slow circle, face
horribly contorted as Amy lies on the floor gagging and crying.
We PULL TIGHT watching him gasp for breath, knowing a
dead man when we see one. He stumbles into the circle of his
own people, everyone backing away from him in horror as he
falls to his knees, then his face.
ANGLE—DENNY. He's on the floor staring in horror, his
face covered in blood. Dead silence surrounds him for several
long, interminable beats.
ANGLE—LIVING ROOM. Everyone is staring down at the
body of the evangelist. Then, a WOMAN SCREAMS.
CLOSE-UP—MAN IN SKI MASK.

MAN

She's killed Dr. Connover. Get her!

ANGLE—CROWD. The mindless beast roars, descending
like a plague of locusts upon Denny and Amy, as the room
becomes a jumble of confused movement.
ANGLE—DENNY. We are on the floor with him, watching as
he's pummeled and kicked mercilessly, the SOUND OF
SIRENS loud in our ears, drowning out everything else.

REVERSE ANGLE. From Denny's POV we are looking through a moving forest of legs at Amy, on the floor, covered with blood, her little face confused, pleading, as she reaches a bloody hand toward Denny as the crowd animal continues to beat and taunt her. The siren sound hurting our ears.

ANGLE—MONITOR. We are watching the death of Amy Kyle, along with an international TV audience.

ANGLE—DENNY. He's trying to rise, but a cowboy boot to the ribs knocks him down again.

REVERSE ANGLE—DENNY'S POV. From flat on the floor we see Amy lying perfectly still across the width of the room. Her eyes are open wide, her face, even in death, seeking understanding. Then we see a pointy boot arcing toward us, then. . . .

FADE TO BLACK.

FADE OUT TO THE SLOWLY DIMINISHING SIREN SOUND.

Scene 3

(several days later)

DAY—EXT—THE JUNGLE. We are looking at a density of underbrush, dried out and dusty. An insistent motor sound, straining loudly, is heard in the bg. The bottom of the screen SUPERS the words ABAYA REGION, ETHIOPIA. All at once, there is the loud crashing of brush, a huge dust cloud billowing through the growth, obscuring our vision for several seconds until a BULLDOZER plows through the dust right in front of us, followed by a convoy of trucks, their headlights on, dust covering them.

ANGLE—A SMALL VILLAGE OF GRASS HUTS IN A CLEARING. The trucks rumble into our vision, passing a dead cow covered with flies as they pull into the village, the dying people of the village moving slowly out of their hovels, their eyes large and round, standing out from sunken skull-like

faces, their bellies swollen up with malnutrition. People jump
hurriedly out of the trucks, the driver of the bulldozer talking
quickly to those gathered in a language we can't understand.
ANGLE—CRATES BEING UNLOADED FROM THE
TRUCKS.
ANGLE—DOCTORS EXAMINING PEOPLE.
ANGLE—CRATES. All manner of fruits and commodities are
being unloaded from the crates and quickly handed to people.
ANGLE—A LINE OF PEOPLE. We are watching food being
distributed to the villagers.
ANGLE—A SMALL CHILD The boy can't be older than five
years. His hair sits in patches on his head, his lips dried and
cracked as flies continually buzz around him, landing all over
him. He's looking pitifully up at someone out of our line of
vision, then reaching out to take a mango, his horribly bloated
lips twisting into the approximation of a smile as he brings the
fruit to his lips and begins to eat. We slowly PAN UP to the
man who gave him the fruit. The man is short and somewhat
squat. He wears khaki clothes and a New York Yankees
baseball cap. He is STARING DOWN at the boy, his own face
drained of color, a hand to his stomach, a sign that is becoming
a universal gesture of fellowship. All at once, he seems to
physically straighten, the hand dropping from his stomach, his
face lost in confusion, then slowly spreading joy, then incredible tears—the pain is gone.
ANGLE—THE VILLAGE. All the people from the trucks are
charging around, embracing, many of them falling to their
knees, tears flowing unashamedly from everyone's eyes as they
understand the extreme importance of what has happened.
The whole world—the whole world—has been fed. No one is
hungry. Life, love, and respect has been shared among every
person on the face of the Earth. There is fellowship. There is
hope. There is God.
CUT TO:
MONTAGE. We are looking at the big hunger board, a man on
a ladder sticking the last flag into the last hunger zone on the
map. He turns to us, beaming, throwing his arms out wide as
a roomful of people begins cheering and embracing, throwing
torn up paper into the air that TURNS TO SNOW as we fly
exuberantly to SIBERIA where we see Russian and American
troops dancing in snowdrifts as the people of a small isolated
village dance and clap their hands. We see nothing but rosy
faces and smiling teeth that are replaced by the laughing face

of a MAN IN TIMES SQUARE as we ZOOM UPWARD looking at a city in absolute turmoil. Millions of dancing people fill the streets as confetti and paper falls from all the skyscraper windows marking a celebration not seen since VE-day. We fly to a PENITENTIARY, where guards and inmates comingle in the yard, celebrating, and see that the gates aren't even closed and then to a kindergarten where the teacher dances, laughing, with her students in a huge ring-around-a-rosy. And we realize that the people are celebrating humanity and its goodness. We realize that human potential for beauty and greatness is being understood by all who live, that all people are the same person, that none of us can be happy until all of us are. Every human being who lives has reached outside of himself and known the beauty of giving.

CUT TO:

A TV SCREEN. We are looking at a shot of the Gayler mansion, a number of ambulances pulled up on the lawn as bodies covered with white sheets are being gurneyed out to the vans.

ANNOUNCER (os)

And here, on the second day of worldwide celebrations, a connected tragedy has occurred. Ted Gayler, media giant under investigation for his role in a CIA drug smuggling operation, was killed last night by a group of men armed with automatic weapons. The killers were all Colombian Nationals and were themselves killed by Gayler's own security force and Dallas police. The leader of the band was none other than Jorge Cardera, brother of drug kingpin Jesus Cardera, who told police before he died that the murder was a vendetta against his brother's former partner, whom Cardera blamed for his capture, saying that Gayler released the information through his own TV station in order to take Cardera out of the picture. In related stories, it appears that the growing scandal may be strong enough to topple the government. There is already a move afoot in the Senate to begin impeachment proceedings against the president for his alleged role in the dope-for-intelligence scam, plus the possible charge of treason for his ordering of foreign troops onto U.S. soil as occupation troops. The president has been in seclusion at Camp David for three days and cannot be reached for comment.

CUT TO:
THE NEW YORK STOCK EXCHANGE. We are looking at a
shot of the trading floor as people move hurriedly around like
the inhabitants of an ant farm.

> ANNOUNCER (cont, os)
>
> On Wall Street, the stock market continues strong
> today as food producers, food distributors, and com-
> modities trading are the big winners. This on the
> heels of this morning's announcement from Allied
> Foods and Empire Distributors, the largest food con-
> glomerates in the world, that their outreach programs
> were being maintained, and that food for the world
> was now the major priority of both companies, form-
> ing the entire core of their management theory. Get
> 'em fed and keep 'em fed seems to be the new
> motto, and the citizens of America and the world are
> rallying around the concept. The results of a Harris
> poll released this morning said that an incredible
> ninety-six percent of American citizens would gladly
> pay much higher food costs at the check-out stand if
> it could keep the rest of the world fed. No one knows
> if this remarkable turnaround will last, but analysts
> agree that the longer it continues, the more perma-
> nently entrenched the system becomes, both intellec-
> tually and economically.

We PAN SLOWLY away from the TV, its sound becoming
indistinct almost immediately. We are in a hospital room, the
blinds closed, the room semidark. The room is stark, no
flowers, no knickknacks or boxes of candy. We finally come to
a stop on DENNY STILLER, who sits back, his bed raised so
he can see the television. A bandage covers his skull and comes
down around the side of his face, under his jaw. Both of his
eyes are horribly blackened. His arm is in a cast, and we can
see bandages peeking through the sides of his hospital gown.
He STARES SADLY at the screen, his face frozen into a tragic
mask. We sense his deep, emotional pain, and wish there was
something, anything that we could do for him.

Denny lay watching the screen, not connecting up to

anything he saw on it, simply hating it for its pretensions of Truth. He couldn't shake the picture of Amy from his mind as she lay on the floor, reaching out to him as they stomped her to death. He hadn't done anything right. He had thrust her onto the public with her power, then taken that power away from her just in time to get her killed. The body count lay heavily upon him—Charlie, Frank, Tawny—all blood on his hands.

He had no idea of how long he'd been out, though the stubble on his chin told him it had been several days. His head throbbed horribly, but he didn't mind it, looking at it as part of the punishment for his sins.

He turned at a sound from the doorway, and saw a white-coated doctor walking in, smiling. "Ahh. The nurses told me you had come around."

"Well, that's more than they'd do for me," Denny replied. "They wouldn't tell me anything."

The doctor walked past the bed to the window. "I asked them not to," he said, drawing the blinds, bright light pouring into the room. "Time to rejoin the living."

"How long have I been unconscious?" Denny asked, although the answer was of no real importance to him.

"I think this is the fourth day," the man replied. "By the way, I'm Dr. Albright."

"Charmed," Denny said, pushing the remote control that turned off the television.

"You haven't asked me about the extent of the damage," Albright said. "I'm surprised."

Denny shrugged. "Are the police waiting for me?"

The doctor came and sat on the bed beside him, taking a penlight out of his lab coat pocket and studiously shining it into Denny's eyes. "You have a broken arm," he said, "three cracked ribs and a broken sternum. Multiple contusions and lacerations, but no lasting internal damage. An eardrum is iffy right now, and the granddaddy of all concussions has kept you in never-never land. In other words, a typical Sunday for a Dallas Cowboy."

Denny smiled despite himself. "Thanks," he said. "What about the police?"

The doctor looked thoughtfully at him, clicking the penlight and sticking it back in his pocket. "Well, they saved your life," he said. "If they'd have shown up a minute later, we wouldn't be having this little chat right now. They swarmed around here for a day or two, but then the belly pain went away, taking everybody's edge off, and I also overheard several detectives talking about going through your videotapes and piecing together the whole story. They still want a statement from you, but I think you can give it to them after you're out of here. It's no big deal anymore. You've actually become the forgotten man."

Denny shook his head. "I've been getting caught up by watching the TV," he said. "Neither Amy nor I have been mentioned at all."

Albright stood, taking a deep breath. "A great thing has happened to the world, Mr. Stiller," he said with solemnity. "A great thing that was accomplished through human cooperation. I don't think that people want to lessen their accomplishment by, how should I say this . . . giving you either credit or blame for it. In fact, the dead have already been quietly buried, Connover blamed for Amy's murder, with no other suspects in custody."

"Isn't that against the law?" Denny asked.

The man smiled. "No one is . . . interpreting the truth of what happened," he said, eyes twinkling. "They are simply reaching out, wanting to keep what is positive going. Can you blame them for that?"

Denny shook his head. "No . . . no, I can't. How soon can I get out of here?"

Albright went to the foot of the bed and picked up Denny's chart, writing on it. "Not long," he said. "Another day of observation should do it . . . by the way, you have a visitor outside."

"Connover," Denny said, his thoughts turning dark. "What . . . *exactly* killed him?"

The doctor looked him steadily in the eyes. "No one ever checked to see," he said. "Now, your visitor— "

"I don't want to see anyone," Denny replied.

"I think you should see this one," Albright said. "She's been here since you were brought in. She's been sleeping in the waiting room and eating every meal in the hospital cafeteria, which should qualify anyone for sainthood."

Denny stared hard at the man. "I said no. I'm just not . . . ready for any visitors just yet."

Albright shrugged. "You're the boss," he said, moving toward the door. "Eat a lot, get your strength up. It's all just a question of healing right now. I'll look in on you a little later."

Denny nodded. "Fine."

The man started out the door, then turned back. "And I want to thank you, Mr. Stiller . . . for what you've done for all of us. I hated you there for a while, but now . . . all's well that ends well, I guess."

Denny watched the man leave, shaking his head over the distance a doctor would go to make a patient feel better, though in his case the effort was lost. He had spent his whole life acting selfishly, arrogantly, leaving nothing but pain in his wake.

"I never doubted that you were hardheaded," came a voice right beside him. "Did you have to go and prove it?"

He looked into the face of an angel. "Molly," he said, his voice catching in his throat.

"So, I disobeyed orders," she said. "Pushy broad—right?"

"I never thought I'd . . . see you again, after . . . after . . ."

"Shhh," she said, putting a hand to his lips, and sitting beside him on the bed. "I've come to tell you that I was wrong. My own fears kept me from understanding what was happening."

"Happening?" he said.

"Your dakini sign," she said. "The changes in everyone's attitude. Life is different now, Denny, fundamentally changed. Hell, the countries of the world are so tied together by trade and food agreements right now that I don't know but that politics as we've come to understand it is a dying art. And Denny, everybody in the world is *eating*. It's incredible."

"I didn't do any of that," he said. "All I ever did was fumble around and make mistakes and get people hurt. You're looking at the wrong man if you're handing out humanitarian awards."

She smiled, pointing a finger at him. She looked beautiful, her eyes wide and bright as a light bulb. "You, sir, are not taking your own advice," she said. "The Truth sits all around you, the Truth that *you* catalyzed. What right do you have to interpret that Truth?"

Denny looked at her, tears coming to his eyes as he remembered his final broadcast. Molly was right. The things he'd said, the thing's he'd discovered through Amy were true and worthwhile. The events that had sprung from that Truth were tragic, but didn't alter the strength of that Truth even a little bit. The pain of the loss of his guilt would never go away.

But those were things that weren't *supposed* to go away, and he embraced them, too.

He reached out and took her hands, Molly smiling, tears coming to her own eyes. "I w-want to tell you I'm sorry for the way I've treated you."

"Don't even think about . . ."

"No," he said. "Listen to the Truth." He found her eyes, held them. "I love you, Molly, with all my heart and all my soul. Somewhere back there in the jumble of the last week, I found a strength, a compassion I didn't know was within me. I guess you could say that I've found God, at least the essence of God. I sure as hell don't deserve it, but I'm still cheeky enough to ask—if you'll give me the chance, I'd like to spend the rest of my life trying to make it up to you and the baby."

She pulled a hand away from his and wiped at her eyes through a smile that refused to fade. "I'd rather you spend the rest of your life sharing the laundry and dishes with me," she said. "Oh God, I love you, too."

Denny fell back on the pillow, staring at the white plaster ceiling, staring past the walls and past the skies to the heart of all mankind. "Thank you," he whispered. "Thank you so much."

CUT TO:

FREEZE-FRAME—DENNY'S FACE. We look at him and see in the infinity of his eyes all the possibilities of mankind, all the glories, all the love. And we marvel at what the dakini has wrought through the all-seeing eye of Truth pumping magically through the airwaves directly to the hearts and minds of billions. And just for fun, we reach out and turn the lens, changing the focus until Denny's features blur out, reducing themselves to indistinct areas of light and darkness—the unseen hand gently guiding the perspective.

FADE TO WHITE.

Glossary of Film Terms
Used in This Book

A.D.: Assistant director.

ANGLE: Camera angle. The field of view of a camera when it is set up to shoot.

BG: Background. The action that takes place behind the main action on screen.

CONT, (cont): Continuing. Term applied to dialogue broken by description of action.

CUT: An instantaneous transition from any shot to the immediately succeeding shot that results from splicing the two shots together.

DISSOLVE: An optical effect between two superimposed shots on the screen in which the second shot gradually begins to appear, at the same time, the first shot gradually disappears.

EXT: Exterior. Any outdoor scene.

FADE: An optical effect occupying a single shot in which the shot gradually disappears into blackness (FADE OUT) or appears out of blackness (FADE IN).

FG: Foreground. The main action that fills the front of the screen.

FOCUS: That position at which an object must be situated in order that the image produced by a lens may be sharp and well defined. An object is spoken of as in focus or out of focus.

FOLLOW SHOT: A shot in which the camera moves around, following the action of a scene.

FRAME: The individual picture on a strip of film.

FREEZE-FRAME: The projection of a single frame of film for an extended period of time.

INT: Interior. Any indoor scene.

MONTAGE: A type of cutting using numerous dissolves and superimpositions rapidly following one another to produce a generalized visual effect.

NETS: Networks. The three major television networks.

OS, (os): Off screen. Term used when a character not on screen at the time is speaking.

PAN, PANNING: Movement of the camera in a horizontal plane, following the action but not moving with it.

POV: Point of view. In film terms, a shot taken, as it were, through the eyes of one of the characters.

REVERSE ANGLE: A shot 180 degrees opposite the shot we've just seen. E.g. if we are looking into a store window, the reverse angle would be looking back out of the store window.

SHOT: An elemental division of a film into sections, within which spatial and termporal continuity is preserved. The common descriptions of shots are necessarily relative to the kind of picture of which they form a part.

   a. CLOSE-UP, (CU): A shot taken with the camera close, or apparently close, to the subject, which is most often a human face filling the screen.

   b. EST: Establishing shot. Long shots, usually in exteriors, which establish the whereabouts of the scene.

   c. HIGH SHOT: Looks down on the subject from a height.

   d. INSERT SHOT: A shot of some object, usually a piece of printed matter, which is cut into a sequence to help explain action.

   e. LONG SHOT, (LS): A shot in which the object of principle interest is, or appears to be, far removed from the camera.

   f. LOW SHOT: A shot that looks up at the subject.

   g. MEDIUM CLOSE SHOT: A shot intermediate in distance between a close shot and a medium shot.

   h. MEDIUM LONG SHOT: A shot intermediate in distance between a medium shot and a long shot.

i. **MEDIUM SHOT**: A shot that shows a person at full height or views a scene at normal viewing distance.

j. **REACTION SHOT**: A shot inserted into a dialogue sequence to show the effect of an actor's words on other participants in the scene. More generally, any shot displaying the reaction to anything.

k. **SLOMO**: Slow motion. Where the action taking place on screen is slower than normal life.

l. **ZOOM**: Real or apparent rapid motion of the camera toward (ZOOM IN) or away from (ZOOM OUT) its object is known as zooming.

SUPER: Superimposition. The intrusion of words or graphics onto a film or video.

VO: Voice over. A voice we hear that has no picture to back it up, an unseen narrator.

ABOUT THE AUTHOR

Mike McQuay's first novel, *Lifekeeper*, was published in 1981. Since that time he has published over twenty-five volumes of novels and short stories, writing in many fields and styles. His works include *Escape from New York, The MIA Ransom* and *Jitterbug. Memories*, the companion volume to *The Nexus*, won the Philip K. Dick Special Award for excellence in fiction in 1987.

McQuay is 39 years old and holding. He is married to novelist Shana Bacharach, and has three children and three cats. He is Artist in Residence at Central State University in Edmond, Oklahoma.

Spectra Special Editions

Bantam Spectra Special Editions spotlight some of Spectra's finest authors in their top form. Authors found on this list all have received high critical praise and many have won some of science fiction and fantasy's highest honors. Don't miss them!

☐ **Out on Blue Six** (27763-4 • $4.50/$5.50 in Canada) by Ian McDonald. On the run in a society where the state determines one's position in life, Metheny Ard takes charge of her fate, turning from model citizen to active rebel.

☐ **The Nexus** (27345-2 • $4.50/$5.50 in Canada) by Mike McQuay. The tale of an autistic girl who can literally work miracles and the reporter who brings her story to the world.

☐ **Phases of Gravity** (27764-2 • $4.50/$5.50 in Canada) by Dan Simmons. An ex-astronaut goes on a personal odyssey to centers of power all over the earth in search of an elusive—but powerful—fate he senses awaiting him.

☐ **Strange Toys** (26872-4 • $4.50/$5.50 in Canada) by Patricia Geary. Winner of the Philip K. Dick Award. A young woman tries to come to grips with the supernatural powers that pervade her life.

Buy Spectra Special Editions wherever Bantam Spectra books are sold, or use this page for ordering:
